LEGACY

Praise for Charlotte Greene

A Palette for Love

"The relationship really works between the main characters, and the sex is steamy but not over the top."—*Amanda's Reviews*

Pride and Porters

"Have you ever wondered how *Pride and Prejudice* would work if it were two women falling in love with a brewery as a backdrop? Well, wonder no more!…All in all, I would say this is up near the top on my list of favorite *Pride and Prejudice* adaptations."—*Amanda Brill, Librarian, Rowan Public Library (North Carolina)*

"Greene's charming retelling of *Pride and Prejudice* transplants the Bennets into the world of Colorado craft beer…The story beats are comfortingly familiar, with the unusual backdrop of brewing and beer competitions, modern setting, and twists on the characters providing enough divergence to keep the reader engaged… Feminism, lesbianism, and class are all touched on in this refreshing update on a classic."—*Publishers Weekly (Starred review)*

Gnarled Hollow

"Greene has done an outstanding job of weaving in all sorts of layers; mysterious patterns in the gardens, missing rooms, odd disappearances, blandly boring journals, unknown artwork, and each mystery is eventually revealed as part of the horrific whole. Combined with intensely emotional descriptions of the fear the characters experience as they are targeted by the tortured spirit and this book is genuinely a page turner…not only could I not sleep after reading it, I didn't want to put it down."—*Lesbian Reading Room*

By the Author

A Palette for Love

Love in Disaster

Canvas for Love

Pride and Porters

Gnarled Hollow

Legacy

Visit us at www.boldstrokesbooks.com

LEGACY

by
Charlotte Greene

2019

ISBN 13: 978-1-63555-490-8

This Trade Paperback Original Is Published By
Bold Strokes Books, Inc.
P.O. Box 249
Valley Falls, NY 12185

First Edition: September 2019

CREDITS
Editor: Shelley Thrasher
Production Design: Stacia Seaman
Cover Design by Sheri (hindsightgraphics@gmail.com)

Acknowledgments

Special thanks to my amazing editor, Shelley Thrasher. This novel had a little more work than usual between the first and final drafts, and I couldn't have done it without you. My very deep gratitude to you and your insightful mind.

Thanks also to my beautiful, wonderful, loving wife, who supports my writing and adds to my happiness more than she will ever know. I love you forever and always, hon.

Finally, thanks to the wonderful rangers at our beautiful national parks, without whom so many of us would be hopelessly lost. Keep fighting the good fight.

For my supportive, dedicated family. You guys are everything.

CHAPTER ONE

Jo grabbed her pack from the back of Ronnie's truck and leaned it against the nearest tree. Ronnie had gotten out of her truck and was bending, side-to-side at the waist, stretching. The air up here was thin, the last of the day's summer heat harsh and uncomfortable, and Jo knew the hike to the cabin would be rough.

Ronnie rolled her neck and shoulders a couple more times and then stopped, peering at Jo, her expression grim. "Are you sure you want to be here by yourself?"

Jo nodded. "I told Carter I'd check out the trail, just in case something's wrong with it, and maybe get started on the cabin. No one's been up there for two years."

Ronnie shuddered, staring into the woods. "Better you than me. I'd never go up there by myself."

Jo camped, backpacked, and climbed by herself all the time, but it was hard to convince most people that it was safe. Even her parents, die-hard mountaineers themselves, often chided her for it. Truthfully, she liked being by herself in the woods. Her cousin Carter and two of their friends were coming up tomorrow, and, knowing the three of them, once they arrived, it would be anything but peaceful. Carter, a lawyer, liked the sound of her own voice. Their grandmother used to say she could talk the bark off a tree.

Jo shrugged. "I'll be okay. It's just one night."

Ronnie was still frowning, staring up the trail, and Jo stepped toward her to get her attention. She opened her arms and they hugged. Ronnie drew back first and squeezed Jo's shoulders.

"Be safe, okay? I don't want Carter to kill me if something happens to you. I'm so pissed I can't go up there with you and help out. Friggin' work." Ronnie had planned to stay through the weekend, but her boss had called her this morning with a last-minute emergency. She was flying to New York later that day.

"I'll be fine," Jo repeated, "and don't worry about it. We can show you the cabin, all cleaned up, when you get back from your trip."

Ronnie nodded, clearly reluctant to go, and then sighed. She gave Jo another tight hug and climbed back into her truck. The windows were down from their drive up, and she put her arm on the edge, grinning.

"Keep your nose clean, kiddo." She gave her a mock, two-fingered salute.

Jo laughed, returned the salute, and then watched as she drove away. Ronnie stuck her hand out of the window, waving, and then disappeared around a curve in the road. Jo waited until the sound of the truck faded, and gradually the silence of the woods overtook her. She closed her eyes, breathing deeply. Down here on the road, the clean air was muddled slightly with the scent of pavement and road dust, but her sensitive nose caught the heady odor of pine and wet leaves from the woods.

She opened her eyes, her stomach lurching with excitement. She'd been looking forward to this for a long time, had saved all her vacation time just in case she could come here for this two-week trip. Now, finally, she was here, and she had an unexpected night to herself. She felt like laughing, almost giddy.

She checked her backpack one more time, making sure the zippers and straps were properly fastened, and then pulled it onto her back, using her core and her legs to stand up with it safely. Tomorrow she would help Carter and the others lug a great deal of equipment up this same trail, but for today she just had her pack—a pack she'd carried thousands of miles at this point. Despite the weight, it was comfortable, familiar, even, like an old friend. She cinched the belt at her waist, adjusted the shoulder straps, and started up the trail, nearly skipping with suppressed joy.

Despite being firmly within the bounds of Rocky Mountain National Park, beyond the little parking lot, the trail Jo was hiking and the mountain itself was family property. In the late nineteenth century, her ancestors had bought this land, long before it was a national park, and built a cabin at the top. When Rocky was first developed, anyone with land inside the boundaries was allowed to keep it through a policy called inholding. While most of the other families inside the park had sold out to the park system long ago, no one in Jo's family had even considered selling, even at the height of the Depression. For generations, her family had spent vacations here, had weddings here, and, in the case of some of her ancestors, had been born and died here. This land and the cabin were the family haven.

Then, after the death of her grandparents, one of her aunts had started arguing with her siblings about the property rights, and no one in the family was allowed to come up here while they duked it out with her in court. The cabin had been virtually abandoned for the last two years, and no one knew how it had held up. Carter, as one of the lawyers in the family lawsuit, had gotten permission for this visit, but it had taken months to sort it out. Now, after all this time, Jo was finally going to see her favorite place in the whole world.

The plan, for the next two weeks, was to assess the trail and the property and start cleaning and repairing the cabin and anything else that needed work. Still, even with what was likely to be a very difficult job ahead of her and the people joining her tomorrow, Jo was thrilled to be here. It had been very difficult to stay away, and being here again was like coming home. A hollow, empty part of her felt fulfilled, whole.

Because of several delays—all Ronnie's—it was now late afternoon, and Jo knew she needed to hike as quickly as possible if she wanted to make it before dark. She was fairly certain she would have to sleep in her tent tonight, as she imagined the cabin was in shambles, but it might just be possible to clean a space inside for a sleeping bag. It was only about a mile to the top, but it was a steep mile, especially the second half. Despite the hour, she started to sweat heavily almost at once. This September had been unseasonably warm, even up here, and the exertion of carrying a heavy pack always made the heat seem twice as intense.

The first quarter of the trail, she walked through a thick grove of aspens, some of the leaves just starting to take on the famous gold they would become over the next month. Then, almost as if there were a barrier, the aspens fell behind, and as she walked farther, she was surrounded by thick pine. Their mountain was covered almost entirely with Lodgepole pine and Ponderosa, and her nose filled with the strong scent of butterscotch and vanilla from the warm trees.

In her jubilance and haste, she ignored the sound in the woods for several yards, stopping only when she heard it more distinctly—a crashing, lumbering sound breaking through the trees and bushes some distance to her right. She peered that way, squinting in the bright sunshine, and waited for the animal to reveal itself. About fifty feet away, the branches of some thick bushes were swaying dramatically, as if something were fighting its way through. Jo expected to see a deer or elk walk through at any moment. Regardless of what animal it was, she was safe at this distance, as even a bear would likely ignore her. The branches stopped moving almost at once, and Jo held her breath, waiting for something to appear. She stood there, motionless, long enough that she began to tremble from suppressed nerves, and she finally let out her breath and relaxed her shoulders.

Despite the thick pine on the mountain, in several spots on the trail, like the one she stood in, the sky opened up entirely above. The trees had either been cut back or grew naturally farther away. As she waited, still hoping for the animal to appear, she suddenly realized that the heat of the sun on the back of her neck was no longer as intense as it had been. Then, as she continued to stand there, she no longer had to squint as intensely, the light gradually dying out of the sky. She glanced upward, expecting a cloud, and had to stare for a moment longer, confused. The sky was clear above her, the fierce blue unbroken, but the light was still fading. She glanced at her watch, confused, but it was much too early for sunset, and anyway, she could still see the sun.

She shivered then, intensely, and rubbed her arms, which had broken out in gooseflesh. A tree branch is blocking the light somewhere, she told herself. She watched the bushes for a few seconds more, still hoping to catch a glimpse of the animal over there, but an acute anxiety was suddenly making the hair on the back of her neck stand up. She felt as if she were being watched.

She shook her head, scolding herself for being silly. Of course she was being watched. Whatever was hiding in the bushes over there was clearly watching her. It had seen or smelled her standing here and was waiting for her to move on, motionless with fright. Still, the sensation was unpleasant, and she had a sudden wild, almost desperate urge to start moving again. She didn't want to see what was out there any longer—no, more than that, she knew she shouldn't let herself see what was there. She understood, with complete conviction, that she wouldn't like what she saw.

Fighting a compulsion to run, Jo turned back to the trail and started hiking toward the cabin with a haste just shy of jogging. Having stopped for perhaps five minutes, total, to wait for the animal or whatever it had been, she was surprised by how chilled she was. Within a few yards, the sun started blazing down on her again, and she was sweating soon after.

By the time she reached the last switchback ten minutes later, she wanted to laugh at herself. There she'd been, not twenty minutes after

Ronnie's departure, creeping herself out. All it had taken was a deer and a shadow, and she'd wanted to run away and hide. She shook her head, grinning sheepishly. At least her cousin Carter hadn't been there to see her make a fool of herself. She'd never live it down.

When the cabin finally came into view, it seemed even smaller than Jo remembered. Some of this illusion was the effect of the trees, whose growth had nearly swallowed it over the last two years. She was used to the sparse, almost desert-like effect of beetle-kill in other parts of the state. The dense pine near the cabin looked foreign, unfamiliar, almost like she had walked out of Colorado altogether. Only the glint of glass and the edge of the porch suggested the presence of a cabin there.

The cabin stood at the far edge of a flat clearing. Her ancestors had cut the woods back to give themselves a kind of yard here on the flattest part of the mountain. Still, the trees grew high on all sides, so that the effect was only slightly successful. Already, just in the last two years, saplings and a few larger young trees grew in several places in the clearing, and Jo was certain that if more time passed without maintenance, the clearing would entirely disappear. The family used this space for larger gatherings, setting up tents around the picnic table and fire pit with only a lucky few able to stay inside. Knowing she was likely staying outside tonight, Jo set her pack down on the table, surprised to find it sturdy and solid, though filthy. She opened the top zipper on her pack and dug around for the keys and a headlamp, then walked toward the cabin's small porch.

The neglect was even more apparent up close. Jo spotted one broken window, suspecting there were more. Glass littered the ground beneath the window, sparkling in the bright sunshine. She frowned, staring at the shards. She would have expected most of the glass to go inside unless it had somehow broken from the inside out. She took a step closer and peered at it, deciding this was what had happened. She couldn't see anything inside that might have broken out, but it was too dark in there to see anything clearly.

The other windows on this side of the cabin were intact but cloudy with dirt and grime. The porch was covered with streaks of mud and little drifts of leaves and pine needles. The furniture on the porch was, in some cases, literally on its last legs, a few pieces already caved in and broken. She would never have thought two years could cause this much damage. She had to struggle with the locks for a few seconds, and the door opened with a loud, piercing squeal.

Inside, it was incredibly filthy, and so dark it might have been the dead of night. The light from her headlamp barely penetrated the murky gloom. Jo walked farther in, pausing in the kitchen, leaving a track of footprints behind her on the dusty floor. From what she could make out in the gloom, the place was in shambles. This was the main room, a combination kitchen and living room. Two closed doors, one on either side of the room to the right and left, led to the two bedrooms. The upholstery of the living-room furniture had been destroyed, likely by animals or insects. Tufts of stuffing poked through the cushions or lay in little white piles all over the room. Dust and dirt coated every surface. The air was dense with it, almost foggy.

The bedrooms were identical, but she went to the one she knew had a broken window, knowing she would likely find real weather damage in there. She had to put her shoulder into the door to open it. The wood had obviously expanded with the summer humidity, and it took all of her strength to force it. Suddenly, almost as if it had been held closed on the inside, the door gave way all at once, and she crashed into the wall, the reverberation sending a shock through the right side of her body. She cursed and rubbed her wrist, and then, as the light of her headlamp penetrated the dark room, she froze.

It took her a long moment to make sense of what she was seeing. All the bedroom furniture had been placed in a large pile from floor to ceiling, stacked precariously on top of itself, but arranged in a way that was almost artistic, not haphazard. Rather than thrown there together in a heap, the furniture had been carefully arranged so that each piece supported something on top of it. The base of the structure was the large, antique dresser that had been in here since the cabin was built. Three twin-sized beds rested upright against it, and they held four upright wooden armchairs, which in turn supported the final twin bed and a smaller dresser, lying upside down. Four lamps sat on the top bed, flush with the ceiling. She moved her light up and down the pile several times, but she stayed where she was, almost petrified with fright.

Unlike the cool darkness of the main room of the cabin, this bedroom was stifling, the heat dense and humid despite the broken window. Jo could just make out the light coming in behind the rungs of one of the chairs, but the room was otherwise closed off, and almost sauna-hot. When she directed her light there, the floor was an unbroken surface of grime. Whoever had done this, it had been long ago, but that recognition gave her no comfort.

"Nope," Jo said, and slammed the bedroom door.

She stood there, breathing heavily, fighting to stop her trembling limbs. Her heart was racing, her body covered in a chilled, sticky sweat. She threw one quick glance at the door to the other bedroom, and shook her head, needlessly, in the near pitch of the room. Forcing herself not to run, she walked back across the small room and out the front door, which, thankfully, she'd left open for the light. In her current state, she wasn't sure she would have been able to open the door. Her hands were shaking too much.

She closed it behind herself and hurried back to the picnic table. She sat down with relief, her legs nearly giving out. She sat there, shuddering, her back to the cabin.

"Stop it," she told herself, suddenly angry. She'd looked forward to coming back for over two years, and now here she was, scaring herself twice inside an hour. She levered her body upright by pushing off the table and stood on legs that felt ready to collapse. Fighting every instinct, she forced herself to turn and face the cabin. Almost as if waiting for her to look at it again, the broken window flashed in the flickering sunlight, winking at her. The strength in her legs gave out again, and she sank back down onto the picnic table bench, this time keeping her eyes rooted on the cabin, watching it for movement.

She'd planned to start the repairs today. The whole point of coming up here was to get the place livable again and ready for the winter. Tomorrow, when Carter and the others arrived, she was supposed to have a list of tasks started for everyone to complete during their time here. Instead, she knew she couldn't go back in there. Not today, anyway. Not alone. At some point since sitting down again, she'd put her hand over her mouth, and a groan escaped her mouth. She squeezed her eyes shut, trying to summon her anger again. She was being irrational. After all, the cabin had been up here, abandoned, for years. Anyone could have broken in and placed the furniture that way at any time. It didn't mean anything.

Irrational or not, she knew what she was capable of, and after a long wait, when her trembling finally stopped, she got to her feet to set up her tent, pitching it as far as she could from the cabin.

CHAPTER TWO

So, you haven't done anything?" Carter asked, hands on her hips.
Jo shook her head. "I worked a little on the trail and cleaning
the camp area. I cut back some of the growth." She pointed at several
piles of sheared saplings and branches around the camp. "I only had my
Leatherman, so I couldn't get through the bigger, new trees. Those two
over there need a real saw."

"You didn't do anything inside?"

"No—there wasn't enough time. Ronnie dropped me off so late
yesterday, I barely had time to set up camp before it got dark. I should
have just waited and come up here with you guys."

Jo was hoping her little white lie would go unchecked. Her cousin
Carter and Ronnie were close friends, so it wouldn't be unheard of for
Carter to ask her about it. Still, even if that was the case, Jo thought it
was possible that Ronnie might mix up the time—she was like that.
Anyway, as there was no cell service up here on the mountain, there
was no way for Carter to ask her anytime soon, and she'd probably
forget in the next two weeks.

Last night had been a long one. She'd stayed up as long as she
could, crouched by a campfire for comfort and warmth, hoping to
tire herself out. Even there, by the fire, she'd felt the cabin's presence
behind her, crouched in the dark as if waiting, watching. Things had
been a little better when she crawled inside her tent, but she slept
poorly, waking up just as the sky started to lighten into dawn. She'd
spent the morning and early afternoon doing exactly what she'd told
Carter—removing larger branches and rocks off part of the trail up the
mountain and cutting down some of the saplings in camp. Still, she'd
had plenty of time to go inside the cabin today, but she'd put it off.

Carter was frowning at her, hands still on her hips. Her short hair, like Jo's, was sticking up on her head, pushed back with sweat. Her eyes were narrow, suspicious. Jo had never been able to lie to her or hide anything from her successfully.

"Is there something you're not telling me?" Carter's voice was quiet, concerned.

Jo's heart gave a big lurch in her chest, and she shook her head, rapidly. "No. Nothing."

Carter stepped closer, still peering into her face. Jo had a hard time meeting her eyes.

"Tell me," Carter said, almost angry now.

"It's nothing. Really. You're going to think I'm overreacting."

"What is it?"

"Inside the cabin—"

A loud crashing sound cut her off, and she and Carter whirled toward it. A moment later, their friends, Meg and Rachel, stumbled into camp. Meg almost literally tripped her last few steps, but managed to catch her balance.

"Thank Christ," Meg said. She slung her backpack off and dropped it on the ground where she stood. She rolled the big muscles in her shoulders and rubbed the sweat out of her short, almost buzzed blond hair. "I thought we'd never get here."

Rachel flicked her long, black hair behind her shoulders and blew a strand of it off her red, damp face. "The last time we stopped, you said you were fine—that you could keep going for hours."

Meg gave her a level stare. "I lied. Ten more minutes, and I was planning on dying, right there on the trail, and making you bury me in the woods. I only said I was okay to help you keep going."

Rachel stuck her tongue out, and Meg swatted at her, playfully.

"Stop flirting, you two," Carter said. Jo's cousin always liked to be in charge, but she was smiling, only half serious. Meg and Rachel had only recently started dating, so asking them to stop flirting was a losing battle. Also, despite being somewhat annoying, they were incredibly cute together.

"We weren't—"

Carter rolled her eyes. "Whatever. Jo—show us the cabin before it gets too dark. The sun sets early up here."

Jo left the keys in the little pocket of her tent, and after she got them out, she saw Carter watching her, clearly confused. Why keep the door locked when she was here? She knew Carter wouldn't understand until she saw what was in the bedroom, so she didn't try to explain.

"Get your headlamps, guys. It's really dark inside."

The others took a couple of minutes to find them and then followed her to the cabin, Rachel and Meg noting the state of the furniture out on the porch. Jo's heart was racing and her hands started shaking again, so she barely heard what they were saying. She took a long, deep breath to steady herself and unlocked the door. The others followed her in and the four of them stood, just inside the doorway, taking in the filth. The spotlights from their headlamps made arcs around the room, revealing years of mess and neglect on every surface and in every corner. With the others here, it seemed even worse than yesterday, almost embarrassing, the air thick, dank, and almost fetid.

"I'm sorry, guys," Carter finally said. "This is a complete waste of time. We'll never be able to stay in here. Jo and I will have to hire someone to do this."

"What do you mean?" Rachel asked, almost whispering, her arms crossed tightly over her body. "It's just…a little dirty."

Carter laughed. "Thanks, Rachel, but come on. It's disgusting."

Rachel's smile was weak. "Nothing a little elbow grease can't cure."

The four of them stayed where they were, no one wanting to move farther inside the gloomy room. Still, Jo thought, Rachel was right in a way. Beyond the cushions, almost everything else appeared salvageable. This room was still dry, the wood sound and sturdy under her feet. The living-room furniture was nearly destroyed, but that could be replaced, and she didn't detect, at least presently, any sign of animals inside. As for what was in the bedroom—that was something else, something only she and Carter should see for now. A little flicker of hope flashed through her heart. With the others here, she didn't have to be afraid anymore.

"She's right," Jo said.

"I am?" Rachel asked, eyebrows up.

Everyone was staring at her now, disbelief in every expression, but Jo nodded. "It's just dirt. We came up here, in part, to clean it out. We can do one room at a time." Saying this out loud made her believe it. That carefully arranged structure in the bedroom, once taken down, would just be furniture again. Nothing scary about that, she told herself, trying to believe it.

Clearly no one wanted to argue with her, but no one met her gaze. Everyone seemed to be waiting for someone else to speak first.

Carter let out a long, whistling breath. "I guess."

The others relaxed a little, and Jo smiled. In any group, whatever Carter said, people naturally went along with. She was just like that.

"What should we do first?" Meg asked.

Carter paused for a long while, hands on her hips. "Well, we definitely can't stay inside tonight, and maybe not for a couple of days. Let's set up the other tents outside and get the rest of camp together before it's too dark. I'll poke around in here with Jo and make a list of the other things we'll need. I can pick them up tomorrow, when Jo and I go get Daniela and the gas for the generator." Carter's wife Daniela had been forced to postpone her vacation for a day.

Despite the thick tree coverage, the sunlight was nearly blinding when they went outside. All of them paused on the porch to let their eyes adjust and took off their headlamps.

Carter pointed. "You can set the tents up over there near where Jo has hers. The ground around it is pretty flat in several places, if I remember right. Put as much space as you can between the tents for privacy."

Rachel giggled and Meg elbowed her, lifting her eyebrows up and down.

Carter sighed. "I meant for the noise, you perv."

"I meant for noise too," Meg said, making Rachel laugh.

Carter smiled and rolled her eyes. "Anyway, Jo and I need to get started inside. Can you guys do my tent, too? It's right on top of my pack."

"Sure," Meg replied.

"Okay. Just holler if you need us."

Jo and Carter watched as Rachel and Meg raced back to their packs. They'd planned for Carter, her wife Daniela, Jo, and their friend Meg to spend the next two weeks up here together, but it hadn't worked out that way. Carter had promised Jo that she wouldn't be the extra wheel, but that was before Meg invited her new girlfriend, Rachel. Jo could hear parts of their back-and-forth banter and laughter. Watching their covert and not-so-covert touches and kisses, Jo told herself she shouldn't mind being left out. With the tension between her and Daniela, she had already expected some awkwardness this week. And anyway, it was nice to see Meg so happy. She hadn't dated anyone seriously in years.

"So," Carter finally said. "What's got you so freaked out?"

Jo met her eyes. "It's in one of the bedrooms."

"Show me."

Jo led her back inside, both of them pausing for a moment to relight their headlamps. They both had to struggle with the bedroom door for a moment again, and then it finally swung open as it had yesterday—all at once. The door swung wide, slamming into the wall, and the furniture structure was revealed once more.

"What do you make of it?"

Carter's head moved up and down, the light from her headlamp eventually crossing every inch of the entire pile. She pointed at the unbroken dust on the floor and Jo nodded that she'd noticed it, too. Carter stepped forward to look at it more closely, and Jo let out a quiet gasp.

Carter turned back. "You okay?"

"Sorry. Go ahead."

Carter approached the furniture structure slowly, walking lightly as if afraid it would fall. With Carter here, Jo wasn't nearly as frightened as she'd been yesterday, and now she actually understood what she was seeing. There were, she saw, too many things in here. Usually, each bedroom held two twin beds, a dresser, and two chairs. Somehow all the bedroom furniture from both rooms had been moved in here and stacked together. Her fright finally began to abate, and she walked forward and touched one of the chairs. The structure held steady. The pile, despite the height, had been well arranged. It was solid and firm.

She and Carter's eyes met, and Jo lifted her shoulders. With Carter here, her rational mind was functioning again, and she tried to think of an explanation.

"Do you think Aunt Nancy did this?"

When the cabin had belonged to their grandparents, it had been a shared space for their entire extended family. Before their grandparents died, everyone in the family took turns visiting it throughout the year on an agreed-upon schedule. Their grandparents had died in quick succession two years ago, and their dad's twin sister, Nancy, had commandeered the keys, setting off the lawsuit that was still in progress.

Carter shook her head. "I doubt it. I can't see Nancy hiking up here just for a prank. She's not the nature-loving type."

"Then why did she take the keys?"

"To be a bitch, as usual."

Jo stared at the pile and then took a couple of steps away from it to view the entire structure again. "Can you think of anyone else who would do this?"

"She was the only one with keys."

"That we know of."

Carter nodded. "That's true. I guess there could be other sets."

"It's creepy either way," Jo said. She paused, trying to think of another explanation. "If it wasn't Nancy, who was the last person up here?"

Carter lifted one eyebrow, thinking. "Nancy claims she hasn't been up here at all, so if she's telling the truth, it would have been Martin right before Grandpa died." Their cousin Martin and his sons had used this as a ski lodge every January.

Jo frowned, confused. "That's even weirder. Why would he do this? He's not the type to do something just as a prank. I guess one of his kids might have done it?"

Carter lifted her hands. "I mean, it could have been someone else, but I'm pretty sure he was the last one here. Let's call him tomorrow when we get cell service again and see what he says." She gestured at the pile. "Do you think we should stop by the forest-ranger station? When we go back down tomorrow? See if they've heard of any vandalism in the park lately?"

Jo considered the situation and then shook her head. "No. Let's ask Martin and the rest of the family first. If it's not one of them, I'm betting some teenagers managed to get in somehow. Or Nancy. If she didn't do it herself, she might have asked someone to come up here."

Carter snorted. "I wouldn't put it past her. She's that petty."

"Should we tell the others—Meg and Rachel?"

Carter paused and then shook her head. "No. It might scare them. I can see now why you were so weird earlier—it kind of creeps me out, too. I'm sure it's nothing but a prank, but I don't know how they would take it. Let's tell them only if we have to."

They spent a minute or two examining the rest of the room, kicking up dust. The structure stood, level, secure, no matter what they did, and Jo found that with extended exposure, she was finding it easier and easier to be in here. It was still incredibly hot in the bedroom, in part because the broken window had been blocked by a curtain and the furniture. This was actually a good thing, as very little moisture had come inside. She didn't remark on the fact that the window had clearly been broken from the inside out, and Carter didn't seem to notice.

Jo followed her cousin out into the main living space again. Carter walked over to the other bedroom to take a peek inside and then closed the door again, nodding that it was okay.

"Totally empty."

Jo thought they were headed outside, but Carter stopped by the front door and turned around, shamefaced and guilty.

"Listen, Jo. I wanted to say I'm really sorry about Rachel. I wouldn't have asked Meg up here if I'd known she was going to invite—"

"It's fine. Don't worry about it. They're cute together."

"I know, but I promised you wouldn't be left out this week. And with Daniela coming up tomorrow—"

Jo squeezed her hands. "Stop. It's okay. It was always going to be awkward this week, no matter what."

Carter's face fell, and Jo pulled her into a hug. "It's okay. I'm doing better now."

Carter drew away, frowning. "Goddamn Elsa. I still can't believe it."

"I'm getting over it. It's been six months."

"I still can't believe she broke up with you on your birthday."

"She always gave the worst presents."

Carter laughed. "Okay. Still, I'm sorry if you feel left out this week."

Jo followed her outside. It was getting late now, but the light outside was still much brighter than in the cabin. They snapped off their headlamps and slid them down around their necks. Meg and Rachel had put four camp chairs around the firepit and already started a campfire. They'd also collected a sizeable pile of wood nearby, ready for the evening ahead. Even now, at the end of the summer, it was cold up here at night at this elevation. The thin air didn't hold the heat the way it did down in the foothills.

"What's the rest of the cabin like?" Rachel asked when they drew closer.

Carter threw Jo a quick glance before responding. "The same— filthy. Only that one window in the bedroom is broken, but luckily the curtain in there blocked most of the weather from getting in. A little dry rot on the sill, but it's minor." She paused. "It's going to be a really big job, though, guys. Are you sure you want to do this?"

"Of course!" Rachel said. "That's what we're here for. We want to help."

"Kind of shitty to make you work on your vacation. Jo and I should be the ones to clean it out."

Rachel put a hand on her arm. "It's fine. I'm looking forward to seeing it restored."

"Thanks, Rachel," Carter said. "I appreciate it. I really do. Once everything's done, you guys can come up here any time it's free."

Rachel and Meg shared a smile, and Carter rolled her eyes at Jo. Sorry, she mouthed. Jo shrugged and made herself smile back.

"You guys all set for the night?" Carter asked.

The tents were already up, and Jo was glad to see that both couples' tents were far from hers. She didn't mind their loving happiness, but she didn't need to hear it in the middle of the night, either.

"Not quite," Meg said. "We don't have our mattresses or sleeping bags out yet. Yours is all ready, though."

"Okay. While you guys finish, I'll get started on dinner. It'll be dark soon, and it's going to be chilly."

"I've got some brats for tonight," Meg said.

"Any of them vegetarian?" Rachel asked.

Meg looked crestfallen, and Rachel laughed. "I'm joking. I brought my own food."

"Brats sound good to me," Carter said. "I can cook up some chili, too, if anyone wants it."

"I brought stuff for s'mores," Rachel added.

Everyone turned to Jo, and she grinned. She'd stored her backpack in the little vestibule by her tent, and she went over to it, dug around, and pulled out an oversized bottle of tequila.

"This is all I brought. That okay?"

Meg stood up from her spot by the fire, walked over to her, wrapped her in her thickly muscled arms, and gave her a long, solid hug, almost popping her back. Meg sobbed and pretended to wipe away a tear. "My hero."

Jo laughed and bent down onto one knee, holding it up in tribute. "For you, my lady. May my offering give you pleasure."

"Hear, hear!" Rachel shouted, and they all laughed.

CHAPTER THREE

Jo sat up, still wrapped in her mummy bag, and listened. She was sure something had woken her, but the silence beyond the tent remained thick and complete. She held her breath, listening harder, but heard nothing. Just as she was certain she'd imagined some remnant of a dream, she heard it again: footfalls, heaving, plodding, somewhere near her tent. Whatever it was, it was a heavy walker, but cautious. It moved a few steps, paused, and then continued. With the moon already set, the animal was likely having a hard time seeing anything. She listened longer until she was sure—a deer, maybe an elk. Sometimes, like any animal, they would risk moving around in darkness if they thought they were in danger. Hopefully it could smell her and the tent and would give the camp a wide margin.

She lay back down, her heart still racing. Now that she was listening for it, the sound of the animal was obvious, clear. A branch snapped, and the footsteps halted again for a long moment before continuing that careful tread through the woods. It was a long time before the sound faded away completely.

She was still wide awake. Her startled fear had faded, but the adrenaline was still pulsing through her, making her ready for flight. She made herself snuggle into her bag, covering her head again, and took several long, deep breaths before closing her eyes. Certain she wouldn't fall asleep again, she was a little surprised when she started to drift off.

When she sat up again some time later, a faint light filtered inside through the tent walls. As before, she was listening, holding her breath, and again she heard nothing. She took a couple of quiet breaths and then held the last one. Still nothing. Just as she was about to make herself lie down again, she heard it—footsteps. Not a deer.

She slipped on her knitted cap and gloves, struggled out of her sleeping bag, and pulled her pants over her long underwear. She scooted the sleeping bag out of the way and grabbed the fleece jacket she'd used as a pillow before unzipping and climbing up and out of her tent. She shook one boot and then the other before putting them on, carefully and quietly closing the tent behind her. The sky was still dim, her watch suggesting that full sunrise was still about an hour away. She'd put her headlamp in her jacket pocket, and she snapped it on. She threw a quick glance at Carter's tent, wondering if she should wake her, too, but dismissed the idea almost as once. It was clearly just an animal, perhaps the same one she'd heard hiking up here today, and a second person would simply scare it away.

She walked into the woods in the direction she'd heard the sound. She paused, listening. A few birds were starting their morning songs, and off in the distance she thought she heard a squirrel chastising something, but detected nothing else, nothing to explain what she'd heard. Unlike the deer or elk from earlier this morning, this sound had been different—lighter, somehow. Still, she couldn't be sure she'd actually heard it. The tread had been much softer and surer somehow, almost as if whatever it was could see where it was going, with none of that hesitation the larger animal had moved with earlier in the night. It had also seemed closer. Much closer, perhaps ten or fifteen feet from the tent. A bear, probably. She didn't want to creep up on it—that would be stupid, but if she spotted it, she would at least know what they were dealing with and wake the others if needed.

It was colder than she'd expected, and she caught a whiff of something foul and rotten. A predator like a mountain lion or bear might have dragged its kill nearby. They would have to get out some of their bear spray to scare it off. She took out her handheld flashlight and shined it on the ground. She bent close, not entirely sure what she hoped to see, and moved the light in short arcs in front of her as she inched forward farther into the woods.

"Lose something?" Carter asked.

Jo shrieked and spun, almost tripping backward over a log. Carter squeezed her lips together, but a moment later she was laughing, hands up in a warding-off gesture.

"I'm so sorry, Jo. I couldn't resist."

"You asshole. You almost scared me to death."

"It was the opportunity of a lifetime. You would have done the same."

"Not likely. Not unless I wanted to give you a heart attack."

"Okay, okay. But seriously—what are you looking for?"

Jo paused, turning slightly and peering into the woods. Her eyes had adjusted a little, and the light had increased in the last few minutes. She could see some twenty feet into the woods but spotted nothing out there—no movement at all in the still, dawn light.

"I thought I heard something. It woke me up."

Carter frowned and walked over to her, staring out into the woods. They both stood there, both holding their breath, but again, Jo heard nothing.

Carter shrugged. "Maybe a raccoon, or a fox. They're attracted to the smell of human food."

"Maybe." Jo didn't actually believe this. While quieter than the deer, the noise had come from something bigger than a fox. She decided, however, to let it go.

"What are you doing up?"

Carter sighed. "I couldn't sleep. Not long anyway—two, maybe three hours."

Jo raised an eyebrow. Carter didn't lose sleep over almost anything. Three years ago, Carter had spent the night before her wedding to Daniela at Jo's place and slept like a log all night. Jo, on the other hand, the best lady, had been pacing and fidgeting until dawn—terrified she'd mess something up. Carter was the family rock—steady, unflappable, dependable, and calm in a crisis.

"You worried about something?" Jo asked.

"Not exactly. At first, I couldn't stop thinking about the furniture in the bedroom. I must have slept a little, because when I checked my watch again, it was almost two. I tossed and turned, and finally decided just to go fix it."

"On your own?"

Carter nodded. "Yeah. I mean, at first I just wanted to see if I could, and wait for you to help me today, but once I got started, I decided to finish. None of it's very heavy—it was just a matter of dragging half of it to the other bedroom."

Jo had a hot flash of relief. After showing the pile to Carter, she'd avoided going inside the cabin for the rest of the day. Though she wasn't as scared of it as she had been, it was still unnerving. She didn't want to see or look at the furniture structure again. Carter had done her a huge favor without realizing it.

She licked her lips and tried to sound casual. "Must have taken you all night."

She could see Carter shrug in the pale light. "I just finished, if that's any indication."

Again, they stared into the woods, and Jo sensed that Carter was waiting for something. They'd spent enough time together that she could tell what her cousin was thinking and feeling. The silence dragged on into awkwardness, and Jo finally forced the issue by speaking first.

"Are you sure there's nothing else? You seem worked up. It's not only the furniture."

After a long pause, finally Carter sighed. "Yes, actually. I'm worried about you."

"What? Why?"

Carter started to shrug again and then shook her head. "You've been so down, lately, and I can't help feeling like I should have done more for you. After Elsa left, I mean. I've been so busy at work, lately, and then there's the weirdness between you and Daniela…but that's no excuse. I should have been there for you, and I've barely seen you for months now. I'm sorry."

A flash of angry resentment—the same feeling Jo had nursed for months now—washed through her in a hot blaze. Carter was trying, and she should let her apologize. She knew this intellectually, but it was hard to let go of the pain with just a few words. She made herself take a deep breath and let it out. "It's okay, Carter. Really, it is. I know I was pretty dramatic when she broke up with me, but I'm feeling better about it—I promise."

"Are you dating yet?"

Jo shook her head. "No. I mean, I've seen a couple of women, but nothing serious. One or two dates."

Carter raised her eyebrows up and down. "Oh yeah?"

Jo laughed. "The answer is yes, if that's what you're implying. But nothing past breakfast." She paused, peering at Carter closely. "Anything else bothering you? My love life can't be keeping you up at night."

Carter sighed and then shook her head, apparently defeated. "It's mostly about you and Daniela. She's my wife, Jo, and I'm worried that when she comes up here, you guys will start fighting again, and then—"

Jo grabbed her shoulders. "Carter—it's okay. Don't worry about it. It's been so long now, I can't imagine it's gotten any worse. I promise I won't start anything with her."

"She won't even talk about you. I know I should have pushed her a little, but I was hoping she'd come around. Then last week, when I told her you managed to get the time off, and that you'd be up here too, she tried to back out. It was all I could do to convince her to come up at all. She's still upset about Elsa."

When Jo had started dating Elsa, Elsa and Daniela had immediately hit it off. The two of them had been like sisters. They took trips together and had eventually ended up working together in a little Mexican bakery and café they co-owned in Longmont. Elsa had sold her half of the business when she and Jo broke up, and Daniela had barely talked to Jo since.

"Do you know why?" Jo asked.

Carter shook her head. "She won't tell me. I mean, I know she was scrambling for a while to get a second manager at the café, but I don't think it has anything to do with that anymore. The new guy is great—better than Elsa, actually. It must be something else."

"So you don't have any idea why she's so mad at me?"

She shook her head again. "No. I was hoping you'd tell me."

The sun finally broke the tree line, and warm light flooded the area around the cabin. The birds ratcheted up, so loud now they almost hurt Jo's ears. She and Carter started at a loud crashing sound, both turning toward it just in time to see the tail end of a deer leaping away. They smiled at each other, both a little sheepish at their fright.

Carter squeezed her shoulder. "Just try to talk to her this week for me, Jo. Maybe you two can make it up. It would mean a lot to me if you guys were friends again."

Jo almost argued with her. She'd tried to talk to Daniela several times over the last six months, in person and via text and email. As far as she knew, Daniela was uninterested in mending fences. Still, seeing Carter's worn, tired face, there was only one thing she could say.

"I promise I'll try. As hard as I can."

"Thanks."

"I'll start breakfast. When are we heading down?"

"As soon as possible. Daniela gets off work at noon today, but I wanted to buy the supplies before we pick her up so we can make it back here before dark." She grinned. "She's not going to be happy about sleeping in a tent, I can tell you."

"Still not a camping convert?"

"I guess she never will be. I mean, she'll do it, to please me, now and again, but it's never her idea, that's for sure. She just likes a roof over her head and flushing toilets. Can't say I blame her, really." She snapped her fingers. "Dang, that reminds me. I need to check the outhouse in the daylight. It was a little smelly last night, which means I might need to buy some more peat and lime when I'm in town. I know it was cleaned out two years ago, but I think the stuff in there needs to be refreshed."

"Sounds delightful."

"Anyway, go ahead and start breakfast. I've almost finished making the list, so I should be ready to hike down right after we eat."

Carter set off for the outhouse, and Jo began pulling the breakfast things out of the bear canisters and coolers. By the time the water for the coffee was boiling, the others had gotten up. Rachel seemed to like having a fire, as she immediately lit a new one, somewhat unnecessarily. It did help with the bugs, but the air was already warming up nicely. In half an hour, it would likely already seem hot.

Soon, Jo was frying eggs on the camp stove, and Meg was helping Carter. Despite the occasional crazed song of the birds, it was quiet here, windless and still. Rachel stood up from the fire and walked closer to Jo, rubbing her thin arms against the last of the morning chill. Her long, black hair was tied back in a loose ponytail today, and she looked a little pale, possibly from lack of sleep or the remnants of last night's tequila. She smiled at Jo, a little uncertainly, neither one of them having much to talk about. They'd met once before, for a couple of hours last week when they were all planning the trip, but all Jo knew about her was that she was a lawyer, like Carter.

They spoke at the same time.

"When I—" Rachel began.

"So you—"

They laughed, awkwardly.

"Go ahead," Jo said.

"You sure?"

Jo nodded.

"I was just going to say that when I woke up and got out of the tent, I thought you were Carter. Do people get you two mixed up?"

"All the time."

"You could be twins. I've seen twins less like you. You're like that old show—that one about identical cousins."

"*Patty Duke*?"

Rachel laughed. "That's the one. I used to watch it on the retro channel when I was a kid. I love those corny old shows."

"Carter and I watched it a lot growing up. We memorized the song and could do that mirror thing in the doorway."

"Oh, that's right—Meg mentioned you grew up together."

"Carter moved in with my family when we were thirteen."

"You're the same age?"

Jo grinned at her. "Close enough to be twins—a few hours apart, same day."

"Creepy," Rachel said, then blushed. "Sorry."

"It's okay. I think it creeped our parents out, too, until they got used to it. It's some kind of genetic fluke. Some people say we look like one of our great-great-aunts, or something, but I don't know. We don't resemble anyone else in the family. Everyone else has really dark hair, and that's just the beginning. Both my sisters look just like my dad's sister."

Rachel inched nearer, peering at her intently. Jo blushed under her gaze, but if Rachel noticed her embarrassment, it didn't stop her. Finally, Rachel shook her head.

"Up close, I guess I can see some differences. Your hair is lighter than hers, and you're obviously tanner. And your eyes are a little different, too. Hers aren't as blue."

"I spend a lot of time outside. And we're pretty different in other ways, too, once you get to know us better."

Rachel smiled. "I hope I do. I'm having fun with you guys."

She laughed. "Oh? Cleaning is fun?"

Rachel shrugged. "Well, maybe not that part—but the rest of it. I still don't know a lot of people here."

"That's right. Meg and Carter said you moved here from out of state."

Rachel nodded. "California."

"Why did you come to Colorado?"

"I wanted a change. I came here for a conference a couple of years ago and kind of fell in love. My parents think I'm crazy. I had a great job in San Francisco, and it paid more than I make now. And all my brothers and sisters live near them in the Bay Area. It's kind of a Korean thing, especially for daughters, to stay close—or at least it is for my parents and their friends. But then, I was already different from the rest of my family when I came out of the closet." She paused. "But you and Carter are kind of like that, too, right? Your whole family is here in Colorado."

Jo nodded. "Yep—every single one of us. And we marry locals, too. People in our family take it as a personal insult if you leave the state. My sister Annie went to college in Wyoming, and my parents almost disowned her. She came back after she graduated."

Rachel laughed. "Yeah, my parents are exactly like that. I've gotten the silent treatment from my mom since I moved."

"Well, Meg's happy you're here, obviously."

Rachel grinned, her cheeks coloring slightly. "I'm so happy I met her. We've been together only a few weeks, but it's going well. I haven't dated anyone like her before. My previous girlfriends were so uptight—career-focused, money-driven, overachievers. I always thought that's what I wanted, but Meg kind of swept me off my feet."

Jo smiled, happy to hear it. Meg was definitely not career- or money-focused. She worked seasonally as a ski instructor or river-rafting guide and lived in a tiny studio apartment. She probably wouldn't work at all, if she could get away with it.

"Carter's glad you're here, too. She can't say enough about you at work. She told me the other day she doesn't know how she ever got along without you."

Rachel grinned and wiped her forehead. "Whew! What a relief. I mean, I thought it was going okay, but it's hard to tell at a new job." She paused. "You know what—I don't know what you do. Are you a lawyer, too?"

Jo laughed. "I wouldn't do that for all the money in the world. I work in the parks department for Fort Collins."

"Oh, cool. That explains why you're outside a lot."

"Almost every day."

They were quiet for a long, awkward pause. Jo was terrible at this kind of small talk. Luckily, Rachel broke the silence.

"What does Carter's wife think of you two?"

"What do you mean?" Jo asked.

"I mean, how does Daniela deal with having two of you? Has she ever mistaken you for Carter?"

Jo laughed. "Once. And it was embarrassing as hell."

"Oh, do tell."

Jo shook her head. "No way—Daniela swore me to secrecy. Even Carter doesn't know." She looked around to make sure she wasn't nearby. "But I will say this. When it happened, Daniela was naked. I know exactly where and what her tattoos are on some fairly private places."

Rachel started giggling, and soon they were both laughing.

"What's so funny?" Meg asked, walking into camp.

"Nothing," Rachel said, giggling again.

Meg cocked an eyebrow her way, which sent Jo into another giggle fit. Meg started laughing simply watching them, and before long the three of them were breathless, clutching their stomachs.

Jo had just managed to calm down and was wiping her eyes when Carter joined them. Seeing their faces, she asked, "What's up?" and it sent them off again.

CHAPTER FOUR

They were about five miles down the road when they heard a loud pop. Jo had to grab the wheel to keep the car from going off the road. Carter screamed, but Jo gritted her teeth and managed to steer over to the side of the road to a stop. They both sat there, quiet, tense, and almost panting. They were parked on the downward side of a very steep hill about twenty feet from a hairpin turn that overlooked the valley below.

"Jesus," Carter finally said. "I thought we were going over the side for sure."

"Me, too."

"Was it a tire?"

"I guess so." But it hadn't felt like a flat tire at all. More like an explosion. Jo had had lots of blowouts in her life, and none of them had ever made her lose control of a car all at once like that. She made herself let go of the wheel, her knuckles actually white. She wiped her sweaty palms on her pants and climbed out of the car. She saw what had happened at once and swore.

"What is it?" Carter asked, getting out.

"Both tires on this side are flat."

"What?"

Carter came around to the driver's side and cursed loudly. "Great. Now what the hell are we going to do? We're in the middle of nowhere!"

Jo paused. If they'd brought a second car, they could have walked back to the trailhead for the cabin, but the three of them had carpooled yesterday to save gas. Their cabin was about twelve miles from the entrance to Rocky Mountain National Park. The road they used to get to the trail to their cabin was almost entirely deserted, especially now at the end of the summer season. Going back toward the cabin was completely pointless—there was nothing in that direction besides hiking trails. This road eventually hooked up with the main one through the park in that direction, too, but in a very roundabout way. If they continued the way they'd been headed, downhill, they would hit the main road in perhaps three or four miles.

"We'll have to walk, I guess," Jo said.

"Are you kidding me? We don't have any gear. It's hot as hell out here."

"We don't have any other choice. Let's take what we have and get going."

"We're going to be so late. Daniela will kill me."

Even a cursory glance inside the car revealed their complete lack of preparation. Jo had brought a banana and the rest of her coffee, but her canteen was almost empty from the hike down to the car from the cabin. Carter was a little better off with more water, but neither of them had a hat or any other sun protection.

"We'll cook out here," Carter said, squinting and shielding her eyes from the bright, cloudless sky.

"Do you have a better idea?"

She shook her head.

"Then let's go."

Jo took the lead, almost storming off. She wasn't angry with Carter per se, but she did hate it when other people gave up so easily. They had to get to the main road and to a phone—no use pouting about it. Carter might not be in the same shape she was, physically, but she was no slouch, either. Three miles downhill was less than an hour's walk.

It was incredibly hot, however, and perhaps ten minutes later, Jo had to fight an urge to drink the rest of her water. It didn't matter whether she drank it now or later, she would get dehydrated either way, but it seemed safer to wait in case she became desperate for something wet. Tiny rivulets of sweat were running into her eyes, stinging, and she cursed herself for acting like such a novice. It was never safe to head into the mountains unprepared, car or no car. She knew better than that.

She was so wrapped up in her thoughts, she missed the first hint of sound behind them, but eventually she heard Carter's footfalls begin to lag behind. She stopped and turned around, almost ready to yell at her, and then she heard it too: a vehicle, heading their way from the direction they'd come. They'd rounded the corner now, so they couldn't see beyond the edge of the curve they'd already walked past, but it was clearly getting closer.

Carter had already stopped, peering up the hill behind them, and Jo retraced her steps a little to stand by her side.

"What is it?" Carter asked. "Another car?"

"I think so. We'll just have to wait and see, and hope they stop for us."

"They'll pass our vehicle, so they'll know what happened."

As if she'd predicted it, Jo was pretty sure she heard the other car slow down and then pick up speed, and a moment later it came into view over the crest of the hill.

"Thank God," Carter said.

It drove closer, and both she and Jo began waving wildly, walking on the road a little to get the driver's attention. He or she apparently spotted them and made for the edge of the road, slowing and stopping some ten feet away. The vehicle was an old Bronco truck, green in places, rusty in others. The sun was shining directly behind it, so it was difficult to see inside, but after it stopped, the door opened, and someone very tall climbed out of the cab.

"Jesus, would you look at that," Carter said, almost breathlessly.

If Jo could have found the air to talk, she would still have been speechless. The woman, when she appeared from behind her door, was a revelation. She was so impossibly tall, she seemed unreal—epic and godlike. Her face was somewhat cast in shadow because she was backlit, but the delicate planes of her cheekbones and her strong jawline were clearly visible. Her hair was a shoulder-length spun gold, and the sunlight that caught it reflected like a halo around her head. She paused, reached into the cab of her truck, and pulled out a wide-brimmed campaign-style hat, putting it on and damping that golden light. Her uniform was drab and shapeless, but the body underneath was anything but—muscular and trim, yet distinctly feminine.

"Can I help you?" the ranger said, walking toward them. Her smile was dazzling underneath a pair of bright, almost fiercely blue eyes. She was some six inches taller than either of them and seemed to gaze down at them from a distance.

Jo let out the breath she'd been holding and heard Carter do the same. Dazed, shaken, Jo was unable to formulate a single answer. She simply stared up at this vision.

"Yes," Carter managed to say. "Please. Our tires—"

"I thought that might be the case," the ranger cut in. "I saw your car back there. I'd offer you my spares, but they're much too big."

Jo licked her lips, her mouth incredibly dry. Her voice, when she finally spoke, was barely louder than a whisper. "That's okay. We just need a lift into town or to the station so we can make some phone calls."

The ranger pointed at her. "I can do you one better. I'll radio down and have someone at the station call a tow for you, save you a step."

"Could you?" Carter asked, her voice still somewhat muted, uncertain.

"I'll do it right now."

The woman walked back to her truck, and Jo almost had to grab Carter's arm to keep from staggering.

"Holy shit," Carter said, eyes stark with disbelief. "Have you ever?"

Jo shook her head furiously. "No. Never. It's not even possible. I'm pretty sure we're both dreaming."

"Well, don't pinch me, 'cause I never want to wake up," Carter said. She grinned, and soon the two of them were giggling like children.

"Damn," Carter said, wiping her eyes. "I'm almost glad we got those flats now."

Jo swatted her arm. "Hey! You're a married woman."

Carter squinted in the direction of the ranger and then back at Jo. "I don't think Daniela would blame me. And anyway, a girl can look."

Jo had to agree. No one could help but stare at the woman. She was standing by her truck, radio receiver in hand, her eyes distant as she talked with someone on the other end, nodding unnecessarily as she agreed with something they said. Jo and Carter watched her hang up her receiver again and walk back over to them. Again, her smile was bright, inviting somehow—friendly, genuine, and warm.

"Shouldn't be long—half an hour, maybe—before we get a truck up here to tow you into town."

"Oh, wow, Officer..." Carter said.

The ranger held out her hand. "Andy Knox."

Carter shook it, pumping up and down with clear pleasure. "I'm Carter, Officer Knox, and we can't thank you enough. It's so hot out here, and my cousin Jo and I—"

"Cousin?" Andy said, then shook her head. "I would have thought you were twins. And it's Andy. None of that officer stuff."

"Okay," Jo said, finally finding her voice. She offered Andy a clammy hand, and they shook. "Thanks so much. We were in a real pickle." She could have kicked herself. *A pickle?* she thought. *The woman's going to think I just crawled out of the 1950s.*

But Andy smiled, if possible, even wider. "It's my pleasure."

They stayed that way for a long beat, staring at each other, hands clasped, and Jo seemed to sink into those cool, blue eyes. She finally made herself let go, her face heating with embarrassment. If Andy had found the exchange strange, she did a good job of hiding it, as she turned to Carter with that same beautiful smile.

"What are you folks up to this weekend? I mean, before the flat tires."

Carter was clearly still struggling to act normally, as it took her a few seconds to respond.

"Uh, well, we're cleaning out our cabin. Up on Glenview Peak."

"Oh yeah? Up at the old Lemke homestead?"

"Yes," Carter said.

"We're both Lemkes," Jo added, unnecessarily, she realized, a moment after the words left her mouth.

"How interesting," Andy said. "Not many people have private cabins in the park anymore. I've always wondered who owned that place."

"Here we are," Jo said, feeling like an idiot again a second later.

The three of them stood there silently, Andy still smiling, and Jo wished very much that she could erase the last three things she'd said. She sounded like a complete and utter idiot.

"What's it like?" Andy asked. "Your cabin, I mean."

"A little run-down right now," Carter said, sounding more like herself. "It's been...abandoned for a while."

"But we're fixing it up," Jo added, unable to keep a hint of pleading from her voice. She couldn't stop herself from wanting to impress this woman.

Andy opened her mouth to respond, but her radio squawked back in her truck. She touched the brim of her hat. "Excuse me for a sec, ladies. I'll be right back."

Again, Jo was unable to tear her eyes away from Andy's retreating form, and she snapped back into reality only when Carter elbowed her, hard.

"Ow!" she said, rubbing her arm.

Carter rolled her eyes. "Get it together, Jo. You've gone all goosy on me."

"Can you blame me?"

"No, but come on. You're acting like a creep staring at her like that. Ask her up to the cabin."

"What?"

Carter laughed. "I'm serious. Ask her up. You heard her—she'll be happy to see it." She raised her eyebrows up and down. "And maybe more."

"Are you kidding me? We don't even know if she's...like us."

Carter gave her an even stare. "You're the one who's kidding yourself, Jo. She was totally coming on to you."

"No, she wasn't. She was being friendly. And anyway, why would she come on to me and not you? She thought we were twins."

"Maybe it's your winning conversation skills."

Jo laughed. "Fuck you."

Carter grinned. "Anyway, what could it hurt? She says no—no problem. But I'm pretty sure she'd like to see it."

"I can't. I mean, we just met—"

Jo stopped talking as Andy rejoined them.

"Can I offer you ladies anything?" Andy asked. "Water, maybe?"

"That would be amazing," Carter said. "I'm parched."

"Yes," Jo said, frowning at Carter's phony enthusiasm. "We'd love some."

The two of them followed Andy over to the truck, and Carter managed to throw Jo a quick wink behind her back before saying, "Say, Andy? Jo and I were just wondering—"

Jo elbowed her, hard, just as Andy turned around. She'd seen the exchange, and her face crinkled briefly with confusion.

"Wondering what?"

Carter took a careful step away from Jo and threw her another wicked smile. "We were wondering if you'd like to come up and see the cabin some time. Since you've never seen it, I mean."

At that moment, Jo would have been happy to have the road open beneath her and swallow her whole.

If Andy found the invitation strange, however, she didn't let on, as she immediately smiled. "Really? I'd love to, actually. Like I said, I've always wondered what it was like. You guys are so lucky to have land inside the park."

As Andy started digging around in the back of her truck, Jo leaned over to Carter and whispered, "I'm going to kill you."

Carter smiled. "You'll thank me later."

"In your dreams, smart-ass."

CHAPTER FIVE

Between getting the car towed and having four new tires put on, it was almost noon by the time Jo and Carter drove out of the garage in Estes Park. They decided it was better for Jo to return to the cabin, as the others would likely start worrying if they didn't show soon—they'd been due back around one. Carter managed to text Daniela and let her know what had happened, but with no way to contact the others up at the cabin, it simply wasn't fair to let them wait up there without any explanation. Carter dropped Jo off at the trail to the cabin and sped away. As late as it was, it would be a miracle if she and Daniela managed to get back before dark.

Carter had given Meg and Rachel assignments to start on while they were gone, and Jo jumped in to help Meg once she returned. Jo and Meg were cutting the branches away from the windows and tying them into bundles that would either have to be burned or hauled down. Rachel was inside cleaning the main room. They'd brought a lot of supplies with them on the way up yesterday, including gardening shears, a broom, and other cleaning materials, but Jo thought the job she and Meg were working on would have gone a lot faster with a chainsaw. She stood on the roof, cutting the tops of the branches off to make it easier for Meg to get the rest of them from below, but the work was slow and physically difficult. She was drenched in sweat and covered in dirt and sap.

"Can we take ten?" Meg shouted from below. "I'm about to fall over dead."

"Sure. Let me climb down."

Meg didn't respond, and Jo took a second to rest. She crouched, resting her arms on her knees, balanced on the balls of her feet.

The view from up here was incredible. The cabin had been built near the top of a high peak overlooking a long, wide valley of aspen and pine in one of the more remote corners of the park. The location had several benefits, including the absence of neighbors for miles in any direction. You could spend the whole year here and never run into another person. For Jo, it was heaven on earth. Before her Aunt Nancy had taken the keys, she had spent almost all her vacation and free weekends up here, on her own or with Carter and Daniela.

"You okay up there?" Meg called.

"Yep. Heading down now."

Jo walked across the roof to the makeshift ladder she'd set up—a log they'd propped up against the side of the cabin. It had several thick branches that functioned like the rungs, and she climbed down quickly. Rachel and Meg were waiting at the bottom, gaping at her.

"You're like a monkey," Rachel said, shaking her head. "You couldn't pay me to, a, go up there and, b, climb that thing. You must be nuts."

Jo shrugged. "Doesn't bother me. How goes it down here? Did we make any progress?"

Meg sighed. "We've almost cleared the front of the cabin, but there weren't as many branches there anyway. We still have to figure out how to clear the vines off some of the windows, and I'm not sure how to do that. There's some poison ivy mixed in."

"We've got some work coveralls and gloves. Just have to protect our skin when we do it."

Meg frowned. "That still leaves the other three sides of the cabin."

"What's it like inside, Rachel? Brighter at all?"

Rachel lifted a shoulder. "Maybe? I still had my light on when Meg came and got me."

"It'll be a little better when we get the generator going again. Carter and Daniela are bringing back some gas."

Rachel shuddered. "I can't imagine how awful it'll be in there with the lights on. The dirt looks bad enough in the dark."

Jo sighed. "Maybe we should have hired someone to do this after all. It's going to be a really big job."

Neither of them replied, and Jo took that as a sign that they were beginning to regret coming up here. The three of them went over to the camp to find something to eat, not talking. She knew they felt defeated by the scale of the job, and she didn't blame them. Even with all five of them working all day, they likely wouldn't finish before most of them had to be back at work.

They flopped into their camp chairs, exhausted. She was so tired the sandwich she'd made tasted like sand, and she set it in her lap, almost uneaten. The others were also sitting, not eating, staring into space. Meg was having a hard time keeping her eyes open, and Rachel was brushing at the dirt of her arms and legs with a sneer of disgust. Jo was about to apologize again when, almost simultaneously, she and the others heard a noise in the woods.

"What is it?" Rachel asked, getting up.

Jo shook her head, listening carefully. It seemed early for Carter and Daniela, but given how Carter drove, not completely impossible, either. After listening a little longer, she was sure from the banging and yelling that it was them. While they had brought a lot of supplies and materials up with them yesterday, Carter and Daniela were bringing the heavy stuff in a handcart. They could hear Carter cursing and swearing down below, and Jo immediately levered herself out of her chair to go help.

Sound is funny in the mountains. Carter had seemed close—within sight even, but it took almost five minutes to hike down to her and Daniela.

"Hey," she said when she finally saw them.

Carter dropped the cart handle. "Thank Jesus. I thought we'd never make it."

Hello, Jo signed at Daniela.

Hi. Daniela looked away immediately, which, when using sign language, is a very effective way to end a conversation.

"Want me to pull the cart the rest of the way?" Jo asked.

Carter clasped her hands together in a silent prayer. "Please, for the love of God. I will be forever in your debt."

Jo laughed. "Okay. Go ahead and head up. Rachel and Meg are taking a break. I'll be up there soon."

Carter and Daniela disappeared up the trail, and Jo started to drag the cart uphill. She'd volunteered in part to give herself more time away from Daniela. They'd barely spoken since she and Elsa broke up, and judging from her response just now, it seemed like they weren't going to become friendly again any time soon.

Pushing and dragging the cart drove that tension from her mind. While the trail's incline started off somewhat gradually—a gentle uphill slope—the last half mile was incredibly steep. There had once been a horse trail, but the family had eventually abandoned it when it started eroding significantly. They'd hired a land surveyor to suggest a better, more environmentally sound route up the hill, and that was the current footpath they all used. As a kid, Jo had spent two weeks with her family up here when they'd dug up the new trail from the little parking lot down on the road. This one went uphill in several, more sustainable switchbacks. But no one had serviced the trail for over two years. Despite the work she'd done yesterday, branches and brush covered a lot of it, and some loose stones had shifted enough that Jo was forced to throw her entire weight into the cart to move it over something in the way. It took her half an hour to drag it up the last stretch, and by the time she made it into camp, she was almost spent. She immediately collapsed into her camp chair, surprised to find herself alone. She took long, deep breaths to slow her racing heart, every muscle trembling.

Eventually, the others reappeared from inside the cabin, pausing on the porch. They hadn't noticed her sitting there, and they were all laughing and talking. Daniela's face was carefree and open, smiling as she hadn't done with Jo in months now. As Jo watched the four of them, she realized how incredibly naive she'd been. When she'd realized Meg was bringing Rachel, she'd told herself she wouldn't mind being the fifth wheel. Now, in the face of that reality, it was like being punched in the gut. They were all happy together without her, and Daniela didn't want her here. She should never have agreed to come.

Rachel spotted her first and waved dramatically. "You made it!"

"Barely."

"What'd you bring us?"

The four of them joined Jo at the campsite, and Carter started unloading the cart, telling them the inventory as she took things out.

"Besides the diesel, some more cleaning supplies—two extra brooms, more rags, more cleaners, more bags, more twine, two more sets of shears, some face masks, some more tools, and a couple of extra coveralls. Oh, and more food and tequila."

Meg took a bottle from her and cradled it like a baby. "Come to Mama, sweetie pie."

They all laughed.

"We'll have to be careful with the gas for the generator, though," Carter said. "I'm going to set the circuits so it'll run only the power in the main room, and I can set it at night to power only the fridge. Still, in two or three days someone will have to go get some more gas. We'll have to try to make as much ice as possible in case we have periods without juice."

"I'll go get it running," Jo said, moving in that direction.

"No, that's fine, Jo. I'll do it. You've been working all day. Show Daniela what you guys are doing so she can help."

Jo's stomach dropped, but she nodded and gestured for Daniela to follow her. Once they were standing by the makeshift ladder, she faced Daniela again.

Rachel's been cleaning inside, if you want to do that. Meg and I are out here. We need to get the branches and vines cleared away from the windows. Meg and I finished the front of the house, but we've barely started on the other sides.

Daniela nodded and turned away, but Jo touched her arm. Daniela flinched and almost recoiled, glaring at her.

Jo held up her hands. *Sorry. I didn't mean to startle you. I just wanted to talk for a second.*

Daniela made a cutting gesture. *I don't want to talk to you, Jo. Not now.*

It's just—

Daniela made the same gesture. *We're not doing this right now. I don't want to talk.* She sighed slowly and with emphasis to show her anger.

Jo's stomach dropped again, and her eyes prickled with tears. *But what will you tell Carter?*

Carter knows how I feel. She has no part in it. This is between me and you.

With that, she turned and marched away, her body rigid and her fists clenched. Jo took a couple of minutes to calm down again, afraid she'd start crying. She took a few deep breaths and wiped at her eyes, then went back to the makeshift ladder and climbed it again. It was clear that Daniela's anger was deeper and more volatile than she'd feared. It would be difficult to be around her. Between that and being the fifth wheel, it might be better if she made her excuses and left. She would have to come up with a concrete reason to leave, though, because of Carter. She didn't want to disappoint her, but it was starting to seem like she didn't have any other choice.

She kept working long after the others had called it a day, desperate to keep away from Daniela's icy glare. By the time the sun had started to set, the others were all sitting around the fire, and Jo was literally shaking with fatigue as she dragged herself into camp to join them.

Carter slapped her shoulder. "Hey, lady. You're working too hard. We made some real progress today. We might actually be able to sleep inside tomorrow."

Jo was surprised. "Really?"

"Once Daniela started helping, it went a lot faster," Rachel explained. "We got most of the main room cleaned. The cushions are a wreck, but everything else is fine. We'll probably want to go over it again more carefully with the lights on in there, but we got the first layer of grime, anyway."

Jo glanced at Daniela, expecting her to add something, but she was watching the fire, not paying attention.

Carter touched Daniela's arm lightly, and she shook her head as if to clear it. *Sorry. What are you talking about?*

"What did she say?" Rachel asked.

"Oh, right," Carter said. "She just apologized for spacing out."

"But you can read lips, right?" Rachel asked her.

Daniela nodded, then gestured at the fire. *But only if there's enough light. It'll be harder when the sun sets.*

Again, Carter interpreted.

"All of you know sign?" Rachel asked.

"We learned after they'd been dating for a few months," Jo explained.

"I'm not great at it," Meg admitted.

"How cool!" Rachel said. "Now I want to learn."

Daniela grinned. *Thanks.*

"How do you say 'you're welcome'?"

You're welcome, Daniela said.

You're welcome, Rachel repeated. "Neat!"

Rachel and Daniela continued to talk, Meg and Carter acting as interpreters, and Jo thought of the birthday party they'd thrown Daniela five years ago. Jo, Carter, and Meg had taken an accelerated course in ASL as a surprise, and Daniela had been so touched she'd spent the first ten minutes of her party crying. More classes and years of study and individual work with Daniela and some of her hearing-impaired friends had made both Carter and Jo nearly fluent.

After that birthday surprise, the four of them had been nearly inseparable. Every weekend, Jo would drive down to see them in Boulder, or they would drive up to see her and Meg in Fort Collins. Since the breakup, she'd seen them perhaps three times, and every time Daniela made her excuses and left early or found something else to do. She knew Daniela blamed her for the relationship between her and Elsa ending and for losing her best friend and business partner. She didn't know what Elsa had told her, but Daniela was furious with her, refusing to listen to her side then or since. Jo had tried several times to patch things up, explain, but Daniela wouldn't talk to her.

"The solution is tequila," Meg said, breaking into her thoughts.

"What?" Jo asked, laughing.

"The solution is always tequila," Meg said, grinning.

"I've got some more lime juice," Rachel said.

I brought simple syrup.

"Sounds like a party to me!" Rachel shouted.

Jo woke instantly when she heard it again—those careful movements in the woods, somewhere nearby. She remembered then the trick of the sound from earlier. Daniela and Carter had been fairly far away when she'd heard them coming up the hill, but they'd seemed much closer. Still, she was almost certain what she heard now was nearer than that—a few yards beyond the tents, at most.

The others had spent the evening drinking heavily, laughing, joking, and eventually dancing around the fire to the tinny music piped out of Meg's phone. Jo had nursed a single margarita, smiling along with the others, but after the first hour, she hadn't been capable of joining in. She was too tired to let herself go and was worried she might say something stupid to Daniela if she got too drunk. As the evening drew on, she'd found herself drawing farther and farther away from the others. Carter threw her a few hurt, questioning glances, but eventually even she got too drunk to notice that Jo was keeping to herself. Daniela, on the other hand, didn't look her way a single time all evening. Jo had left the others when they started slow dancing, knowing they wouldn't miss her. She'd been forced to listen to what followed after the couples went to their tents.

The sound in the woods, if possible, grew louder, closer, and Jo was certain she'd heard what she'd thought she heard—footsteps, soft and even, moving carefully through the trees. She sat up, squinting, but couldn't detect any light source beyond the walls of her tent. Whatever or whoever it was could somehow see in the dark.

After carefully scooting out of her bag, she put her hand on the zipper of her tent and inched it open, moving as slowly and carefully as she could. She muffled the zipper's swish with her other hand, but it was still clearly audible in the dead silence of the night. She paused with the flap about halfway open and listened again, but the footsteps had stopped. Grabbing her flashlight, she jerked the zipper open and sprang out of her tent, running in the direction of the footsteps.

The light from her flashlight barely penetrated the dark. The woods were so dense her line of sight was significantly shortened—maybe ten feet, at most, in any direction. The air was strangely hazy, almost foggy, and surprisingly cold. That sour, rotting stink she'd smelled before was stronger, closer. She paused, standing still, and shone her light in a wide arc around her, expecting to see some kind of carrion. She took a few seconds to slow her breathing and crept forward into a cluster of trees, carefully stepping over branches in her wool socks. She winced when a rock bit into her foot but managed not to call out. She paused again and turned off her light, then waited a long while for her eyes to adjust to the dark. Moving as silently as she could, she inched forward, feeling her way with her hands. She managed to maneuver around a large pine tree and stopped, her back to the tree. She held her breath, listening, but heard nothing. She made herself stand there, hand over her mouth to muffle her breath, and waited. Five minutes. Ten.

Nothing.

She took a deep breath, the stench assaulting her at once. She let out the air in a loud cough, almost gagging, and covered her nose with a chilly hand. She listened again, stifling more coughs. Whatever had made that noise had apparently had enough time to escape when she'd opened her tent. It was gone now.

Or perhaps, a tiny part of her said, there was no noise. You dreamt it.

Arguing with herself, she shook her head in the dark. She was certain she'd heard something. The smell alone suggested that some kind of animal had hidden its dinner somewhere nearby. More than likely, however, it was farther away from her than she thought. Sound and odor traveled far in thin, mountain air. Still, she knew now she'd probably never catch it like this—not unless it came back and she slept outside her tent. It was always going to hear her getting out.

She shivered, hard, from exhaustion and cold. She should go back to her tent, sound or no sound. The ground here was very dry, but her feet were still uncomfortable on the rocky soil beneath her socks. She hadn't taken her fleece, either, and the temperature had dropped some twenty or thirty degrees since the sun set. Her legs felt weak and limp, and her arms were aching from the work on the cabin. It had been reckless to run out here in the dark. Why had she done that again? It had seemed important, crucial somehow, but now, standing here in the dark, she just felt stupid, impulsive. Twice today she'd acted without thinking things through. That wasn't like her at all.

Disgusted with herself, she pushed away from the tree, fiddling with her flashlight in the dark. Just as she managed to turn it on, she heard a loud snap behind her. She was spinning that way when something hit the back of her head, and then she was falling.

CHAPTER SIX

When Jo woke up, people were screaming her name. She immediately tried to get up, but her arms and legs, cramped from lying on the ground, were uncoordinated, stiff. After she finally managed to lever herself to her feet, she swayed, dizzy. That rancid smell was back, filling her nose and mouth, and then it was gone, almost as if she'd imagined it. The pain finally registered, and she touched the back of her head. It was wet and her hair was matted, and as she held up her fingers, the blood on them was a thick, clotted red. She took a stumbling step forward, almost went down, then grabbed the nearest tree for support.

"I'm here!" she shouted.

The screaming stopped, the voices a jumble of confusing words as they came in her direction. She spotted Carter first and gave her a weak wave with her free hand, still too dizzy to let go of the tree.

"Jesus, Jo. What are you doing out here?"

"Your tent was wide open," Meg added. "Your shoes, your jacket—you left everything behind."

Rachel and Daniela were silent, a few feet behind. Rachel appeared scared, pale, and Daniela looked almost violently angry.

When they were a few feet away, Jo saw Carter's face clench with concern. "Why are you leaning on that tree like that?"

"Because I'm about to fall over. I'm dizzy."

Carter and Meg immediately leapt forward to help her, propping her up between them and nearly carrying her under each arm. She was surprised to find how far she was from the camp. It took several minutes for them to help her back. Reviewing what had happened, she thought she'd walked, at most, twenty feet from camp before she stood in the dark, listening. Instead, it appeared she'd traveled quite far into the woods. How had that happened? The memory was dim, almost dreamy. She remembered the sound, remembered feeling like she needed to find whatever was making it, and then things began to get hazy. She recalled a smell, but what else?

She winced when they set her down, her whole body complaining. The cut on the back of her head was throbbing, the pain sharp and biting.

Meg and Carter were breathing heavily, hands on their knees. Daniela stepped in front of her. *What were you doing out there? No coat, no shoes—you could have gotten hypothermia.*

Again, her expression seemed less like concern and more like anger, almost rage.

Jo waited, trying to formulate a response. Thinking back, what she'd done was pretty ridiculous. Why had she run out into the woods on her own in the middle of the night? What had she thought to accomplish? Her motivations were as hazy as her memory. Still, she had an explanation of sorts.

"I heard something. In the woods. So I went to check it out."

"Without a coat?" Carter asked, clearly baffled.

Jo shook her head and then winced again, her fingers straying up to the back of her head.

"Is that blood?" Rachel asked, her voice high and scared.

"Yes. Something hit—I mean, I must have hit something. That's why I was still in the woods."

"You mean you passed out?" Carter asked, her voice rising.

"I guess so. I don't really remember."

Carter put one hand to her forehead. "So let me get this straight. First, you run into the woods without shoes or a jacket, all because you heard something. What did you hear?"

Jo shrugged and again shook her head, forgetting, too late, how much any movement made it hurt.

Carter's frown had deepened. "So you run into the woods, no coat, no shoes, and then you hit your head on something. And you hit it hard enough to pass out. That's what happened?"

Jo wasn't sure how to respond. Something warned her not to tell them what she thought had happened—that something or someone in the woods had attacked her. She knew simply from the way they were all staring at her that they wouldn't believe her. She wasn't even sure she believed herself. She remembered trying to turn the flashlight on, she remembered the smell and hearing something behind her, and then what? She'd moved toward the sound, quickly. Had a branch been there, in the dark? Had she hit her head on it? Or had something or someone hit her? She didn't know for sure. The whole incident seemed like it had happened weeks ago, not hours.

Jo sighed. "I don't remember. But yeah, I think that's basically it."

Carter was speechless, her face mottled red with anger.

"What the hell, Jo?" Meg finally asked.

"Daniela's right—you could have been killed," Carter said, her voice low. "You might have gotten hypothermia or fallen down the hill and broken your leg."

Or your neck, Daniela added.

"What were you thinking?"

Jo peered up at the four of them, all angry and upset with her. No way could she convince them that the sound had been compelling enough to risk what she'd done, when she knew herself how stupid she'd been. Even if, as she'd suspected last night, someone was walking around their camp, the last thing she should have done was run after them in the dark, giving herself away. Why had she done that? She could remember thinking it was a good idea—no, more than that, it had been almost a compulsion. She'd *had* to do it. But why?

Carter finally sighed and lifted her hands. "Anyway, it doesn't matter right now. We're going to have to take you down to a hospital, Jo."

"What? No way."

"Yes way. You probably have a concussion, and you're going to need stitches. That's more than my little first-aid kit can handle."

"Oh, come on. It's not that bad. I'll be fine if I just sit here for a while."

"What is it with butches and doctors?" Rachel asked.

Carter spun toward her angrily, and then her expression seemed to fight with itself. Finally, she laughed. Some of the tension drained out of everyone, and Jo gave Rachel a quick, thankful smile before she touched Carter's hand.

"Isn't there an emergency clinic at the ranger station? Couldn't I go there first? See what they say? I don't want to drive back to town if we can avoid it."

Carter stared at her evenly and then nodded, clearly reluctant. "Okay. If you want. But if they tell us we need to go to the hospital, we're going. No arguments."

"Okay."

Carter continued to glare a while longer and then shook her head. "I still don't understand why you did that, Jo. You're lucky to be alive."

"I know. I'm sorry."

They were quiet, staring at each other, and Jo could see the clear worry in Carter's eyes. Ashamed of herself, she couldn't understand why she'd been so reckless. Had she wanted to hurt herself? Her actions made no sense now.

Carter, as if sensing her thoughts, suddenly grinned and winked at her. "Of course, this also means another chance to see that hot forest ranger, Andy."

Last night, deep into their margarita party, Carter and Jo had told the others about the gorgeous forest ranger who had saved them on the side of the road. They might have exaggerated a little for laughs, but the others hadn't believed most of what they'd told them.

Daniela swatted at her. *Hey! I'm right here, jackass.*

Carter laughed. *Sorry, hon. But if you saw her, you'd understand what I mean.* She turned to Meg. "It's gonna have to be me and you taking my genius cousin down to the car, lady. Think you can handle it?"

Meg flexed her arms a couple of times. "Oh, yeah. Let's do it."

Carter stepped toward Daniela and touched her face briefly. *Will you and Rachel be okay up here on your own, or do you want to come with us?*

We'll be fine. We'll finish cleaning the main room and start setting up in there. Just get back soon, okay?

Carter kissed her and motioned to Meg. "Come on. Let's get this over with."

❖

The trip down the mountain went far faster than Jo had feared. After a shaky start, her head had cleared a lot, and by the final stretch, she was walking, for the most part, on her own, only occasionally holding Carter's arm for support. The main thing now was the pain. In addition to the cut on her head, lying on the ground all night had made her neck and limbs cramp. She didn't know how long she'd been there, but from the way she ached, it must have been hours. By the time they reached the car, her legs felt quite a lot better from the exercise, but her neck still hurt, and her arms were spasming and painful to move.

Their family had been given permission from Rocky to make a

little two-car parking lot at the foot of their hill, which was technically public land. Private-property markers in front of the trail to the cabin warned off the public, but this far from the main highway through the park, they weren't that necessary. Few people drove up this way, and even then, they headed to the marked trails farther up the road. Most people would miss it if they didn't know where to look.

The road from their parking lot went downhill from their land through the park for almost ten miles before it intersected the main, two-lane highway that stretched most of the length of the park. The ranger station was located about two miles beyond this toward town. The station here was sizeable, with a small public building and several others around it that housed equipment and staff. Still, when they pulled into the parking lot, she saw only one vehicle there—the old green Bronco truck with park-service symbols on the doors.

As they were getting out, Officer Knox opened the door and came outside, smiling as she walked over to meet them at their car.

"Jesus," Meg whispered to Jo. "You weren't kidding."

Jo nodded, trying not to smile.

"Nice to see you again," Andy said. "What can I help you with today?"

Carter shook her head. "My idiot cousin here managed to hit her head on a branch running around in the dark and spent the night passed out in the woods. We're wondering if there's someone here who can take a look at her."

"Sure. Come on it. I just made some coffee, too, if anyone's interested."

They were led into the public building. It was dark inside, the small windows doing little to light the room, but the place was cozy, warm, all of it made from the same light-colored pinewood. This first room had a counter that stretched the length of one wall, as well as rotating stands with maps and pamphlets, and some tables and shelves with an assorted collection of souvenirs. There was a small sitting area near an empty fireplace.

"You guys can wait here. Coffee's on the hob there." Andy pointed and then led Jo behind the counter and through a door into a small, one-room clinic. No one was here.

"Is there a nurse somewhere?" Jo asked.

Andy shook her head, grinning. "Nope—just me. Have a seat."

"But are you…"

Andy laughed. "A doctor? No. Paramedic."

Jo sat down on the edge of the examining table, the blue paper cover crinkling loudly in the small room. The clinic was bright and white, a marked difference from the other room. She watched Andy wash and dry her hands and begin to set up a little tray of equipment. She moved with precision and slow, careful certainty. Something about the way she handled herself was surprising from someone as tall and clearly muscular as this woman—a kind of unexpected grace.

Despite the awful glare of the overhead lights, Andy's skin was luminous, tanned a dark golden brown. She had little laugh lines near her startling blue eyes, and Jo thought she might be older than she'd first guessed—late thirties or even early forties, perhaps, a few years older than her. The muscles on Andy's forearms bunched and shifted under her skin as she placed things on the tray, and her hands, which were large and finely muscled, still seemed strangely delicate as she pulled on gloves. Even beyond her stunning face, Jo sensed something absolutely compelling, almost mesmerizing about her—a kind of presence that drew the eye. She found, as she had yesterday, that she couldn't look away.

She realized Andy had asked her something, and she snapped into reality again, wrenching her eyes away from those hands. "I'm sorry, what?"

Andy grinned. "Do you have any confusion? Memory loss?"

She started to shake her head and stopped with the sharp bark of pain this motion caused. "No—none."

"Feel nauseated at all?"

"No."

"Dizziness?"

Jo hesitated and then nodded. "Not anymore, but I was really dizzy when I woke up."

"That's not good. Okay—let me check you out."

Andy set the trail of equipment down on a little table and then sat on a stool near her. She rolled closer and leaned in, peering into her eyes with that fierce, icy gaze long enough that Jo's face started to heat.

"Your pupils are okay," Andy said, moving back a little. She grabbed a pen off the tray. "Follow the tip of this with your eyes." She moved it around, up and down and side to side before setting it down. "How does your head feel? Do you have a headache?"

Jo shook her head. "Not exactly. The back of my head hurts like hell when I touch it, and I'm stiff all over."

Andy winked at her. "That will happen if you sleep on the ground."

She reached over to her tray and picked up a little rubber mallet. "I'm going to check your reflexes now." She tapped each knee, making Jo's legs jump, and they both laughed.

"It always looks so silly," Jo said.

"I'm going to check for muscle weakness now," Andy said. She put her hands on Jo's thigh. "Push up." She did the same with the other leg. "Okay," she said, grabbing her forearm. "Pull." They repeated the process with her other arm.

Andy rolled a little farther away and smiled. "Things seem pretty good. You have no memory loss, no headache aside from the wound, your reflexes and muscles are fine. If you have a concussion, it's very minor, but I'm pretty sure you don't have one. Let's see that cut now."

She stood up, moving behind Jo, her body brushing hers as she examined her head. Jo went rigid, expecting pain, but Andy's fingers only brushed her hair aside, gently avoiding the actual cut.

"I need to clean this out to be sure, Jo, but I don't think it's as bad as I feared. Head wounds bleed a lot, so it's always hard to tell how big they are." She grabbed a towel. "Here—put this around your shoulders." She picked up a large, clear squirt bottle full of liquid and showed it to Jo. "This is mostly water, but it has a little astringent in it, so it will probably sting. Is that okay?"

"Yes."

It stung much more than she expected, and the liquid was surprisingly cold. Andy touched the wound, making Jo gasp.

"Okay, it's like I said—not bad at all. I don't see anything we can't treat here."

"Why does it hurt so much?"

"It was hard to tell with your hair, but I think the whole area is a little bruised, which, of course, makes sense if you hit your head on a big branch or a rock. But it only punctured the skin in one place. We can put a butterfly bandage on it, and it should be fine. If you're really worried about it, it certainly wouldn't hurt to have a doctor check it, but you seem to have lucked out." She paused, meeting her eyes. "Still—you should be careful for a couple of days. Try to sleep sitting up as much as possible, and have someone check on you every two or three hours tonight.

"Take it easy physically, too. No heavy labor for a few days—nothing too strenuous and nothing that gets your heart rate up too high. If you get dizzy again, or start getting nauseated or have a bad headache, go into town and have a doctor examine you." She paused again, and

Jo was surprised to see her face color. She cleared her throat. "Also, if you want, you can use my shower before I put the bandage on. Get that blood off you. Just don't shampoo, okay? Water only for today."

Jo's own face went hot, and she couldn't wrench her eyes away from Andy's. She managed to nod. "A shower would be great."

Andy looked away. "It's in a different building. I'll show you where and then go talk to your cousin and your friend."

She led her out the back door and up to a long, low wooden building at the back of the complex. There were several doors, which, Jo assumed correctly, led to staff housing. They stopped at one of the doors, and Andy gestured. "Let me get you a towel." She went inside, and Jo, curious, peered inside. The room was somewhat spartan—a narrow twin bed and a chair, a small dresser, and nothing else, nothing personal. It was tidy, everything in its place, just as she would have expected from this woman. Andy got a fresh towel out of her dresser and handed it to her.

"Shower room is just down there," she pointed, "the door with the long handle. You'll find soap and stuff in there in my locker." She frowned. "Do you have any clean clothes to change into?"

"No, but that's okay. I can change when we get back to the cabin."

Andy's eyebrows shot up. "You're going back up there? Camping?"

"Well, yes. You said everything was okay."

Andy shook her head. "Not for that—not for sleeping on the ground. Not for hiking. All of that could be bad for you."

"We've almost got the cabin ready. We should be on the beds tonight. Inside."

Andy frowned. "I don't know, Jo. I think you should go home. Ask a friend to come over and check on you overnight."

Jo sighed. "I'll be fine—really. You said so yourself. And I promise I'll have the others keep tabs on me tonight."

Andy was still frowning, and Jo had a wild impulse to laugh. She was beginning to find her careful concern endearing and almost, she was forced to admit, as attractive as the rest of her.

"I'll be okay. I promise to be careful. There's no difference between sleeping in a cabin and sleeping in town, and I'll have four of my friends watching me."

Andy's face and body relaxed a little, and she nodded. "Okay. But I'm going to come see you, too."

"Come as often as you like," Jo said, then nearly bit her tongue to keep from laughing. Despite everything, she was coming on to her.

Andy nodded, smiling a little. "I will. I have tomorrow afternoon off, and I'll visit then. Is that okay?"

Jo grinned. "Of course."

They stared at each other for a long time, and Jo knew that Andy had understood the clear invitation she'd just given—it wasn't only to check up on her head wound.

Andy broke eye contact first, that slight color back in her cheeks. "I'll go tell the others what I found."

Jo watched her walk away, back toward the other building, her long, fine legs bunching under her khaki slacks. If she knew Jo was watching her, she didn't let on, and Jo had to grin to herself. Maybe she wanted Jo to watch. The sight was absolutely worth it.

When Andy disappeared into the other building, Jo finally remembered what she was doing and headed into the shower room. It apparently served for the whole staff, as there was a bank of ten lockers, each with a little name label. She opened the one labeled A. Knox, which was, of course, immaculate, everything inside folded or stacked neatly and even, as if by a professional cleaning service. She saw a travel bottle labeled Soap, which, when she held it up to her nose, had a strangely delicate, natural odor—chamomile, perhaps, and something else, something floral.

She set the bottle and her towel beside a shower stall and, after turning on the water to warm up, suddenly caught sight of herself in a mirror over one of the sinks. Her short, blond, wavy hair was matted, greasy, and sticking up all over her head—the back wet from the astringent Andy had poured over it. Her face, normally tan and healthy, was strangely pale and streaked with dirt and blood. Her eyes were bloodshot, the whites almost entirely dark red. She looked tired and worn, far older than she actually was.

Her hopes about Andy sank. Who was she kidding? Andy was probably just trying to be nice.

CHAPTER SEVEN

The electricity was on now in the whole cabin to help with cleaning, and Jo, sitting quietly with her book and a cup of tea, finally felt as if their little place was coming together again. She'd managed to sleep on the couch last night, but eventually they would have to replace all the cushions on it and the armchairs. Otherwise this main living room was almost as nice as it had been two years ago. She felt a little guilty just sitting here, but she also wanted to make sure that when Andy showed up in a couple of hours, she would be doing just as she asked—absolutely nothing.

Jo set her book down on the little side table next to her and closed her eyes, picturing the moment Andy appeared at the cabin later this afternoon. She would be wearing her regular clothes, not her uniform, but somehow Jo couldn't imagine her without her ugly brown pants and button-up work shirt. Her fantasy version of the woman was even wearing her brown campaign hat. She would be smiling with that same inviting warmth, and Jo would walk up to her and...

Here the fantasy broke down. What would she do? It had been hard enough to talk to Andy yesterday when they had a topic of conversation—her head wound. What on earth would they discuss? She would make some initial introductions, since Daniela and Rachel hadn't met her yet, but what would happen after that? It seemed ages ago that she had needed to talk to a woman she was interested in. True, since Elsa, she'd gone out to the bars a few times, and had even picked up a woman on a couple of different occasions, but that had been different. Those encounters hadn't needed conversation beyond the merest initial greeting. How did you talk to someone you actually wanted to get to know?

It didn't help that, before Elsa, she had still been in something of a wild oats phase, sleeping around, not actually dating anyone. She'd had one serious girlfriend in her mid-twenties before that, but no one else had lasted longer than a month or two. And Elsa had been the one to pursue her, not the other way around. Jo had no idea how to ask someone out.

She sighed and opened her eyes again, giving up. Most likely Andy would show up, and she'd make a complete ass of herself and never see her again. That was the most realistic scenario she could picture right now. And anyway, regardless of what Carter had said, she wasn't sure Andy was actually interested, or even a lesbian, for that matter. There were plenty of straight women in Colorado like her—a little butch, a little outdoorsy, a lot hot.

She reached for her book and then frowned. It wasn't there. She looked around next to her, on the couch she'd slept on and the floor, and didn't see it. She stood up, moving the little pillow she'd been leaning on to the side, but it wasn't underneath either. She got down on her knees and peered under the couch, but didn't see anything. She stood up again and paused, frowning deeper. She'd been sure she set it down right next to her on the table. She would have heard it fall.

The door to one of the bedrooms opened, and Daniela came into the room, holding Jo's book. She handed it to her with a strange expression.

Is this yours?

Jo nodded, completely confused. She set it back down on the side table before asking, *Where did you find it?*

Daniela shook her head, frowning. *That's the weird thing. I was cleaning in there, getting the beds set up, and then suddenly it was on top of the sheets I set on the dresser. I swear I'd just looked at them, and I didn't see the book then. One minute it wasn't there, and the next it was. I can't figure it out.*

How did it get in there?

Daniela seemed just as confused as she felt. *Don't you know?*

Jo shook her head.

They both stood there, staring at each other, and Jo's heart rate picked up a little. There was absolutely no way her book could have gotten in to the bedroom without someone carrying it there. She hadn't been in there since the first day Carter was here. Consciously or unconsciously, she'd been avoiding that room.

Weird, Daniela said.

No kidding.

Jo thought of the creepy, almost sculpture-like pile of furniture she had found the first day. She hadn't told anyone how much it had upset her at the time, and she'd avoided thinking about it since. The idea that someone had broken into their place and done that was unsettling, at best. Though Carter had dismantled it, moving half of the cots, lamps, and one of the dressers into the other bedroom, something about the artful way it had had been arranged had been bothering her on some deep level ever since. She would catch herself remembering it and begin to feel that same sick dread again—a violation in some undefined way. Their cousin Martin had claimed ignorance when she called him, and Jo believed him. Neither she nor Carter had told the others what she'd found, but she suddenly wasn't so sure they'd made the right choice to keep quiet. And then there was the noise in the woods—those careful, certain footsteps she'd heard inside the tent. She hadn't imagined those, either. All of it felt connected somehow, similar in some way, but she couldn't quite tell why. Almost as if the person and the woods and the furniture sculptor were one and the same, but not quite that either. Anytime she thought about either incident, that same chill seemed to wash through her. Even now, goose bumps were standing up on her arms, but why?

Daniela finally shrugged. *Who knows? Maybe I accidently picked up the book earlier with the sheets.*

Jo knew for certain that wasn't the case, but she nodded. *Maybe.*

Daniela was frowning again, clearly sensing some of Jo's uncertainty. *You think it was something else?*

Jo was suddenly anxious that she would give something away. *What else could it be?*

Daniela continued to meet her eyes, squinting a little now as if trying to read her thoughts. Finally, she shrugged.

Okay. Well, I better get back to work. I'm almost done in there, and I want to set up the other beds for tonight.

She turned to leave, and a sudden surge of sorrow swept through Jo. This conversation, strange as it'd been, was their longest in months. Always, like now, like the last two days, Daniela avoided talking to her for any length of time. At one point, Jo had considered her another cousin, a best friend, and now this fury had risen between them. After the initial heartache of the breakup, with Elsa moving to Denver and leaving both of them behind, Jo had actually felt worse about Daniela's anger than about being single. She'd tried several times the first few weeks to talk to Daniela about it and then had given up, avoiding both her and Carter, hoping Daniela's rage would die down. She realized now she should have pushed harder, as, instead of better, things had simply grown worse between them with time.

Daniela was almost to the bedroom now, and Jo nearly decided to let her go. The last thing anyone needed was a fight or hurt feelings, most of all Carter, who couldn't help but feel like she was in the middle of whatever this was. But she had to try.

She jumped into action, quickly catching up. Daniela must have sensed her coming. Her face was hard when she met Jo's eyes.

Not now.

No—we need to talk, Daniela. I know you said this was just between us, but how could it be otherwise? Carter knows you're mad at me, and she's upset about it. I don't want this to get between us. More importantly, I want you to stop hating me.

Daniela shook her head. *I don't hate you, Jo. I'm just disappointed. Elsa was my best friend.*

So, what am I? We're family, at the very least.

Families fight. And I'm not ready to forgive you, Jo.

For what?

You know.

I seriously have no idea what you're talking about.

The front door opened, and Carter came in, blinking to adjust to the relative darkness inside. The lights were on, but they were nothing compared to the bright sunshine outside. She frowned.

"Are you two fighting?"

"No."

Yes.

Carter sighed. *Daniela—*

Forget it, Daniela said. *I knew you'd take her side.* She went into the bedroom and slammed the door behind her.

Carter's face fell, and Jo walked over to her swiftly, pulling her into a hug. Carter pushed her away.

"What did you say to her?"

"Nothing! All I said was I wanted to talk. She won't listen to me. She won't even try."

"Goddamn it, Jo, don't put me in the middle."

"What do you want me to do? You asked me to talk to her—I've tried. Twice now. She's not interested. I don't know if she ever will be."

Carter's eyes welled with tears, and then she furiously wiped at them before shaking her head, hard. "What do you want me to do? That's my wife in there. You can't ask me to—"

"I'm not asking you to *do* anything, Carter. I'm just telling you how it is. She's furious, and she won't tell me why."

They stared at each other for a long, silent spell. Jo watched as several expressions passed across her cousin's face—anger, sadness, anger again. Then a deep weariness seemed to settle on her. Even her shoulders sagged.

Finally, Carter spoke. "Maybe you should leave."

Jo felt as if she'd been slapped. It was all she could do not to burst into tears. Again, they stared at each other in silence, and Jo blinked a few times to clear her eyes.

"Okay. I'll go pack."

She started toward the door, but Carter touched her shoulder, making her turn around.

"I'm sorry. I just don't know what else to do. I'll give you a ride when you're ready."

Jo forced herself to nod and then went outside.

She stood on the porch, taking deep breaths to calm down, a deep depression now settling on her like a heavy weight. Just yesterday, she'd been thinking she should leave the four of them up here, but she hadn't wanted this. She hadn't wanted to be forced to go. She should have left on her own when she first thought of it.

She headed toward her tent, passing Rachel and Meg, who were taking a break by the fire pit. They both called out to her, but she wasn't capable of talking right now. She waved at them and kept walking, sure that if she said anything to either of them, she'd break down crying.

She knelt down by her tent to unzip it and pulled out her air mattress and sleeping bag, looking around vaguely for the stuff sacks they both traveled in. She was stunned by what had just happened.

"Going somewhere?" a voice said behind her.

It was Andy—Andy like she'd never seen her. It was no wonder she hadn't been able to imagine her like this. Her maroon shorts revealed a set of impossibly long legs—legs that seemed to go on and on the farther and farther her eye climbed. Andy was wearing a light-blue T-shirt made of a thin cotton that hugged all her many curves. No one could dream up a woman as gorgeous as the vision in front of her. She positively glowed with a radiant, healthy beauty, her skin kissed by a thin sheen of sweat from her hike up the mountain.

Jo found herself completely unable to respond, but she somehow managed to climb to her feet. Desperately, she sought to put the words together in her mind. "I, uh…"

Andy's brows knit. "Are you confused? Do you need to sit down?" She put a hand on Jo's shoulder as if to steady her.

An electric shock ran through her at Andy's touch, and Jo almost shuddered with the warm heat that passed through her. She made herself take a slight step away to stop from melting into the ground.

"No. I'm fine. I just—"

"She's just packing up to bring the rest of her stuff inside," Carter said, appearing behind Andy.

"Oh good," Andy said, smiling. "I was worried there for a second. You should be sitting down, anyway, Jo. You're a little pale. I want to take another look at that cut."

Rachel and Daniela were standing a little farther away, close to the fire pit, both of them gaping at Andy like they couldn't believe what they were seeing. Andy, as if sensing this reaction, turned toward them with a smile and walked their way, holding out a hand. Jo began to follow her, but Carter grabbed her arm and pulled her to a stop.

"Hang on a second, Jo. I'm sorry. I don't know what I was thinking. I don't want you to leave. I should never have said that. I don't know why I did."

A wild rage surged up in her breast, and she shook herself free of Carter's hand. A second later the rage was gone, and she finally burst into tears. Carter pulled her into a rough hug and then steered her away from the others, back into the trees for a little privacy.

"Christ," Jo said, shaking her head. She wiped her face angrily with her arm. "Andy's going to think I'm a real catch. I can't talk to her, and now I'm crying."

Carter smiled. "She won't think that. And anyway, she didn't see, and nobody else noticed."

Jo smiled. "Not with Andy around—that's for sure. Did you see their faces? Rachel almost fell over at the sight of her."

Carter waved a hand in front of her face. "I don't mind admitting that I felt about the same. Damn. You really have to ask her out."

They were quiet for a long spell, and then Jo hugged her again. She was no longer angry or upset about what Carter had said, just sad. For the last six months, she'd done her best to avoid thinking about the situation between her and Daniela, but now here it was, out in the open, and it had been festering all this time despite her best intentions.

"I don't want you to feel like you're in the middle of it, Carter. Maybe it's like Daniela said—it's between us, not you."

Carter nodded, her eyes still worried.

"Just give us some time, okay? Neither one of us wants to fight, and I know neither one of us wants you to feel badly about this, either. Maybe Daniela will talk to me, and maybe she won't. But either way, we both love you."

Carter sighed and tried to smile. "Okay, Jo. I just want you both to be happy."

Jo peered around Carter, catching sight of Andy towering above the others. They were all clearly flummoxed, gawking at her like they'd never seen a woman before, and a little thrill of excitement rippled through her at the thought of getting to be around her again.

Carter turned to follow her gaze and laughed. "Can't keep your eyes off her, can you?"

"Nope."

Carter pushed her a little toward the others and Andy. "Go get her, tiger."

Jo staggered a little, straightened her shoulders, and winked at Carter before heading Andy's way.

CHAPTER EIGHT

A nd this is the second bedroom," Jo said.

"Nice little place you got here," Andy said, peering around the room.

"Supposedly our great-great-grandmother built it."

Andy grinned. "On her own?"

"That's the story, anyway. I don't know if it's true, since we're pretty sure her husband is buried up here, but that's what we've been told. I keep meaning to research the details."

They stood there silently for a long, awkward pause, and Jo desperately sought a new topic of conversation. Carter had been the one to suggest the tour, but with a three-room cabin, there wasn't much to show. The others were outside.

"Can I offer you a drink? Water? Soda?"

Andy smiled. "Water, thanks."

Jo led the way back into the main room, grateful that the kitchen, at least, was in good shape. She filled a glass with ice and water and handed it to Andy.

Watching her drink made Jo's stomach feel funny, but she couldn't look away. Andy's long throat was exposed, the bronze, flawless skin bunching as she swallowed. Jo's mouth went dry, and she licked her lips, unconsciously mimicking what she'd like to do to that skin.

Andy set the glass down on the counter and smiled at her again. "Thanks. It was a hot hike up here."

Jo nodded, speechless.

Andy turned around, taking in the room, hands on her hips. "So your whole family owns this cabin and the land?"

"Not quite. It's still in probate. Carter's trying to arrange it so that we all own it equally, but for now it's just a verbal agreement. Carter and I offered to clean it out in exchange for getting one of the summer months scheduled up here for the two of us to share every year."

"Well, it's really wonderful. I can't tell you how much I envy you guys. You couldn't buy anything like this now in this part of the state."

"You have a nice place at the station, too," Jo said, feeling like an idiot the second she spoke.

Andy shrugged. "It's okay. Better than some of the housing I've had in the past. My apartment in town is better."

"You've worked at other parks?"

She nodded. "I was at Yellowstone before this, and in the army before that."

"Oh?"

"Medical corps."

"Ah."

Again, Jo felt like a complete moron. Get it together, she told herself. Give her more than one-word responses.

"So how long have you been in Colorado?"

Andy counted on her fingers briefly. "Going on five years now—five years in November."

"So how does it work? Being a ranger, I mean. Do you work here all year?"

"For the most part. I'm occasionally rotated for a week or two to another park, sometimes longer, but I volunteer to do that. Works kind of like a paid vacation."

"That's really interesting."

"What do you do?"

"I work for the city in the parks department."

"Oh! That's cool. Down in Estes?"

"No—Fort Collins. I love Estes, though."

Conversation dried up, and Jo couldn't help but feel like this opportunity was slipping through her fingers. Here was a gorgeous woman, clearly interested in getting to know her, and she was acting like she'd never talked to anyone before. Scrambling, she finally thought of something.

"Do you want to see the best part of being up here?"

Andy smiled. "Better than this?"

Jo grinned and grabbed her hand before she thought better of it. "Follow me."

They went back outside, the sunshine now so desperately bright and hot it felt like walking into the desert. The others were back to working on clearing the vines and branches on the outside of the cabin, and Carter threw her a quick wink as they walked past them toward a small trail.

"I don't know if you should be out here," Andy said. "You should be inside taking it easy in this heat."

"It's just up ahead," Jo said, still pulling her along. Andy hadn't tried to free her hand, so she took that as a good sign.

The cabin had been built on the highest flat part of their small mountain, but it wasn't quite at the top. Jo led the way to the peak, some hundred feet up a steep trail, and when they reached a small, rocky plateau, the trees opened up, revealing the entire valley. She heard Andy's breath catch at the sight, and the two of them stopped to take it in. From here, the view was unbroken—no roads, no buildings, no power lines, nothing but trees and hills and the steeper peaks of higher mountains, a vast sea of green and yellow in all directions. The sky was a crystalline, cloudless blue, and the sun shone down as if on heaven itself.

Andy was standing next to her now, holding her hand as comfortably and naturally as if she'd always done it. Jo gave it a slight squeeze, and Andy grinned down at her, her eyes the same intense blue as the sky.

"It's amazing."

Jo nodded in simple agreement, and they continued to stand there in silence, the majesty of the view not needing an explanation or conversation.

"Sorry to interrupt," Carter said behind them.

They both jumped a little and turned around. Andy's hand slipped from hers, and Jo had a stab of regret. Carter was grinning, and Jo knew she'd seen them.

"What's up?"

"We're missing some of our equipment. I just wondered if you put it somewhere."

"I didn't move anything. What's missing?"

Carter waved a hand dismissively. "It's fine. We'll keep looking. Just wanted to ask."

"We'd be happy to help," Andy offered. Jo warmed with pleasure at the word "we."

Again, Carter waved. "No, no, really, it's fine. I must have put it down somewhere and forgot."

"No, please. Let us help."

Andy started toward Carter, and Jo regretted the interruption before moving after them and down the trail. At least she knew now what it took to impress Andy—the very thing she loved herself.

The three of them joined the others, all of whom were searching around the camp, lifting tarps that had been set up around the camp to cover various piles of equipment to keep them out of the weather.

"What are we looking for?" Andy asked.

"Some shears and a little saw I brought up. They're all bundled with a red bungee cord. I thought I put all the stuff over there on the porch when I was unloading the cart, but I guess not."

Jo could remember seeing the bundle Carter was describing. They'd tied the tools together to keep them from rattling too much up the hill. Jo also remembered seeing the bundle on the porch this morning with the rest of the outdoor supplies. She went there first but didn't see it. She walked around the outside of the cabin, moving loose, leafy branches and pine boughs aside, raising piles of branches and vines they'd already tied together with the twine, but by the time she'd circled the whole cabin, she still hadn't found the missing shears and saw.

Carter was standing by the porch, hands on her hips, frowning.

"I would have sworn they were right here," she said, pointing at the spot Jo remembered.

"I saw them there, too," Jo said.

"So where did they go?"

Jo shook her head. "I don't know, but it can't be far. I'm sure they'll turn up eventually."

She heard laughter and saw Rachel and Andy talking by the fire pit, both of them smiling and gesturing wildly. They were a little too far away to hear clearly, but she could detect a hint of excitement in their tone and movements. Meg was standing near them, smiling slightly at the two of them.

Jo and Carter walked closer, and Andy and Rachel stopped talking to smile at them.

"You'll never believe it," Rachel said.

"What?"

"Andy and I went to the same high school."

"Back in California?"

"Yeah! Talk about a weird coincidence."

Andy nodded and laughed. "We even had some of the same teachers."

"Including Ms. Preble, the lesbian band director."

Andy fanned her face as if it were hot. "I was in band just so I could look at her."

Rachel laughed. "Me, too. Three years of the flute."

"The oboe!"

They both burst out laughing again, and Jo and Carter shared an amused grin. Carter lifted one eyebrow and nodded slightly at Andy. Jo winked in return.

Everyone turned at the sound of the cabin door opening, and Jo saw Daniela come outside, her expression dark and troubled. She lifted a hand briefly and then signed, *Hey, Jo, could I see you for a minute?*

Jo glanced at Carter and then at Andy. "Excuse me."

"No problem."

Jo walked over to Daniela on the porch.

What's up?

Can I show you something inside?

Jo nodded and followed her in. Daniela led her into one of the bedrooms and then pointed. The bundle of tools was sitting on top of the antique dresser.

Jo frowned at Daniela. *What the hell?*

Daniela shook her heard. *I don't know. I can't figure it out. That's why I wanted to show you.* She stared at her, hard, before continuing. *You didn't do this, did you? To scare me?*

A flash of hot anger swept through Jo. *No! Why the hell would I do that?*

Daniela continued to stare at her, her face still dark and almost angry, before her expression cleared and she nodded. *Sorry. I just had to ask. You and Andy were the last people in here, and I just thought...* She shrugged.

Jo spun away and closed her eyes, clenching her fists. She took a couple of deep breaths to calm down and made herself let go of the anger. After all, it was true—she had been the last person in here. That earlier sorrow threatened to sweep over her again. Daniela clearly thought very little of her to suspect her of this. She turned back to her.

Well, it wasn't me, and it wasn't Andy.

So how did it get in here?

Jo paused, thinking. The others had been looking around outside for the tools, too. If any of them had put the tools in here, they wouldn't have been searching outside. That or someone was trying to play a trick on everyone, but that seemed pretty far-fetched. Meg had a silly sense of humor, so it could be her, or maybe Rachel, but she couldn't imagine Carter doing this for any reason.

I don't know, Daniela. I really don't.

Well, they didn't move here on their own.

I know. That's why it's so weird.

Should we tell Carter?

She'd asked Carter the same question about the pile of furniture—the pile that had been in this very room on top of this dresser. Now three things had happened in here—the weird furniture pile, her book, and the tools. She glanced around, trying to understand what was happening. This bedroom was just like the other one, both of them still somewhat darkened by the branch-covered windows. Still, the longer she was here, the more it seemed like this room was different somehow—lighter and warmer than the rest of the cabin. The other rooms were cool, almost chilly, but this one seemed almost as hot as it was outside. Her skin began to crawl, and she shuddered before shaking her head hard to clear it. She told herself she was imagining things, making herself feel things that weren't there. Still, she couldn't help but take a few careful steps away, back and out of the bedroom. She didn't want to be in there.

Daniela was hugging herself, her face creased with concern, eyes frightened. Jo touched her arm.

It's going to be okay. There must be some explanation.

Daniela shook her head. *But what?*

Jo had no response, and she waited as Daniela picked up the tools and followed her out into the main room. Daniela set them down on the couch and turned toward her as if expecting a response. Again, Jo knew she was imagining things, but she felt a great deal of relief being out of that bedroom.

Who's sleeping in there? Jo asked. Yesterday, after they'd returned from their trip to the ranger station, Jo had fallen almost instantly asleep on the couch. Carter and Meg had woken her throughout the night, as Andy had directed, but she hadn't noticed which room they were staying in.

Me and Carter.

Jo thought that might be a bad idea, but she couldn't think of any real reason for why that would be the case. In fact, she thought, no one should be staying in there. But again, she couldn't come up with a way to convince the others of that without telling everyone what had happened. She certainly didn't want to scare anyone unnecessarily. There must be some kind of explanation.

Daniela was slightly pale, her lips pinched. *I don't like this, Jo.*

Jo suppressed a shudder. *Me, either.*

I don't know why, but I'm scared. Something's wrong. I feel like something happening, like someone—

The front door opened, making both of them jump. Carter came in, blinking again in the dim light. She frowned, and then her face cleared when she saw the bundle of tools near them.

"Oh good, you found them. Where were they?"

Jo threw Daniela a quick glance, and Daniela shook her head, almost imperceptibly.

"In here, for some reason. I guess I must have brought them in without thinking about it."

"That's weird."

Jo nodded.

"Anyway, you should come back outside. Andy's making us mid-afternoon cocktails as a treat." She paused, smiling. "And Jo—if you don't ask her out, I'm going to kill you."

Daniela smiled at her. *No shit. Ask her out before one of us does it first.*

"Okay, okay, I'll do it. Jesus. You guys have no chill."

Carter smiled. "There's no such thing as chill with a woman like that."

None, Daniela said.

The three of them went back outside into the intense heat of the late afternoon, and Jo found Andy's eyes once she was clear of the door. Andy had been cutting something on the little table they'd set up, and she paused at the sight of Jo, lifting a hand and waving, her smile warm and open.

"Do you like mojitos?" she yelled.

"Hell, yes!" Jo yelled in response.

Carter gave her a slight push. "Ask her now, you chicken, before you lose your nerve. She's obviously into you."

Jo squared her shoulders, took a deep breath, and walked down the little steps of the porch, feeling distinctly like she was heading into battle.

CHAPTER NINE

Jo frowned at her reflection in the mirror of the gas-station restroom. She looked like shit. For one thing, because there were only four beds, she'd been forced to continue sleeping on the couch the last three nights. The tattered cushions, which they hadn't replaced yet, were even less comfortable than sleeping outside. Also, following Andy's strict directives, the others had taken turns checking on her every other hour. It had been difficult to sleep knowing they would just wake her up again, which meant she hadn't slept well in days. The others had finally let her start working on the cabin again yesterday, so her lack of sleep coupled with the physical exertion had clearly taken its toll on her face. The only consolation was knowing that she probably didn't have a concussion. She felt completely fine now, and she could report that much to Andy. Still, this knowledge didn't help with the problem she had right now. How could she go on a date looking like this?

The cabin had one working sink in the kitchen, powered by a pump when the generator was running. The pump drew directly from their well. They had to be a little careful with the water, though, as the water table was refreshed only by snowfall and the very occasional rain, so their family had never bothered to install a shower or a toilet. Jo had a camp shower she used sometimes, but she hadn't brought it this trip. Now, staring into the mirror, she cursed herself for being so lazy. She was filthy.

Rather than try to clean up at the cabin, knowing she'd only get dirty again on her hike down the mountain, Jo had decided to stop in Estes and wash there as best she could. She'd spent a fruitless hour trying to find a public restroom with a mirror before parking here at this gas station. The flickering neon light in here was doing nothing for her appearance.

She spent a long minute scrubbing her hands, clearing out the black gunk under her fingernails, and then washed her face and wetted down her hair as best as she could. She'd forgotten to bring any soap down with her, so she had to use the pink powdered crap from the dispenser in here. Luckily, she kept her hair short, and the little black comb she remembered to bring made quick work of taming her loose curls. Wet, her hair was almost brown, but it always dried into a sandy blond. As Rachel had pointed out, her hair was lighter than Carter's, but only just. Now, frowning at the mirror again, she thought that anyone seeing them side by side would genuinely believe they were twins.

"That'll have to do," she told herself.

Despite the relatively early hour, the sun outside was blindingly bright and already hot. Down here in town, some two thousand feet below their cabin, it was always warmer than up there, but Jo could hardly believe this heat wave. Weather in Colorado had warmed and dried over the course of Jo's lifetime, but she'd never seen a September like this one. Usually this was the only time of year they got any significant rainfall, but not a single drop had fallen since the beginning of last month. The air was dry, the water levels low all over the state. All it would take was one careless cigarette butt thrown out a window, and they'd have a major forest fire.

She reached into her pocket and pulled out the little note Andy had given her. Andy and another ranger shared an apartment here in town on their off days. After she'd finally nerved herself up to ask her out— this after one strong mojito the other afternoon—Andy had offered to cook her breakfast today, her next morning off. It had seemed like an easy, casual thing at the time, a nice idea for a first date, but now Jo could feel her nerves starting to knock at the corners of her mind. Doubt was leaking in, and she started to wonder why Andy had suggested something so intimate, so private. There were plenty of nice restaurants here in Estes, so why meet at Andy's place?

Jo went to her car and pulled out her map of town, finding Andy's street a few seconds later. Her phone worked here in town, but it hadn't occurred to her to turn it on again for navigation. A week without using it had already broken the habit.

Ten minutes later, she pulled into the guest parking spot in Andy's apartment complex and sat in the car for a minute or two, trying to calm down. Her heart was racing and her hands shaking. She bunched and unbunched her fingers, trying to get them to still, then made herself get out of the car. If she waited too long, her nerves would just get worse.

Andy's apartment was on the second floor, and she stood outside the door without doing anything, trying to work up her courage. Finally, she knocked lightly and waited, realizing she should have used the bell. The door opened, and a man stood there, grinning at her.

"You must be Jo," he said. He held out his hand. "I'm Drew—the roommate. But don't worry. I'm on my way out."

Jo relaxed and shook his hand. "Nice to meet you."

She followed him in, and he closed the door behind her before looking her up and down. He let out a low whistle and winked at her. "Oh, you're cute. Totally cute."

She laughed. "Thanks?"

"I can see why Andy likes you. Just her type."

Jo laughed again, the remains of her nerves leaking away. Drew was slight, almost delicate, his face elfin and mischievous. Even in his drab uniform, he managed to be somewhat stylish—the cut of the shirt tailored, perhaps, to his small frame. He was shorter for a guy, about Jo's height at five-seven, his hair a silky, peroxide blond that draped down over one side of his forehead. Jo couldn't be sure, but she thought he was wearing bronzer on his cheeks.

"She's just finishing now," Drew said, pointing down the hall. "I've got to jet." He paused, peering at her closely. "You know, if this goes well, we should all go out sometime. My boyfriend would get a kick out of you."

"How can you tell?"

He laughed. "I just can. I can read people, and you two would totally get on. He's like you and Andy—the outdoors type."

"Aren't you?"

He shrugged. "Yeah, but I'm more of the working-with-the-public type of ranger. I do easy nature walks with old people and talks with the kiddies." He gave her arm a brief squeeze. "Anyway—good luck. Hopefully I'll see you again soon."

"Bye."

She watched him leave and then stood there by the door, taking calming breaths. Her stomach was doing those funny flips and turns again. She made herself walk down the hall, the smell of cooking meat growing stronger and stronger the farther she walked. The hall opened into a combined kitchen, eating, and living room. Andy had her back to Jo, cooking something on the stove. She had earbuds in, and Jo heard her humming softly to herself. Jo could have stood there watching her the rest of the morning. Like the other day on the mountain, she was dressed simply in dark shorts and a T-shirt, but she made her simple clothes look better than they had any right to be. Her hair was clipped up on top of her head in a messy, loose bun, a few tendrils of that spun gold hanging out in little careless wisps on the back of her neck. Even cooking bacon, she was a vision.

Andy turned around and jumped at the sight of Jo, almost dropping the pan. She grinned and set the pan on a trivet before taking out her earbuds.

"Drew let you in?"

"He was on his way out."

"Oh, that's too bad. Still, I'm glad you got to meet him. He's the best roommate. And a good friend. I don't know what I would do without him, sometimes."

"How long have you guys lived together?"

Andy looked at the ceiling. "Two years? About that anyway. We've known each other longer than that, though." She indicated the two chairs at the small breakfast-nook table, and they both sat down.

"Living with him works out great. Rent up here is really high, so we save money splitting this place. And then we're both up at the park three or four days a week, so most of the time just one of us is here. We only overlap maybe once a week."

"So you get three days off every week?"

"Or two and a half and an afternoon, like this last week."

"That's nice."

Andy nodded before waving a hand at the food. "Anyway, help yourself. I always like a little bit of both—savory and sweet—at breakfast."

The spread was impressive. Every breakfast food imaginable was here on the table—two different kinds of eggs, bacon, sausage, pancakes, waffles, crepes, and a quiche, as well as homemade jams, fruit, yogurt, and fresh granola.

"I think I might have gone a little overboard."

Jo laughed. "Not at all. I was looking forward to a fresh breakfast."

"It did seem a little primitive up there."

Jo nodded. "Yes—you can't do a lot with a fire and a camp stove. There's a wood-burning oven inside the cabin, but this time of year it's way too hot to use it."

They ate in companionable silence. Jo wasn't surprised to find that the food was incredible—she had expected it with the offer. She ate an enormous amount and was pleased to see that Andy did the same. She always had a hard time with women who didn't like to eat very much—it made her feel like a pig. She finished before Andy and had the distinct pleasure of watching her polish off the rest of the food.

Andy, sensing her gaze, met her eyes and then blushed slightly. She finished chewing and set her fork and knife down.

"What are you staring at?"

"You," Jo said simply.

The color in her cheeks heightened, and she laughed nervously. "What? Why? Do I have jam on my nose or something?"

Jo shook her head. "No. I just like looking at you."

Andy smiled and took Jo's hand. She rubbed her thumb along the back of Jo's, making her entire arm tingle.

"I like looking at you, too."

Jo barked a laugh. "Like this? I'm filthy."

Andy shrugged. "All the better. If you're like this now, I can only imagine how much better you are cleaned up. And anyway, I like a girl who doesn't mind a bit of dirt."

They continued to hold hands, smiling at each other, and the remains of Jo's nervousness began to ebb away. It was easy being with her—far easier than she could have ever imagined. Despite the fact that Andy was quite possibly the most beautiful woman she'd ever known, it seemed like she was actually and genuinely interested in her.

"So," Andy said, releasing her hand before folding hers together. Her face settled into something like mock-seriousness, but a hint of a smile lingered in her eyes. "Let's get the obvious out of the way: twenty questions."

Jo laughed. "Shoot."

"Age?"

"Thirty-five."

Andy's eyebrows shot up. "Really? I thought you were younger."

"Is that a good thing or a bad thing?"

Andy pretended to consider for a moment and then smiled. "Good thing. I was worried I was too old for you. I'm thirty-eight. Parents?"

"Still alive, still married. They live down in Loveland. Dad's a service technician, Mom's a former nursing assistant. You?"

"Similar. They live in Freemont, in California. Dad just retired—former chemist. Mom was a homemaker."

"Siblings?"

Andy shook her head. "Only child. You?"

Jo grinned. "Four—two sisters and two brothers."

"Yikes! What are you—oldest, middle, youngest?"

"Second to youngest. I have one little brother, Justin."

"What about Carter? You said she's your cousin? It's hard to believe. You're so much alike."

Jo nodded. "We're close, too, more like sisters. Closer, really. She moved in with my family when we were thirteen."

"Oh?"

"Her parents are religious, and they kind of freaked when she came out."

Andy grimaced. "That sucks."

Jo nodded. "It was really tough for a while there, but they've gotten over it. Her mom's even in PFLAG now."

Andy's eyes were thoughtful. "Were you out at that time, too?"

Jo nodded.

Andy shook her head. "That's amazing. You're both gay, and you could be twins. What are the odds?" She paused. "Does just your family own that cabin, or is it your extended family?"

"All of us, eventually. Like I said, the legal stuff hasn't been formalized yet. There are four people in my dad's generation and ten of us in mine. Eventually we'll each get part of a month of the year up there, with two open months in the summer to fight over."

Andy laughed and then slapped her forehead. "Shit, that's right. I almost forgot." She got to her feet and went down the hall, returning with a manila file folder. She handed it to Jo. "I printed this for you last night."

Jo opened the folder and frowned in confusion. Inside was a printout copy of an old document. It had several columns, each of which had been filled in with fancy, almost illegible handwriting. It took her a few seconds to realize what it was: an old census record.

"Oh, wow, is this…?"

"It's the 1890 census for the area. We have access on our computers for the history buffs researching the park." She pointed at column. "Read that one, there."

Jo squinted and finally began to understand the loops and curls of the old-fashioned handwriting. She read aloud. "Adult males: zero. Adult females: Mrs. Aurora Lemke, née Anderson, thirty-eight, pioneer woman; Miss Sarah Bell, thirty-five, spinster. Male children: John Lemke, twelve; Robert Lemke, five." Jo looked up at Andy. "How cool! Robert is my great-grandfather."

"You know his name?"

Jo nodded. "It's on his grave, and my parents are really into genealogy. But I've never seen his mother's full name before—she went by a nickname—Rory, if I remember right." She smiled at Andy. "Thanks! This is very interesting."

"That was all I could find online, but I bet there's more stuff in the physical archive at the museum, if you're interested."

"I am, thanks. I'll have to check it out." She paused, rereading the entry to herself. "I wonder who this Sarah person was. A servant, maybe? I'll have to see if my dad knows anything about her."

"I like that they called Aurora a pioneer woman. Has a nice ring to it."

Jo grinned. "Right? Sarah just gets spinster."

They laughed.

Jo was touched. She couldn't remember the last time anyone had done something like this for her. The gesture suggested time and care. Even if it was just a printout from the internet, it meant that Andy had been thinking about her last night. Her ex had never been this thoughtful.

She closed the file and reached for Andy's hand again, squeezing it slightly. "Thanks again. This was really nice of you."

Andy flushed slightly and shook her head. "It was nothing."

They continued to stare at each other, and Jo went hot under the direct gaze of Andy's fierce blue eyes. It had been a long time since she felt this kind of attraction, and it seemed almost as if her whole body was waking up after a long sleep. She'd rarely had this kind of visceral reaction to someone before, if ever.

"Do you want to take a walk downtown?" Andy asked. "I could use one after gorging myself like that."

Jo's stomach dropped with disappointment. "I'm sorry, but I can't."

"Something to do?"

Jo nodded. "Yes—shopping. I have to drive down to Longmont for some new couch cushions."

"Mind if I come along?"

Jo laughed. "Really? I can't imagine it will be that interesting."

Andy's smile, as it lit her face, was like the sun rising in the mountains—a glowing, beautiful warmth that stretched across every plane of her pretty features.

She squeezed Jo's hand. "I wouldn't say that. After all—you'll be there."

Jo's mouth went dry and her stomach dropped. She had to swallow, once, to find her voice again.

"Then yes. Please come."

CHAPTER TEN

Jo struggled up the trail toward the cabin in a daze. It didn't matter that she was dragging the little handcart, stocked and loaded down with the new cushions and more gasoline and food. It didn't matter that the heat was so intense she was almost baking, her face and body drenched with sticky sweat. It didn't matter that every flying pest within a hundred miles had decided that she was today's special. What mattered was she had just had one of the best days of her life. Her time with Andy had been so simple, so comfortable, it was almost as if they'd always known each other. Any awkwardness was one-sided on her end. Andy was friendly, open, and, in a strange way, calming. She made Jo feel reassured in a way she hadn't realized she wanted—protected, watched after, even.

When she'd broken up with Elsa six months ago, she'd gone into a kind of self-doubting spiral. It hadn't been about the breakup so much as it had been about the fact that she was actually relieved to be free of her. It had taken a couple of months to get over the guilt she felt about that relief, not sure what it meant about their relationship or about her, personally. Now, in the greater span of time between now and then, and in the light of a new relationship, she knew what she had been struggling with. Her guilt had come from the realization that she had wasted so much time with the woman. She and Elsa should have broken up long before their final fight.

Now, with the memory of Andy's warm body against hers when they hugged good-bye, all that angst and guilt about Elsa seemed trivial—a thing of the past. The only remnant of it now was this strange distance and anger between her and Daniela, and even that didn't seem so insurmountable. Daniela would eventually forgive her. Somehow Andy made that seem possible again.

She saw the steepest part of the hill coming, the last stretch, and cursed. Andy had offered to help her bring this stuff up here, but Jo, wanting to be chivalrous, had declined and downplayed the difficulty. Now she realized she'd made two mistakes: not asking for help and declining more time with Andy. Talk about stupid.

She saw movement up ahead and froze with startled fright, relaxing a moment later when she recognized Daniela coming down the hill. Strangely, she was alone. Everyone at the cabin knew Jo would be bringing this stuff up with her, so it seemed odd that a couple of them—Daniela and Carter at the very least—hadn't come to help when someone heard her.

She waved and Daniela waved back, and a minute or so later, she was standing next to her, breathing heavily from exertion. Her expression was troubled, and she threw a furtive glance up the hill before turning back to Jo.

Hey. I wanted to catch you before you got back to camp.

What's up?

Daniela frowned and lifted her shoulders. *It might be nothing, but it's strange. It made me think about the book and the tools moving around on their own. I don't like this, Jo. I'm starting to freak out.*

What happened?

It's still happening. The water in the cabin keeps turning on by itself. Carter hasn't been able to figure out why. She finally had to turn off the pump to stop it.

They stared at each other, and Jo's heart seemed to skip a beat. *Do you think it's all connected?*

Daniela hesitated and then nodded. *You should have seen it, Jo. It's really creepy.*

Daniela crossed her arms over her chest, almost as if to hug herself. Her face was scared and pale. Jo put her hands on her hips, thinking hard. All of the things that had happened at the cabin could have a logical explanation. It was possible, after all, that some vandals had piled the furniture in the bedroom, that the book *had* been moved inside the bedroom with the sheets, or that someone *had* put the tools in there as well. Her accident in the woods was also explainable. She'd been walking around in the dark, after all—no wonder she hit her head. She'd been a complete idiot to go out there on her own in the middle of the night. And now this: an old faucet that was malfunctioning. The thing was fifty years old, for goodness' sake—no wonder it was breaking down. But all of these things together and all at once? Except for the thing in the woods, all of it was rather minor, somewhat benign. But what did it mean?

Daniela still looked troubled, upset, and Jo squeezed her shoulder. *Hey. It's going to be okay.*

Should we tell Carter?

That question again. Jo was tempted to shake her head and leave Carter out of this. After all, what did they know for sure? All of it could be explained away. But hiding their suspicions from Carter was clearly adding to Daniela's nerves.

Yes. Let's tell her. But not the others. Not yet.

Daniela nodded, a wan smile rising to her lips. Jo stepped forward, arms open, and they hugged, Daniela squeezing her. When they pulled apart, Daniela's eyes were sparkling with tears.

I'm sorry, Jo. I've been a complete asshole.

Me, too. It's okay.

Daniela shook her head. *No. It's not. We should have talked months ago.*

Jo made herself dismiss a tiny flash of anger. She'd tried, over and over again, to talk to her. But it wasn't the time to point this out.

I'm ready any time you are, she said instead.

Daniela smiled at her and indicated the cart. *Let's get this goddamn thing up the hill first.*

It was easier with two of them tugging and pushing at it, but still incredibly awkward and difficult. By the time they finally cleared the edge of the trees into the campsite, Jo's muscles were screaming with pain, and her shirt was soaked through with sweat. Daniela's face was flushed with effort, her brows furrowed with something like anger. Finally, they pushed it into the clearing by the fire pit and collapsed into their camp chairs.

I'm not going to do that again any time soon, Daniela said.

The others were conspicuously absent. Clearly, they had heard her coming. Otherwise, Daniela would never have known she was hiking up the hill. Their little disappearing act was completely transparent. They simply hadn't wanted to help. Daniela was right—it was totally someone else's turn next time.

The cabin door opened and Carter came out, polishing a wrench with a dirty rag. She waved and walked over before sitting down.

"You guys look beat."

They both glowered at her, and she laughed, holding her hands up. "Hey, don't blame me. I was busy."

"At least one of you was. Where are Meg and Rachel?"

Carter smiled. "Up at the peak. They're having a little alone time."

Jo rolled her eyes but smiled, letting go of her annoyance. At least it was a good excuse.

Carter flicked her knee with the dirty rag. "So how did it go with Andy?"

Daniela sat up, leaning forward, and Jo had to laugh at their identical, eager expressions.

"It was great. Really great."

Is she a good kisser?

Jo shook her head. *I don't know yet.*

Daniela rolled her eyes but smiled, slightly.

Carter's smile was broad and happy. "Are you going to see her again soon?"

Jo nodded. "She's coming up on her next day off. She wants to help."

This time Carter rolled her eyes, making Jo laugh out loud. "Great idea, cuz. Get your new girlfriend to work for us."

"Hey! She offered."

Carter looked skeptical and then shrugged. "Okay—but it's your funeral. If she was my girlfriend, all I'd ever want to do is put her on a throne to worship and admire."

Daniela nodded eagerly.

Jo smiled. "That's just it, though. She's so nice, you almost don't realize that she's helping you, or offering to help, until afterward. We went shopping today—"

"What?"

Jo laughed. "We went shopping today, and she found the best stuff without even seeming to try. It would have taken me hours, or I would have bought the wrong things."

Daniela stood up and went over to the cart. She flipped the little tarp Jo had tied over everything to reveal the new, stylishly striped, gray-and-yellow chair cushions for the armchairs and the couch.

She nodded her approval. *Good choice.*

"Like I said—you can thank her for it, not me. I wanted some brown ones."

Daniela grimaced. *Thank God she was with you.*

"These look great, Jo," Carter said. She paused. "Did Daniela tell you about the faucet?"

Jo threw Daniela a quick glance. "Yes. It's running on its own?"

Carter raised her shoulders. "It's the weirdest thing you ever saw. I don't even know how it's possible. I was just working on it. I took the whole sink apart and tightened the valves for the faucet, so hopefully that will do it. I was just going to turn it back on."

Jo rolled her shoulders and got to her feet. "I'll help you."

I'll unpack.

That reminds me, Jo said. *Meg asked me to get something for her when I was in town. It's a surprise for Rachel. Could you hide it somewhere? It's in the cooler.*

What is it?

Jo laughed. *A jar of kimchi.*

Daniela smiled. *Will do.*

Jo followed Carter around the side of the house to the fuse box. After over sixty years as what amounted to a primitive three-room shack in the woods, the cabin had been updated to its present condition in the mid-fifties. Her grandfather had put in more windows and replaced the old ones, making them bigger and with better glass. He'd also re-insulated the entire cabin and installed generator-powered electricity and the water pump. The family had to replace certain parts of everything over the years, but much of what he'd put in was still functioning, if old.

"Okay," Carter said, pointing at the fuses. "This is the fuse for the pump. I'm going to throw it now, and we'll see what happens. I seriously hope it works, or we're going to have to get someone up here to fix it."

"Does the old hand pump work?"

Carter sighed. "As far as I know, but talk about a pain in the ass. Let's worry about that if we have to."

She flicked on the fuse, and they walked back around to the porch and inside. Daniela was already there, replacing the cushions, and the three of them walked over to the sink together. They stood there watching it, but nothing happened.

Carter let out a long breath. "Thank God."

Jo tested the faucet, and they heard the pump kick on, just as it was supposed to do. The water sputtered for a moment and then came out in a steady stream. She shrugged at Carter and turned it off, and they heard the pump shut off. They continued to watch it for a few seconds, and again, nothing happened.

Carter put her hands on her hips. "Before you, you see a god: the god of home maintenance."

Daniela fluttered her eyelashes and clasped her hands next to her face. *My hero.*

The door opened and Meg came in, closing it behind her quietly. She put a finger to her lips and peered out the window for a second before turning around, grinning.

"Okay. She won't hear me. Did you get the stuff, Jo?"

Jo pointed at the cooler. "It's still in there."

Meg rubbed her hands together and then got the kimchi out of the cooler. She looked around the room, frowning. "I don't know where to hide it. I want to give it to her as a surprise." She paused, her eyes sliding to the floor. "Next Wednesday's our two-month anniversary."

Daniela clapped her hands together a couple of times before saying, *That is the cutest thing you've ever said.*

Jo held out a hand. "Give it to me—I know a couple of places. Just ask me for it when you want it."

They heard footsteps outside, and Meg's eyes became huge. She threw the jar of kimchi at Jo, who just managed to catch it and put it behind her back before Rachel came in. Rachel paused in the doorway and looked around at them, clearly confused by their guilty expressions.

"What's up?"

"Nothing!" they all said in unison.

Rachel frowned at them. Her eyes settled on Jo, who still had the kimchi behind her back.

"What are you hiding?"

"Uh, Rachel," Meg said, "didn't you say you wanted to see the cemetery?"

Rachel glared at her, suspicion in her eyes, but her face finally cleared and she smiled. "Do you guys really have a cemetery up here?"

Carter nodded. "Yep. Five people were buried there. There would be more, but the plot isn't big enough."

Rachel shuddered dramatically. "Creepy."

"I can show you if you like," Jo said. She'd inched backward, closer to Carter, and felt Carter take the jar from her. "Let's go."

Rachel was frowning at Carter now, having seen something happen behind Jo's back. "Okaaay," she said. "You guys are acting really weird."

Meg grabbed her arm and steered her toward the door. "I'll tell you later. Let's go see it before it gets dark."

Rachel threw Carter and Daniela one more puzzled look before turning to follow Meg outside. Jo pretended to wipe her brow in relief and then followed them.

It was late afternoon, but if anything, it was hotter than it had been earlier. Usually, once the sun moved out of its zenith, it started to cool quickly up here, but that wasn't the case today. Jo closed her eyes, letting herself enjoy the warmth. She loved weather like this. Sure, they could use some rain, but unless it was summer, it was often too cold here to spend very much time outside.

Rachel and Meg had already disappeared down the trail to the cemetery, and Jo wondered if she should let them go on their own. Meg appeared behind some trees a moment later, waving and gesturing for her, and she raced ahead to catch up with them. She passed the old well on the way and paused to check that the cover was still in good shape. It looked better than she expected, and it was firmly locked. She caught up with the others a few yards from the graves.

Rachel's eyes were huge, and she was hugging herself. She turned her gaze to Jo.

"Do you mean we've been up here with these dead people the whole time?"

Jo laughed. "They're nice dead people. Ancestors."

Rachel relaxed a little and followed Jo over to the graves. They were all located on a tiny flat area overlooking the valley below. It wasn't quite as grand as the peak of the mountain, but Jo couldn't think of a prettier place to spend eternity. A large, leafy maple tree shaded the graves, and the cool shade was a relief from the intensity of the sun.

"So who's buried here?" Meg asked. "I know you told me once, but I forgot."

"That's our great-grandfather, Robert, and his wife, my great-grandmother, Estele." She pointed. "That one is his older brother, John. We've always thought this last grave must be his parents, but now I'm not so sure." She told them about the census record she'd seen this morning. "The family legend was that our great-great-grandmother built the cabin on her own, and now I think we actually have some proof. The census didn't list her husband. But it's kind of confusing, too."

"Why?" Rachel asked.

"Read the inscription on the gravestone."

Rachel crouched down next to the grave, puzzling over it. The weather had worn the grave over the years, but the lettering could just be made out. Rachel read the inscription out loud.

"*Together in Life, Together in Death, Love Eternal.* And then some dates, birth and death." She looked up at Jo. "Two sets of them." Jo nodded. "Exactly, just like Robert and Estele. That means two people are in there. Again, I always thought it was my great-great-grandparents, but now I'm not so sure. No one knows who's in that grave, since it doesn't have any names."

Still, Jo realized, it wouldn't hurt to investigate, find out once and for all who was buried there. Everyone in her family had wondered, but as far as she knew, no one had ever determined who they were one way or another. They might be able to find more records somewhere in town, even beyond the census records. Maybe the deaths had been noted down somewhere, too. She didn't know if people did that back then, but they probably had. There'd been a census by that time, after all.

Rachel stood up, stretching, and walked closer to the edge of the cliff. She threw one quick glance over the edge and backed away, eyes wide.

"Sheesh, that's a long way down. Seems even farther down than up at the top. I'd hate to fall off. You should look, Meg."

Meg shook her head. "Nah—I'm good. I'm okay with heights, but only if I have a rope tied on." She turned to Jo and elbowed her in the ribs. "Say, I forgot to ask. How did your date go?"

Jo's face warmed a little with pleasant embarrassment. "Amazing."

Meg lifted her eyebrows up and down. "Oh yeah?"

Rachel pushed her arm. "Hey. Get your mind out of the gutter." She frowned at Jo. "At least, I think so."

Jo laughed. "We didn't even kiss, yet. I chickened out."

They both looked disgusted and she laughed again. "Hey! Don't worry. I'll get another chance. She's coming up here in a few days."

"Oh, thank God," Rachel said, sagging with mock relief. "I wasn't sure we'd ever get to see her again."

Meg's eyes sparkled with mischief. "Yeah, Jo. We totally thought you'd screw it up."

Jo gave her a level stare. "Gee, thanks."

CHAPTER ELEVEN

With the new cushions on the armchairs and the couch, a final cleaning, and the dim warmth of the electric lights, the cabin was finally comfortable inside. In fact, it was almost as good as it had ever been in there—better in some ways with the updated furniture. Jo was surprised by how quickly it had come together. They would want to do another finish in here, preferably with wood oil to get the remaining mustiness out of the room, but it was livable again. They also still needed to do a lot of work outside—the trees and vines were cut back from the cabin itself, but they needed to let more sunlight in. She and Carter were actually planning to decide which trees might need to be cut down altogether, especially in the back, which was still very dark. The one broken window needed new glass, and a couple of spots on the roof required repairs, but overall, it was almost done.

Just ten days ago, the place had seemed almost hopeless, and now here they were, playing cards in the living room. Jo had forgotten the special, cozy feeling she had sitting in here when visiting with friends and family years ago, all of them gathered around this same little coffee table. Part of her wondered why she and Carter hadn't pushed Nancy for the keys sooner. Being here was like coming home again.

Meg threw down her cards in disgust. "Well, that does it. I'm all out."

"We could open the bag of pretzels," Rachel offered. They'd been using potato chips as their stake all evening.

"No, no, it's okay. I'll just watch you guys."

Carter checked her watch. "It's still early, but I'm really tired. Maybe we should wrap up now, anyway."

Daniela rolled her eyes. *You would say that. You're winning.*

"She always wins," Jo said. "I've always said she should quit practicing law and move to Vegas."

Rachel yawned, loudly. "I'm tired, too. I guess that's what happens when you get up at dawn. And I need to go to the bathroom. Will you come out there with me, Meg?"

"Sure."

"Thanks. It's creepy there." She shuddered. "I hate it when I wake up in the middle of the night and have to go on my own."

Meg grabbed her hand. "You can always wake me up, hon. I'll be happy to listen to you pee."

Rachel swatted her arm. "Yuck!"

Meg grabbed a flashlight, and the two of them went outside. Jo started collecting the potato chips as Carter washed their cups and glasses in the sink. She could hardly believe how tired she was. Her mind was muddled and thick, and she felt clumsy. She had to pause to stifle a loud yawn.

Daniela touched her arm. *Can I talk to you for a minute after the others go to bed?*

Of course. She threw Carter a quick glance and saw that she'd witnessed this exchange. Carter gave her a hopeful smile and turned back to the sink.

Jo's heart was racing. She'd been wanting this conversation for months, but now that it looked like it might actually happen, she was nothing but nerves. It was crucial that she and Daniela figure this thing out, and not just for Carter's sake, but for her own. She wanted Daniela back in her life. She'd missed her. She told herself to be patient, to see Daniela's side of things with as much objectivity as she could summon. Clearly, whatever she thought had happened between her and Elsa had been enough to make Daniela sufficiently angry to cut her out of her life. She wasn't the kind of person to do that lightly, so it must be serious.

After the others had gone into the bedrooms, she and Daniela sat across from each other in the living room. Daniela was fidgeting, clearly as nervous as she was.

I'm going to get right to the point, she said.

Jo nodded. *Please.*

Even before you and Elsa broke up, she was complaining a lot about you and the way you treated her.

Jo's temper rose, but she made herself stifle it. *About what?*

She said you weren't being honest with her, that you hid things from her.

Again, Jo had to clamp down on her anger. *Like what?*

Your new car, for one.

Jo sighed. *I can't buy a new car with my own money?*

You were living together, Jo. Big money decisions should at least be a topic of discussion, if not a debate.

Jo had disagreed then and she did now. What she did with her money was up to her.

What else did she complain about?

Your trip to Detroit.

Jo flashed back to that argument. It had been a bad one—yelling, screaming, Elsa throwing things and slamming doors. About four months before they broke up, Jo's boss had asked her to attend a conference on urban landscaping. She'd forgotten to tell Elsa about it until two days before she left.

That was just a mistake. I didn't think she'd want to go.

Daniela frowned. *So you didn't even ask? And you didn't think to tell your girlfriend you'd be gone for two weeks?*

Jo flushed with guilt. At the time, she'd thought herself completely justified in what she'd done. She'd thought she was in the right. Now, objectively presented with the facts of the matter, her actions did seem fairly cold, almost heartless.

No. I guess not.

Daniela continued to stare at her, that troubled expression clouding her face. Finally, she shook her head.

There were other things, too, Jo. Lots of things. You got that promotion and didn't tell her you got a raise. You lost all that money in the stock market and only let her know when she found out by accident.

Jo hardened with anger. Again, she thought that in both cases, it was her own damn business how much money she earned and how she lost or spent it.

Anything else?

Daniela nodded, her face now filled with regret. *You had that scare, with the lump in your breast, and then you told me and Carter. She heard it from me before you said anything to her. Talk about putting me in an awkward position. I would never have thought you hadn't said anything to her yet.*

Again, Jo's stomach sank with something like dread. Even at the time, she'd known she should tell Elsa, but she kept putting it off, first after the biopsy, then during the wait for the results, and then later when she found out it was benign. It was true—she hadn't wanted to talk to her about it at all, and might not have if she hadn't been forced. That had caused another bad fight.

Daniela touched her knee. *I know you don't want to think about all this, Jo. I'm just sharing what she told me, and how she felt about it. The point is, you hid a lot from her. You didn't trust her enough to share your life with her. Even before you finally broke up with her, she was a wreck.*

Jo sat there for a long while, thinking back on the last few months with Elsa. They'd been bad, but it had been bad before that, too. Daniela was right, and, by extension, Elsa had been right to be upset with her. Jo hadn't trusted her, hadn't wanted to share things with her. That was true. Part of her relief, when they finally broke up, had come from the fact that she wouldn't have to hide things from her anymore—she was tired of sneaking around. The rest of it had come from something else, something darker, that she hadn't wanted to admit then and didn't now. She had fallen out of love with Elsa long before they'd broken up, but she'd been too much of a coward to do anything. She'd been convinced that if she did, she'd end up alone, forever. Still, she wasn't alone in her guilt. Elsa hadn't been a saint, either.

She sighed again and squeezed Daniela's knee. *You might be right about a lot of things. I didn't trust her, especially at the end, and I did hide things from her—too many. But did she tell you why we finally split?*

Daniela's face creased with obvious confusion. *All of that wasn't enough?*

Jo shook her head. *I'm sure we would have eventually broken up. It couldn't have gone on like that, but it might have dragged on another few months if not for Maggie.*

Daniela still looked confused. *Maggie? Her physical therapist?*

Jo nodded. Elsa had a lot of old injuries related to a car accident and about a year ago had finally decided to do something about her aches and pains.

I think it started out fairly innocently. They were meeting once or twice a week, for coffee, drinks, after their sessions. Then it was more. They're living together now.

Daniela was clearly thunderstruck and didn't reply.

I know I was distant with her. I knew it then. But I was hoping things would get better. Of course, if you never talk about anything, things only get worse.

Daniela's face was pale in the dim light. Slowly, as Jo watched, her expression began to transform, first into something like pain, and then into a dark, indignant anger. She stood up and moved toward Jo, arms open. They embraced, Daniela hugging her so tight she could barely breathe. When they drew apart, she had tears in her eyes. She wiped them away, her face mottled with emotion.

Oh God, Jo. I feel like such an idiot.

It's okay.

She shook her head. *It's not. Really, it's not. She lied to me, and I should have known better.*

What do you mean?

Her face was dark with sorrow and regret. *She sort of implied that you and Jackie from work...* She shrugged.

What? Jackie? Are you kidding me? She's twenty-five, for God's sake.

Daniela shrugged. *I guess it was the crock calling the kettle black.*

And you believed her?

Daniela's shoulders went up again. *I mean, she didn't come out and actually say you were sleeping with her, but she did talk about how much time the two of you were spending together.*

Yeah—we work together. That's what happens with coworkers.

She implied a flirtation, anyway. Then, when you broke up, and she quit the bakery, I thought... Daniela shook her head. *I'm so sorry.*

Jo was hot with anger, and her heart was beating hard. She closed her eyes, forcing herself to calm down. She wasn't angry with Daniela. After all, the rest of what Elsa had told Daniela had been true. Why shouldn't she believe this last, final betrayal of trust?

She opened her eyes and met Daniela's, which were worried and almost frightened. She hugged her again and then made a cutting gesture.

Don't worry about it. Neither one of us was innocent in all of this. I'm just sad you and I waited so long to clear the air.

Daniela nodded, still looking troubled and upset, like she might start crying any moment.

I just feel so guilty now, Jo. I should never have believed it of you.

Jo made the cutting gesture again. *Let it go, and please don't feel guilty. It's over now, and we can move on to better things.*

Daniela gave her a wan smile. *Okay. I'll try.*

Jo yawned, her exhaustion now something pressing, weighty, dragging at her shoulders. *Let's hit the sack. We can talk again when we're not so tired.*

She turned to get her bedding out of the ottoman, but Daniela touched her shoulder.

Just one more thing, Jo. I know it wasn't your fault, what Elsa did, but I have to ask something now, okay?

Jo nodded, but Daniela hesitated. Jo could see her wrestling with something. Finally, her face hardened into a clear resolve.

Just make sure you tell Andy everything, okay? I mean, if you really want things to be different this time. Tell her every little thing, no matter how you think she'll react. That's how love works—with trust. If you want love, you have to trust each other.

Jo made herself think about this suggestion before replying.

Okay. You're right. I'll try.

Daniela smiled. *Good. I know you just met, but I like her.*

Jo smiled back. *Me, too.*

Jo brushed her teeth and set up her bed as Daniela took a quick trip to the outhouse, and they hugged in that same fierce way before they finally said good night. For a long time, Jo lay awake in the dark, staring at the ceiling, exhausted but too wound up to sleep. Finally, a warm relief swept through her. It was all going to be okay again. She and Daniela had finally made up. Their relationship might even be stronger for it.

Her clamoring nerves finally started to quiet, and her eyelids began to grow too heavy to keep open. She let herself start to drift asleep, and seconds later, she was out.

❖

The water was running, full blast, and Jo sat up on the couch with a start. Usually the water came out of the faucet at a rate hardly strong enough to clean things off a dirty dish. The family had installed a water-saving device a long time ago to make sure the well lasted the entire dry season. This, however, sounded much stronger. Water was gushing out and hammering the steel sink, very loud in the still, dark night. Jo saw a light go on in Carter's bedroom. Then her bedroom door was flung open, and she came out.

Jo cursed, switched on the lamp near her, threw off her blankets, and got up.

"Goddamn it," Carter said.

"It's doing it again, I guess," Jo said.

The two of them walked over to the sink, and Jo turned the faucet off. They stood there together, elbow to elbow, and then Jo watched as the knob to the faucet moved on its own, opening again at full power. The sight caused chills to race up and down her back. Daniela was right—it was difficult to see how it was possible to do that on its own. The sink only had one mechanism for turning on the water—one old, cross-handled knob. To save electricity, there was no water heater, so they didn't need a second one. To turn it on, you had to spin the cross toward you, often with a little muscle behind it—the knob was tight on purpose to avoid leaks. How could it possibly move like that?

Carter reached for the knob and then hissed when she touched it, shaking her hand. "Shit! It burned me." She grabbed a rag to protect herself and turned off the water. "It's the weirdest thing, right?"

Jo nodded. She thought it more than weird, more like terrifying. She'd already taken a few steps away, scared to see it again.

"So it'll just keep doing that? Turning on again?" Her voice sounded sharp, frightened, even to herself.

Carter threw her a confused look. "That's what it did earlier this week. I guess I need to go switch off the fuse outside again."

"I can do that." Anything, Jo thought, to get away from it.

"You sure?"

"You did it last time. Stay here and turn it off again if it comes back on. Use an oven mitt if it gets hot again."

Jo slipped her boots on and remembered at the last second to grab her fleece before heading outside. It was always hard to remember how cold it got out here at night. It was, perhaps, only a few degrees away from being chilly enough for a heavy coat, hat, and gloves. Her breath was misting the air, and she shuddered against the cold seeping into her skin. It was surprisingly cold, even for September, especially considering how hot it had been earlier today. She could even see her breath in the dim light from the window.

She had a little flashlight in her jacket pocket, and she switched it on a couple of feet from the porch. The night was incredibly dark. The moon had already set, and the only light above was starlight. This far from Estes, there wasn't even any light pollution. Her little light was a powerful LED, but it still did little to penetrate the solid blackness.

It seemed to get even colder as she walked. Moving quickly, she went around to the far side of the cabin to the fuse box. She opened it, found the right one, and flicked it off. Even from out here, she could hear the water pump running, and a second later, it stopped. She closed the box again and started heading back toward the front of the house and then paused, listening.

She heard footsteps, somewhere nearby.

"Carter?" She'd said it at a speaking volume, not yelling, afraid to wake the others inside. She waited, hearing nothing, and then, just as she began to think she'd imagined it, she heard the footsteps again, louder this time, and closer, coming from behind her. She spun that way, her flashlight making wide arcs of light, but saw nothing but trees that way, and no movement. Once again, the footsteps had stopped.

"Carter, if that's you trying to scare me, I'm going to kick your ass."

Again, nothing.

She took a wary step toward the woods, moving as quietly as she could, tempted once again to turn her light off. She'd had just about enough of this, whatever it was, and she was starting to get angry. She seized that feeling, letting it push away the remains of her fright. Before, when she'd been in the tent and heard the footsteps, she'd almost managed to convince herself she'd been dreaming. After all, she'd been asleep, or nearly asleep, every time she heard them. But this was different. She was wide awake, and there was no mistaking that sound. Something or someone was out there, and it was up to her to put a stop to it.

She stopped a few feet from the tree line. Unlike the last time she went into the woods at night, she was wary of what she might find out there. She still didn't know if something had attacked her or if she'd hurt herself, but she also didn't want to find out. She smelled a strange odor out here, too, and wondered if it might be an animal after all, giving off some heavy musk. It was terrible, whatever it was, and she wrinkled her nose in deep disgust. It reminded her of something, that smell, but she couldn't remember what it was. A memory of something similar in the woods the night she was hurt nagged at her mind, but the harder she tried to remember it, the foggier that memory became. She shook her head angrily to dismiss it. It didn't matter now, anyway.

She decided to wait until she heard it again before heading in there on her own, frightened now that she might get attacked by whatever smelled like that. If it was a skunk, it would take days to get that smell off her skin and out of her hair. Several long seconds passed, and she was just about to give it up as an animal when she heard it again. Something was moving around in the forest, just out of sight. Using her anger to bolster her courage, she stepped forward and pushed a large pine bough out of the way. Her light immediately revealed what lay beyond.

She screamed, letting go of the branch and leaping backward before tripping on her own feet. She landed hard on her tailbone and bit her tongue, cutting off her scream. Her flashlight bounced out of her hand, rolling away, and she scooted away as quickly as she could from the trees.

"Jesus Christ, Jo. What the hell are you doing down there? And what the hell is that smell?"

Still on the ground, Jo wheeled around to see Carter standing a few feet behind her. She was holding the kerosene lantern.

"Someone's there! In the woods!" Jo said, pointing.

Carter frowned and lifted her light. "Who?"

"I don't know! I heard something moving back there, and when I looked, I saw him right there—two, three feet behind that tree."

Carter took a step forward, and Jo scrambled to her feet, grabbing her arm. "Don't!"

Carter stared at her. "Why not?"

Jo didn't know why she'd stopped her. She only knew that one sight of him had scared her more deeply than she'd ever been before. She hadn't found anything specifically sinister about him—he'd just been a man, after all, but she had seen something in his eyes. Something she didn't like. Her mind reeled at the mere memory of his expression.

"Come out of there!" Carter shouted at the trees.

"Shh!" Jo said, still clutching at her cousin's arm. "He'll hear you."

Carter shrugged her grip away. "Of course he'll hear me, doofus. Why do you think I'm calling out?"

"Be quiet!" Jo said, and grabbed her cousin's arm again. She dragged her away from the trees. "Let's go inside. Please, Carter."

Carter lifted the lantern, lighting Jo's face. "What's the matter? Why are you so scared?"

Jo shook her head. "I can't explain. Please, let's just go inside. We're not safe out here." Her heart was hammering so hard she was having trouble breathing. It was everything she could do not to run away, screaming.

Carter peered once more at the trees and then nodded, frowning. "Okay. Have it your way." She raised her voice in the directions of the trees. "But I'm calling the police, tomorrow, you asshole! Get the fuck off our property!"

Jo found as they walked back to the cabin that her legs and hands were trembling. Shaky all over, almost unstable, she had difficulty getting her feet to cooperate with her. She almost tripped going up the stairs, but Carter grabbed her right before she went down.

Inside, all the lights were on again, the others standing there, confusion and fright on their faces.

"What happened?" Meg asked.

"We heard yelling," Rachel said.

Carter sighed. "Someone was out there. In the woods. A man." She locked the front door.

"What? Who was he?"

Everyone looked at her, and Jo shook her head, unable to explain what she'd seen. Still, they needed an explanation, and she swallowed her fear to speak. "I don't know. Some stranger. Homeless, I think."

Daniela's face was pale and drawn with fright. *What makes you say that?*

Jo thought for a moment and then shook her head. She'd seen him for only a couple of seconds. "I don't know. His clothes, maybe. They were really dirty. And he reeked—like horribly bad BO or something. And his beard was a mess."

The five of them were quiet, each of them peering at the others, equal expressions of confused fright on their faces.

"Well, that's creepy," Rachel said. "What are we going to do about him?"

"I'll have to go down tomorrow and talk to the police," Carter said. "I don't know that they can do anything about him, but maybe he has a squat somewhere nearby, or something. It's illegal to camp without a permit in the park, so they should be able to get rid of him. No one's been up here at the cabin in a while, so maybe he got curious or something when he heard us over here. He could have come to see if he could steal something while we all slept. I'm just guessing, of course."

Jo didn't think this explanation fit the man she'd seen, but she couldn't explain how she knew this. Some covert thief in the night wouldn't have stared at her with that dark hatred. He hadn't looked frightened or surprised at all. He'd seemed angry, dangerous even. The image of him in her mind made her heart rate pick up again, and she peered out the window, trying to see if he was out there now, watching them.

"Let's get back to bed," Carter said. "I can't imagine he'll try to get in here, but just to be safe, make sure your windows are locked, too."

The others headed off toward their bedrooms, but Carter hung back.

"Are you okay? Do you want to put the couch cushions into the bedroom and sleep in there with me and Daniela?"

Jo hesitated and then shook her head. Much as she wanted to do just that, she would never intrude in that way. Now, inside, she was beginning to find her fright a little silly. Maybe it was like Carter had said—he was just some squatter. Some part of her knew that was wishful thinking, but she pushed the thought away and tried to smile.

"No, it's fine. I'll be okay. Let's go back to bed."

Carter was staring at her, critically, but she finally nodded. "Okay—whatever you say. But wake us up if you change your mind." She paused, still looking at Jo with a puzzled expression. "It was really dark out there. Are you sure you saw someone?"

"What? Of course I am! You smelled him, didn't you?"

Carter continued to stare at her but finally nodded. "Okay. We'll poke around a little together tomorrow, see if we can't find some trace of him, and I'll hike down and call the police in the daylight."

She gave Jo's hand a quick squeeze before heading into her bedroom, and Jo saw the lights under both bedroom doors go dark, one after the other. She was left on her own in the dim light of the living room.

It was a long time before she made herself sit down again on the couch, and even longer before she switched off the lamp and lay down. She was fairly certain she would never get to sleep, but it wasn't long before she was drifting off again, fear fading with her exhaustion.

CHAPTER TWELVE

The next morning, dawn seemed reluctant to make its appearance, and Jo realized upon waking that the weather had finally turned. It was cloudy for the first time in weeks, and when she went outside on the porch, the morning air was almost frosty. It was very unusual to get snow up here on their mountain this early in September, but Jo wouldn't be surprised if they had a cold rain or possibly sleet later this morning or afternoon. With no internet access, none of them had been able to check the forecast in days.

The idea made her worry about Andy, who was heading up later today. She might take one look at the sky and decide a hike up here was dangerous. And, Jo had to admit, she would probably be right. She herself had made the mistake of heading into a storm a few times, only to regret it every time. Andy couldn't cancel, but Jo knew she was smart enough not to take chances.

Despite the relative gloom, Jo found that in the light of the morning sun, clouds or no clouds, she was no longer afraid of the man she'd seen last night. She remembered being afraid, but last night's fear seemed misplaced and overwrought. When she'd spotted him, she'd been tired, and he'd surprised her; that was all. If she'd detected something sinister in his eyes, it was probably either a trick of the light or he had simply been angry at being caught. She was certain he wouldn't make an appearance in the daytime, and she wasn't afraid to be outside on her own. Carter might get mad at her later, but she wasn't scared. She picked up the metal bucket they planned to use to carry water and headed outside to pump some for breakfast.

Jo cursed. The hand pump for the well was rusty and overgrown with weeds. Before Nancy had taken the keys, the electric water pump had functioned almost perfectly. It had been replaced in the mid-nineties, when she was up here with her family. She'd been about fourteen at the time. All of them—her parents, her siblings, and Carter—had taken turns pumping water until her dad replaced the electric one. As far as she knew, no one in the family had needed to use the manual one since, and she couldn't remember the last time she'd even looked at it. They were all going to pay for that neglect now.

She set down the bucket and dug out her little pocket knife, then cut away the vines. They had wrapped themselves around the pump entirely and were surprisingly thick and tough, difficult to cut through. Something in the rust must be a food source for them, she thought. She struggled until her hands grew raw from pulling at them, and finally found the edge of the handle. She focused the rest of her efforts there until the handle was completely revealed and then put her knife away. She gave the handle a hard yank, but nothing happened. Cursing again, she set both of her feet on either side of the pump for leverage and pulled on the handle again. It didn't move.

"Fuck me," she said, rubbing her sore hands. She gave one more try, but the handle didn't even wiggle in her grip.

She heard the door to the cabin open and saw Meg sneaking outside. Meg peered around furtively and then spotted Jo. She lifted a hand before jogging over to her.

"Out here on your own? After last night?"

Jo nodded. "He won't come out during the day."

Meg accepted this statement without comment. "What are you doing, anyway?"

Jo pointed. "I was trying to get water, but the friggin' thing is rusted shut and won't budge."

"Let me try. Your little noodle arms have nothing on these guns." She kissed each of her bulging biceps.

Jo laughed and got out of the way. Meg squared her shoulders and rolled her neck a couple of times. She took several deep breaths, held the last one, and crouched down over the handle as if lifting a deadweight. Her face got redder and redder as she pulled, and she let out a long, low groan, teeth gritted. Nothing happened. Meg finally let go, breathing heavily, her hands on her hips.

"You were saying?" Jo said.

Meg laughed. "Yeah, yeah, yeah. Laugh it up."

They stood there staring down at the pump.

"What removes rust?" Meg asked.

Jo shook her head. "No idea. Can't even look it up without my phone."

"Can we use the old water well?"

Jo raised her eyebrows, surprised. She hadn't thought of that. The hand pump had been put in along with the drilled well in the early twentieth century, right around the time her great-grandfather inherited the cabin in the 1920s. Before that, however, her ancestors had relied on the traditional dug well, the kind with raised, stone sides. The old well opening was still there, covered over with a circular wooden cover. They'd passed it yesterday on the way to the cemetery. Her family had debated having it filled in several times, but it was cost prohibitive. Filling it meant getting a construction crew up here as well as their equipment, which would not simply be difficult and costly, but nearly impossible without flying some of it in. They'd all agreed to simply leave it there, covered and locked. All her nieces, nephews, and her cousins' kids had been warned not to play around it.

"The old well is definitely worth checking out," Jo said. "I mean, I can't imagine there's even water in there with how hot it's been this summer. It's filled by the water table near the surface, so I'm sure it goes dry this time of year. We also don't know what kind of quality that water is. It has a cover, but it's still basically open to the elements. The drilled well has filters and things, so you don't get bugs or mud."

"Or drowned chipmunks."

Jo laughed. "Exactly—though the cover keeps out larger animals."

Meg frowned. "I have my backpacking filter here. It's always with my camping supplies."

"Me, too."

"So if there's water, we could get some out of the well and filter it. I've definitely had to get some pretty dank stuff from rivers and lakes before, and my filter completely cleared it. It's better than having to lug water up here from town, anyway."

"Sounds like a plan. Let's see if Carter has the keys."

They started to walk back toward the cabin, but Meg suddenly stopped. Jo raised an eyebrow and waited. Meg was quiet for a long time, but she finally sighed as if reluctant. "I came out here to ask your opinion about something." Her face was slightly pink, and her eyes were rooted to the ground.

"What?" Jo asked. Meg looked up, and Jo realized that she was embarrassed about something. She touched her arm. "It's okay—just tell me."

Meg shifted from foot to foot, glancing away again. It took her a while to speak, her gaze darting everywhere by Jo's face. "All right. So you know how tomorrow is my two-month anniversary with Rachel?"

"Yes."

"Well, I got her some presents. I mean, besides the kimchi. Earrings, a scarf, my favorite novel." Her eyes met Jo's before sliding away again. "Do you think it's too much? I don't want to scare her away—look too needy, or something."

Jo had to force herself not to laugh. Meg was not only embarrassed; she seemed genuinely scared. She grabbed both of Meg's broad shoulders and made her meet her eyes.

"Listen to me, now, Meg, and listen well. You're not going to scare her off. That woman is crazy about you."

Meg's face brightened. "She is?"

Jo nodded and let go of her. "She totally is. A few presents will only make her happy. Nothing else."

"You're sure?"

"Completely."

"I was going to give it all to her up at the peak. She really loves it there." Meg looked shamefaced again.

Jo smiled. "That's a great idea."

"I even bought a little gift bag. With a bow. Carter hid everything under her bed."

Jo had a hard time picturing Meg buying something like a gift bag. Her butch swagger was so rigid, she usually avoided anything "girly." The fact that she was willing to go into a store and get something like that spoke volumes about her feelings for Rachel.

She squeezed her shoulders again. "She'll love it. I promise."

They continued toward the cabin, and Carter came out just as they reached the porch.

"Everything okay out here? Any sign of him?"

Jo shook her head. "I don't think he'll come back during the day. He was just some bum. We probably scared him off."

"I think that, too. Still, I should probably report him, anyway. He shouldn't be up here in the park or on our property, for that matter." She frowned when she saw the empty bucket. "What's wrong? Is the hand pump broken?"

Jo nodded. "It's rusted shut. Won't budge. Even Miss Muscles here couldn't move it."

"Did you try vinegar?"

Jo laughed. Of course Carter knew what to use. "Can't say I did. Didn't have any on me. We were going to check out the old well." She explained their idea about using their water filters.

Carter lifted her eyebrows and nodded. "That could work. But yeah, only if there's water in there." She unclipped a set of keys from the carabiner on her belt and held it out. "One of these fits the locks for the cover. Do you have a flashlight?"

Jo took the keys. "What for?"

"So you can see down inside the well."

"Oh, yeah, didn't think of it." She checked her pocket. "Yes—I have one."

"I'll see if I can find any vinegar inside. Maybe we won't need to use the old well."

Jo and Meg headed down the trail to the cemetery together, Jo in the lead. It was now getting into morning proper, but the sky was still so dark it seemed much earlier. It was a little warmer than when she'd first come outside, but Jo still wished she'd thought of bringing her hat and gloves. Her exposed hand, the one holding the bucket, was painfully cold, and she was forced to switch back and forth to give the other one time inside a pocket.

"Damn," Meg said when they finally reached the well. She blew out her breath, and it misted in the air. "Friggin' freezing out here."

"No kidding. Let's get this over with so we can get back inside."

They found two locks on the cover, one on either side to keep it down and closed. It took her a couple of tries to find the right keys, and both locks opened with reluctance. It might have been twenty years since anyone needed the hand pump, but Jo knew it had been even longer since anyone had opened this well. It took both of them to lift the enormous wooden cover off, and they set it down next to the well, propped on its side against the stone lip around the well.

Despite its age, some hundred and thirty or forty years, the well seemed in good shape. The stones that ringed it were still solid, still flush with each other, and filled in with something like concrete. This kind of well, when used, had to be dug deeper and deeper as the years passed and the water table dropped. That was why the drilled well they used at the cabin now was so much better—it went much farther into the ground than anyone with a well like this could ever hope to dig. The rim of stones rose about three feet off the ground. She knew from old pictures that a kind of hand crank used to hang over the top for the bucket, but that was long gone. Now, without the cover, it was simply an open hole.

The well was some four or five feet across, and the light from the sun penetrated ten or fifteen feet below the stone rim. Jo leaned forward a little and shone her flashlight down inside, but the angle was awkward. She would have to lean over much farther than she was comfortable doing in order to see down in it properly.

Meg crouched down and picked up a little pebble, then flicked it into the well. It seemed like a long time before they heard a splash.

"Wow. I would never have thought it was that deep."

Jo shook her head. "Me, either. But at least we know there's water in there. We should have brought a rope. Then we could lower the flashlight into it. We'll need a rope for the bucket, anyway."

"I'll go grab one."

Jo watched her disappear down the trail back toward the cabin. She rested her lower legs against the rim of the well, not quite daring to actually sit on the ledge. She took the opportunity to warm both her hands, cramming them into her pockets, and frowned up at the sky. She was starting to hope Andy would decide to stay home. As much as she wanted to see her, it seemed as if it might snow sometime today, and maybe soon. It would likely be flurries, if anything, but the trail up here would be slick and dangerous. That old adage about Colorado was true, especially in the mountains: wait ten minutes, and the weather will change. A cold snap like this was extreme, but again, not necessarily unheard of at this elevation this time of year. Two years ago, Jo had been caught in something like a blizzard hiking Long's Peak, and that had been in September, too. She'd been lucky to make it out alive.

She heard something splash in the water below and jerked away from the well, standing up and staring at the opening, wary. It had likely been a frog, or she might have knocked a loose stone off the edge, but the noise was unnerving, anyway. She took a couple of careful steps toward the edge, peering down, and listened. Nothing. She set her hand on the rim and then leaned over to see inside better.

Her vision began to cloud, and the world took on a surreal, cloudy haze. The cold, which had been a nagging, painful sting in the air, deepened, and she shuddered, hard. Her breath, which had been misting the air, now swirled out of her mouth and nose in billowing clouds.

Even stranger, the day, which had been unusually dark, seemed to be losing light and color. She took a couple of steps away to peer up at the sky, part of her confused to see the same uniform bank of clouds that had been there above her all morning. If anything, the sky was lighter than it had before—a glimpse of sun peeking out here and there—yet it was incredibly dark down here on the ground, almost like she was standing in the shadow of something that loomed over her. She looked around, thinking she might spot it, but the shadow seemed to be cast from something that wasn't there. It extended some thirty feet outward in a circle from the well.

Her stomach gave her a kind of funny, frightened lurch, and she refocused on the well. Suddenly, she wasn't scared of it anymore. She could sit down on the edge, no problem. In fact, if she sat on the edge with her feet inside, she'd be able to see down inside, all the way to bottom, rope or no rope. She took another step closer to the rim of stones in order to do just that, but her legs felt stiff—almost numb. She staggered a little and had to grab the edge of the well to keep from falling. She chuckled. She felt drunk. She started to lift her leg in order to climb up on the rim, then paused. Something was wrong. The impulse to get up on the ledge was strong, however, and she raised her leg again.

She heard voices behind her, and as she turned her head in their direction, the world snapped back into reality with an almost audible pop. She staggered and almost sank to the ground, once again grabbing the edge of the well to keep from falling. She was buffeted by a warm, blowing wind, and the light around her brightened perceptibly back to its former cloudy gloom. The voices were still far away but coming her way.

She peered at the well again and then leapt backward, almost tripping. What had she almost done? The idea of climbing onto the ledge and dangling her legs inside was absurd—insane, even. Why had she wanted to do that? She backed away from the well warily, keeping her eyes on it the whole time. She half expected it to start calling for her again.

She recognized the voices a split second before Meg and Andy appeared, and she made herself smile and wave at them. Andy was dressed appropriately for the weather, her blond hair tucked up in a woolen skull cap, her figure shrouded under a gray, waterproof jacket and hiking pants.

Andy lifted a hand in reply, but her brows knit concern as she got closer. "Are you okay? You're as white as a ghost."

Jo made herself nod. "I'm fine. Just super cold."

She peered at her, her fierce gaze critical, suspicious. "Really?"

Jo nodded again. After all, it wasn't exactly a lie. She was incredibly cold, even worse than before, her limbs almost stiff in the frigid morning air. This wasn't the deep, arctic frost she'd felt inside that foggy shadow, but it was still very cold out here.

Andy stared at her, evidently still puzzled. "Okay. But let's go inside and warm up. Carter told me to let you know they got the water back on inside the cabin, so you don't need to bother with this."

Meg nodded, grinning. "It was Rachel, actually. She figured out how to turn the water pump on and off from inside, so no one will need to go back and forth to the fuse box. It's kind of annoying, but it works."

Jo laughed, weakly. "You've got a smart one there."

"Yep." Meg smiled, her face radiating pride. She made a shooing gesture. "Go ahead inside, guys. I'll get this closed up again."

"No!" Jo said, almost shouting. Meg and Andy stared at her, both of them clearly baffled by her response. She licked her lips. "I just mean…it's too heavy. To do on your own."

Andy obviously didn't believe this explanation, but Meg nodded. "Okay. You head in, and Andy and I will be right behind you."

Jo shook her head. "That's okay. I'll wait." No way she was leaving anyone near that thing on their own. It was too dangerous.

Both of them seemed to know better than to argue with her, and it took them a couple of minutes to maneuver the wooden cover up over the top of the hole again. They both had to fiddle with the locks, which, while difficult to open, were even harder to close. One of them proved impossible to shut fully.

"Damn it," Meg said.

Andy took it from her and examined it closely. "Some WD-40 would loosen this right up."

"There's some inside. Let's take the lock with us," Jo suggested, desperate to get away from the well. Even covered, it was like a grave.

Andy was staring at her again, eyebrows lowered, a slight frown bringing down the corners of her mouth. "Are you sure you're okay?"

Jo nodded and tried to smile. "Just cold—like I said."

Andy smiled in return and put one arm around her shoulders, her taller height making this gesture seem easy and natural. Her body was warm, almost hot. "Okay, Jo. Whatever you say."

"Carter said she was getting the stove on in there, so it should be nice and toasty by the time we get back," Meg added.

They started walked toward the cabin, and Jo threw one glance back at the well before it disappeared behind them. The cover was on—she'd seen them put it on—but the well nevertheless looked like a squatting, open mouth, the stony rim a set of sharp, jumbled teeth.

CHAPTER THIRTEEN

Ten minutes later, Jo was still shivering, clutching a cup of coffee in both hands near her face. The stove worked quickly inside a space this small, and it was obviously warm here inside the cabin, but the cold skulked deep inside her, settled in the core of her body like a stone. Andy had put a blanket around her shoulders and was on the other side of the room in the kitchen with the others, all of them chattering away and laughing. She and Rachel already seemed like close friends. Jo was glad she was distracted. What had happened had shaken and terrified her.

But what *had* occurred? Her memory, like the shadow that had attacked her, was foggy. In fact, the harder she tried to remember why she had been about to climb onto the edge of the well, the less she could understand what she had almost done. She did recall, however, that strong urge, almost a compulsion, to get up and put her legs down inside that hole. She had felt like she had no choice. She shuddered and took a long pull on her coffee. The sooner she forgot it, the better. If she told anyone, they would think she was losing her mind.

Jo shook her head slightly to clear it and made herself focus on the conversation in the kitchen. Carter was telling Andy about the man Jo had seen last night in the woods. Andy nodded when Carter suggested he might be a squatter.

"We get a lot of that up here, unfortunately. Just last week, I had to help evacuate a whole family camped out in the woods near the west entrance—parents, three kids. It was heartbreaking."

"Why would anyone do something like that?" Rachel asked. "With kids, I mean?"

Andy shrugged. "Lots of reasons. Those people—the parents, I mean—were survivalist types. They'd even built a little Walden Pond–

type cabin, of sorts, though it was falling apart when we found them. They had a garden and everything. They'd been up there for months." She paused. "Luckily the parents surrendered their guns without a fight."

"Jesus," Meg said. "That's terrifying."

"Definitely. But since the guy you saw came only at night, and only the once, I think you're right, Carter. He probably has a squat nearby and got curious when he heard all of you over here, especially if it's been a couple of years since you were up here. With your permission, I'll make some phone calls when I get down and set up a search, but I would imagine you scared him off."

"Oh, look!" Rachel said, pointing out the window. "It's snowing!"

The flakes were coming down hard and fast outside, the air almost white. Jo was surprised. Usually, if it snowed this time of year, it was flurries at most, and generally not even that—just a few snowflakes in the air for ten or fifteen minutes. The size of these flakes and their fury suggested a real snowstorm. If it kept up they could get snowed in here for a day or two, maybe longer.

"I can't believe it's snowing in September," Rachel said.

"It's unusual, for sure, but I've seen it happen before," Andy said. "Two years ago, some parts of Rocky had snow in August. It was totally fine down in Estes before I headed up here. A little cloudy, but I didn't expect this at all."

Rachel was staring out the window, her expression wistful. "I haven't seen snow in years. That was one of the things I was excited about, moving here. I saw it only when we went up to Tahoe when I was a kid."

"Wow," Carter said. "It's really coming down. It's already sticking out there."

"Snowball fight!" Meg shouted.

Rachel shrieked and clapped her hands, and they raced into their bedroom, coming out a quick minute later wearing their coats. Carter and Daniela were right behind them, all four of them running outside in a flurry of childish giggles.

Jo hadn't moved, and when Andy turned around, her smile died and her mouth creased with concern. Jo made herself grin, but Andy's expression remained serious. She could clearly see that Jo was faking it. She walked over and sat down next to her on the sofa, taking her hands in hers. She rubbed them a couple of times to warm them.

"You must have caught a chill. Your hands are like ice."

Jo nodded, unable to reply. Andy's face darkened even further. "Are you okay? Do you feel sick or something?"

Jo opened her mouth to reassure her and then snapped it closed. The memory of her promise to Daniela last night rose in her mind. Did she want to start a relationship with this woman telling lies? Still, even she knew that what had happened out there at the well had been the behavior of a crazy person. She settled on a half-truth.

"I had a scare, out there by the well. I was leaning on it and almost fell in."

Andy drew away a little, appearing stunned and surprised. "Why didn't you say anything before?"

"I don't know. I felt like an idiot, I guess. Careless. I was afraid…I don't know what I was afraid of. That you'd worry about me, I guess. But I don't want to lie to you, either."

Andy nodded, her eyes dark. "Okay. How did it happen? Did you feel dizzy? Is that what it was?"

Again, that wasn't precisely true. She'd felt drunk, if she remembered it correctly, or drugged. But that was similar to dizziness, so she nodded.

Andy stiffened. "How long has this been going on?"

Jo shook her head. "That's just it. I felt fine all week—more than fine, really. My head barely hurt after that first day, and the cut stopped bleeding right away. I feel fine now, too. I don't know what happened."

Andy looked positively frightened. "We should get you to a doctor. I don't like the sound of this." Her gaze drifted to the window. "But it might not be safe to hike down in this. Maybe I should radio it in. Get search-and-rescue up here to bring you down."

"You have your radio with you?"

"Always. I have to carry it at all times, except on vacation. For emergencies, fires, that kind of thing."

Jo was starting to regret speaking up. She didn't want a big rescue team to come up here. It would scare the others, unnecessarily, and she would have to admit what had happened at the well, or at least what she'd told Andy had happened there. Carter would be very upset.

"Do we have to?" Jo asked, trying not to plead and failing.

Andy nodded. "Yes. It's just not safe to wait. You could have internal bleeding or swelling. We can't risk it."

Without waiting for a reply, Andy stood up and walked across the room to pick up her backpack. Seeing it now, Jo realized it was no simple daypack, but a large-capacity gear sack. It clearly held a significant amount of equipment, the straps and buckles stretched to the max. Jo found it strange that she'd brought it with her just for the day, but Andy was obviously the kind of person who always came prepared. Andy dug in her pack and pulled out a large, walkie-talkie-type radio. Jo watched her fiddle with it for a few seconds, and then Andy cursed.

"I can't believe it."

"What?"

She shook her head and sighed, frowning deeply. "The battery's dead. I don't know how that's even possible. I checked it this morning—I know I did. I always do. No way would it lose power that quickly, especially turned off."

"Bad battery?"

Andy shook her head. "Couldn't happen. This is a new one."

Jo stood up and walked closer, holding out her hand. Andy gave the radio to her, and she examined it, spinning the little power knob on and off with no result. She handed it back.

"How do you charge it?"

"It has a special docking mechanism. At home." She cursed again. "I can't believe how careless I was."

Jo grabbed her free hand and squeezed her fingers. "Hey. Don't blame yourself. It could happen to anyone."

Andy set the radio down on a little side table and grasped both of Jo's shoulders.

"Jo—I don't think you understand how serious this is. If your brain is bleeding, you could slip into a coma and die. I can't let that happen. I won't let that happen."

Again, Jo wanted to protest. The incident at the well had nothing to do with her head injury. In fact, she would have been relieved if it were that simple. What had happened had seem to come from outside of her, almost as if something was controlling her. That compulsion had been like a hand drawing her inside the well. Still, she couldn't convince Andy without spilling the whole story, and she couldn't do that.

"So what should we do?"

Andy stared at the floor. "The rest of us will have to carry you down."

"What? No way."

Andy stared at her levelly. "If your brain is bleeding, exercise will only make it worse. You need to keep your heart rate down as much as possible."

Again, Jo was about to protest, when the door was flung open, and Rachel, Carter, and Daniela spilled into the room. Their faces were pale, their eyes terrified.

"Quick! Help us!" Rachel screamed. "Meg's missing!"

"What?"

Carter's eyes were brimming with tears. "One second, we were all screwing around, throwing snowballs, Rachel and Meg on one side, me and Daniela on the other."

"We dodged behind some trees to take cover, and then she disappeared!" Rachel said, her voice still high, near hysteria.

We looked everywhere, Daniela added. *Nothing. No footprints, no marks in the snow, not one sign of her.* Carter interpreted this information for Andy, who paled considerably.

"Jesus Christ. Of all the days for my radio to go out."

"Do something!" Rachel screamed.

Andy paused, her eyes dark and thoughtful. Finally, she pointed at Carter and Daniela. "You two, come with me. Show me exactly where she was before she went missing." She pointed at Jo. "You stay here with Rachel."

"No," Rachel said, shaking her head. "I'm coming with you. I have to find her."

Andy approached her and squeezed her hands. "No, Rachel. You need to stay here. You're too upset right now. You'll only make things harder for me. I need clear heads."

Rachel seemed about to protest, but she finally nodded and burst into tears. Jo walked forward and put an arm around her shoulders, steering her over to the couch before sitting down next to her. The others geared up, Andy pulling on waterproof pants again and lacing on a pair of gaiters. She picked up and cinched the straps on her backpack. Carter and Daniela also grabbed some heavier clothes and coats from their bedroom before rejoining her.

Andy handed Daniela a whistle. "Blow this if you see something and I'm not there, okay?"

Daniela nodded and looped its string over her neck.

The three of them stood there staring at each other, their expressions grim and severe. Rachel was sobbing into Jo's neck, her tears wet and hot against her skin.

Andy met Jo's eyes. "Try to stay calm."

Jo knew she was also talking about the other thing—her supposed dizziness—and she nodded. "Okay. We'll be here."

"Get her to drink something warm. We'll be back soon."

With that, the three of them marched outside into the storm.

The next hour was the longest of Jo's life. It went against her every instinct to wait, warm inside the cabin, while the others hunted outside. She was not the kind of person to shrink from a challenge, and she was not one to abandon a friend in need. The very fact that the others didn't find Meg right away meant that she was in serious danger. If she'd fallen and hurt herself out in the snow, things could get bad fast. She'd been wearing a heavier coat, but if she wasn't moving around, she could easily and quickly get hypothermia or frostbite.

More than once as they waited, Jo had been about to suggest that she and Rachel gear up to help the others, but one look at Rachel's face stopped her. Andy was right—Rachel was nearly hysterical. She would only get herself hurt if they went outside. They had to wait until the others came back. Jo's job right now was to keep Rachel safe and warm inside. Still, knowing this fact and accepting it were two different things. She itched to stand up and run outside.

Just when she thought she couldn't take it anymore, at almost the exact moment she was about to open her mouth and tell Rachel to stay here and then join the others outside, the door opened, and Andy, Daniela, and Carter spilled into the room. They obviously hadn't found Meg, and Rachel immediately burst into tears again, almost wailing. Jo pulled her back into a rough hug under one arm and cradled her face against her neck.

"We're just here to warm up," Carter explained, stamping her feet to knock the snow off her shoes.

Daniela slipped off her boots and gloves and walked directly to the stove to warm her hands. Unlike the others, her coat was not suited to the weather, and her lips were almost blue. Jo knew from experience that it was hard to sign with cold, numb hands.

She turned to Carter. "Did you find anything? Any trace of her?"

Carter paused, her gaze falling on Rachel's sobbing form, and then shook her head.

Daniela rejoined her wife, her lower lip trembling with suppressed tears. *It's like she disappeared, Jo. There was nothing out there—no footprints, no trail of any kind. We looked and looked. There's nothing.*

Jo's stomach dropped. "Nothing?"

Daniela and Carter shook their heads.

"We need to check a couple of places," Andy said. "Carter mentioned them. If we don't find anything, we'll have to get down the mountain and send a search team up here."

"You have to let me help," Jo said.

Andy shook her head. "No way. You're in no shape to be out there."

"What?" Carter asked. "Why not?"

Jo ignored her, still staring at Andy. "I know this mountain better than anyone here. Let me help. I'll be careful."

Andy was clearly intending to shut her down, but Carter, missing this interaction, said, "Fine. Get your shit on." *Daniela, stay here with Rachel and warm up. You're way too cold to go out there again so soon.*

Jo barely caught the last of this remark, as she almost leapt from the couch and over to her backpack. She pulled out her heavier coat, gaiters, gloves, and a woolen hat, racing to put them on before Andy could say something to stop her. No way did she intend to sit here and wait when the others went outside again. Andy must have sensed her determination, as she didn't attempt to stop her. She appeared, however, when Jo finally glanced at her, troubled, almost angry, but Jo decided she could live with that for now.

Mostly to avoid upsetting Rachel further, the three of them went outside together to discuss their plan. They stood on the porch, and Jo was relieved to see that the snow had lightened significantly. A lot of flakes still whirled in the air, but experience told her the storm had almost passed. It had coated the ground with perhaps two or three inches. Jo could see the tracks the others had made coming in and out. They would be impossible to miss. So where, then, was Meg? A terrible thought occurred to her then: the well. A ripple of horror swept through her, and she turned to Carter.

"Where have you searched?"

"Everywhere but the cemetery. I figured if we didn't find any trace of her there, we would need to start down the mountain."

"We roped up and looked off the far side of the peak," Andy said. "No sign of her, thank God."

"But she might have fallen down somewhere a little closer— maybe down the trail to the road a bit," Carter suggested. "There's that one steep part some hundred yards down or so."

"Let's check the cemetery first," Jo said, trying to keep her voice calm. The trail to the cemetery went right past the well, so searching in that direction would serve both purposes. She had no way to explain why she wanted to stop there, but she would have to figure out some way to convince the others it was worth a try. A deep, awful dread swept through her at the thought that Meg could be down in the well, alone in the dark.

They started walking, and Jo had to grab Andy's elbow to keep her from going down on a slippery patch of ground. She was still carrying her backpack, and it must have thrown off her balance. Andy gave her a grateful smile before moving on. The relief she had at the sight of the smile was fleeting, however. Andy might have forgiven her, but whether Meg was in the well or not, she must be hurt out here somewhere. Otherwise, she would have come back.

The well was looming ahead of them on the trail, but seeing it calmed Jo's nerves. The cover was firmly in place and coated with two or three inches of unbroken snow. It clearly hadn't budged since Andy and Meg put it there this morning. Her relief at this realization was almost staggering. If Meg had fallen or climbed in there for whatever reason, she probably would have died.

Suddenly Carter let out a whoop and started running down the trail. Jo and Andy saw why an instant later—they spotted footprints on the ground, leading away from them toward the cemetery. As the others hadn't been this way earlier in their search, it could only mean that someone else had. She and Andy both started running at the same time, Jo's mood lifting as they raced ahead.

They caught up with Carter a couple of minutes later. She was standing in the middle of the three graves, frowning. She pointed at the ground.

"The footprints just stop. Right here."

Andy glanced around. "It could be from the tree. There's not a lot of snow under here. Everyone spread out and look at the ground. Something should show us where she went."

Jo crouched down, her nose almost to the ground, and waddled forward, keeping her eyes rooted to the ground. The three of them started in the same spot where the footprints disappeared and then walked away from each other, outward, like spokes on a wheel. They did this twice on different paths with no success, but on the third try, Jo paused, picking up a soft noise. She stood up, her movement so quick and abrupt the others stopped and turned her way. She held out a hand to silence them and listened again, hearing the noise again a few seconds later. It was coming from the edge of the cliff.

She dashed over there, throwing herself down on her stomach, and inched her head over the edge, peering down. Meg lay some twenty feet below on a little shelf of stone. She was on her back, but her eyes were open. She waved one arm wildly when she saw Jo above her.

"I'm down here!" she said. Her voice was hoarse and broken, but loud enough to carry up to them. The others had crouched next to Jo and were peering over the side with her.

"Jesus Christ," Carter whispered. "How the hell did she get down there?"

"We're coming, Meg! Hang on!" Jo shouted.

The three of them sat back on their haunches and stared at each other.

"How are we going to do this?" Jo asked.

"We have to be very careful," Andy said. "She could have a neck or back injury. We might make it worse if we try to move her."

"But if we leave her down there, she'll die of exposure," Carter said.

Andy nodded. "Exactly." She paused. "The best thing is for me to go down there and assess. I have the training. I'll do what I can to immobilize her, and then we can decide how to get her up here. At that point we'll need to make some kind of stretcher to carry her down to my truck." She shook her head and held up a hand. "Sorry—one thing at a time. First things first—I need to rappel down there and check her injuries. Jo, help me set up the line on that tree over there. Carter, call down to her and ask her where she's hurt."

As Jo helped Andy, she couldn't help but admire her calm efficiency. She went through each step with her climbing gear as carefully as if a life weren't in jeopardy. Jo's hands were shaking, hard, and twice Andy covered them and squeezed them to calm her. It worked, if only for a minute or two, as if Andy's serenity was catching.

Andy's gear was well-used but well cared for. She was also an obvious expert. Even Jo could see that. Jo knew how to climb, had taken advanced classes, but she was, at best, modestly skilled, nothing like this woman or even Carter, who climbed almost every day of the week at the gym. As with everything Jo had witnessed, Andy ran through her safety checks with grace and composure, and Jo's hopes finally started to rise. If anyone could save Meg, it was this woman.

"Okay," Andy finally said. "I'm ready. I don't like doing this when it's so wet, but we have no choice." She shook her head, appearing angry. "I can't believe I let my battery go dead."

Jo squeezed her hand. "It's okay. She's going to be okay."

Andy stared at her levelly before nodding. "Yes. She is. I swear it." She pointed at the tree. "Keep an eye on this for me, will you? Shout to Carter if you spot a problem. There shouldn't be one, but you never know."

Jo barely had time to agree before Andy walked over to the edge of the cliff. She buckled her harness onto the rope and then carefully threw the rest over the side. She and Carter spoke briefly before she went over, walking backward, and disappeared from view. Carter got down on her stomach, her head over the side, peering down. The wind was just strong enough that Jo, from some fifteen feet away, could catch perhaps only one word in ten from the shouted exchange. Jo knew when Andy reached the ledge with Meg, however, as the line slackened. She stood there, shivering, wondering if she could join Carter on at the edge, and then the rope became taut again. Carter got up and walked over to her.

"She's coming up."

"How's Meg?"

"She's okay."

A rush of relief swept through Jo, and she almost started crying. Carter gave her a weak smile. "She's scraped up a bit, and I think she hurt her wrist, bruised some ribs, and probably sprained both ankles. She didn't hit her head or back at all, and she has feeling in all her limbs. Andy's going to set up some kind of pulley system and get her up here. You should go back to the cabin to get our rope and gear and tell the others."

Jo knew this was the best course of action—Carter was the expert, after all. But again, knowing this didn't help the fact that she wanted to stay here and wait for Andy to return safely.

Carter, as if reading her thoughts, gave her a weak smile. "It's okay, Jo. I'll keep an eye on both of them for you. Hurry back."

Jo gave her a quick, thankful hug and then took off down the trail back to the cabin, running as hard and as fast as she could over the slippery, snow-covered ground.

CHAPTER FOURTEEN

It was late afternoon by the time the six of them were together inside the cabin again. Getting Meg off the cliff face and back inside had taken a great deal of effort. Once she was on safe ground again, Jo, Carter, Andy, Rachel, and Daniela had carried her the quarter mile or so between them on a space blanket, rotating for breaks. Finally in the cabin, they'd moved her bed out into the living room by the stove, and she was lying on it, bandaged and in a deep, peaceful sleep brought on by hot tea with a little tequila. Rachel had dragged a chair next to her and was holding her hand. Jo and the others sat about ten feet away on the couch and armchairs, too exhausted to do anything but stare or doze.

Still, Jo thought, things could have been much worse. If Meg had been more seriously hurt, she would have been in a great deal of trouble. No way were they strong enough right now to convey her all the way down the mountain after what they'd just done. Already, the light outside was starting to acquire the soft, hazy glow that preceded sunset. The storm had completely cleared, the sky almost entirely free of clouds, but it was still chilly, and the trail down would be slick and wet, dangerous to walk on, especially carrying someone. If they rested long enough, they might have been able to reach Andy's Bronco, but it would probably be dark by the time they got there. Not necessarily having to do this was a great relief.

Andy let out a long sigh and rolled her shoulders. She slapped her knees and rose. "Okay. Enough of this. I'm hiking down to my truck to get search-and-rescue up here."

Jo stood up. "I'll go with you."

Andy stared at her, frowning slightly, then finally nodded. Clearly, given the physical acrobatics she'd just witnessed as Jo helped save Meg, Andy had decided she was okay, but she also seemed uncertain, and Jo knew she was wondering if she was making the right choice to let her help.

Andy turned to Carter and pointed at Meg. "Make sure she gets lots of fluids when she's up. In fact, if she doesn't get up on her own in twenty minutes or so, wake her and give her a glass of water and some weak tea, if she'll take it."

"Okay."

Jo and Andy started gathering their gear from the various places they'd set it out to dry. Most of it was still damp, but at least it was warm. By the time she had her boots on again, Meg was stirring on her bed. Rachel let out a little gasp and then leaned down to kiss her.

"Where am I?" Meg asked. The question came out muddled, almost slurred.

"You're safe, baby," Rachel said. "Back in the cabin."

Meg tried to sit up, winced, and lay back down again. "How did I get here? The last thing I remember is getting hooked up with the ropes..." She shook her head. "Then nothing."

"It doesn't matter. You're here now. We got you back inside, safe and sound." She picked up a glass of water. "Drink this."

Rachel took a couple of pillows off the couch and propped them under Meg's head to raise her head. Everyone had gathered closer to her bed, and as Meg finished her water, she peered up at them, obviously still confused. Her eyes stopped on Andy and Jo, who stood a little behind the others.

"Why are you dressed like that? Where are you going?"

"To get help," Andy said. "You need to be in a hospital."

Meg shook her head emphatically and tried to sit up. She let out a little hiss of pain and lay back down. "No! You can't do that."

Rachel grabbed her hand again. "They have to, Meg. You're really banged up. This is no time for butch heroics."

Meg shook her head rapidly. "It's not that. It's not that at all. You can't go out there. It isn't safe." Meg, clearly seeing their puzzled expressions, began to plead. "No, please—listen to me. You have to believe me! I didn't fall down that cliff. Someone pushed me off."

Jo was stunned into silence. Carter crouched down next to the bed so Meg wouldn't have to crane her head. "What are you talking about? Who pushed you?"

Meg paused and her face crumpled as she fought back tears. Finally, she took a deep breath and met Carter's eyes. "It's hard to explain."

"Try."

Meg looked around the room, terror in her eyes. "I don't know if you'll believe this, but you have to. Every word of it is true." She paused, her eyes down and inward. She licked her lips, and then her face hardened with determination.

"It started right away. We were all out there, goofing around in the snow. You and Daniela were hiding behind that boulder, and me and Rachel were hiding in the trees."

Carter nodded.

She turned to Rachel. "Then I heard something. Remember?"

Rachel frowned with apparent confusion, and then her expression cleared. "Oh my God! Of course. How did I forget that?"

Meg held up a hand. "I think I know why, but I'll get to that in a minute." Her eyes seemed to darken and lose focus, her thoughts turning inward as she relived the memory. She continued to stare at her legs as she spoke. "I remember telling Rachel I was going to check out the sound. It was like someone crying."

Rachel shook her head. "I don't remember that at all."

Meg nodded. "I thought you wouldn't. Things were already starting to go hazy at that point."

Jo's stomach dropped. She knew exactly what Meg meant by "going hazy." The same thing had happened to her at the well.

"The weather started getting colder—even colder than before," Meg said. "Then, as I walked toward the sound, the day grew darker and darker, almost like nighttime, but not quite. Twilight, sort of? The air was funny, too, thick, almost, and kind of hard to breathe, like somewhere humid. It was hard to see very far. Like I said, it was hazy, like I was walking in fog. I don't know why I kept going. Part of me knew something was off about everything, but it was like I couldn't stop. I had to see what that crying sound was.

"Before I knew it, I was standing in the middle of the cemetery. I don't know how I got there. I really don't. I was just there, all of the sudden. It was freezing cold, with almost no sunlight. I could barely see anything."

"We saw your footprints on the trail," Carter said, her voice gentle and soothing. "You took the path there, Meg."

Meg lifted an eyebrow and shrugged. "I kind of expected that.

Like I said, I'll get to it. I had a long time on that cliff to think, and I have some ideas. Anyway, I was standing in the middle of the cemetery, surprised but at the same time not surprised to find myself there.

"The crying was coming from the cliff. I started walking over there, but it was getting harder to move. It was so cold, and the air was kind of heavy. I felt more like I was swimming than walking, or maybe wading through mud. Also, I thought I heard someone else—Rachel, I think—calling my name, somewhere behind me. I tried to turn around but couldn't. Then, like a second later, I didn't want to find her anymore. I *had* to look over the side of the cliff. It was like... like—"

"A compulsion," Jo said.

Meg nodded. "Exactly like that, like I had no choice."

Jo went cold. She remembered that feeling with crystalline clarity. It had seemed like a perfectly reasonable thing at the time to climb up onto the edge of that well. Some part of her had known that it was wrong and dangerous, but the majority of her had considered it a great plan. If Andy and Meg hadn't appeared, she would have climbed up there and jumped in. It had been as if she had to do it, like she had no choice.

"What did you see? When you looked over the edge?" Rachel asked.

Meg frowned, appearing almost angry. "That's the thing I don't remember. I keep trying to, but it's hard—almost like that fog is still there, but inside me. I remember seeing a face—a scared, pale face, down there on that ledge you found me on, and then someone pushed me from behind. I slid all the way down but managed to land on my feet, which is probably how I hurt my ankles. Then I fell over and passed out."

"So you didn't see who pushed you?" Carter asked.

Meg shook her head and then hesitated. "No, but there was something—a tall shadow, and a strong smell right before it happened. The smell was really bad, terrible, like something rotten."

Jo's stomach fluttered with horror. Despite everything, she'd almost forgotten that smell. She hadn't detected it at the well, but last night, and last week in the woods, it been overpowering. How had she forgotten?

"I'm just so glad you're okay," Rachel said, her eyes welling with tears. "That you'll be okay, I mean."

"So how do you explain the footprints we saw?" Carter asked, sounding angry. Jo thought she might be scared, too—anger was her usual response to fright.

Meg stared at her, her expression determined and serious. "That haze, or whatever it was, fooled me. It made me think I was seeing and hearing things that weren't there."

"Well, that's obvious!" Carter shouted. "None of this actually happened. It's not possible, Meg."

Daniela touched her arm, and Carter's face relaxed a little. "Sorry. I didn't mean to yell. I'm just…having a hard time believing you."

Meg shrugged. "I knew you would, but it's true. I lived through it, so I'm certain. It was showing me something for a reason, but I wasn't actually there—I was here that whole time, walking down the path to the cemetery and then to the edge of the cliff, but the whole time, until the last second, I was also somewhere else, somewhere cold and dark. Whatever it was confused me on purpose, just like it did Rachel. It made her forget that I told her I heard something. It's sneaky, whatever it is, and it's rotten."

Rachel let out a little gasp of fright and leaned down to hug her. They continued to hold each other, Meg's hands, bandaged and scratched, tight across her back, both of them shaking with sobs. Andy touched Carter and glanced at Jo and Daniela, motioning toward one of the bedrooms. They followed her in there, and she closed the door behind them. Andy looked troubled and pale.

"I'm really worried now. It's imperative that we get her out of here and to the hospital. She's clearly delusional."

Jo shook her head. "No. She's not."

Andy and Carter looked stunned. "You believe her?" Andy asked.

Jo nodded and turned to Daniela. *We should tell them. Everything.*

Daniela seemed to have trouble meeting Carter's gaze. *We were going to tell you.*

Tell me what? Carter was clearly angry now, her brows knit, and her lips curled in a deep frown.

Andy cut in. "Can someone tell me what you guys are talking about?"

With Carter acting as interpreter, Daniela began their story. *It started when Jo was reading in the living room and I was in the bedroom, doing the last of the cleaning in there.* She told the others about the book that seemed to relocate on its own and the tools that appeared in the bedroom without help.

And then, of course, there's the faucet, she said.

"What about the faucet?" Carter asked. "It's just a mechanical malfunction."

Daniela stared at her levelly. *Do you really believe that? You saw it move on its own, too.*

Carter laughed. "Because it was malfunctioning! That's all. Water pressure could easily turn that handle. There's nothing supernatural about it."

I think there is, and I think you know it, too. You just don't want to admit it.

Carter put a hand to her forehead. "Hold on a second, here. I'll admit the moving book and tools are a little weird, but there's clearly some rational explanation. And the faucet is not haunted. It's broken."

"What about the weird furniture sculpture I found?" Jo asked.

Carter seemed taken aback, and Jo had to explain what they'd seen to the others.

Daniela frowned at Carter. *You never mentioned this.*

Carter sighed. *We didn't want to scare you.*

Jo took a deep breath and let it out. "There's more."

Carter's head snapped her way. "What?"

Jo told them about hearing footsteps in the woods, about how she had felt somehow compelled to go look for whatever was making that sound out there. She hadn't felt the same overwhelming compulsion she had at the well, but it had been strong enough to get her to run outside of her tent without a coat or shoes.

"And I don't think I was alone out there, either. And I'm not sure I hit my head."

"What do you mean?" Andy asked.

She met her eyes. "I believe someone hit me."

Andy and Daniela were clearly stunned, but Carter's face went a mottled red. "What? This is the first time you've told us. Why didn't you mention it before?"

Jo shook her head. "I didn't want to scare you. And I didn't think you'd believe me."

"And I don't."

She nodded, expecting and accepting this reaction. Carter's anger came from a deep sense of the rational and made her such a good lawyer and a good, clearheaded friend. Her rationality was being shaken, and she didn't like it. Part of Carter knew that what Meg, Daniela, and now

Jo had said was true, but she wasn't willing to accept it. Her rational brain was too strong. Still, Jo knew she had to try.

"There's one more thing," Jo said, then glanced at Andy. Her heart broke a little when their eyes met. Andy's were filled with pity, but she was also clearly skeptical. If Jo continued, she was pretty sure that expression would stay there forever. Still, it needed to come out, all of it, if they had a chance to figure this thing out.

"It happened at the well," she said, then told the whole story. The others listened and watched her patiently. All of them, however, did this with clear and deep skepticism in their eyes, especially Andy and Carter.

"Don't you see?" she said. "It's just like what Meg told you. The same thing happened to me."

They stared at her and didn't reply. Daniela was obviously upset, her eyes red and wet, but, Jo suspected, she was halfway convinced. This made sense—she'd seen the book and tools move on their own, or had at least seen them after they'd relocated. Carter, on the other hand, was even angrier than before, and Andy's expression was hard to read—concerned, perhaps, or worried, her eyes not meeting hers.

"Look," Carter said, breaking the silence, "I don't know what happened to you, and I don't know why you feel the need to tell us this fairy tale—"

"It's not a fairy tale, Carter. It happened. I swear to God, it happened."

Carter shook her head briskly. "No, Jo. It didn't. You're imagining things."

Jo opened her mouth to protest, but Andy raised a hand. "This is getting us nowhere, folks, and it's not going to help Meg. I need to go to my truck and get some help up here. Her condition might not be critical, but she needs X-rays and better medical attention than we can give her up here. Jo, are you still coming?"

She tried to smile. "As long as you don't think I'm crazy."

Andy gave her the kind of warm smile Jo had feared she'd never see again. But when she spoke, what she said broke her heart. "I don't think you're crazy, Jo. You obviously believe what you're saying, but I can't believe it, not based on what you've said. You know that, right?" She touched her shoulder briefly and then dropped her hand.

Jo nodded, her stomach clenching with sorrow and dread. She was fairly certain she'd just been dumped.

"Okay then," Andy said. "Let's get going. The sunlight will last only another hour or two."

Jo barely heard or acknowledged this remark, but she followed her out of the bedroom and outside into the brisk air, a deep part of her knowing that she'd blown it.

CHAPTER FIFTEEN

It was dark by the time Meg and Rachel disappeared down the mountain road inside the ambulance. Once the search-and-rescue team had come, the evacuation went fairly quickly, despite the slick trail. Jo and the others helped as they could, leading them up or down the trail, but generally stayed out of the way. Andy spent most of this time on the radio in her truck, relaying messages to the various task forces involved, as well as park officials. The other cars and trucks from the rescue team disappeared one by one until only Andy's and Carter's vehicles were left. Jo waited for Andy to finish from inside Carter's car, dozing off now and again.

She'd slipped into a deep sleep when Andy knocked on her window, startling her awake. She opened the door and climbed out, stretching.

"Everyone's gone. It's over," Andy said, her voice weary and hoarse. "What do you want to do now? Go to the hospital?"

Jo shook her head. "Meg begged us not to come. She said we can visit her tomorrow, if she's still there. Otherwise she and Rachel were heading to her place as soon as possible. I'll call them in the morning."

"Are Carter and Daniela still up at the cabin? I didn't see them come down the last time."

"Yes. The three of us still need to finish a few things up there."

Andy's face darkened, and her eyes strayed up the trail, which disappeared in the dark some twenty feet away. Down here, it hadn't snowed at all—just a light rain, and even that had mostly dried up hours ago. Still, the trail seemed somehow menacing in the dark, and Jo could see that Andy was a little afraid of it now, too.

"Are you sure that's a good idea? Going up there again?"

Jo laughed. "It's our home. My family's, anyway. I'm there only a few weeks a year, but it's part of me, part of all of us. And anyway, you and Carter seem to think Meg and Daniela and I are imagining everything. What's the problem?"

Andy looked worried, her brows low. "I don't know what I think, Jo. It's all just so…fantastic, I guess. I mean, really—ghosts?"

Jo shrugged. "I don't know what it is, Andy. Ghosts seem like a silly way to describe what I saw and felt. But something is up there. I swear it."

Andy hesitated and then nodded. "I know you think that's true, so I won't argue with you. But whatever it is, I don't think you're safe there. You might want to end this trip before you get hurt again. I don't like the idea of you going back."

Jo didn't respond. It was impossible to explain why she felt like she needed to, had to go back, even. She didn't have any choice. Beyond the fact that the cabin was her favorite place in the world, she was certain now that something was wrong with it—a kind of illness that had blossomed in the years it was neglected up there on its own. When she'd been up there before, she'd never felt or experienced anything like the odd happenings during the last week, and she knew one else in her family had, either. Something had changed, something had come through. But the place was hers—her family's. More than a vacation home, the cabin was a kind of refuge, and it had been for generations before her. She had to stop whatever was happening.

Andy stepped closer to Jo and met her eyes. "Look, I get it—you think you have to go back, but please wait until morning. You're too tired for that hike tonight."

Jo hesitated. Actually, she felt a lot better now after her nap in the car, but Andy was clearly determined and glared at her as if waiting for her to protest. When she didn't, Andy smiled, obviously relieved.

"So where will you go tonight?"

It would take at least an hour and a half, perhaps longer, to drive to her little house in Fort Collins, and though she felt fairly rested, that would be pushing it. She shrugged. "Get a hotel room in Estes, I guess."

"No, you're not. You're staying with me. I have a sofa bed." She glanced up the trail. "Will Carter be worried?"

"No. She knows I'm with you. She'll figure it out."

They walked together to Andy's Bronco and climbed in. Jo was pleased to be here. She hadn't been inside a Bronco since she was a kid, and this was an old one—late 70s, if she had to guess. It seemed strange that the park services held on to this old relic, but perhaps that was Andy's doing. The truck was clearly well-maintained as the engine turned over at once, rumbled into life, and settled into a comfortable low hum.

"Music?" Andy asked, pointing at the radio.

"Sure. What have you got?"

"Look in that case there," Andy said, pointing. Despite the fact that they were alone out here, Andy put on her directional before pulling out into the road and heading down the mountain.

Jo picked up a large, zippered case on the floor and opened it. Inside, she found 8-track tapes and laughed. "You must be kidding me."

Andy grinned. "Not at all! They're the best."

Jo laughed again. "What are you talking about? 8-track sounds like crap. Just because it's old doesn't make it better. It's not like vinyl."

Andy rolled her eyes. "Oh, I see. You're one of those."

"One of those what?"

"One of those vinyl snobs." She began mimicking someone with a much higher voice. "'Only vinyl sounds good. Music should be listened to only on vinyl. That's why I have a portable record player in my car.'"

Jo laughed again. "Don't exaggerate. Any music expert would tell you vinyl is best."

"Oh? Do you call yourself an expert?"

"Well, no, but—"

"Aha!" Andy shouted. "So you're no expert, but you have an opinion." She shook her head. "Typical."

"Okay, then, smart-ass, let me prove you wrong." She examined the tapes in the case. "What have we here…Kenny Rogers, Dolly Parton, Hank Williams, Johnny Cash, more names from the sixties and seventies…Gee, it's like no one in the last forty years is making 8-track albums anymore."

"Hey!"

Jo laughed again and touched her arm. "I'm kidding. I'm sure these guys sound great, even on tape."

"They do. Choose one and play it, wise guy."

Jo hesitated before pulling out Dolly Parton, knowing this was some kind of test. It took her a while to figure out how to put the tape in the player, and the music began only after a long pause. Dolly's voice came out of the speakers in a sweet, melodic croon. They listened in silence for a while, the trees and road flashing by, barely visible beyond the headlights in the dark.

When Jo glanced over at Andy, she was smiling, her eyes distant, fingers tapping the steering wheel. Jo's stomach fluttered with warm, pleasant nerves. Whatever Andy thought about what she'd said up there at the cabin, it clearly hadn't changed anything. They were comfortable with each other again. As if sensing Jo's gaze, Andy glanced over and then back at the road, one eyebrow crooked up in a question.

"So. What do you think? Are you an 8-track convert?"

"Dolly would sound good on cassette—it's hardly a fair question."

"True. Well, we'll just have to listen to some more in my apartment so I can prove it to you."

"You have a player in your apartment, too?"

Andy glanced over at her and grinned. "Of course!"

Jo was sweating. Andy had built a large fire and the heat was on, but Jo was still wearing her heavier hiking clothes—long underwear underneath her pants and sweater. She'd taken off her coat, but that was the only layer she could remove modestly. Still, the heat felt good on her tired muscles. Andy was clearly the kind of woman that liked to keep her place as hot as she could. Jo found something comforting in that, something unexpected. Andy was so precise and practical, this detail about her seemed out of character, but humanizing. Music was playing softly on the 8-track player, and Jo was drinking a glass of dark beer. She relaxed for the first time in hours.

Andy reappeared from the bedroom, toweling her hair. She was wearing a full set of green flannel pajamas and wool socks. Jo's stomach dropped at the sight. Even in the least revealing clothing imaginable, Andy was incredibly attractive. Clothing that would look baggy or dowdy on anyone else might have been custom-made for her tall, strong figure.

"So what do you think?" Andy asked, gesturing at the sound system. "Pretty good, right?"

Jo had to stifle a laugh. In fact, Johnny Cash sounded tinny, his voice even scratchier as it was piped through the 8-track and out of the speakers. But Andy had a point. Because the album was older, the dampened quality of the sound on the tape seemed almost natural, old-fashioned, which was somehow acceptable with the music, nice even. It wasn't the original sound, no—that could be heard only on vinyl. Of that, Jo was certain. But the music from the tape had a warmer, cozier quality.

She gave Andy a quick smile. "I like it."

The smile Andy gave her warmed her all the way through. "I told you so."

Jo couldn't respond, so she nodded.

"How do you like that porter?"

Jo had forgotten about it as she stared at Andy. Andy's hair was damp and messy, in desperate need of a comb, but Jo could hardly tear her eyes away from it. Like her heavy pajamas, Andy's hair was somehow sexy despite the mess.

"What?" Jo asked, dazed.

Andy smiled, as if reading her mind. "The beer. Do you like it?"

Jo looked down at it absently, trying to remember. Her last sip seemed like hours ago, lost in the fantasy of running her fingers through Andy's hair.

"It's great," she said finally, taking another shaky sip. "What is it?"

"A friend of mine in Loveland brews it. She and her sister have a nice little taproom together on Fourth."

"My friend Ronnie lives in Loveland," she said after a long pause. She was having trouble focusing. Andy's hair was mesmerizing.

"Oh yeah? That's cool. I bet she knows the place. We should all go over there sometime, and you guys can meet my friend. I think you two would really hit it off. You and Carter remind me of her. Maybe Ronnie would like to join us. Does she like beer, too?"

"Mmm," Jo said, simply to be agreeable. Andy was talking, but the sense of her words was muffled in Jo's head. Her snarled, damp hair was making it hard to follow her.

Andy yawned, stretching. "Boy, am I beat. We should go to bed." She blushed slightly at the implication, her eyes darting away from Jo's. "Want a shower?"

Jo's heart was racing. She'd heard and seen Andy's anxious slip. She licked her lips, her face hot and feverish. "A shower would be great. But I don't—"

"I put some pj's on a chair in there for you. I'll get the sofa set up while you're in there." Andy still couldn't meet her eyes, and she spoke quickly, her voice shaky.

"Thanks."

Jo had to walk right by her to get to the bedroom, and Andy stopped her as she passed, touching her arm. Jo met her incredible eyes, and they both stood there, staring at each other for a long pause. Jo was sinking into those eyes again. She swallowed.

"Yes?"

Andy shook her head as if to clear it. "I was going to ask you something..." Her voice sounded weak, her words halting. Jo let her gaze drift up to that wet, tousled hair and had to fight the urge to touch a loose, damp curl on Andy's forehead. Her fingers itched to do it, to touch her, and to run her fingers across her face and along the side of her jaw. Jo bunched her fingers into a fist to stop herself.

They continued to stare at each other, and something passed between them—a kind of electrical charge. A great surge of desire washed over her, and she stepped closer, staring into her eyes, waiting for permission. Andy's lips parted slightly, and that was enough.

The beginning was gentle, hesitant. Their lips met briefly, like they were strangers. Andy's breath was a sweet, clean mint, her lips soft and delicate, a hint of cherry ChapStick coating their surface. The heat that came from the kiss was instant, however, and a moment later, Jo lost control, crushing those lips against hers. Andy's hands were on her back, pulling her closer, and the kiss turned hard, reckless, their lips brutal and unforgiving. Their tongues met and the heat racing through her caught fire. She pushed herself into Andy, who lost balance slightly, stumbling backward. They had to brace themselves on the doorframe to keep from falling. Jo hardly noticed their unsteadiness, her desperation now so great she was disintegrating.

Their bodies were flush now, and Jo could feel the crush of Andy's full, long length against her. Her body was warm, firm, solid, not an ounce of anything soft on her except the swell of her breasts against Jo's. Her thighs were strong, the muscles bunching under Jo's hand when she gripped one of them and then slid into the warm space between her legs. Andy's lips released hers, and Andy gasped, whipping her head up and back in pleasure. Jo kissed her throat, then nibbled it, sucking slightly. She moved into her again, grinding the palm of her hand between Andy's legs. She gripped Andy's back with her other hand, pulling her forward, and trailed her tongue down the length of Andy's long, gorgeous neck.

"Wait, wait," Andy said, grabbing her wrist.

Jo stopped and pulled her hand away, staring up into Andy's flushed face. Andy's eyes were bright, almost surprised. Had Jo gone too far? Then, almost as if she could read Andy's mind, she saw something there—a dark, deep desire bordering on panic.

"Bedroom," Andy finally said, and Jo followed her in, closing the door behind them.

CHAPTER SIXTEEN

A nd who is this?" Jo asked, holding out the photo in the frame. It had been sitting on the nightstand next to Andy's bed.

Andy took it from her, blinking to clear her eyes. "That's my mother. She's about my age in this—late thirties."

Jo took it back and moved her eyebrows up and down. "Hubba hubba."

Andy laughed and pushed at her shoulder. "I'll have to tell her you said that."

The sun was just coming up. The bedroom window faced the mountains that lightened as the sun broke over them. The sky was still fairly dark, a vivid orange suffused with purple. They'd slept, on and off, the last few hours, but for hardly more than an hour at a time. First Andy woke her up, her body hot and strong in its desperate need, and then, some hours later, Jo returned the favor. Still, despite her broken sleep, she felt rested and sated, relaxed.

Andy finally sat up, the sheet falling to reveal her naked chest. Her green pajamas lay on the floor in various places around the room, jumbled with the clothes they'd torn off Jo. The heat was still on at perhaps eighty degrees, so they didn't need a blanket, but at some point during the night, Andy had pulled a sheet over them. Her body, revealed, was breathtaking. She was muscular, her shoulders and arms well-defined, and her abs were taut and firm. Her skin was a universally honey color, like she suntanned in the nude. Her golden hair was even more tangled and mussed than it had been last night, and Jo, staring at it, felt that same dropping feeling she'd had in her stomach last night, like she was falling off a high cliff.

Andy, clearly seeing something in her eyes, shook her head. "No way, lady. I have to get to work soon. Don't stare at me like that."

"Like what?" Jo tried to make herself sound innocent and failed.

Andy grinned. "Like you want to eat me for breakfast."

Jo sat up and kissed her. "I do want to eat you for breakfast. A part of you anyway."

Andy pushed at her again and then pecked the tip of her nose. "You're dirty. I love it. Now get up and shower. We have to leave in less than an hour."

"Are you coming into the shower with me?"

Andy gave her a level stare. "What do you think? I'll go use Drew's."

By the time Jo finished her shower, she could hear voices in the kitchen—Andy's and Drew's, probably. She hunted for her clothes, finding everything but her pants and socks. The clothes had come off here and in the doorway to the bedroom, so she was fairly certain the missing pieces were beyond the closed door somewhere in the living room. Jo spotted the pj's Andy had set out for her last night, unused, folded neatly on a chair in the corner of the room. Feeling distinctly ridiculous, she pulled on the bottoms with her sweater and opened the door. Drew and Andy gave her equally mischievous grins, and Jo knew they'd been talking about her.

"Well, look what the cat dragged in," Drew said, smiling at Andy.

Jo colored and tried to smile back, not sure how to react. It had been a long time since she'd had to deal with a roommate the morning after.

Drew was in his uniform, looking a little bedraggled. His shirt had lost the crispness she remembered from the last time she'd seen him, and his eyes appeared tired and red. His hair was still styled and cute, however, that peroxide blond shining like a halo.

He held up his hands. "Sorry, sorry. I'm being rude. Haven't slept in a couple of days."

"S'okay," Jo mumbled.

"Coffee?" Andy asked, holding up the pot.

"Yes. Please," Jo said. Andy handed her a large mug and filled it to the top. Jo sat down on one of the chairs at the breakfast table, and the others joined her soon after.

Drew, watching Andy drink her coffee, shook his head in seeming wonder. "It's been crazy this week with school groups. I don't know how you're going to get through the day today, missy, with no sleep."

"We slept," Andy said, then smiled. "A little."

Drew laughed. "Sure you did." He closed his eyes and inhaled

deeply. "That coffee smells divine. Way better than that swill at work."
He opened them and winced. "But I need to go to bed. I'm exhausted."

"What's that all about, anyway? Why were you up all night?"

His expression darkened. "Friggin' tourist tried to get a picture with a bear last night at one of the campgrounds. Got a little too close."

Andy seemed equally angry now. "Did the tourist get hurt?"

Drew nodded. "So did the bear, of course. That idiot got scratched, and now a bear is dead, all thanks to him and his damn social-media accounts." He paused and looked over toward the front door. "I think I just heard Kevin's car."

"He's coming over?"

"Yes. We've talked on the phone, but we haven't seen each other in a few days, so we're going to have breakfast before he goes to work." He yawned and stretched. "I hope I can stay awake long enough to say a proper hello."

"That's our cue, Jo," Andy said, standing up.

"Hey!" Drew said, laughing.

Andy grinned at him. "I've heard your 'proper hellos' before. I have to save Jo's ears."

Drew laughed and touched Jo's hand. "At least stay long enough to meet him."

"I'll go finish getting ready," Andy said.

Kevin walked in a moment later, filling the entrance to the hallway almost to the ceiling. He had to be well over six feet tall, maybe closer to seven. He was in a light flannel shirt, jeans, and work boots, and had a neat, stylized beard and closely shorn, dark, curly hair. A small pair of wire-framed spectacles perched on his nose, almost primly. Drew rocketed to his feet and ran at him, launching himself into Kevin's arms. Kevin swung the smaller man around in a long hug before setting him down and kissing him deeply.

"God, it's good to see you," Kevin said, his voice low and thick with emotion.

"I missed you so much," Drew said. He grabbed Kevin's hand and pulled him over to the breakfast table. "I want you to meet Jo—Andy's new piece."

"Hey!"

Kevin rolled his eyes. "Forgive my boyfriend's antics, Jo. Nice to meet you."

Jo's hand was swallowed in his as they shook. "Same here. And I hope I'm a little more than a piece."

"I'm sure you are." He paused. "So Drew tells me you actually own a place in Rocky?"

Jo nodded. "Family cabin."

He shook his head. "How lucky. It must have been there a long time."

"Yes—going on a hundred and thirty. It's been updated, but it still has a lot of the original wood and character."

"I'd love to see it sometime."

"Kevin's a local history buff," Drew said, the pride in his voice clear.

Kevin glanced at him and blushed. "It's a hobby of mine." He seemed embarrassed to admit it.

"That's really interesting," Jo said. "I'd love to talk to you about it. I've been wondering about a relative of mine that lived there. She built the cabin, actually. Or her husband did—one of the two. We don't know for sure."

"What's her name?"

"Aurora Lemke."

His expression grew thoughtful. "Lemke, Lemke…why does that sound familiar?" He finally shook his head. "I'm sure I've heard her name before, but it's eluding me."

The door to the bedroom opened, and Andy stuck her head out. "Hi, Kevin. Nice to see you. Hey, Jo. Could you come here a minute?"

Jo went into the bedroom again, and Andy closed the door behind her and grabbed her arm, pulling her into a long, slow kiss. When Jo drew back, her heart was racing, and she was hot and trembly again, weak at the knees. Andy was smiling, a knowing look in her eyes, as if she knew how the kiss had made her feel.

"I just wanted to do that one more time before we left."

Jo nodded, unable to respond.

Andy leaned down and picked up Jo's pants, handing them to her. "I hate to rush you, but I really need to head in to work, especially if I'm dropping you off first." Her face clouded. "Though I wish you weren't going up there again."

Jo squeezed her shoulders. "I'll be fine—we'll be fine. We just need to get the place together before the winter starts up, and it's not quite there yet."

Andy nodded, clearly still troubled, but didn't reply. She was watching as Jo pulled on the rest of her clothes, the long underwear and pants much too hot in the stifling bedroom.

The men were gone by the time they returned to the kitchen. Jo heard laughter coming from the second bedroom, and Andy hustled her through and down the hall before they could hear anything more.

In the car, Jo used Andy's phone to call to the hospital. Meg had been released early this morning. She tried to reach her on her cell, but either her phone was off or she wasn't answering. She tried Rachel with the same result. She left a quick message for both, letting them know that Carter would be down in town later today or tomorrow to get supplies and check on them.

Andy pulled into the little parking area next to Carter's car but kept the engine running. Jo turned to her, heart sinking. Now, suddenly, she realized they had to part. Andy's somber eyes reflected her mood, and Jo took her hands in hers.

"When will I see you again?"

Andy sighed. "I'm working until Saturday."

"The whole time? You don't get any time off at all?"

She shook her head. "Not really. I can have people visit at the station, but I'm technically on duty." Her eyes became slits. "No overnight visitors."

Jo smiled. "But I can stop by?"

Andy shrugged. "I might not be there. If we have a call, we all have to go out. You saw Drew this morning. Things can happen any time." She paused, her face lined with regret. "I also have to be on fire duty soon."

"What's that mean?"

"I get sent to a special lookout for two weeks. No visitors at all, there."

"Jesus. How soon?"

"Next week—Thursday."

They sat there for a long time in silence, simply staring at each other. What they'd started was already strong, already easy and comfortable, but could it survive a long absence so soon? Her own feelings wouldn't change, but Andy was acting strange, guilty even. Her eyes kept flickering away, and her hunched, tense shoulders made her appear troubled, wary. Jo squeezed her hand, hard.

"Hey, don't worry about it. We'll just have to spend your next break together before you head to the lookout."

Andy's eyes lit up. "Yeah? You sure? Don't you have to go back to work?"

Jo shook her head. "I'm flexible. I have a lot of PTO built up, and my boss is a good guy. He won't mind if I come back Wednesday instead of Monday."

Andy's smile faded. "But what about after that? You live so far away. I know you're up here a lot, but—"

"Hey," Jo said, pulling her into a hug. "What's all this? We'll make it work. Fort Collins isn't Borneo. It's less than two hours away. No big deal."

Andy nodded and then rubbed her hands over her face. "Sorry. I'm really tired. It makes me insecure, I guess."

"We'll make it work. I promise."

They kissed then, and Jo was fairly certain that if Andy wasn't already running behind, they might have made use of the large back seat. As it was, Andy had to forcefully disengage herself, almost scooting away from Jo and holding up her hands.

"Okay, okay. If you don't get out of here, I don't know if I'll ever leave."

Jo was out of breath, her heart hammering. "Do you have to?"

"Yes. Now get out of here before I tear your clothes off again."

"You make that sound like a bad thing."

"Go!"

Jo laughed and climbed out of the truck, waving as Andy drove away. As Jo watched Andy disappear down the road, a sinking depression struck her so hard she almost cried out. Andy was right—this wasn't going to be easy.

She sighed and turned to the trail. Judging from the way the air and the sun felt already, it was going to be another warm day—probably not as hot as it had been two days ago, but certainly uncomfortable in these clothes. The trail was just shy of a mile to the top, but that would be enough. She'd be filthy with sweat by the time she got up there. Still, with no backpack or clothes to change into, she didn't have any choice but to head up as she was.

The trail was populated by aspen almost exclusively at the bottom, near the parking area, but as she traveled up, pine and a few maples gradually replaced them. Fruit trees had grown here once, but they had been cut down long ago, sometime in her father's childhood. Even now, this close to the park road, she might have walked into another time. Nothing here suggested that she was actually in the twenty-first century.

She was perhaps halfway when she heard something and stopped so quickly she almost fell over. She instantly held her breath, listening hard, and heard it again. Footsteps, off in the woods to her right. She spun that way, peering hard, and saw a bush some fifty feet away moving slightly. She waited, tense, but the bush stopped, and the day became quiet again, the sound of birds her only company. In all the hubbub of yesterday, with the well and Meg's fall, she'd almost completely forgotten about the man she'd seen in the woods.

"I heard you, you bastard!" she called. No response. The bush remained still.

"You don't scare me. Do you hear me? You don't scare me! This is our place, not yours!"

Again, nothing.

Her heartbeat was pulsing through her as she stood there tense and ready. She'd rarely felt this angry. Should someone appear, she would definitely chase them. She glanced around her and saw a large branch on the ground by her feet. She picked it up and took a couple of steps toward the bush.

"I'm armed, you sonofabitch! Get the hell off our land!"

If he heard her, he didn't respond, and again, the bush remained still. Her breath was still whistling in and out of her open mouth, and she was rigid with fury. She waited long enough to calm down, hearing and seeing nothing, and threw the branch down on the ground.

"Fucking coward," she whispered, and continued to hike up the trail.

CHAPTER SEVENTEEN

Jo sat on the porch, the late-afternoon sun directly on her face and almost blindingly bright without her sunglasses. Today was warm, but the intense heat from earlier in the week was probably gone for the season. They might have one or two more days up here in the upper seventies this month, but the little storm two days ago had most likely marked the end of the real summer heat. It might be another month before the snow started to fall in earnest, but autumn had definitely begun.

She held the second lock to the well, twisting it back and forth to lubricate it with oil. It squeaked in protest despite her efforts, but at least she could move the locking mechanism again. Like the water pump, it had been crusted with rust, and after she'd cleaned that away with vinegar, she'd oiled every inch of it. She knew she should go, immediately, and put the lock back on the well cover. Even though one side was fastened, it could come up on the other and let animals or anything else fall in. But she waited. She wanted company for that task.

The cabin was almost back in shape, better, perhaps, than it had been before Nancy took the keys. After she'd gotten back yesterday, she, Carter, and Daniela had cleared the remaining branches and vines from the final window and patched part of the roof. It would have to be replaced next summer, but she and Carter surmised it would make it through one more winter. Even if it didn't, Jo's siblings and other cousins would be up here on and off during the worst of the winter weather, so someone would always be there to check on it if it needed any immediate or major repairs.

Carter and Daniela were working on the broken window right now. They'd taken it off the frame and were putting a temporary plastic tarp over the hole, intending to take the window into town to have the glass replaced after they finished. It would also give them a chance to check in on Meg.

Jo stood, stretching, bending back and forth at the waist. She felt better than yesterday, but she was still sore and tight from all the activity before and during her overnight with Andy. When she'd come back, she'd felt strange—woozy and spacy from lack of sleep. Everything was taking longer to do, and when they were working on the roof, Carter had to call her name several times to get her attention.

She planned today, while Daniela and Carter were elsewhere, to take care of some of the smaller tasks inside the cabin, but mostly to take it easy, maybe read or simply nap. She'd earned a rest. She only wished Andy were here with her, relaxing in this gorgeous sunshine. She smiled at the memory of Andy's body in the morning sunlight— that golden skin warm and smooth and inviting.

"Hey, now," Carter said as she came around the side of the house. "I know that expression."

Me, too, Daniela signed. *The "I'm thinking of boobs" look.*

Jo couldn't help the heat in her face. "Yeah, well, it's hard not to."

Daniela touched her arm. *I meant to ask you yesterday: are you and Andy okay? I mean, you spent the night, but did you talk about the stuff that's happening up here?*

Jo made a seesaw motion with her hand. *Yes and no. She doesn't believe me, but she also thinks it's dangerous up here. She didn't want me to come back.*

Daniela nodded. *It is hard to believe.*

They both turned to Carter, who was holding the window in her hands. "Hey, don't look at me. I don't know what to think."

"Do you think I'm crazy?"

Carter hesitated, then shook her head. "No, but I do think you and Daniela are jumping to the wrong conclusions. Everything that's happened has a rational explanation."

Jo made herself bite back a retort. There was no use arguing. She wasn't even sure she wanted Carter to believe her. Bad enough that she, Daniela, and Meg had been affected by whatever was happening up here. No one else needed to be involved, let alone an outsider.

Will you be okay up here by yourself? Daniela asked. *You could come with us.*

Jo shook her head. *I'll be fine. I'll stay inside and lock the door.*

Daniela hesitated before nodding. *If you're sure.*

She made a shooing motion. *It's fine. Go ahead. Have a real meal somewhere.*

Daniela's eyes seemed dreamy. *And a shower. An honest-to-God shower. I've never wanted one more in my life.*

You could use one.

Hey!

She followed them to the top of the trail down the mountain, and the three of them paused, enjoying the sunshine.

"You sure you wanna stay?" Carter asked. "We might get a place for the night, depending on how long this takes to fix. You'll be okay overnight?"

"It's fine," Jo said. "I'll be fine. Say hi to Meg for me, though, okay?"

Carter nodded, and Jo watched for a while as they hiked down. Daniela paused and waved before they disappeared behind some trees.

Jo turned around, taking in the cabin as a whole. It looked much better than it had when they'd come up here, but it still seemed a little lonely, abandoned and lost in the trees hovering over it. With the tarp over the window frame, the cabin seemed almost wounded, bandaged with plastic.

"Stop it, Lemke. You're creeping yourself out."

She started walking toward the porch and realized that the lock to the well was still in her pocket. She took it out and peered down the trail to the cemetery, wondering if she was brave enough to replace it on her own. She shook her head. Not today. It was less about being afraid than realizing her own limitations. The memory of that feeling, that compulsion, was becoming harder to recall, but she remembered how strong it had been. She couldn't argue with it and would have jumped into the well if she hadn't been interrupted. She put the lock back in her pocket and walked to the cabin, up the porch steps, and inside.

Although all the windows were clear now, it was still relatively dark inside, and she switched on a lamp, searching for her book. She couldn't remember the last time she'd seen it, but she was sure she'd left it in here in the living room. She hadn't been in any of the bedrooms for more than a few seconds for days. Someone else could have picked it up to read, but she didn't think so. Unless Rachel was into nineteenth-century French literature, no one else would be interested in perusing it.

She spotted a piece of paper on the coffee table. Carter had left a list with a few minor tasks to complete, and Jo decided to do them now before she relaxed for the rest of the day. She scrubbed the inside of the fridge again, scoured the windows in the living room inside and out, and polished all the wooden furniture with the organic lemon oil they tried to use for everything in here. They had already done most of these chores once, but given the neglect during these last two years, she and Carter agreed that they needed to do everything twice to remove the deeper grime. After a couple of hours, her work rags were black, suggesting they'd been right. It probably wouldn't even hurt to do everything a third time, but not today. She could barely keep her eyes open. She checked her watch. Three o'clock seemed a completely reasonable time for a long nap.

She yawned loudly, almost yodeling. The bed they'd dragged out for Meg still stood by the stove, and Jo sat down on it, testing its give. It was little more than a cot, but it felt comfortable enough. She'd slept on the couch again last night, but since Meg and Rachel most likely weren't coming back, she could safely commandeer this one. Eventually she would have to drag it back into the second bedroom, but it was fine here for another night.

She remembered something then and stood up, walking over to Carter and Daniela's room. The door was open to let in more light, and the twin beds had been pushed together in the center of the far wall. The tarp-covered window frame was in here, the plastic flapping slightly from the breeze outside. The light that came through it looked strange, almost gray. She knelt and peered under the beds, seeing the gift bag Meg had assembled for Rachel.

"Dang it," she said, pulling it out. If she'd remembered earlier, she could have sent it with Carter and Daniela. She rose to her feet again to leave and then paused. She turned, slowly, peering around the room. Something was different.

She stood there, trying to figure out what it was, but she couldn't pinpoint the change. Had something moved? No. Everything was right where it had been, or if something had changed, the difference was imperceptible. The plastic tarp flapped again, but that wasn't it, either. Something was different, something hugely different, but she couldn't see it. She started backing out of the room, darting her gaze everywhere, watching for movement, and then froze when she spotted it.

A padlock was sitting on top of the dresser.

Her free hand went to her pocket, the one where the lock had been, and she knew even before she probed it that it would be empty. Her heart was hammering now, as if catching up, and she backed up farther, peering around, anxiously expecting to see something. Back in the living room, she closed the bedroom door and stood there, frozen, her hand on the knob, uncertain what to do. She was still holding the gift bag, clutched to her chest, and she made herself walk backward a little farther and set it down on a side table. She kept her eyes fixed on the bedroom door, certain it would open on its own.

Her hands were shaking, and she felt weak with terror. She backed up a little more and sat down, heavily, on the sofa, still staring at the door. She was quaking now, almost shuddering. She made herself take three deep breaths, holding them before letting them out in a long, shaky rattle.

"Get it together," she told herself. Her voice was harsh in the quiet room, but hearing it seemed to help, and she continued to take long, deep breaths until her heart started to slow. She eventually stopped shaking, but her hands were still trembling when she held one of them up.

"It's just a lock. You're safe." And, on saying this, a little more of her fear dissipated. After all, what she'd said was true. It had been true before, when her book moved, or when the tools had appeared in there in the very same place on the dresser. This was a different feeling than the one she'd had at the well, or even when she'd gone looking for someone in the woods on her own. No overwhelming will was forcing her to do something. This was not the same. She didn't know why she knew this, but she did.

The rest of her fear fell away, and she sat there without moving, thinking hard. She was no longer frightened, but her heart was still racing. It took her a moment before she realized that she was curious now, almost excited.

You're losing your gourd, she thought, then stifled a laugh. She and Carter had used that phrase on each other over and over again as teenagers. Anytime one of them did something silly or fell for the wrong person, the other one would say exactly that. She hadn't thought of it in years.

She wasn't frightened anymore, but a kind of impatient anxiety still roiled her stomach. It was doing the little flippy butterflies she had when she was about to do something exciting. Or stupid.

She rose to her feet, found her legs solid again, and walked over to the bedroom door, opening it carefully. The lock still lay on the dresser. Nothing had changed. She walked over to the dresser and picked it up, slipping it back into her pocket. As she started to leave, she paused, letting her gaze drift back to the dresser. It was the only actual antique left in the house. All the other furniture had been replaced over the years due to the usual wear and tear, as well as the simple need for an update for the sake of comfort. This dresser, on the other hand, had traveled all the way from Estes with her ancestor, Aurora. She couldn't even begin to imagine how she'd gotten it up that hill.

She ran her hand along the smooth, clean surface, smiling. It wasn't anything special—Sears Roebuck, she thought. It was old, but not worth much of anything since thousands of them had existed at one time. She didn't have to have it appraised to know that. It was functional and solid, but nothing more. Still, it had lasted this long, and no one in the family would ever think of getting rid of it.

She frowned. The furniture had been piled up around this dresser. The book had appeared there, then the tools, and now the lock, all in this same spot. She rested her hand on the surface. Did all of this mean something? Was the dresser important somehow?

She shrugged and started to leave again, but this time she felt it— an overwhelming gust of warmth from behind her, and then her leg felt funny, almost as if it were being tickled. She whirled, almost falling in her haste as she jumped back and away, then clapped a hand over her mouth to stifle her scream.

The lock was back on top of the dresser. As she watched, the little locking arm moved slightly, squeaking in protest.

She ran then, fast, out of the room and then the cabin. She didn't look behind her, racing to get away. She reached the trail in seconds and ran down it, realizing in some distant part of her brain that it was reckless to take the trail this quickly. She was nearly leaping down it in her fright, sailing over rocks and branches and taking long, careless strides that were half jumps.

About halfway down the mountain, she finally made herself pause, leaning against a ponderosa to catch her breath. She had both her hands on the tree, bent at the waist, and she made herself wait there, taking deep breaths, until she calmed down a little. Breaking her neck running down this hill wouldn't help anyone.

Calming, she stood upright, staring up the hill behind her. She couldn't see anything, but that didn't mean it wasn't there. Except for the lock moving on its own, she hadn't seen anything in the bedroom, either—just felt it. She started walking down the hill soon after that, careful where she put her feet. A little shaky again, she worried now that, even being careful, she might still fall and hurt herself. She stopped and closed her eyes, putting her hands on her waist to ease the cramp forming there.

"Cool it. Take it easy. You're almost there."

Yes, she thought, but where? To the road? This time of year, that stretch would almost certainly be deserted, especially on a weekday. Running into Andy last week had been a complete anomaly. Once she reached the road, she would have a long hike down to the main highway, on her own. She had no water, no supplies, and it would undoubtedly be dark by the time she got there. Even then, would anyone stop for her? If they didn't, it would be even longer before she made it to the ranger station.

"Fuck, fuck, fuck," she whispered.

She opened her eyes and started moving down the trail again. Regardless of what she found at the road, anything would be better than going back to the cabin. If she'd remembered to grab her phone, she might have tried it a few miles down the road—she and Carter had found service there before, but that didn't matter since she didn't have it.

"Stupid, stupid, stupid," she said, her words in rhythm with her marching feet.

She was almost to the line of aspens that marked the last quarter mile of the trail when she heard footsteps, off in the woods to her right. The sound of them came from almost the exact spot she'd heard them yesterday on her way up. She paused, too tired to be frightened or angry like she'd been when she'd heard them before.

This time a man appeared, walking around the edge of foliage and into the sunlight. It was the same one she'd seen before, in the woods in the dark. He was perhaps fifty feet away, but even at this distance she could recognize him easily—same disheveled, dirty clothing, same dark beard. The quality of the light around him was strange, almost foggy, much darker than in the woods near him. He said nothing, simply watched her.

"Who are you?" she called.

No response.

She took a few steps toward him. "What do you want?"

Again, he was silent. He was just far enough away that Jo had trouble reading his expression, but she could see lowered brows. Confusion, she thought, or anger. But why?

The shadows around him seemed to shift a little, grow. They drifted outward, almost slithering away from him, and as they caught the trees and bushes, they too grew hazy, shrouded almost, as if in a dream. Jo watched the darkness creep toward her, fascinated. It reminded her of something, but she couldn't remember what. Colorado could be hazy, yes, in the wet season of late summer, or from dusty dry spells, but this haze was different somehow, almost dense. The trees inside the shadows coming from him were almost misty, cloaked with that foggy, blurry, diminishing light.

She gasped when she remembered where she'd seen that shadowy haze before—at the well. After letting out a low, frightened groan, she backed away, up the hill toward the cabin. Going farther down would mean walking directly into that darkness. She threw one look behind her, up the trail, and stopped, frozen with indecision.

She could go back and face whatever was moving things inside the cabin. On the other hand, she could walk into the powerful, cold, dim haze, the one that clouded her senses and made her do careless things. Leaving the trail, even this close to the road, could mean a real risk of getting lost. She'd seen too many newspaper articles about lost hikers to do that, especially without a compass. After all, no one would know she was missing until later today at the earliest, more likely tomorrow.

The shadows were creeping closer now, perhaps thirty feet away, and the man stood, still watching her, still silent. The dark haze came from him, she was certain. Even if she did leave the trail, she didn't think it would matter—he would find her. She didn't have a choice after all.

She turned and headed back up the trail toward the cabin, forcing herself not to run.

CHAPTER EIGHTEEN

Her return to the cabin was careful, slow. Now that she had decided to go back, she didn't want to risk hurting herself on the way. She would need every ounce of strength to face what was inside, waiting for her. She threw several wary glances behind her, but if the darkness emanating from the man was following her, she could no longer see it when she couldn't see him. She didn't know what that meant, or why that should be, and she didn't want to. She was certain he was still down there, somewhere, watching for her.

She'd left the door to the cabin open in her haste, and she stood at the foot of the stairs to the porch, peering cautiously inside. The lamp was on, and the door to the bedroom stood open. She jumped when the tarp over the window shifted and had to put a hand over her heart to stop it from racing. She had to force herself to take the three little steps up onto the porch and inside. She closed and locked the door and stood there staring at the bedroom door.

Her legs were trembling as she took the five or six steps toward the bedroom. She threw one terrified glance inside and slammed the door, breathing heavily. She closed her eyes, taking deep breaths again to calm down, and waited, her hand still on the knob. Nothing happened. She opened her eyes and took a few wary steps away, sitting down on the sofa, where she could look at both doors. From here, she would be able to see both visitors if they came—the man in the woods and the thing in the bedroom.

She paused then, frowning, forgetting her fear for a moment. Could she be right? Were two different things happening here—one inside, and one out? If so, what did that mean? If it was true, she realized, whatever was inside hadn't tried to hurt her. Seeing things move on their own was frightening, but it wasn't the same as being compelled to climb into a well or hit on the head or pushed off a cliff. Maybe whatever was inside wasn't dangerous. Maybe it was trying to show her something.

The feeling she'd had earlier, when she was staring at the dresser, washed over her again—that curiosity, that familiarity, almost as if the dresser was part of the cabin. Antique or not, it was strange that it was still here. It took up a lot of space in that bedroom, more than was comfortable, actually. You had to turn sideways to get past it to the far side of the room, an awkward maneuver in the middle of the night. She'd stubbed her toe on it countless times, and she knew everyone else had, too, when they stayed in there. So why hadn't they put it in a bigger room?

She was breathless, on the brink of understanding something. She rose, almost without realizing she was doing it, and walked toward the bedroom door. She could stop herself. Unlike at the well, she was in complete control of herself. She felt hot, almost feverish, with excitement.

After placing a hand on the door, she jerked it away. It was warm to the touch, impossible in this dark, chilly room. She put a careful hand on it again and waited. The warmth spread, first from her hand up to her arm and then throughout, like she'd been blown with dry, balmy wind. Her fingers stopped trembling, and she calmed again, relaxing. She opened the bedroom door.

Temperate sunshine suffused the room, so bright she might have been outside. Even with the window replaced, this room would never be this bright, even at the peak of summer—the angle to the sun was wrong. At best, it was bright enough to read in here, but never like this. She paused, waiting for the feared compulsion to wash over her again, but nothing happened. Unlike that dreamy, removed feeling she'd been gripped by at the well, her senses felt sharp, acute, her vision crystal clear.

The lock twitched on top of the dresser again, but this time, though it made her jump slightly, she wasn't afraid. She walked over and put her hand over the lock. It was almost hot, moving under her hand as if alive. She picked it up and it stopped, but when she put it back on the dresser, the little arm began to squeak again as it turned in its socket.

"I don't understand," she whispered. "What do you want from me?"

The lock picked up speed, thrumming in place, the arm rotating back and forth wildly. Beyond the squeak of the hinged arm, it was knocking on the wood, rattling loudly. She picked it up again and then dropped it on the floor with a hiss, shaking her hand and clutching it to her chest. She looked at her palm. A heat blister was rising in the center, red and already starting to peel open.

The dresser emitted a long, low groan, and the bottom drawer began to slide out toward her legs. She jumped back and away, almost falling onto the beds, and stood still, watching it reposition itself on its own. As if two hands were pulling it, the drawer inched out one side at a time, until it was open. It finally stopped, and nothing more happened.

Still clutching her hand, she walked toward the dresser, peering inside the open drawer. She gasped and jerked her head back and away, retreating to the safety of the doorway. She'd caught only a glimpse, but she had spotted her book in there, sitting on top of Carter's and Daniela's clothes. Her breath whistled in and out of her nose as she tried to draw air into her lungs. She squashed her lips together, holding back a scream. If only she could leave and never return.

A hammering at the front door made her let out a wild shriek, and she spun toward it. He's come for me, she thought wildly. I'm going to die up here.

The hammering continued, and then she heard Andy's voice. "Jo? Open up. It's me."

She let out a sob and rushed toward the door, unlocking it and throwing it open. She was in Andy's arms in one leap, crying hysterically. Somehow, Andy led her to the couch, and both of them sat down. She nestled into Andy's neck, still crying, and felt Andy's hands running up and down her back, soothing her.

"Shh. It's okay. I'm here now."

Eventually Jo drew away from her, letting her gaze drift to the open doorway to the bedroom. The light in there had faded back to normal. If she went in there again, everything would be as it was before—no moving locks, no moving dresser drawers. A normal, everyday bedroom.

She frowned. "How did you get here? I thought you had to work today."

Andy smiled. "I did. I left as soon as I could when I heard you were up here on your own."

"How?"

"Carter and Daniela stopped at the station to use the restroom this morning. Carter mentioned you were here."

Jo flushed with pleasure. "So you left? You just came here?"

Andy grinned. "Yes. I had to call in my relief, and I'm sure he's going to kill me later."

"Drew?"

She nodded, and they grinned at each other. "I'll be stuck on dish duty at our apartment for months."

"I bet."

They were quiet for a spell, Andy's arm still around her shoulders. She felt better now but couldn't stop looking at the open doorway to the bedroom.

"Do you want to talk about it?" Andy finally asked.

"About what?"

"Why you were so upset when I got here. It was like you'd seen a…well, you know."

Jo managed a weak smile. "Something like that."

They were quiet again, but eventually Andy nudged her. "That's all you're going to say?"

Jo looked up into her eyes, her own welling with tears. "You won't believe me."

Andy squeezed her shoulders. "Try me."

Jo hesitated. This hadn't gone well before, and she had no reason to expect it would this time. Still, she'd already committed to being honest with Andy, regardless of consequences, so she cleared her throat and told the entire story—the man on the trail, the lock, the dresser—all of it.

After she finished, Andy was peering at her burned palm, her face dark and troubled. "See," Jo said. "You don't believe me."

Andy shrugged, shook her head. "I don't know what to say. It's not easy *to* believe."

"You didn't see anything on the trail up here? Nothing?"

Andy hesitated, and Jo leapt on it. "You did see something."

Again, Andy hesitated, her eyes distant. "I didn't see anything, but something happened."

"What?"

"My radio." She pulled her backpack off and set it in her lap before digging around inside. Eventually, she held up her radio. She clicked it on and off, but the light didn't turn on.

"I checked it on the trail, and it was working fine at first."

"And then?"

"I hit the edge of the aspens, checked it again, and it wasn't working anymore."

Jo's stomach sank with something like relief. "Are we out of service range?"

Andy shook her head. "Radios don't work quite like that, and anyway, even if that were true, it would still turn on. This little light would be green, but it isn't. It's like the battery is dead."

"And it's not?"

Again Andy hesitated, her eyebrows low. "No. That's the other part. I experimented by walking back down the trail, toward my truck. I left the radio in the on position."

"And?"

"It came back on, maybe a hundred feet down toward my truck—full battery, completely functional."

"And it stopped working again when you walked this way?"

Andy nodded.

The radio was the key to getting Andy to recognize what was happening up here, but Jo needed to let her get there on her own. Andy was still staring at her radio, her fierce blue eyes almost angry, as if she couldn't believe it didn't work, couldn't comprehend what she was holding in her hand.

She seemed to snap out of it, and she gave Jo a broad, gorgeous smile. "Well, anyway, I'm here now, and you don't have to be by yourself. Let's take care of that hand." She kissed it, and a flash of heat rushed through Jo. Her hand and arm tingled in Andy's grasp.

She moistened her lips, her heart pounding so hard she could feel it in the back of her throat. "So you admit that it's burned?"

Andy laughed. "Yes, Jo, I have eyes, but it could have happened in a number of ways. Maybe the lock was too close to the heater, or maybe the sun was on it—I don't know."

"Ever the rationalist."

"We need to run it under cold water, and then I can bandage it."

"Always prepared."

"I was a Girl Scout, after all."

They walked to the sink together, Andy leading her by her uninjured hand. Jo couldn't keep her eyes off the back of her figure, and when Andy turned toward her, she colored slightly as if she could read Jo's mind. She shook a finger at her.

"None of that right now, missy."

"None of what?"

Andy grinned. "You know. Now put your hand in here. We're going to flush it for a while. The blister's on the surface and pretty small. First-degree, almost second. You'll be okay in a couple of days."

Jo showed her how to turn on the water, and it came out in a gush the second they flicked the switch. The water was so loud in the metal sink, they couldn't hear over it. Andy made her hold it in the stream for a full minute before turning it off.

"There," she said, drying it gently. "Let me wrap it."

Jo followed her wordlessly back to the couch, and they sat down next to each other, so close their legs touched. At the feel of her hands, heat and desire began to inch through her, from the hand Andy was holding into her deepest center. Her heart rate was racing again, and she could hear herself breathing heavily. Andy's cheeks were slightly pink, but she kept her eyes on Jo's hand as she wrapped it lightly with sterile gauze. When she finally looked up, her pupils were dilated, and that was all it took. Jo launched herself forward, pinning Andy back, and started kissing her all over. Andy laughed, relaxing into the sofa and tilting her head back for easier access.

They both jumped at a loud screeching slam that came from the bedroom. Jo leapt out of Andy's arms and raced into the room, scrutinizing it. She saw what had happened immediately.

"The dresser closed," she told Andy as she came up behind her.

Andy frowned and pushed past her. Jo grabbed her arm, but Andy shook off her hand. "No, Jo, I have to see."

She walked closer to the dresser and then pointed at the bottom drawer. Jo nodded, and Andy got down on her knees, pulling at the handles. She had to edge it open, one side at a time, the wood warped with time and moisture. She stopped, staring into it, then back at Jo.

"Nothing in here but clothes and a book." She held up the paperback. "Emily Zola."

"Emile," Jo said absently, and walked closer to take it from her. She flipped the book around in her hands, scrutinizing it. It seemed fine—the same as it had been before. It was a used book, slightly musty, the spine cracked and the cover peeling. She shrugged.

"I don't get it," Andy said. "What are we supposed to see? It's just socks and underwear. What's the point?"

Jo shook her head. She had no idea. She walked the couple of feet closer and knelt next to Andy. "So you believe me now?"

Andy appeared uncertain, wary, but Jo thought she saw something deep in her eyes, a dawning acceptance. "It would be pretty hard for this thing to close on its own," Jo said.

"Impossible," Andy whispered, then shook her head, hard. "No, not impossible, but definitely difficult."

"And then there's your radio," Jo added. "That's impossible, too, right?"

Andy started to shake her head and then stopped, tilting it. "Do you hear that?"

"What—" Jo said, and then she heard it, too. They both jerked away from the dresser, almost simultaneously. A soft knocking was coming from inside the drawer.

"Jesus Christ," Andy whispered. Her face had gone the color of rotten cheese, pale and a little green.

Jo gripped her hand and squeezed it before letting go to take the clothes out of the drawer. She set them in a large pile next to her, finally revealing the entire drawer. The knocking grew louder, coming from the bottom panel.

Andy's eyes were huge, terrified. She'd shrunk back into herself, away from the dresser. Jo started feeling the bottom of the drawer, digging her fingernails into the edges. The panel finally gave way a bit, and she pulled it up and out, revealing a shallow compartment. The lock lay inside, the arm twisting back and forth with desperate speed, but she saw something else in here, too: a flat wooden box. The surface of the box had been carved and painted with delicate flowering vines. Though it was caked in dust and spiderwebs, Jo could see that each vine was a different, delicate color.

She reached for the box, and Andy gasped, grabbing her arm. "Don't touch it!"

Jo lifted an eyebrow. "Why not? It's obviously for me."

With that, she reached in and pulled out the box.

Chapter Nineteen

Jo carried the wooden box into the living room, set it on the coffee table, and sat down. Andy remained in the doorway to the bedroom for a long time, her eyes still wide, her face still pale, almost sickly. Jo's fear had completely disappeared. Everything made sense now—the furniture, the book, the tools, the lock—everything. Someone had wanted her to find this box.

She smiled at Andy and patted the spot next to her on the sofa. "It's okay. Come over here."

Andy hesitated and then joined her, sitting down, but back and as far away as she could from the box. Jo squeezed her knee and turned her attention to the mysterious object. She ran a hand across the top and brushed off more dust, revealing more of the delicate floral design. After feeling around the edges, she found no hinges. She did, however, detect a seam that ran all the way around, and she fitted her fingernails inside and lifted it. Next to her, Andy gasped as the lid came off.

Inside, she found a long-desiccated bunch of dried, pressed flowers and two small bundles of papers, each tied with a ribbon. The ribbons, one blue and one red, were surprisingly sound, not frayed in any way. Jo held the blue bundle up to the light, revealing envelopes with old-fashioned stamps.

Andy relaxed a little next to her, the tension leaving her body. She leaned forward, a tiny line between her eyebrows. "Letters?"

Jo nodded. She pointed at the addressee. "These were sent to Chicago." The three or four letters were bound together so tight, Jo was afraid to bend the corners back and count them.

Andy frowned, lifting a brow. "What are they doing here?"

Jo shook her head, also confused. These letters had been mailed back East—the postmark showed that they'd gone out—but they had ended up here.

"Maybe Aurora brought them with her?" Jo suggested.

"Can you read the name?"

Jo scooted closer to the lamp and frowned. She couldn't decipher either name on the address line, but the last name was not Lemke—that wasn't an *L* at the beginning, though she couldn't be sure.

"I can't make it out."

She picked up the second bundle with the red ribbon. This pile was smaller—only two letters. The address line, however, was easier to read.

"To Mrs. Aurora Lemke, General Delivery, Estes Park." She grinned at Andy. "How cool!"

"Should we read them?"

Jo smiled, her heart swelling with relief. Andy looked excited now, just like Jo felt. The incident with the dresser had shaken Andy, but she'd recovered. Jo leaned over and kissed her.

"Of course."

"Which ones?"

Jo considered both bundles and then pointed at the larger one with the blue ribbon. "If the red bundle is *for* Aurora, this one might have been *from* her."

"Could be," Andy said. She motioned back and forth between the piles. "You think this is some kind of correspondence?"

Jo nodded. "Between Aurora and someone in Chicago. Makes sense—that's where she came from. I just don't know how her letters came back to her."

She picked up the larger bundle and fiddled with the ribbon. It was strong, the knot tight. She had to pick at it for several seconds before it loosened slightly and she could untie it. She set the slip of blue cloth carefully aside, still surprised by how well it had held up.

Four letters, each approximately the same thickness, nestled inside the little envelopes. On first sight, the handwriting on them was almost universally illegible except for the word Chicago, but she could make out the dates on the postmarks.

"May 1888, July 1888, September 1888, and April 1889." She looked up at Andy. "I guess I'll start with the earliest one."

Andy nodded and then held up a hand. "Wait a sec." She turned to the little side table next to her, where her first-aid kit was still sitting. She'd used it earlier to bandage Jo's hand. She dug around in it and pulled out a pair of latex gloves. "Wear these. The paper is probably delicate."

"Good idea," Jo said. All the envelopes had been sliced open with a knife or letter opener on one end. She snapped on the gloves and then, as carefully as she could, eased the first letter out of the envelope. Two sheets of paper were inside, folded together. She set them down on the coffee table, then picked up the lamp and set the light directly above the letter. She crouched down on her knees and carefully unfolded the paper, holding it open by the corners as gently as possible. Her stomach was fluttering with nerves and excitement, and she threw Andy one quick smile before focusing on the words scrawled on the page.

Like the envelopes, the handwriting was difficult to read, and it took her a long while to puzzle out what she was seeing. The scrawl reminded her a little of her own handwriting, or Carter's. They'd both gotten terrible grades in handwriting as children and never improved. Gradually, the script began to make sense, words starting to rise and form from the messy, blotted ink. She licked her lips and cleared her throat, suddenly nervous.

"My Dearest Sarah," she read aloud.

❖

May 1888

My Dearest Sarah,

My darling, my love, it went exactly as planned. The boys and I caught the morning train from Chicago and began our journey in high spirits. Even John seemed to recover some of his vigor. The station and the train were loud and chaotic, but that didn't bother us. Everything was so new, so exciting, we began to sing as the city dropped behind us. The whole coach joined in at one point, and though many of our fellow passengers didn't speak any English, they sang along, the tune if not the words, all just as happy as we were to be on our way. I've never been gladder to leave the city, and I think more than a few of us felt the same way.

The windows did little to keep out the damp, however, and with the constant rain and chill, John began to suffer later that same day. I think the dust and the coal smoke were already too much for him, not to mention the excitement and disturbed sleep. By the afternoon, he was coughing so much the other passengers began to move away. I told him not to fret, as it meant we had an entire area of the coach to ourselves—a relief from the cramped seats we'd had before. He was embarrassed, but just like the little soldier he is, he never complained, even when it was clear that he was suffering. Robert was much fussier, carrying on and on, crying and sobbing, setting off many of the other little children traveling with us. Their parents didn't appreciate it, I can tell you that much. I had to give both of my boys some of that soothing syrup you found, and they drifted right to sleep. I even thought of taking some myself! All told, I managed one or two hours of dozing that first day, a little more the next. I know I'm safe now, but it's hard to accept that he is no longer a threat. I'm still sleeping fitfully, afraid he will appear and bring us back.

Our train was stopped many times to make way for express and freight trains. At one point we were halted in Lincoln, Nebraska for almost five days. I was upset by this until I saw the great opportunity it gave us for John. I found a hotel that would admit us and put him to bed the entire time. The rest did him wonderful good, though his color was still poor when we returned to the train.

All told, it took us fifteen days to reach Denver, not including the delay in Lincoln—longer than you and I had figured, but only just. We found Dr. Jacobs's sanatorium the same day, and John is there now, resting comfortably. I also managed to find a little room for Robert and myself very near the sanatorium. I told the house mistress that my husband had died in a streetcar accident back home, and she was kind enough to allow a single woman and child to rent from her. I get the impression that Denver is full of women like me, as she was neither surprised nor suspicious of my story. I see many women like myself in the streets around here—single, on their own, many with children. Perhaps their husbands are sick like John, but I don't think that's always the case. I believe your friend was right—Denver is different for people like us. A haven. You and I will have to find something bigger when you arrive, but it will do fine for Robert and me until then. The room is clean and warm and almost homey—more than I could have hoped for. Robert has his own area and a little window to look out, and there is some pretty open land not far from here that he loves to run through. Even before his illness, John was not playful like he is, even as a small child.

You will have already received the telegram I sent at the train station to let you know of our arrival. You will be angry at the waste, as you told me to use the postcard, but our food and board costs less than we budgeted, so please don't fret. I promise not to send another unless it's an emergency. The woman that runs this house has already indicated that she knows of some needlework I might take in, so perhaps our lack of money will not be as dire as we'd feared.

I know this letter will take some time to reach you, and that we agreed to keep our correspondence infrequent lest we be caught, but I do hope you are well and happy, or as happy as you can be in these trying circumstances. Just remember that I love you eternally, that you are the only reason I'm alive to write this. But also remember, my love, that he is always watching, and he will watch you forever until you can escape safely. That is the kind of man he is. Only when you are certain that he is otherwise occupied can you risk joining us, not before.

It will be very difficult not to contact you again until the agreed-upon date, my darling girl. I will send you a postcard once a month, as we decided, but I will be thinking of you always. Please be careful—he's watching. Send response to General Delivery, Denver 2.

Your love,

Rory

"Holy shit," Andy said after she finished.

Jo was speechless and nodded her agreement.

"So this means…"

"My great-great-grandmother was bisexual, or a lesbian."

They both stared at each other for a long beat and then burst out laughing. Jo got off her knees and sat on the couch, snuggling under Andy's arm.

Andy held up a finger, still grinning with suppressed laughter. "At that time, people didn't say 'bi' or 'lesbian.' They said two women were in a 'Boston Marriage' when they lived together."

Jo grinned up at her. "I love that." She looked down at the letter on the table, her heart swelling with pride and happiness. She'd always been close with her family, and she'd always loved this place more than any other, but these letters made that connection between her, her family, and this cabin feel like it was somehow central to her as a person—like everything was linked, meaningful. She had to blink back tears, every ounce of her spirit brimming with emotion.

"What do you suppose she was talking about when she said 'He's watching'?" Andy asked.

Jo frowned. "I don't know, but it doesn't sound good, does it? I guess that's why Sarah had to stay behind? This guy, whoever he was, was stalking them or something?"

Andy nodded. "That's what I thought, too. You don't know who she means?"

Jo shook her head. "Like I said, the family legend said Aurora arrived here on her own, built this cabin by herself. Nobody knows why she came. I guess most of us assumed it was for cheap land."

Andy nodded, her face troubled. She picked up the first sheet of paper and pointed at a couple of lines. "Here she says she's having trouble sleeping, even though he's no longer a threat. That must be the same guy, right? The one that's supposedly watching Sarah?" She paused, her face pale and tense. "Kind of sounds like she was running away from him."

She didn't continue, and Jo's stomach dropped at the implication. Two years ago, Amy, one of her best friends from high school, had run away from her abusive husband, hiding in a shelter with her children for weeks, and then a halfway house for even longer. It had been months before Jo had received even so much as a phone call from her. Even now, Amy was afraid to share her address with people in case he found her again. It was still difficult to see her with any frequency, and Amy always insisted on meeting in different places, different towns, always in disguise. Her husband had spent very little time in jail.

"Maybe Aurora's husband…" Andy said.

"My great-great-grandfather…" Jo shook her head. "God, I hope not."

They were quiet for a long time, and Jo couldn't help but feel a desperate kind of shame roil her stomach. The explanation fit. Many women had to run away from their abusers, even in the nineteenth century. She felt ashamed of him, however, and horribly sad for Aurora.

Andy touched her knee, making her meet her eyes. Hers were dark, compassionate, and she held her arms open for a hug. Jo squeezed her hard, closing her eyes against the tide of emotions washing through her. She stayed there in her arms long enough to let Andy's embrace warm the cold dread in the pit of her stomach.

"It's okay," Andy said, her voice low and soothing.

Jo drew back and wiped her eyes. "I'm sorry. I guess every family has its share of skeletons."

Andy looked strangely stricken and pale. She seemed anxious, almost guilty, her eyes distant and sad, that fierce blue almost icy, removed. Finally, after a long, anxious pause, her expression began to clear, and she almost appeared to shake herself out of it. She gave Jo a weak grin. "And hey, at least you know the other part now. She left him—she got away."

"With a woman," Jo said.

Despite Andy's smile, Jo could feel tension radiating off her. Her back was straight, her hands clenched in fists on her legs. Jo was about to ask her about her reaction when Andy said, "Read another."

She almost refused. Andy's tension was palpable, strong. Something was clearly bothering her. Jo opened her mouth, ready to question her about it, but Andy refused to look at her. Jo decided to let it go for now and focused on the next letter.

❖

July 1888

My darling girl,

I was incredibly grateful for the postcard I received today. You have no idea how relieved I was to receive it. All this time, I have been wondering, waiting, hoping against hope that you were safe, that he hadn't done anything to you. It is a great weight off my mind to know that you are well.

You will note from the date that I followed your instructions and waited as you asked to send this letter. I wrote many earlier versions and discarded them over the last seven weeks, which kept me from sending one to you. I am glad now that I didn't post them, as they were blubbering, weak things, full of my fears and terrors. I feel almost safe again, I assure you, so you needn't worry on my account.

As this letter will take some time to reach you—the last took, I believe, three weeks—I have sent another telegram with the barest information and our new address. I write this letter to explain our move, which has everything to do with John's health.

In his first weeks at the sanatorium, John rallied. In fact, Dr. Jacobs was so impressed with his progress, he indicated that it might be possible for us to experiment with outings, in town, at least on a small scale. I took him to a little Wild West show, with cowboys and gunslingers, and I can't remember the last time I saw him so lively, so healthy, nor can I remember him laughing quite as much on any other occasion. It was, perhaps, one of the best days of my life.

Things changed, quickly, as they often do with John, and he started to fail again. Dr. Jacobs and I were so afraid, that by early June I began to fear the end was near. Dr. Jacobs suggested that I consider seeking out final arrangements should he slip away in his sleep. There was so much blood, my dear, so very much blood. The poor boy never complained, but he was a wasted, pathetic little thing, indeed.

Then one morning, about three weeks ago, Dr. Jacobs pulled me aside and told me about something he'd been thinking on for some time. Denver, he said, was well and fine for most consumptives—the air is thin and dry here— but some patients, he'd found, needed more than Denver provided. He even admitted that he is beginning to believe that because Denver has built up so much in the recent past, the city might be dangerous to some of his patients' health, what with the increased use of coal and the heavy dust from the horses and carriages.

He told me then that he has sent some people farther into the mountains, in the past, with marked success. Glenwood Springs, a town some hundred and fifty miles west of Denver, is well developed for treating cases like John's, but he also knew of a place to the northwest that was much closer, one that had recently saved one of his adult patients. This man had been on death's door and had completely revived when he went there. The town itself, he explained, is hardly more than a cluster of cabins, and land there almost for the taking.

Despite the greater distance, I was at first tempted to move our little family to Glenwood Springs. There is a lovely sanatorium there which is far less expensive than Dr. Jacobs's. The town also has a train line directly in town, so making the journey would be easier for John. Thus, I began to inquire at the station regarding tickets.

Then something rather queer happened. This man Albert, the former patient of Dr. Jacobs, came to town for business and dropped by the clinic for a visit. Dr. Jacobs brought the man to me, and I could hardly believe the sight of him. If Albert was ever consumptive, there is no evidence for it now. He looked as healthy as you or I! He assured me that he'd been quite ill, almost dying, before deciding to brave the journey north to Estes Park. One month later, he was walking around again, and two months later, he'd been nearly cured.

I don't mind admitting that Albert charmed me, my dear, though not in any way you might worry on. He has been a gentleman from the moment I met him and seems to take my "widowhood" as a mark of my purity. He convinced me almost at once to travel back with him to Estes Park, and even offered to foot the bill as a courtesy to a fellow "lunger" and his family. I didn't take him up on the offer, of course, but I mention it to help you understand his character.

The journey was arduous, my love, and several times I believed that John would perish. However, almost the very hour we reached Estes Park, he began to revive. It has been a little over a week now, and his color has already returned. He can sit up in bed again for a few minutes at a time, and this morning he and Robert played a game of cards. I am certain this was right.

The three of us are staying with Albert and his spinster sister while we seek out private accommodation, but as there is very little here besides guesthouses, we have not had a great deal of luck finding anything. As before, I won't give you our direct address. Please address anything you send to General Delivery, Estes Park. The mail will likely take a great deal longer to arrive here than in Denver, but there is a telegraph machine should you need to reach me quickly.

With love and longing,

Rory

CHAPTER TWENTY

Jo stood in the kitchen watching the electric kettle, waiting for the water to boil. Her mind, however, was elsewhere, on the past. She'd seen the graves out there on the cliff face, in the little cemetery, a thousand times. She'd heard the names of her great-grandfather and his brother over and over again growing up—her dad and grandfather had hundreds of stories about Robert and John. She'd heard the family legends about their mother, the pioneer woman who had moved to and conquered the West, yet she had never heard even a hint about the history she was reading in the letters. Even in a family as close-knit and liberal as hers, Aurora's past, a major component of her inner life, had been virtually erased from family knowledge.

It was depressing. All those queer lives lost to the ages, all those women longing for other women, men for other men, women and men who knew they didn't belong in the bodies they were born in—so many of their stories gone, as if they'd never happened. Whether Aurora's story had been forgotten or suppressed didn't matter. In the end, it had been lost.

She shivered, running her hands up and down her arms. Despite the warmth of the day, with the sun setting, the cabin was losing the remnants of its heat. It had been chilly every evening she'd been up here, and outright cold in the middle of the night, but that was only part of what she was feeling now.

This chill was deeper, from her heart, which was full of sorrow and regret. When she and Carter were first coming out, they had clung to each other with a kind of fierce desperation, in part because they'd felt so alone. Her parents and siblings had been more understanding than Carter's, but that didn't help either of them in the real world, where all they ever saw were straight people—in every movie, every TV show, every commercial.

There had been few exceptions when they were coming of age, and those exceptions were usually hard to find. All of the couples they saw holding hands in public were straight; all their teachers were straight; everyone, it seemed at the time, was straight but them. It had taken both of them many years to understand that they could be both part of their family and separate from it as lesbians.

How would they have felt to learn that their great-great-grandmother had been something like them? The very idea made Jo almost dizzy with joy, even now, over twenty years after her turbulent adolescence.

The front door opened, startling her out of her daze, and Andy came inside, closing it after herself and locking it again.

"See anything?" Jo had been afraid to let her go to the outhouse on her own, but more afraid to go with her.

Andy wrinkled her nose. "No, but I smelled it."

Jo laughed. "Yeah. It's not great."

"You guys really need to put in a septic tank."

Jo sighed. The family had been arguing about this very thing for years. The cost would be immense. They would have to build a temporary road, schlep the equipment up here, and bring in workers. Every part of the project made it more expensive than putting one in down in town. Jo and Carter were all for it, but getting the rest of the family to chip in their part of the cash was another story. Carter had offered to pay for the whole thing outright, but Jo refused to let her.

"Tea?" she said, holding up the kettle.

"Yes, please," Andy said.

Andy's earlier tension, whatever had caused it, had entirely disappeared. Jo was still tempted to ask her about it—it seemed related to the first letter somehow—but she couldn't think of a way to bring it up. At best, it would seem like a non sequitur, and at worst, it would seem nosy, maybe even intrusive. Either way, Jo decided to try to forget it. Andy seemed like herself again, after all.

They took their mugs back to the sofa, careful to set them far away from the letters on the coffee table. Jo spent a couple of minutes starting the stove. It heated the entire cabin efficiently, but it could be difficult to adjust the temperature with any accuracy. It tended to either be too hot or too cold, but it was much cleaner than the fireplace, which hardly anyone used except during winter. Remembering the sweltering temperature in Andy's apartment, she put some extra wood inside the stove and set the vents fully open. It would be hot in here in no time.

Andy was sitting forward on the couch, bent over one of the letters. She had her own set of latex gloves and still wore her uniform, having rushed up here without changing. But her shirt had short sleeves that revealed the long, sinewy strength of her forearms. The light in the room was dim, the sun setting now, but suddenly the sunset flooded the room with a warm, golden hue. Andy's blond hair and skin almost glowed, making her look like an angel sitting there. Her angel.

Andy smiled at her, the expression so beautiful that tears immediately prickled at the corner of Jo's eyes. Andy's smile faltered. "You okay?"

Jo nodded, embarrassed now. "I'm fine. More than fine. I'm just happy—that's all."

That smile again. "Good. Now come sit here and read the rest."

Jo sat, taking the gloves Andy held out, but didn't immediately grab the next letter. "Don't you think we should wait? Save some? Drag this out a little?"

Andy shook her head. "No way. I want to know what happens next."

Jo grinned. "Oh, I see, you're one of those."

"One of what?"

"One of those people who has to read it, watch it, whatever, all at once."

Andy nodded. "I am. Netflix is a gift from God. I hate waiting for the next episode of anything, or the next book in a series. It drives me nuts."

"I'll keep that in mind," Jo said, and reached for the next letter. She wanted to read the rest of them, too. She just liked having permission.

❖

September 1888

My dearest heart,

I did not receive a postcard from you last week as we agreed on, which sends a dread right through me. Albert and his sister have explained that there are often delays with the post here, but that does little to ease my mind. Upon receiving this, I beg you to send me a telegram reply, simply to let me know that you're alive and well. You have no idea how much I long to hear from you, or how much I struggle to sleep at night knowing that the eyes of that monster follow you from place to place. I pray that it is only his eyes and that he has so far left you bodily alone. Please send word soon.

We are still living with Albert and his sister Anne. They have been wonderfully understanding of our predicament, and more neighborly and charitable than I have any hope of ever repaying. The two of them are the very definition of living saints. That said, the close confines we share have begun to wear on all of us, though neither of them would ever say anything about it. I very much believe that they would allow us to stay here the rest of our lives without actually complaining about it.

I have, however, endeavored to make myself useful. Albert owns and runs a small ranch, and he has been teaching me animal husbandry. I am especially fond of the sheep, but have also made a great deal of progress with the horses, of which I am no longer afraid. Imagine me working with animals! After a lifetime in that filthy city, I now look back and wonder why anyone would care to spend their life there when such places as this exist.

For it is a very heaven, my love. The mountains surround our valley like sentinels, protecting us from the fiercest winds and weather. They break free from the land in ever climbing peaks, capped with snow even now, at the end of summer. The valley itself is a pristine, open paradise, with verdant greens and crystalline mountain streams. I never in my wildest dreams believed such places existed.

The town itself is as it was described to me—barely more than a collection of guesthouses, some cabins, and a few more prosperous ranches, like Albert's. There are, however, several small-goods stores for the prospectors, visitors, and year-round residents. The largest one sells ready-made clothing and functions as the haberdasher. I found some lovely silk ribbon there the other day, as fine as any I'd ever seen in a Chicago store. Indeed, now that I am *here, I want for nothing but your company. That would truly make this place a veritable heaven on earth.*

You will wonder at the fact that I have yet to mention my boys, but you see, my love, I have saved the best for last. John is a new boy—no, he is a new young man now. It happened faster than I was prepared to believe. One week he was too ill to rise from his bed, and the next he was outside, helping Albert with the last of the summer calves. One day he could hardly hold his little bowl of milk, and the next he was running—yes, running!—to catch Robert in a game of chase. He has gained so much and grown so much that I dare say he would be unrecognizable to anyone who had seen him three months ago. Even you, who love him so dearly, would be hard-pressed to pick him from a line of other boys.

Albert believes it is the air that has cured him, and Anne claims it is the clean mountain water, but I have come to believe that it is both this and more. This place has cured my little man. It has saved him. As I watched him this morning, running and playing with his new little dog, you would know immediately that he will live a long, healthful life.

Please send word soon, my love. I know we agreed to wait until the new year to consider your move to join me, but my patience wears thin. If you can, come sooner, and if you can't, please send word. A short missive, a postcard, a telegram, anything to ease my empty, anxious heart. The mountain pass to Lyons will likely soon be impassable with the snow, but Albert has said that some winters are milder and the mail shipment can occasionally get through. Regardless, the telegram will function even if the mail is delayed.

In yearning,

Rory

❖

"That's funny," Jo said, picking up the last envelope in the pile written by Aurora. "I didn't notice this before, but look."

Andy took it from her and peered at it closely. "What does that mean? RTS?"

"Return to sender, I think. The last one didn't make it there, I guess, or came back."

"It's so much later than these others, too. What is that, eight months?"

"About."

"Wonder why."

Jo pondered the question. "She said something about the mountain pass. I guess it would have been difficult to get mail up or down to Estes during the winter, with no plows or anything."

"But that doesn't explain why this last one came back. It should have been clear by April, right?"

Jo nodded and picked up the last letter.

April 1889

Dearest Sarah,

I write this with a heavy heart and little hope. My last three letters have been returned, marked undeliverable, and I have no reason to believe that this one will be any different. When Jack, our mail carrier, finally appeared after the worst of the snow had melted, after almost three months with no mail, I expected at least a short note from you, or a postcard, but I have had nothing from you since July. Albert, Anne, and even the boys have encouraged me to give up. This is understandable advice from the adults, who didn't know you, but the boys love you still, yet they see how your absence tortures me. Even Robert, who is now just four, is heartsick for me. Anne has even gone so far as to suggest that my pining for you has made the boys suffer, but I had to try one last time to contact you. Again, should you receive this letter, please send me a message, even briefly, to let me know that you still live and breathe. Even if your heart has changed, I need to know that he has not hurt you, that you are still safe.

My heart has not changed and never will. There are plenty of available men here, some of whom are quite amiable and handsome, some with great prospects, some with wealth, and all of whom would be happy to take on a widow with two boys who could grow into easy labor for them. But I will

*never take them up on a proposal of marriage, even should I
know that you have moved on. You are the only person I will
ever love.*

*I will continue this letter under the possible delusion
that you still care for me and wish to hear about our lives
here. It is the only thing I know how to do. But as I said,
this missive will be my last. I agree with the others in that
regard—I must stop this. Please unburden my conscience if
you are living but loving someone else. That pain will be
bearable, but this unknowing is not. If he hurt you, or worse,
I would never forgive myself.*

*These months have been prosperous for me, my love,
in ways you would hardly believe. I only wish you were
here to share in my newfound wealth. It began simply. As I
said, Albert had been training me last summer in the skills
of animal husbandry. I made a small investment with some
of the last of our money and bought three animals, horses,
on my own. Albert and Anne helped me set up a carriage
company for the towns' visitors, and even before the first
of the snow fell, I had a nice, tidy income. I bought more
animals and have been renting them out to prospectors and
explorers ever since. I pay Albert a small fee for boarding
them, but as the renters also take on the care of the animals
as part of their contract, the cost is minimal, and the profits
are high. Even in the bleakest part of winter, I was rarely in
stock even a single horse. And now, at the beginning of the
summer season, I am constantly deluged with requests for
animals. I have had to order several more from Denver.*

*I have done all of this for my boys, yes, but also for us. It
is, I am beginning to realize, a twisted, bleak hope that keeps
me going, and one that I will soon have to dismiss. This is
not because I love you any less, but because I simply must.
Writing this, I begin to believe Anne. Longing for you has
made me colder toward the boys, and that is not fair to them.
They deserve a mother who gives them her whole heart.*

*I have already spent some of my earnings and will soon
spend them all on my next endeavor. To the west some fifteen
miles lies a very pretty piece of land that was selling quite
cheaply. The mountain has no gold, very little flat land, and
little to speak of in terms of obvious attractions. But Albert,*

who is friends with the man who sold the parcel to me, took
me and the boys up there when he viewed it as the possible
sight of an orchard. He decided it was too far from town, but
the boys and I were entranced. The view near the top, the
very place where I intend to build our new home, is the most
magnificent on earth. We break ground next week. Albert has
already begun to explain the methods for cultivating fruit
trees at this elevation, and he will be guiding me in every
regard. He has not done me wrong before, so I trust him
wholly. He even offered to continue my horse-rental business
while we get settled, the lamb. Never was there a better man
on this green earth. Despite your general abhorrence of their
sex, I believe you would love him, as I have grown to, as a
brother. He is certainly the best father figure the boys have
ever had.

If you are able, please send word. I am willing to let
you go if that's what's in your heart, but I cannot continue to
live in this uncertainty and keep the remains of my sanity. If
I have not heard from you by the end of this summer, I will
know that one of two things have happened: you have moved
on, or you have died. I cannot imagine anything else that
would prevent a simple note.

Please write,

Aurora

CHAPTER TWENTY-ONE

Jo put the letter down, her eyes filling with tears. Even though she knew the end of this story—Sarah had, after all, been on the next year's census—she couldn't help feel the desperate sorrow and worry that poured off those pages and into her heart. She got up off her knees again and sat back on the couch.

Andy put a hand on her knee and squeezed. "Are you okay?"

Jo started to nod and then shook her head. "No—not really. I mean, I know everything was okay in the end, but I feel terrible. Empty. Almost like I'm feeling what she felt." She frowned at Andy. "Does that make any sense?"

She nodded. "Of course. It's hard to see someone suffering, especially someone you identify with. She was clearly crushed and lonely. There she was, in a new place, raising two boys basically on her own." She shook her head. "That's rough." She scooted closer on the couch and put her arm around Jo's shoulders. "Just so you know, I'd never do that to you."

Jo stomach clenched, and the tears that had been threatening spilled down her cheeks. She turned into Andy, face in her hair, and sobbed. Andy squeezed her, and the warmth of her was comforting, soothing. Jo pulled away, wiping her tears.

"I don't know why I'm crying. That's twice today. You must think I'm a basket case."

Andy shook her head. "Not at all. You feel for her, that's all. It's a good thing to have empathy." She leaned forward and kissed the tip of her nose. "Loving other people is the best part of life."

Jo nodded, a hot flash of recognition piercing her heart. Andy was right. She loved this woman, Aurora, whom she'd never met, could never meet—a person she had barely even heard of before today. She wanted the best for her, wanted her to find happiness. In part, it was because of the similarity between them, their family connection and what they shared, their love of other women, but it was also more than that. No, in fact, the link seemed to reach through time, like a thrumming heartstring across the many decades that separated them. Aurora felt like a kindred spirit, her spiritual ancestor in addition to a blood relative.

"What do you suppose happened?" Andy asked, gesturing at the second bundle of letters. It was still tied together with the red ribbon.

Jo grinned. "Let's find out."

She sat forward and reached for them, but Andy put a hand over hers. "Could I read these?"

Jo flushed with pleasure and nodded. "I'd love that."

That gorgeous smile flashed across her face, and then Andy knelt down, untied the ribbon, and centered two envelopes under the lamp. She held one of them up to the light.

"This one's earlier, and it's a telegram." She slipped it out of the envelope and read aloud: "Safe. More Soon. Love S. Bell." She looked back at Jo. "That's all it says."

Jo held out her hand for it and examined it. Rather than the typewritten telegrams she'd seen before in movies, this one was handwritten, by the operator, she assumed. It was dated May 1889.

"Well, at least Aurora didn't have to wait very long after that last letter," Jo said.

"See the transmission line?"

It took Jo a moment to find it. She frowned at Andy, puzzled. "It says this telegram was sent from San Francisco. What the heck was she doing there?"

Andy shrugged.

"Is the next one a telegram, too?"

She shook her head. "No—it's a letter. It's thick." She turned the envelope over in her hands. "Also from San Francisco. June 1889."

"Well, don't keep me in suspense!"

Andy laughed and then slid out and unfolded the letter, holding it under the brightest part of the lamplight.

❖

June 1889

Dearest,

You will receive this letter with surprise. No doubt, you have moved on. No doubt, some cowboy has swept you off your feet. All the better, if it means that you are safe and cared for. You are too beautiful, too lovely to live on your own or toil too heavily in this sad world of ours. In the last words I read, you had arrived with Albert at Estes Park. I have no doubt that he or someone else has claimed you for his own. I don't make the same kind of claim on you, fruitless as our love was or ever could be. I only send this in hopes that you wintered well and that the boys are still alive and safe with you. I think on John often. John, who is so much like my little brother Jacob, lost to that same insidious disease. I pray John and Robert made it through the winter in that bleak, harsh climate, better and stronger for having survived.

I do, however, hope that the memory of our love—for it was love—has left you some fondness for me, such as for a lost friend, if nothing more. I struggled for a long time deciding whether to send you word. I knew it was best to leave you be, let you live on without guilt, without blame, as I blame myself for what happened. That is my burden, not yours, and I hope you can accept that. I weakened, however, and sent you that telegram last month when I got here, and now I find myself wondering if I should continue this letter or desist. I promised you more, however, and that promise compels me to continue.

My life has been an empty, worthless thing without you. Moreover, it has become a thing of horrors. If you could see me now, you would not recognize me; more, you would run screaming from the sight of me. I cannot even recognize myself. I struggle with whether to tell you of it. I cannot explain what has happened without, perhaps, causing pain, and I cannot bear to think of you in pain. Even if your heart has changed, I don't believe you could ever be callous to another human being, even one as lowly as I am, and not perhaps feel some sorrow on my behalf. I also delude myself that perhaps you have wondered about me some little bit, but that is likely my own vanity. Therefore, if the above was enough, know that I am alive and as well as I can be and discard the rest of this missive. I will never bother you again, and you can live the rest of your life with a clear conscience. If, however, your curiosity, prurient or otherwise, leads you to wonder how I find myself in this strange, floating city so far away from where we began, I provide the story here.

It begins when I received your last letter in September. You may have sent another letter after that, but I did not receive it. I could go into many excuses as to why what follows happened, but the main cause was impatience. That impatience, which you have often chastised me for, was my own doom. Rather than follow the clear directives you gave me, to move from the post office quickly, to take a meandering path back to my apartment, in sum, to do all the things that would hinder him from following me, I made a terrible mistake. I tore your letter open right there on the street and read every word of it. I have it now, as well as your other letters, both as a reminder of your former feelings for me and as a kind of albatross—the cause of all of this. Again, I don't blame you, my darling, or the letters you sent. What I reveal here is not your fault—you gave me clear instructions on how to avoid him. I simply didn't listen.

He followed me home that very day. I had been careful on every other occasion leaving work, leaving the post office— the only places he might have seen me. I wore disguises every time, just as you told me to do, but I was careless that day. I was near the post office too long reading your letter—long enough for anyone to see through my disguise. Then, walking home, I didn't take the usual precautions. There is no other explanation, so again, you can see that it is my fault that he found me, not the letter you sent.

I must pause here to reassure you. I had a little hiding spot in my apartment where I kept all your letters and mementoes, so you needn't worry that he knows where you are. Indeed, it is the next part of my story that will explain how I came to be here in San Francisco.

He followed me home, and then he waited until I was asleep to make his attack. He slipped in the window like a *fiend, and the hours that followed are something I cannot bring myself to describe. He beat me, Rory, and cut me, among other things too horrible to say.*

I had been reading about San Francisco that week. There was a series of articles in the Times that discussed its connection with Chicago on the new train line, and I met a girl at work whose brother had recently struck it rich out there in the goldfields. You might, then, say I had that city on my mind, which is how I managed to convince him that you had moved there. After the first hour of torture, I knew I needed to say something, some place you had gone, so I told myself to simply repeat that same city's name, over and over again. I claimed that you'd met a prospector and had set off with him to California. It took until morning for him to believe me, and he did believe, which I will explain. Still, I think he might have killed me, but for a most fortuitous event—the rent collector came that very morning. Your husband was scared off and escaped the same way he'd come.

The next few months are lost. I was locked in pain, my bones broken, unconscious, and then delirious with fever. After the fever passed, I recovered, albeit slowly, with the help of my sister, Beth. I am, however, a shadow of myself, and my face is a horror to behold. Children shudder and groan at the sight of me, and grown men and women cringe and look away. I also acquired a tremendous opium habit. I took it up to help mitigate the pain, and the drug was, briefly, my master.

When I could, I did some investigation at his work and home, and found evidence three months ago that he had gone west, to San Francisco, in search of his lost wife and children. I had to use the last of the money we'd saved to come here myself, and it was quite easy to find him. I haunt him and watch him as he did to us for so long. I know you are safe as long as I observe him here.

I have a purpose now and no intention of harming myself more than I already have—you can rest easy in that regard, if it was a concern. I have managed to pass myself off as a man, which means I have work, and I have a more important task: to observe Henry for the rest of his life. You will never see him again, I swear it. Even if I have to kill him, he will not cause you harm or come near you again.

You would find me a changed woman in every way but one: my love for you, which has never wavered, never paused. Even now, if you should send word, I would come at once. I don't expect that you would keep me as I am now, a broken, hideous thing, but if you would allow it, I should dearly love to see you and the boys one last time.

My love to you and yours,

Sally

They were quiet for a long time after Andy finished. Jo took the letter from her, eyes burning, reading it to herself over and over again. She was dimly aware of Andy getting up, going into the kitchen, but she didn't focus again until Andy brought back two toasted bagels and some hard, sharp yellow cheese. They ate in silence.

Jo felt drained, worn. She'd heard the name Henry Lemke before, knew that he was the original patriarch, the son of the first immigrant to America that had started their family line in the States. Again, family legend had it that Aurora came to Colorado on her own with her children, and these letters proved exactly that fact, but everyone had always assumed that she came alone simply because Henry had died. The revelation that he was an abusive, violent psychopath was gut-wrenching. It cast a pall over everything she ever knew about her family.

"Hey," Andy said, touching her knee.

Jo looked at her, blinking through her tears. "What?"

Andy's face was pale, almost sickly, and her eyes seemed almost sunken. The tension Jo had seen earlier was back, Andy's shoulders and movements stiff and unnatural. "It's a terrible truth, but this happens in a lot of families." She pursed her lips, frowning deeply. "More often than you think."

Had Andy's father been abusive? It seemed as if she'd found this revelation personal, somehow. Jo told herself not to pressure her about it, that it was Andy's story to tell or not, but she hoped she might say something.

"I didn't know about Henry until now," Jo said.

Andy nodded, once, her eyes still sad and sympathetic. "People, especially women…cover this kind of thing up. No one likes to talk about trauma. Your great-grandfather Robert might not have even known it happened. He was pretty little when they left Chicago."

"But John knew. He would have remembered. He and Robert spent their whole lives together. John lived here with Robert and Robert's family until he died."

"That doesn't mean he wanted to bring it up again. No one does, Jo." Her gaze seemed to shift inward. She swallowed, eyes on the fireplace. If something like this had happened in Andy's family or to someone she knew, that would explain why she seemed so reluctant to say anything.

A flash of frustration, for both Andy and for her family's silence, made Jo clench her fists.

"So much is lost because people are too afraid to talk about things, to face facts. My great-great grandmother was queer, for God's sake, and no one knew it."

"There were laws—"

"Fuck laws!" Jo shouted. She closed her eyes and took a few deep breaths. "I'm sorry. I didn't mean to yell. It just pisses me off. I hate secrets. I always thought of my family as open, caring. We share everything with each other. It would have been very easy for Carter to keep her mouth closed—not come out to her parents until college, but she couldn't. That's the kind of people we are, or at least that's the kind of people I thought we were."

Andy nodded and gestured at the letters on the coffee table. "So this is something to share with them."

"What do you mean?"

Andy's smile lit her up from within, some of the tension seeming to melt away. Her eyes were warm with compassion and sympathy—whatever she'd been worrying about, forgotten. "Think about it, Jo. These letters hold a secret that has been sitting inside this cabin for generations. It's been literally hidden from everyone in your family, and now here it is, out in the open, ready for you to reveal. It showed itself to you for a reason, because you're the one it feels connected to."

Jo's heart seized, and her lungs constricted. She felt a momentary terror, so deep and so strong she would have cried against it if she could breathe. The terror passed almost as soon as it had come, and she took in a large, gulping breath, her entire body relaxing. Andy was right. It *had* chosen her. It was now her secret to share.

She pulled Andy into a tight hug, kissing the side of her head. "Thank you."

Andy laughed. "For what?"

"For calling me out on my shit. I needed that."

Andy nodded in simple agreement. "What are you going to do now?"

Jo shook her head helplessly. "I don't know. I mean, I'd like to know what happened next. Aurora must have sent word to Sarah to come to Colorado, but there's no record of that here. She's on the census in 1890, and I'd bet money she's the one buried outside with Aurora, but again, I can't know either way from these letters."

"Kevin, Drew's boyfriend, might know how to find those records, if they exist. I'm pretty sure we can find death certificates all the way back to that time, even in a small town like Estes."

"I wish we had more letters, or at least some photographs," Jo said. "It would be nice to know what everyone looked like. My dad has a couple pictures of Robert and John, but not many. Too expensive at that time, I guess."

Andy frowned, seeming thoughtful and far away. "It's funny you should mention photos, actually. You know the Stanley Hotel?"

The Stanley, an Estes Park landmark, had been famous for over a century, but more recently due to its association with the author, Stephen King, who'd set his famous novel *The Shining* at a hotel based on it. It was one of the main tourist attractions besides Rocky Mountain National Park.

"Sure, of course."

"Well, the Stanleys were originally famous inventors, especially of two things: a steam-powered car and a photographic method that they eventually sold to Kodak. It made taking pictures much cheaper and easier. They used some of their wealth to build that hotel. Anyway, I think I read that one of the brothers did a photographic series of the entire population of Estes in the early 1890s. Maybe your great-great-grandmother was in it."

Jo smiled. "How cool would that be? If she is, do you think I could get a copy? I'd love to hang it up in here."

Andy shrugged. "No idea. But let me ask Kevin about it—he knows all about that kind of thing. He might know how to get the photos for you, at least."

Jo stared her, her heart swelling with simple joy. Here Andy was, in the midst of what was clearly a family drama, ready and willing to help. No, more than help, she was instrumental to this discovery. Jo would never have had the courage to look in the dresser on her own—she would have sat, terrified, waiting in the living room until Carter and Daniela returned, then possibly run away forever. Now here she was, relaxed, sitting in front of a treasure trove of family memories, on the brink of uncovering a major part of their history. Already, Jo felt closer to Andy than she ever had with any previous girlfriend or lover. They'd known each other less than two weeks, yet she was certain that close, tight feeling in her chest wouldn't change. She was already hers and hers alone.

"What?" Andy said, her smile uncertain.

Jo shook her head. "Sorry. I was staring. It's hard not to stare at you."

"Oh?" Andy's voice was coy, quiet, her lashes lowered.

"Impossible, in fact. I could look at you all day."

Andy's color heightened a little, and she made a face. Jo laughed.

"I mean it. You're beautiful. What's more, you're kind, generous, decent. I don't know what I did to deserve you, know you, I mean."

Jo bit her tongue, realizing she'd said too much, but Andy's lips parted, and she licked her lips, sending a bolt of desire racing through Jo's blood.

"You're going to turn my head," Andy whispered.

"I was planning on it."

Andy stood and held out her hand. Jo took it and followed her into the bedroom.

CHAPTER TWENTY-TWO

Daniela sat back on the sofa, seemingly stunned. She held the last letter, her knuckles white and rigid. She set it down and wiped her hands on her pants.

Carter had finished reading before she had and was now pacing the living room behind the sofa, hands crammed in her pockets. Jo had rarely seen her this agitated.

"You found these in the dresser?" Carter asked again.

Jo nodded. "Like I said."

Carter and Daniela had arrived perhaps ten minutes after Andy had left this morning—they'd passed on the trail—and Jo had immediately given them the whole story before they read the letters themselves. Carter had seemed incredibly dubious until she finished them, and Jo could see that she was still struggling to come up with a rational explanation for all of this. Her entire body seemed to thrum with suppressed nerves.

"And the lock was in there? Moving on its own?" Carter asked. "That's how you knew to look under the panel?"

Again, Jo nodded. She almost said something more but realized that Carter needed to accept the story as she'd already told it. Adding details would only make her more reluctant to believe her. She wished Andy were here, at the very least to act as backup for what they'd seen. But Carter knew Andy would vouch for her story. This explained the nervous agitation. How could she help Carter, a rational person, accept the unacceptable, the unexplainable?

Except, of course, there was an explanation. Aurora had shown her where to find the letters, of that much Jo was certain. She didn't know how she knew this beyond the fact that the letters dealt with her and Sarah, but she was sure, deep inside, that she was right. She was as certain as if Aurora had told her. But Carter didn't need to hear this explanation right now.

Carter sat down on the chair nearest to her and dragged it closer. She took both of Jo's hands in hers.

"But how, Jo? How is it possible?" Her pupils were so dilated her eyes were almost black.

Jo squeezed her hands. "I don't know, Carter, but it is. It happened."

Carter rocketed to her feet again and began pacing. "But that would mean the rest of it is true as well—the thing that pushed Meg, what happened to you at the well..." She stopped, looking hopeless and lost.

Daniela stood up and approached her. She pulled Carter into a quick embrace and then drew back. *I know this is hard for you to accept, but maybe you can think of it as a puzzle.*

Carter frowned. *A puzzle? What do you mean?*

Something for you to solve—something for you to figure out.

"But how do you solve the unsolvable?" Carter asked. The fact that she'd said this aloud was telling, Jo thought, since she rarely spoke to Daniela, especially when it was just the three of them.

If Carter's slip bothered her, Daniela didn't show it. Instead, she gave her wife a warm smile. *But that's just it—some pieces are missing. Don't you see?*

The lost, frightened look gradually died out of Carter's eyes. Jo, watching from a few feet away, thought she actually seemed to grow taller as she relaxed. Finally, Carter nodded.

"Yes," she whispered. "A puzzle." She turned to Jo. "For example, the man, or whatever he is, outside. You think he's responsible for the rest of it?"

Jo nodded at once. "Yes. I know he is. It would be too much of a coincidence, otherwise, and anyway, I have a strong feeling about him."

Carter dismissed this remark with a cutting gesture. "Feeling or not, we need to try to make certain. Who do you think he is?"

The three of them paused, waiting for someone to say it. Finally, Daniela shrugged. *I mean, I thought it was obvious. He must be Henry, Aurora's husband.*

Jo had thought the same thing, but she was glad Daniela had suggested it first. Carter, however, seemed grim. "But do we know that for sure? How did he get here? He thought Aurora was living in San Francisco."

Maybe he came after.

"After what?"

Daniela lifted one shoulder, appearing uncertain. *After he died.*

This time Jo shook her head. "I disagree. I think he found them somehow, when they were all still alive."

Carter pointed at her. "I think so, too."

Now Daniela looked lost. *Okay, but how would we ever find out? We don't have any more letters, so we don't have any way to know.*

Again they were all silent, but this time Jo didn't have a response. She was pretty sure the others didn't either. She'd felt similarly last night, when she and Andy finished the final letter. How could they get the rest of the story when there might not be more to uncover?

Carter sighed. "Of course, he might still be outside somewhere, right now. Jo, you said when that thing happened at the well, you couldn't stop yourself. Meg said something similar."

"Yes. But it seemed to go away after Andy and Meg showed up— the compulsion, I mean. It was like I woke up when other people were nearby."

Carter's eyebrows knit in concentration. "And with Meg, it happened when she was by herself, too."

So we should be careful when we're on our own outside, Daniela suggested.

Yes, but that's not enough, Carter added. She still seemed restless, refusing to sit down, but the fact that she remembered to switch back to sign showed some progress, Jo thought. Presenting all of this as a puzzle to solve had been a good idea. She'd have to thank Daniela for it later.

We need to stop him, Carter said, *or someone else might get hurt.*

Jo laughed. *What are we talking about—an exorcism or something?*

Carter gave her a withering stare. *Of course not. I don't believe in that garbage, and neither do you.*

Then what?

Daniela shifted a little and gestured at the letters on the table. *If we solve this part of it, we might be able to stop him. Jo, you said maybe Andy's friend Kevin could find some of the records related to Aurora and Sarah?*

Jo shrugged. *Maybe. I won't know for sure until we talk. Andy gave me his number.*

Daniela nodded. *Then you should call him. Today, if possible.*

Jo weighed her options. It was true that she didn't want to wait, but on the other hand, she wasn't even sure if Kevin could help. Hiking down and driving into cell-phone range would take a lot of time, maybe for nothing. It was a weekday, after all, so he was probably busy. And the hike down would mean risking a run-in with whatever or whoever was on the trail again.

We can go down to the car with you, Daniela suggested.

What? You just got here.

She's right, Carter broke in. *Talking to Kevin is the first step. You should go right now.*

The air had a definite nip today. The hike down had warmed Jo, but now, standing next to the car as they made their good-byes, the heat leaked out of her into the thin, chilly mountain air. Daniela was bundled up, almost comically overdressed, but Carter wore a short-sleeved shirt, clearly comfortable. Every couple seemed to be like this. She smiled, remembering Andy's overheated apartment.

Uh-oh, Carter signed. *She's got that look in her eyes again.*

Daniela grinned. *That Andy look.*

Jo rolled her eyes. *Are you sure you don't want to come?*

Carter shook her head. *No. It's almost the weekend, and we're running out of time up here. I have a big case coming up, so I have to be back at work Monday. I want to take care of the rest of the cleanup and repairs before we leave. I can stay only till Sunday. We could come back the next weekend, I guess, if we have to, but I kind of need a break.*

Jo knew what she meant and felt a little pinprick of sorrow at the idea. Normally she couldn't get enough of the cabin. Usually she went up almost every weekend when the rest of the family wasn't using it, which generally meant she got the place to herself at least once a month. The idea that she might want to avoid it depressed her greatly.

Come back soon, okay? Daniela asked.

Jo nodded. *I'll try to be there before sunset. If it's going to be later than that, I'll get a hotel.*

Damn, Carter said, frowning. *That means hiking up on your own. Didn't think of it. Maybe we should go with you.*

Jo shook her head. *I'll be fine.*

She got in the car before Carter could argue with her, waving once before she headed down the road. She didn't know why she hadn't taken Carter up on her offer, but something told her it was unnecessary. She might be fooling herself, but she thought she would be okay if she kept her wits about her. Now that she knew what to watch for, it would be harder for him to sneak up on her.

She pulled over a few minutes later onto the side of the road. She and Carter had gotten cell service in this little pull-off before, and when she checked her phone, she saw that she had it again. It was strange, since most of the time it was impossible to get any service up here at all, but this little spot somehow allowed it. She took out the little scrap of paper with Kevin's number and dialed, her fingers clumsy on the screen after all this time.

Kevin answered almost at once. "Hello?"

"Hi, Kevin? This is Jo."

"Hey. I was expecting you."

"Oh?"

"Andy called me this morning on her way to the station. She said you might be contacting me."

"Are you at work?"

He laughed. "No. I'm at the museum. Can you meet me here?"

"Of course."

"Good. Drew almost killed me when I told him I was leaving this morning. He'd only just come home, and he said I love this place more than him."

"Sorry to cause trouble."

"He'll get over it. He was already asleep again before I left, and I'm sure he's still in bed—he spends most of his time off there. Anyway, I've already found something you'll love to see. I'll hang up so you can drive over here."

"Be there in twenty."

Jo threw her phone down and peeled onto the road, little rocks and stones flying up. She drove much too quickly, taking the curves far faster than the posted limits. She was excited, thrilled even, but also agitated, nervous—both sets of emotions fighting for control. She slowed outside the park, but only because the police liked to ticket tourists.

An older red pickup truck was parked in the little museum lot, but hers was the only other car here. She saw, as she approached the door, that the museum wasn't even open today, but lights were on inside. Kevin must have heard her, as he appeared inside and opened the door for her.

"I have a key," he explained, giving her a brief, one-armed hug. Jo had forgotten how impressively huge he was. When he hugged her, he put his arm around her shoulders without bending down. Like the last time she'd seen him, he wore a flannel shirt and work boots, appearing every bit like a lumberjack.

He closed and locked the door behind them and then led her back into a smaller room behind the public displays. The room was plain, almost entirely empty except for a large table covered with stacks of papers and leather-bound albums.

"Please, sit," he said.

"What is all this stuff?"

He grinned and gestured at one of the chairs again. They sat, and he slid an open photo album in front of her.

For a moment, Jo couldn't breathe. It was a group photograph of four people—two women and two boys in front of an empty field. The quality of the photograph was stunning—she had no idea that photos like this had existed so early. She recognized Robert and John instantly. She'd seen one or two pictures of them in the past, and they also resembled her father as well as one of her brothers. She had never seen the women, before, but she knew them at once.

"Holy shit," she said, bending over and peering closely. Her voice was shaky, hoarse. Her stomach knotted, a little like she'd been punched there—that same, low pain in the middle of her body. "I can barely believe it."

Kevin grinned. "You could be twins."

He was right. Seeing Aurora was like peering into a mirror, or, as she did all the time, it was like looking at Carter. In fact, the resemblance was so strong she had trouble accepting the small differences between them and this woman. Aurora seemed older, for one thing, or at least more careworn and weathered, and she had what appeared to be a long, thin scar that ran the length of her face, giving the right side of her mouth a kind of twist that made it seem like she was grinning at them. Her light hair was very short—a man's haircut at the time, Jo presumed. Her clothes were also masculine. It helped, of course, seeing a version of her own face there, but even in 1893, the year in the note under the photo, Jo had a hard time believing anyone would have actually thought she was a man, masculine presentation or not. All she needed was a different set of clothes, and she would have blended into any contemporary lesbian bar in the world.

"Who is the other woman—the one in the dress?" Kevin asked.

A note beneath the photo listed four names, and he read them. "Sarah Bell? Who's that?"

Jo smiled. "Her lover."

Sarah was very pretty. She had small, delicate features, with large, almost wet-looking eyes. She was very short compared to the olderer boy and Aurora, and her hair and brows were dark and thick. Like Aurora, she seemed to be grinning at the camera. Her dress was plain, but clearly neat and of good quality. Despite her fragile beauty, something in her face suggested strength, resilience, a set to her mouth, perhaps, that forbade underestimating her. Strangely, she somewhat resembled Jo's sister Annie, and she was certainly more like the two boys than Aurora.

"Wow," Kevin said. "You mean they were—"

"A couple, yes. Aurora left her husband and came here with her children. Sarah lived with them."

"Incredible. What a story. I'll have to tell the museum director about it. Maybe we can do a special exhibit on them or something."

Jo nodded, vaguely, her mind and eyes still locked on the photograph. For some reason, she had pictured the two women in a different way, with opposite gender presentation. It had been Sarah, after all, who had passed as a man in San Francisco. She could hardly even fathom the idea that anyone would have believed that little, delicate, pretty woman was a man, regardless of how she'd cut her hair or what clothes she'd worn.

And, Jo thought, frowning, Sarah had been the one attacked. She was perfectly fine in this photo—nothing like the monster she described in her letter. Aurora had the scars. But maybe Sarah had recovered. This photograph was taken over three years later, after all. Anything could have happened between that last letter and this picture.

With effort, she wrenched her eyes away from the photograph and physically pushed the album away. She could spend all day staring at that thing, but now was not the time.

"What else do you have for me?" she asked.

"I pulled the death records for the years between 1912 to 1945. If these women are in here, it shouldn't be that hard to go through them and find them. Do you know when they died?"

"Yes. According to the grave, anyway. One of them died in 1914, and one in 1920. I don't know which person goes with what date—the grave doesn't say."

Kevin stood up and moved some of the folders aside until he

found both years. When he sat back down again, his eyes were shiny and the color in his face was bright. He was clearly eager to track down the facts.

"You check that one, and I'll look in here. Not many people were dying, so it shouldn't take very long."

It didn't. The death notice for Sarah Bell, who'd died of what was called "Oedema" in 1914, was the second one in the folder. They listed her as "spinster" on this form as well, and Jo smiled a little at the word. It also listed the interment as "Lemke Mountain." She pointed out that detail to Kevin.

"Oh, of course!" Kevin said, slapping his forehead. "I knew I'd heard that name before."

"Really? I never have."

Kevin nodded. "That's because the park service changed it, after the park was developed in 1915."

"How cool!" Jo said. "I didn't know the mountain had an older name. Have you heard anything about it before?"

Kevin laughed. "Do you mean you haven't?"

She shook her head.

"It was a famous campsite, for tourists, both before and after the park bought out that whole area around it. I imagine that's how they made their money." He paused. "Though I remember something do with horses, too."

"She rented horses. Aurora did. In town, I mean."

"That's right. I didn't realize a woman ran things, but I knew it was called Lemke Horses. She also rented horses up there in the park. Lemke's was the first horse-rental place in Rocky. I think they also gave tours, through the park, on horseback. She must have made a fortune."

Jo flushed with pleasure. It would have been very difficult at that time for a woman to make a decent living, or any kind of living, besides factory work or clothes-making. The fact that Aurora had been something of an entrepreneur made her incredibly proud.

"Did you find anything about Aurora? When she died?"

"I didn't see anything in the file, but that's not uncommon," Kevin said. "If she died up at her cabin, there might not be any record. At that time, only people who died in town got those official records like Sarah. They must have brought Sarah down to town before she died. If I remember right, a doctor came up here sometimes from Longmont— so maybe they wanted to see him. But yeah, if Aurora died up on the mountain, I don't think we'll find a record anywhere."

"What about newspapers? Did any exist at the time? Maybe there's an obituary or something."

He grinned. "Yes, in fact there was one. It's even digital, if you can believe it. And you're in luck—the paper came out only once a week, and it's not usually very long."

He opened his little knapsack and pulled out a tablet computer before turning it on. It took him a couple of minutes, but eventually he had the link for the issues in 1920. He scooted his chair closer to hers so they could look together, and again, Jo had to smile at his enthusiasm. With his huge, impressive physique and his thick, mountain-man beard, he seemed like the last person on earth who would be into this kind of thing.

The newspaper was interesting—more than interesting, captivating. The paper had clearly been aimed at tourists, most of whom were visiting the relatively new national park. It did contain, however, some local news, and Jo found it incredible that they could search it online. Pictures of old stores, old advertisements, directions to trails and fishing spots—all the things that wouldn't be nearly as interesting now were incredibly absorbing as they read each issue. The sidebar on the screen had a searchable interface, and when Jo realized what that meant, they were able to find the obituary easily—in May 1920. It was very short, with minimal details of Aurora's life, but Jo had what she wanted—proof that Aurora had died and was buried up on their family's land.

"So it is them. In the grave, I mean," Jo said quietly. She'd expected this news, but it still caused her heart to lift. Her great-great-grandmother and her female lover were buried together up at the family cemetery. The very notion was so incredibly, wonderfully touching, she felt like crying.

"This is amazing, Jo. You really have to let me talk to the director. I've been wanting to do a little exhibit here on queer history, and Aurora and Sarah could easily be the centerpiece of that show."

"I'd love that."

His smile was catching, and they continued to grin at each other.

"What else did you want to know?" he finally asked. "This was all the stuff I pulled on short notice, but there's more in the archive."

She shrugged. "It's hard to say where to go from here. I don't know what to search for."

"What do you mean?"

She thought about this question, trying to think of a way to tell him the story of Henry Lemke without actually giving away any of the details. It was too personal to reveal much, for now anyway. She liked Kevin, but she barely knew him, and she hadn't even had a chance to confide in the rest of her family.

"Well, you see, we think my great-great-grandfather came up here too, but we don't have any evidence."

He frowned, obviously puzzled. "Why do you think he was here?"

Jo sighed. This was going to be difficult. "Just some stuff up at the cabin."

His frown deepened. "What kind of stuff?"

Jo waved her hands dismissively. "Okay, let's back up. How about I put it to you this way. Can you track who came into town?"

"What, like visitors?"

She nodded.

He started to shake his head and then stopped. "Well, I guess there might be one way. It depends, though. Some of the early hotels kept records. Do you think he used his own name?"

Kevin had clearly picked up on some of her reluctance, so she shrugged. "I guess not. But that's all I have: Henry Lemke of San Francisco or Chicago."

He, too, seemed uncertain, but he nodded. "I can try. It might take a while for me to check, though. Any idea what year we're talking?"

She too started to shake her head and then paused. The man she'd seen in the woods had been dirty, careworn, certainly, but he had also been relatively young. And it had to have been before Aurora died, or he would never have come here, right? These guesses had a lot of "ifs," but, she realized, ifs were all she had.

"I'm going to guess early—1890s. Maybe early 1900s, but I don't think it was that late."

Again, Kevin raised his shoulders. "It wouldn't hurt to check, I guess. But just so we're clear—he would have had to have stayed in one of the hotels with records, and a lot of them didn't keep them or they were lost." He paused, tapping his lips with his fingers. "I might call a friend of mine in Denver, too. He works with the Colorado Historical Society, so he might know more options. Maybe a different way to track him down. You said he was from San Francisco?"

"Well, Chicago, but he would have come here from San Francisco."

He seemed undaunted, his eyes bright and excited. Like Carter, he apparently liked a puzzle. "Like I said, I don't know if I'll find anything, but I'm happy to look into it for you."

She grabbed his hand, squeezing it. "Thank you, Kevin. For everything. I never thought I'd see photos of either of them, and I'm so happy to know they ended up together."

He made a flapping gesture with his hand. "It's nothing. Really, you're doing me a favor. I love this stuff."

She gave him a quick hug and stood up. "Can I make a copy of that photo? I want to get it framed for the cabin."

"Absolutely. Let me show you the scanner."

CHAPTER TWENTY-THREE

By the time Jo had the photograph printed and framed, it was late afternoon. If she headed directly to the cabin, she could make it up there long before sunset. Instead, as she entered the park, she hesitated at the turnoff onto the road that led that way and then continued to the ranger station. Andy was working, but she couldn't help herself. Even if she got to only say a brief hello, she had to see her, at the very least to show her the photograph.

But it wasn't simply the picture, Jo realized. Her desire to be with Andy was like an empty, hungry need, as strong and as vital as breathing. She wouldn't be able to relax until she saw her again, and it would be hard to do it even then. What would she do when Andy was gone for two weeks? She shook her head. Better not to think of it.

It was long past the regular tourist season now, so the parking lot at the station was almost empty—just three cars with out-of-state plates. The old green Bronco was also there in the lot, and Jo's spirits rose with hope. She parked next to it and got out, grabbing the framed photo.

She was surprised to find a large number of people inside the public room of the station—at least two families. She didn't immediately see Andy for all the bodies in there and had to peer around the side of one of the men to finally spot her. She was behind the little counter, bent down a little and talking with a family, pointing out something on the map. As always, Jo's breath seized at the sight of her. Andy's voice was low and almost soothing, too quiet to make out the words, but it sounded like the sweetest music she'd ever heard. Jo's palms broke out in sweat, and she made herself look away, staring at the guidebooks on the little rotating stand near her.

Finally, one family left and then the other. A couple of men were still at the counter, so Andy hadn't seen her yet or was pretending she hadn't. Jo didn't want to intrude, but she also wanted to make sure she had a chance to say something to her before someone else came in, so she walked closer to the counter behind the men, as if waiting in line.

The movement must have caught Andy's eye, as she immediately stopped talking, locking eyes with her. They must have stared at each other for a long time, as, when Jo finally broke contact, the two men in front of her were looking back and forth at them, their heads rotating comically from one person to the other.

Andy shook her head as if to clear it, her eyes refocusing on them. "I'm sorry. What were we talking about?"

The taller one laughed. "Oh, don't worry about it, honey. We're not in any hurry."

"Always nice to find family, even in the sticks," the shorter man said.

"We'll go check out the hats," the taller one added, and he grabbed his partner's arm, leading him a few feet away.

Jo grimaced. "I'm so sorry. I didn't mean to interrupt. I was going to wait, but—"

Andy gave her that broad, heartbreaking smile, and the words died on her lips.

"I'm glad you came," Andy said quietly, leaning forward across the counter. "I missed you."

Heat flashed across the surface of her skin, the blood rising in her face. "Me, too."

They continued to stare at each other, wordlessly. Jo thought she saw that same raw hunger in Andy's eyes. Had they been alone, there was no question what would be happening right now.

Finally, Andy gestured at Jo's hands. "What's that?"

Almost dizzy, Jo found her thoughts were muddled, and it took her a few extra seconds to remember what she was carrying. "Oh, gosh, that's why I came. Kevin found it." She put the framed photograph on the counter, facing Andy.

Andy stared at it for a long time, her eyebrows so high they nearly touched her hairline. "Wow," she finally said.

"Right?"

"She looks exactly like you and Carter. It's eerie."

"Everyone in the family has always wondered. I'm nothing like my parents, and neither is she. We're the only blondes, for one thing, but there's more. Everyone else has a similar face, even—nothing like Aurora's or ours."

As she said this, something tugged at Jo's memory—an idea she'd had earlier, when she and Kevin had examined the photograph together. That sense, when she first saw the two women, that something was off, that something that didn't add up with her own preconceptions.

"Must be the lesbian genes coming out," Andy said, smiling broadly. She glanced over at the men, both of whom appeared to be browsing the clothing section but were clearly listening to them.

She rolled her eyes. "Why don't you go wait in my room? I'll finish in here, and then it's almost my dinner break. My relief will be here soon."

Jo blushed again. "I thought you said you couldn't have guests."

Andy's head tilted a little. "I can have guests, just no *overnight* guests. It's still daylight, so we won't be breaking any rules. Well, technically."

"How long will you be?" Jo managed to ask, beginning to tremble.

Andy checked her watch. "Less than an hour. Depends on when she gets here."

"Is it okay if I take a shower while I wait?"

"Of course."

Their voices had grown quieter as they spoke, so Andy's last words came out barely above a whisper. Jo knew the men were listening to them, but she also felt rather breathless. She thought Andy might feel that way, too.

She took the photograph back to her car and then went around the back of the station to the staff housing and into the shower room. She stood just inside the door, with its bank of lockers, inhaling the fresh, clean, lemony air.

She was shaking all over now, and it took her a long time to take off her clothes, her trembling hands clumsy on the buttons of her shirt. She threw a quick glance in the mirror, saw that eager, barely suppressed excitement in her eyes, and almost laughed at herself. She grabbed Andy's soap and went into the nearest shower stall. It closed with a vinyl curtain, and she stood there under the water, doing nothing to actually clean herself.

She heard the door to the shower room open and jumped a little. "Is that you?"

The curtain was ripped aside a moment later, and Andy came into the water with her, pulling her into a rough embrace. They began to kiss, Jo so desperate for her lips, for the taste of her, it was as if she couldn't kiss her quickly enough, hard enough. Andy shoved her into the wall, her sheer physical presence so overwhelming, so hot and needed, Jo let out a long, low moan.

Finally, she managed to pull away, and she pushed Andy's shoulders a little to get her attention. Andy's hair was plastered to her head, the water still streaming down on them, and her clothes were soaked through.

It took Jo a great effort to say, "Take me to bed. Now."

❖

"Will you get in trouble?" Jo asked several hours later. The two of them were scrunched into the tiny twin bed in Andy's staff bedroom. Andy was spooning her from behind, playing with a lock of her hair.

After her dinner break, Andy had gone back to work for a few hours, and then she came here again, where Jo had waited. When she'd finally returned back, she'd slammed the door and launched herself at Jo without a word. Afterward, they'd dozed off a little, but now they were both awake again.

"Hmm?" Andy replied, her warm breath tickling Jo's ear.

Jo squirmed, heat beginning to gather inside her once more. She scooted out of Andy's arms and turned around, their faces inches apart.

"Won't you get in trouble? For having an overnight guest?"

Andy sighed. "Probably, but maybe not. Only if someone rats me out."

"Will they?"

They could see each other, dimly, but the room was almost completely dark now. She felt Andy's shoulders lift. "Maybe, maybe not. I've covered for a few people before, so maybe they'll let it slide. Karen had her boyfriend over just last week."

"So I don't have to leave?"

Andy shook her head. "No. Never. I want you to live here, in fact. I want us both to stay in this bed forever."

Jo's stomach dropped. "That's what I want, too."

"Good. It's settled, then. Welcome to your new home."

Jo laughed and then nestled into Andy, slipping her head under her chin. She inhaled Andy's clean scent, catching a hint of chamomile and something else, something sweet. She kissed the little notch between Andy's collarbones and felt her shiver in response.

"Be careful, or you'll get me going again," Andy said, her voice dark and low.

"That's the plan," Jo said, and kissed her there again.

"Wait," Andy said, her body suddenly tense. "I wanted to talk to you about something."

Jo didn't reply, surprised, and Andy scooted away, reaching for the lamp. The light made Jo's eyes dilate with some pain, and she blinked at Andy, squinting. Andy's hair was mussed, sexy, but her expression was serious, a trace of something worrisome in the downturned corners of her mouth. Andy lay down on her back and motioned for Jo to come closer. She put her head on Andy's shoulder and waited. Andy's body was hard and rigid beneath hers.

Jo made herself laugh. "Must be serious."

Andy sighed. "It is and it isn't. I just don't know if I should say it."

Jo propped herself up on an elbow. "What is it?"

"Look, Jo…the thing is, I like you. I like you a lot, in fact."

Jo's stomach lurched. This sounds bad, she thought. She made herself smile. "I like you a lot, too."

Andy smiled for a moment, but then that troubled, worried strain reappeared, her lips pressed tightly together. Jo squeezed her arm. "What's bothering you?"

Andy's eyes darted away from hers, and she appeared almost guilty. "I guess I'm just wondering where this is headed. What we're doing."

"We're having the greatest sex of all time," Jo replied. She spoke lightly, but anxiety made her heart hammer.

Andy grinned. "It *is* good, isn't it?"

"Do you even need to ask? Didn't you hear me? I think I ripped my vocal cords." She nudged her. "You weren't exactly holding back, either."

Andy's smile was more genuine now, and her body relaxed a little. "No. I wasn't."

She touched her cheek. "So what's the problem?"

"I'm just wondering if this is something more than that. If…I mean something to you."

Jo laughed and then shook her head. "I'm sorry. I don't mean to laugh, but that's silly. Of course it's more than just sex." She leaned down to kiss her once, quickly, and then met her eyes again. "You mean a lot to me."

Andy looked hopeful, and then her gaze darted away again. Jo gently lifted her chin, making her meet her eyes. "Andy, I'm telling you the truth. Can't you tell I'm falling for you?"

These words had an instantaneous effect. Andy's eyes filled with tears, and she pulled Jo down into an embrace, kissing the side of her head over and over. Jo laughed and kissed her mouth, giving her a tight squeeze before meeting her eyes again.

"Did I do something, say something to make you feel like I wasn't?"

Andy shook her head, her eyes still wet and dewy. "No."

Jo stared at her for a long time. This insecurity surprised her so much she didn't know how to respond. She'd seen a little bit of it in Andy before, and it had surprised her then, too. Andy was gorgeous, by anyone's standards, as well as smart, kind, and caring. She had a cool job and was clearly dependable, trustworthy. Any woman would be lucky to have her. Even now, Jo could hardly believe they were in bed together.

Something occurred to her then, and for a moment it was as if someone had knocked the wind out of her lungs. Of course, Jo thought. That explained things. It even explained something she'd sensed yesterday, when they were reading the letters together—that horrible tension she'd felt when Andy heard about what Henry had done to Aurora and Sarah.

"Did someone hurt you?" she whispered, trailing her fingers along the side of Andy's face.

Andy tensed again but nodded. The tears that had been threatening to fall began to slip down her cheeks.

"A girlfriend?" Jo asked.

Again, Andy nodded, almost rigid now beneath Jo.

Jo leaned forward, close enough that she could feel Andy's breath. She had to get this right, had to make her believe. She stared into her eyes until she saw Andy focus on her and her alone.

"I will never do that to you, Andy. I will never hurt you."

Andy sobbed, once, choking it off a second later. "How do you know?"

Jo had a little flash of guilt at the memory of her ex, Elsa. She'd certainly hurt her, that was true. But this was different, this feeling she had for Andy. It made her want to be a better person, the kind of person who would sacrifice anything for Andy's sake. She knew she could spend the rest of her life proving that to her, if that's what it took, and never lose patience with her in the process.

"I just know," she said.

Andy sobbed again, and Jo lay down into her arms. Andy's grip was hard, almost painful, but Jo didn't complain, letting her cry herself out. She made little soothing sounds and rubbed her hands up and down Andy's back, reminded, suddenly, that Andy had done the same thing for her before. The idea was comforting, somehow, as if they were in this together, supporting each other already. The idea that someone had hurt this woman enough to make her feel this way was awful, gut-wrenching, even, but she knew she could help Andy regain her confidence with enough time together.

"I'm sorry," Andy finally said, pulling away to wipe her face. "I'm kind of a hot mess."

Jo winked at her. "But you're my hot mess."

Andy smiled, her eyes growing distant and uncertain again. Jo touched her shoulder. "Do you want to talk about it?"

Andy shook her head. "No. Not right now. Some other time, maybe. But maybe not. Is that okay?"

"Whatever you want, Andy. You don't have to tell me anything you're not comfortable talking about."

Andy's eyes searched her face, and she nodded. "Thanks. It's just...I've spent too much time thinking about her already. I've let her ruin...things before." Her face constricted with pain. "It's not something I'm proud of."

Jo sat forward and kissed her. "Well, I'm proud of you."

"You are?"

"Yes. I can't wait to show you off to the rest of my family."

Andy almost flinched. "All of them?"

Jo laughed. "Yes—all of them. Even the Republicans."

"Wow. You are brave."

Jo grinned at her. "No, seriously, I want you to meet them. We're having our annual family reunion in a couple of weeks—we could get it all done at once. Like ripping off a Band-Aid."

Andy's face crinkled with pleasure and then fell. "Oh, shit. I can't. I'll still be on fire duty."

Damn, Jo thought. She'd forgotten about that.

Andy looked worried again. "I can see if I can switch with someone, but I don't think I'll be able to do it so late."

Jo squeezed her hand. "It's fine, Andy. Don't worry about it. We have our reunion, but almost all of us get together during the holidays, too. Maybe you could come to Thanksgiving. You've never seen so many German-Americans outside of an Octoberfest."

Andy smiled, but weakly, and Jo saw that worried uncertainty start to creep into her eyes again. Jo had to do something to get rid of that, once and for all. She put her hand on Andy's naked thigh. Andy's eyes widened, and a little color rose to her cheeks.

"Lights on or off?" Jo asked, keeping her voice low and commanding.

Andy licked her lips. "On."

CHAPTER TWENTY-FOUR

Jo let her arms go slack, the muscles in her shoulders burning with exertion. The window looked good—better than it had before, in fact. They'd had to replace the whole frame in addition to the pane of glass, and she was painting it with an all-weather sealant. Carter and Daniela were sealing the other windows and were almost finished. This was the last task on Carter's list, and a funny, almost delirious jubilance built in the pit of Jo's stomach. They'd worked hard, the five of them.

Two weeks ago, when they'd first gotten here, it hadn't seemed possible that the place would ever be livable again. Now here they were, and the cabin had never been in better shape. Sure, the water faucet still turned on by itself, and, by the newest estimate, the roof would take thousands of dollars to replace properly, but both of those things seemed minor in the face of what they'd accomplished together. She only wished Rachel and Meg could see it now.

Meg had gotten out of the hospital with minor injuries, but, from what Carter had reported after she and Daniela visited her yesterday, she wasn't willing to come back up here. Jo knew why—she understood better than anyone else. She'd felt that powerful, compelling will bending her into submission. Meg didn't have the same connection to this place that she did, so she didn't have any reason to return.

Still, Jo thought, things had been quiet since she found the letters three days ago. Nothing had happened inside or outside the cabin to suggest anything strange. Nothing moved on its own, and she hadn't had the faintest sensation that the man was still in the woods. Now that they had most of the story of the cabin's past, she was beginning to wonder if it was all over, back to normal. Maybe it was safe to be here on her own again.

She wouldn't have to worry about that any time soon, however.

Andy, Drew, and Kevin could be here at any time. The six of them planned to have lunch and let Kevin see the place. Then the others would leave together, and she and Andy would stay. Jo had called her boss at home yesterday morning and asked for and received three more days of vacation. She and Andy would be here together until Wednesday, and Andy would help her take some of the equipment down and back to her place in Fort Collins. Andy would leave for fire duty Thursday, and Jo would go back to work. Just the idea of parting for two weeks made Jo feel a little sick, so she kept driving the idea of it to the back of her mind. They would have these three days together, anyway, and she planned to enjoy every minute of it.

Carter appeared from the side of the house, looking bright. "I'm done!"

"Me, too."

Carter was grinning, almost wildly. "I can't believe it. I really can't. If you had told me two weeks ago that we would finish—"

"I know. It's hard to believe."

"Even with all that shit happening."

This was as close as Carter had come to admitting something *had* happened in days, and Jo almost called her on it. She let it go. Carter had to come to things on her own terms, not hers.

"When will they be here, again?"

Jo glanced at her watch. "Any time now."

"Good. Daniela's inside getting lunch together, so it should be ready for them."

"She's the perfect housewife."

Carter grinned. "Not really. She's just the only person who can cook worth a damn." She put a hand up to shield her eyes, squinting into the bright sunshine. "The picnic table is filthy. I'll go wipe it down so you can get ready."

Jo glanced down at herself and then wrinkled her nose. "Thanks. I'm a mess."

"Hell, yes, you are. I'm embarrassed to be seen with you."

"Gee, thanks."

Carter laughed. "But seriously, go change. That shirt looks like you're splattered with blood."

The wood stain *was* bright red on her shirt and pants. "Thanks. I'll do that."

With the windows cleared of brush and branches and cleaned, the cabin was much brighter inside than it had been, but it was still much cooler and darker, and it took her eyes a moment to adjust. Daniela had her back to the front door, so she didn't notice Jo come inside. Jo stomped her feet a couple of times, and Daniela jumped slightly before turning around, a knife in one hand, a piece of bread in the other. She made a face at Jo.

Jo laughed. *I know, I know. I'm changing my clothes.*

Daniela put the knife and bread down. *Good. Andy would probably just leave if she saw you like that.*

I love all the support I'm getting from my family today. Really makes me feel good about myself.

Daniela's face split into a mischievous grin, and then she walked across the room, pulling Jo into a hug before stepping away. *You know I'm kidding.*

Jo nodded, smiling now. Daniela began to turn away but then paused. She looked hesitant, uncertain, her face clouded and her lips downturned.

What's the matter? Jo asked.

Daniela's eyes were a little wet now. *I'm just so happy we're friends again, Jo. I'm sorry I let all those hurt feelings go on so long. We should have made up months ago. That was my fault, not yours.*

Jo shook her head. *No way. It was both of us. And I'm glad, too. We're more than friends, Daniela. We're family. Family sticks together.* She squeezed her shoulder. *It's over now, okay? No more guilt.*

Daniela nodded. *Agreed. Let me finish lunch so you can get ready.* She paused, smiling. *I'm so glad for you, you know. Andy is really great.*

Jo simply smiled and headed toward the second bedroom. As she walked past it, her gaze was drawn to the photograph of Aurora and Sarah and the boys, now hanging in pride of place over the fireplace. Carter and Daniela had been just as pleased with it as she was. She couldn't wait to talk with her family about it later this week, knowing they would be as surprised to see the family resemblance. She had asked Kevin to make another, smaller copy to show them.

She closed the bedroom door behind her, smiling at the memory of a very embarrassing incident about three years ago. She'd told some of the story to Rachel two weeks earlier, but Daniela *had* sworn her to secrecy.

She, Elsa, Carter, and Daniela had been up here together for the Fourth of July weekend. That afternoon, Sunday, the four of them had been doing different things. Elsa and Carter had been climbing together somewhere in the park, and Daniela had been pruning some of the trees around the cabin. Jo knew Carter and Elsa would be gone for hours yet, and it had been very hot. She'd come inside after working on one of the fences and taken off most of her sweaty clothes. She'd thought she was alone, so she lay down on the sofa in her bra and underwear and dozed off.

The next thing she knew, someone was kissing her, and when she opened her eyes, Daniela was partially draped over her, kneeling on the ground, entirely naked. Their eyes had met, and Daniela had suddenly realized her mistake, jumping up and running away. Jo had pulled on her shirt and shorts as fast as she could, and when Daniela emerged from the bedroom, fully dressed, they'd stared at each other for a beat before almost falling down with laughter.

When they were rational again, Daniela had made her swear on everything sacred to her that she would never tell anyone about what had happened. And she hadn't. Their secrecy had less to do with any jealousy their respective partners might have felt, and everything to do with the fact that the experience had been theirs and theirs alone. Sometimes, when she was out with Carter and Daniela, she and Daniela's eyes would meet, and she would see Daniela suddenly stifle a giggle, clearly remembering that moment. It was their private joke.

Jo sat down on the edge of one of the beds and pulled off her clothes, throwing them in a heap in the corner. The cabin was always cooler than it was outside, but the room was positively chilly right now. It was much darker back here, as well, at the rear of the house, and Jo reached over to switch on the bedside lamp. Goose bumps rose on her arms, and she rubbed them, hard, to warm them. She got to her feet and jumped up and down to warm up. The day was fairly warm, and it hadn't been this cold in here even last night, as far as she could remember. It was strange.

She had a little basin of water with soap in here, and, moving as quickly as possible, she used a rag to wash her face and under her arms, shivering as the cold water touched her skin. She'd taken a shower before she left the station, but she'd been outside, sweating, most of the time since. Her fingernail beds were filthy and her hands covered in stain, so it took her a couple of minutes of hard scrubbing to get them clean again. She ran some water through her hair and sighed. It would have to do. Hopefully Andy wouldn't mind. She must be getting used to my filth by now, Jo thought.

She was also approaching the last of her clean clothes. Originally, she'd planned to go home today, so she'd brought only one extra pair of underwear. She sniffed a few of her shirts, chose the cleanest, warmest one to re-wear, and had just pulled it over her head when someone grabbed her from behind. She let out a shriek of surprise, and suddenly a hand was over her mouth, sealing it off. She struggled, but the strong arm around her arms and waist pinned her arms inside the shirt.

The hand over her mouth tasted bitter, sweaty, and was frigidly cold. She bit into it as hard as she could and heard a grunt of pain. The hand clamped down harder, painfully pushing her lips into her teeth, and she jerked harder, swinging her head backward. It connected with what she thought was likely a chin and heard a crack. Another grunt of pain followed, and then the arm around her tightened, squeezing her so fiercely and with such viselike strength she began to have trouble breathing. She struggled harder, trying to twist free, her muffled screams barely audible. The grip on her body was too strong—she was nearly immobilized.

Little stars began to appear in her vision from lack of air, and she made herself stop struggling. Her nose was uncovered, but the arm around her chest was so constrictive she could hardly expand her lungs. Her nose whistled with the effort of trying to get enough air, and the stars increased and began to cloud her vision. Any second now, she realized, she would pass out.

Her assailant's hand, the one around her body, started to slide up, moving up from her stomach. She bucked as hard as she could, again bringing her head back with all her might. She kicked backward with one foot, connecting with a leg. None of this did anything to stop the hand, which was now clamped painfully over one of her breasts, squeezing.

The assault stopped as soon as it had begun, and her scream finally broke free. She quieted almost at once, struggled to get her arms into her sleeves, and whirled around, looking everywhere for him. The room was brightening, almost as if a cloud had moved away from the sun, but the sunshine had nothing to do with what was happening. He had come, and now he was gone again, just as he had before. He brought those shadows with him everywhere he went.

She caught a whiff of the air and wrinkled her nose. She smelled a sour odor in here—fetid, rotten, like carrion on a hot day. The room was even colder than before, and she shivered hard in the chilly air. She blew out her breath and saw it swirl in a billowing cloud in front of her face. She backed away from the smell and cold until she hit the door, still searching the room, but saw nothing there.

A knock behind her made her jump and jerk away from the door, and Daniela opened it, peering in.

Hey. I saw the others arrive out front. You ready to eat?

Daniela hadn't heard her, of course, and neither had anyone else. Jo made herself stand upright and nodded. *Sure. I'll be right there.*

Daniela's face creased with concern. *Are you okay? You're...I don't know. Different, somehow. Worried?*

Jo shook her head. *I'm fine. Just nervous.* She hated lying, but she also couldn't bring herself to tell Daniela what had just happened. The experience was still too new, too raw, and too terrifying.

Daniela nodded, and then she recoiled in disgust. *Jesus. What the hell is that smell?*

The outhouse, I think. It's just outside that window. Needs more lime.

Daniela's face was still pinched, but she seemed to accept this explanation as she walked away, leaving the cabin out the front door.

Once she was gone, Jo relaxed, almost sobbing with relief. She didn't want anyone to know what had just happened. She started shaking then, her knees going weak, and stumbled over to one of the beds, sitting down on it heavily just as her legs gave out. She continued to sit there, trembling, adrenaline coursing through her.

Finally, when the room warmed again, and the smell dissipated, she took several long breaths and rose. Her legs were a little weak, and she was worn and tired, but she felt relatively steady on her legs again. She threw one more glance behind her and left the room, closing the door behind her.

CHAPTER TWENTY-FIVE

"So you'll be in touch?" Carter asked.

"Yes, of course. I'll call you when we reach my place. Should be Wednesday evening some time."

Carter was frowning, her gaze darting back and forth between Jo and the cabin. She seemed afraid of it. Jo felt that way herself, especially after what had happened in her room this morning, but Carter's fear was somehow worse. Even with the evidence of the letters and the hidden compartment in the dresser, even with the nearly identical stories she and Meg had shared, Carter had remained a skeptic. Now, as she prepared to leave, she finally seemed to believe—almost as if she could believe now that she wouldn't be staying here any longer.

Andy put a hand on her shoulder. "Don't worry, Carter. I'll keep an eye on her."

Carter looked up into her face, and some of the fear in her eyes seemed to fade. "Okay, but please be careful."

"Don't let the ghosts get you!" Drew said, then made a spooky, ghostly sound and wiggled his fingers.

Kevin batted at his arm. "Hey! Don't be rude." He smiled at Jo. "I'm sorry. You would think he would be more understanding, given that he's so superstitious."

"Am not!"

Kevin pulled out Drew's necklace—a four-leaf clover sealed in rosin. Drew snatched it back and stuffed it under his shirt again. "So sue me. I'm Irish—we're all superstitious. That doesn't mean I believe in ghosts."

Kevin rolled his eyes. "Anyway, Jo, thanks for having us up here. I'd love to come again sometime and get some photographs for the exhibit."

Kevin was already coordinating an exhibit at the museum next summer featuring Aurora and Sarah. It would form part of a series on the queer history of Estes Park, set to run all of June.

"Your family has kept the cabin in such great shape," he said. "I don't think there's another one like it this old still standing in the whole state—maybe anywhere in the US."

Jo felt a distinct sense of pride. "Any time you want to take photos, just call me, and we'll set it up. We have to work around my cousins' schedules up here, but usually at least one weekend a month is free. You should get pictures in every season. It's gorgeous all year."

"Great. I'll call you soon, then. I'm still searching for more photographs of your great-great-grandmother and Sarah in the archive, but so far, I've found only the one you have hanging inside. The museum director mentioned another batch of photographs from that time somewhere, but we haven't uncovered them yet."

"It's possible my dad has some. I've never seen any of her before, but he inherited everything from my grandfather, so maybe we missed something."

"I'll let you know if I come across more in the archive."

All six of them were quiet for a while, staring back at the cabin. Once again, Jo couldn't help but feel a deep stab of something like betrayal. This place had been a haven her entire life. She'd looked forward to coming up here for two or three weeks with her family every summer her entire child and young adulthood. Then, when she became an adult and could come on her own, it had been like having a vacation home to run away to almost every month. Everything that had happened this week had tainted the place, possibly forever. While she would always be grateful to have learned about Aurora, an air of foreboding, of danger, now existed that hadn't been here before. She knew Carter and Daniela could sense it, and she was fairly certain the others did, too.

"Okay, then, be safe," Carter said, and gave her one last hug.

Daniela hugged her next. *Make sure you the two of you stick together. Don't do anything on your own.*

"Don't strain yourself," Drew told Andy.

Kevin sighed, giving both of them a solid hug. "Have fun. I'll call you soon, Jo."

Andy slipped an arm around her waist as they watched the four of them hike down the trail. Jo could hear Drew chatting away and the others laughing long after they'd disappeared.

Finally, Andy let go of her and walked over to the picnic table, sitting backward on it with her elbows propped up behind her. She tilted her head upward toward the sun, and Jo simply stood there, watching her, for a lengthy, breathless minute. With her long, sun-kissed neck exposed, she might have been posing for a photo shoot in a high-end beauty magazine.

She opened her eyes and grinned when she saw Jo watching her. "What?"

Jo shook her head. It was too much to put into words. "Nothing."

Andy patted the spot next to her on the seat, and Jo joined her.

"Want to tell me what's wrong?" Andy asked.

Jo flushed with guilt. "What do you mean?"

Andy frowned. "Something's been bothering you since I got here. Tell me what happened."

Jo hesitated. She looked up into her eyes, hoping she might be able to stay quiet, but Andy's face was determined, serious. She hadn't planned to tell anyone about what had happened this morning, but on the other hand, if she had to confide in one person, that person should be Andy.

"I was…attacked. In the bedroom."

"What?" Andy turned toward her fully and grabbed her hands. "What happened?"

Jo described the arm that had pinned hers and the hand clamped over her mouth, as well as the horrible stench in the cold, darkened room.

"It was him again," she said. "No doubt in my mind."

Andy's eyes were huge, frightened. "He's inside now? I thought you said he was always outside the cabin."

She shrugged. "Something must have changed."

Andy spun around, staring at the cabin. Her eyes were still wide, still scared, but as she continued to stare at it, her expression began to change. Gradually, she seemed to become determined again, and when she met Jo's eyes, Jo saw something else there, too—anger.

"Fuck him," Andy said.

The curse, coming from her, was so surprising, Jo laughed. The anger in Andy's eyes died a little, and she smiled.

"No, but seriously, Jo, fuck him. It's obvious what's happening here, right?"

She shook her head. "No. What?"

Andy took her hands again. "He's trying to scare you away. He's trying to scare everyone away. And it's working. Pretty soon, this cabin will be his, not yours."

Jo weighed these words for several seconds, recognizing the truth in them almost at once. She'd been thinking this very thing, just not quite in the same way. True, she felt differently about the cabin now— she was afraid of it, and Carter was, too. That fear came from him.

"Agreed," she finally said. She raised her shoulders. "But what are we supposed to do about it?"

"About him." Andy's voice was firm.

Jo nodded. "Right. About him."

Andy peered into the woods, her eyes distant and unfocused. A little line of concentration appeared between her eyes. Finally, she focused back on Jo.

"We drive him away."

"That would be nice, but how?"

"Listen—you found those letters, right?"

Jo nodded.

"You found them, and then suddenly everything was normal again inside, right?"

Jo nodded again.

Andy's expression was bright. "It's almost like because you found the letters, everything was okay. Like Aurora wanted you to find them—that's what you said."

"Right…" She could almost follow where Andy was going, but not quite.

"So you found them, and Aurora was finally quiet again. You found the letters, you discovered her secret. She showed it to you on purpose."

"Okay, yes, I agree. But where does that leave us now? What does that have to do with Henry?"

Andy's eyes were still bright. "Don't you see? It's the same thing! We have to—"

Something finally clicked, and Jo cut in. "We have to find—"

"Exactly! We have to find—"

"Whatever he left."

It all seemed so simple now. Aurora had shown her how to solve the problem in the only way she knew how—by revealing her own secrets. She, or whatever was left of her, had waited, all this time, for the perfect audience for her story—a descendant very much like herself.

Jo had squeezed Andy's hands, but now, as she realized the

implications of this idea, her stomach dropped. "Okay, but how? Where do we look?"

Andy's face fell, and she shook her head. "I have no idea. But there must be something. Don't you think that's what this is all about?"

Jo sighed. "I do. I totally agree, but that doesn't help us. Aurora showed me over and over again how to locate the letters, and even then, I was almost too stupid, too scared to find them. I don't have any idea where to uncover whatever Henry left. He hasn't given any signals." She gestured around them, at the cabin and then at the woods. "Whatever he left could be anywhere."

"You don't have any ideas?"

Jo started to shake her head and then paused. She'd felt a version of Henry's compelling force when they'd been camping outside the cabin. It hadn't been very strong at the start, but in retrospect, he had probably been the reason she'd wandered into the woods on her own in the dark. She'd recognized his compulsion as an outside force, as something strong and dark and evil, lurking in the woods. And Meg had also felt it—at the cemetery.

She got to her feet. "Follow me."

She walked with purpose, Andy behind her. Now that she had a plan, she wasn't afraid. Like Andy, her feelings had drifted into something like anger. Henry had been abusive in life, and he was apparently still abusive in death. She refused to let him ruin this place for her or anyone else. It didn't belong to him. It was hers as much as it had been Aurora's. He had no part in it except through force.

Andy was right. Fuck him.

They passed the well, and Jo edged around it, walking off the side of the trail to put as much space as possible between it and her. She refused even to look at it. Her experience with the well was still too frightening to think about, and she didn't want to let it distract her.

The day was sunny, the sky almost cloudless, but the summer heat was definitely a thing of the past. It happened that quickly up here, one season turning into the next within a few days. Jo had experienced it before. It was still fairly warm out, but nothing like it had been even a week ago.

Andy was staring around the little cemetery, curious. Watching her, Jo had a flash of déjà vu. It had been just two weeks ago when she was here with Rachel and Meg, but it seemed like forever. This had been one of the longest two weeks of her life. Like Rachel, Andy knelt down next to each grave, reading the inscriptions. She paused the longest at the grave for Aurora and Sarah, tracing the words with her fingers. She looked up at Jo with tears in her eyes.

"It's so beautiful. What a lovely remembrance of them."

Jo was more touched by Andy's emotion than the words, but she nodded. "I couldn't be happier for them. They get to spend eternity here, together, in this beautiful place."

Andy got to her feet. "After all they went through—they deserve it."

They were quiet for a while, and Jo let the peace of the space settle into her. After a while, she was no longer angry or afraid. Henry couldn't do anything to Aurora and Sarah now. This spot was theirs, absolutely.

"You think there's something here?" Andy said, gesturing around them.

Jo sighed. "No—not any more. It's too nice. I guess I just thought, since Meg was pushed over here…"

"Ah. Okay, you're right. That makes sense."

Jo let her gaze drift over to the edge of the cliff, and she suddenly didn't feel as certain as she had a moment ago. She'd never been afraid of heights, but something about that edge made her stomach feel tight and sick. She glanced at Andy and saw her eyes rooted on the edge as well.

"I feel it too," Andy whispered.

Jo started walking toward the cliff, and Andy gasped and grabbed her shoulder. Jo turned to her, confused.

"Sorry," Andy said. "Just…be careful."

"I will, but stay here in case something happens."

Jo continued toward the drop-off, getting down on her hands and knees a couple of feet from the edge and crawling the last of the distance. That scared, nauseated feeling was even stronger here, and she swallowed the bile rising in her throat. She peered over the edge, spotting the ledge Meg had landed on some fifteen or twenty feet down. Nothing there. She inched back and away from the precipice again and sat back on her heels, shaking all over, a deep terror rising in her like a frigid wind.

"See anything?" Andy called.

Jo kept her eyes forward and shook her head. "Nothing. Just the ledge."

"I didn't see anything down there, either. I mean, when I went down to get Meg."

"I don't think it's down there."

"What?" Andy asked, obviously closer than before.

"Whatever it is must be here somewhere. Up at the top, near the edge. Otherwise, it would stand out."

She licked her lips, swallowing again, suddenly afraid she might throw up. It wasn't exactly nausea per se. It was simply a horror so deep inside her that she reacted with something like illness. Every inch of her screamed for her to run away, but she wouldn't let that happen.

She looked around on the ground near the edge, searching for some sign of something different—some disturbance that might suggest that something had happened here at one time. The ground, however, was a uniform, rocky earth. So close to the edge, there was almost no grass, nothing growing—nothing but sand and soil. Except for one little red bush, the ground here was barren and dead.

She focused on the bush and frowned at it. That feeling, the cold terror, grew stronger, rising in her throat, threatening to send the contents of her stomach up and out at any second. She pushed down on the feeling and continued to stare at the bush. It was strange—the only living thing for several yards—and scraggly—three or four branches, maybe two feet high. It would have to be something hardy to live here, so far from the water or good soil. She was no botanist, but she did work with plants a lot at her job, and she'd never seen this kind before.

She tried to grab what she thought was a leaf and then hissed with pain, pulling her fingers away.

"What?" Andy said, just behind her now.

"Thorn," Jo said, peering at her fingers. The thorn had torn the skin on three of her fingertips. Blood was already rising and beading at the surface. She sucked on her fingers, but the blood returned at once when she pulled them away from her mouth.

"Son of a bitch," she whispered.

Suddenly Andy knelt down next to her. Jo watched as she dug around in her jacket pockets and pulled out a set of thin, woolen gloves. She shrugged. "Better than nothing," she said and held them out for Jo.

Jo slipped them on and inched a little closer to the bush. She leaned closer, searching for a good place to grab it, and from there she could see that the entire thing was made of thorns and brambles. It was the color of old, dried blood, a murky, brownish red. She'd rarely seen anything so ugly.

She threw a quick glance at Andy, grabbed the bush at its base, and yanked upward. The gloves snagged on the thorns, which tore into her skin beneath, but she continued to pull on it, wrenching back and forth to loosen the roots. Gradually, the bush came up and out of the ground, first with reluctance, and then all at once, sending bits of rocks and soil flying off the edge of the cliff. The thorns were stuck to her gloves, and she slid them off her hands as she tossed the bush aside.

"Bastard," she told it.

"You okay?" Andy asked, taking her hands. They were covered in tiny jagged cuts, all over her palms and fingertips.

"It's fine. I'll wash them later."

Andy kissed them and let them go. "What's in there?"

Jo turned to the hole she'd made and spotted something at once. Like the bush, it was dark brownish red, but only a little corner of it was visible in the hole the bush had covered. She tried to see it more clearly by moving closer, but it was almost entirely covered with dirt. Gingerly, she brushed some of the dirt away, revealing a cylindrical container. Hesitating no longer, she grabbed it and pulled it out of the hole.

It was an old coffee can. Unlike the vacuumed-sealed containers of today, it had a circular, metal lid. The brand was unrecognizable, and the cylinder had rusted with time.

Jo inched away from the edge before getting to her feet again, too wary to be caught standing anywhere near the precipice. It would take only a second, and then she would, at best, end up like Meg. And at worst...

Andy had gotten up as well and was staring at the can. Jo held it out for her, and she took it, frowning. "What on earth?"

"I don't know. Maybe something's inside. But let's look at it in the cabin."

Andy nodded, quickly. "Let's." Her eyes drifted to the drop-off. "I don't want to be here anymore."

Jo couldn't agree more.

CHAPTER TWENTY-SIX

Using a vinegar solution and a cotton ball, Jo was able to loosen the lid of the coffee can after about a minute of trying. It came off with a screech, and she set it down on the coffee table in front of her. Though still early afternoon, the weak daylight coming in through the windows made it difficult to see, so she and Andy dragged all the lamps out into the living room. Their warm light of the lamps made the room feel much homier, much safer, somehow, and her anxiety settled down into something more like excitement at their find.

"What's in it?" Andy asked, her impatience clear in her voice.

Jo peered inside the coffee can, confused. It appeared to be an opaque cellophane bag, but that shouldn't be the case. She didn't know when exactly plastic was in wide-scale use, but it was long after her great-great-grandparents were around. A distinct regret made her stomach sink. Despite the seemingly supernatural guidance she'd been given in order to find this can, maybe they'd just found some old trash.

When she reached in to get out the plastic bag, however, she realized her mistake. It wasn't plastic at all, but rather a package of waxed paper. She set it down on the coffee table, moving the coffee can aside, and she and Andy stared at it for a long time. Finally, Andy nudged her.

"Well, go on, then. See what's inside."

The waxed paper had been wrapped in such a way that it resembled a kind of large envelope. Jo was afraid that if she tried to open it, it would rip, perhaps destroying something crucial. Now she wished Kevin were here to help—he would probably know how to do this in a way that preserved the packaging. But then again, he wasn't here, and the wrapping did in fact look like normal waxed paper—a bit thicker than that sold in stores today, but plain nonetheless.

She flexed her fingers a couple of times and then picked up the package again, spinning it slowly to search for seams. The movement loosened one corner on its own, and she used that as her starting point, setting the package down on the table again and basically unrolling the waxed-paper covering.

Several papers were stuffed inside, each preserved in nearly pristine condition. Jo recognized one of them as a telegram from seeing one a few days ago. She picked it up first, holding the little envelope up to the light.

She read aloud what she saw. "To Mr. S. Bell, San Francisco, and then there's some numbers. Some kind of postal code, I think, and the words General Delivery."

"That's to Sarah, right?" Andy asked.

"Yes. She used that alias in the last telegram we saw."

She met Andy's eyes, and they frowned at each other. Jo didn't know what she'd been expecting inside this can, but it certainly hadn't been more of the correspondence between Aurora and Sarah. All their hypotheses about what they would find had just been thrown out the window. They'd been hoping to find something Henry Lemke had left behind, not more from the two women.

"What's the date?" Andy asked.

"Doesn't say on the outside. Let me see the telegram." Carefully, working as gently as she could, she slid out a small folded, yellow sheet from inside the envelope. Like the one she'd seen before, this telegram was handwritten, but far more difficult to read. She puzzled over the letters, trying to make sense of them.

"I think it says, 'Come at once. Love, Rory.'" She stared at it a while longer. "I can barely read it." She squinted at the words. "Looks like it was sent from Estes in July something—12 or 13, I think—1889." She paused and counted on her fingers. "That would make sense. Sarah sent her letter to Aurora in June, right? So assuming the letter got to Estes by the end of the month or early July, Aurora could have sent this when she got it."

Andy smiled. "She didn't waste any time, that's for sure. Sarah must have come right away."

"Oh?"

Andy nodded. "Remember, she's on the next year's census—1890—which was probably done in January, February, or March, at the latest. She must have set off for Colorado right away.

It would have taken a while to get from California to Estes Park in those days, even with trains. I know there were some fast trains, but those were very expensive. Aurora wrote that it took a long time from Chicago, and I'm sure it was even worse from San Francisco. Sarah must have gotten here by the end of the summer, or early fall, though, or she wouldn't have been here in time to show up on the census. The roads were closed in the winter, after all."

Jo nodded, though still perplexed. "I still don't get why this telegram was buried out there in a coffee can in the cemetery. Why not keep all their letters together? It's weird."

Andy gestured at the other papers. "Maybe the rest of this explains it."

Jo set the telegram aside and examined the next thing she found inside. "Oh wow, how cool!" she said, showing it to Andy.

"A train ticket?"

"Yes. Isn't it neat?"

"What's it say?"

The ticket was surprisingly small, and the print so fine, Jo had to hold it up mere inches from her face. "It's a kind of fill-in-the-blank deal, I guess, so the railroad could change things for each passenger. I can't quite read the first line, but the next says second class, and the last one is Salt Lake City. I assume that's the destination."

"Maybe the route to Colorado went that way, rather than through the mountains," Andy suggested.

Jo nodded, still squinting at it. "Yes, exactly. I think this first line says Sacramento. So the train went almost due east between those two cites. We'd have to find a train map for that time to make sure, I suppose, but I'm betting that's how it worked."

"Any dates on there?"

Jo shook her head. "That's all it says, but there are more tickets here." She picked up the next one. "This one is a different train line. It says Salt Lake to Cheyenne, second class again." She read the last line and frowned. "But this doesn't make any sense." She held the ticket out to Andy, pointing at the confusing line.

Andy had to hold it close to her face to read it, and when she finished, she frowned at Jo, her brows knit. "No, it doesn't. The year must be wrong."

"Right? We know Sarah was here by 1890, so how could she have traveled later? That ticket says 1891, right?"

Andy nodded, her brows still lowered. "I mean, I guess the one could be a badly written nine. It could say 1889."

Jo picked up the last ticket in the pile and shook her head. "This one says 1891, too. Cheyenne to Denver."

"But how could that be? Did Sarah go back to California for some reason?"

Jo lifted her shoulders. "It's possible. But why?"

"Maybe to check in on Henry?"

Jo shook her head. "That seems dangerous. I mean, he was clearly off track. He either thought he'd eventually find Rory in San Francisco, or he might have given up by then. Why would she go there and risk being seen or caught?"

"It *would* explain how he managed to get here, though. Maybe he did see her and followed her here."

"I suppose." This explanation didn't seem to fit, somehow, but Jo didn't have any other ideas, so she didn't argue.

"What's that last thing?" Andy asked, pointing.

Besides the tickets and the telegram, the package from the coffee container held a large envelope. It had been folded in half to fit inside, but the waterproofing from the can and wax paper had preserved it perfectly—better, in fact, than the yellowing letters between Aurora and Sarah. The paper was also a better quality than those letters—the envelope thick and solid. Jo read the front and back folds, and her stomach dropped.

"Holy shit. It's addressed to Henry Lemke in San Francisco."

Andy sat forward, seemingly enthralled. "Who's it from?"

"Pinkerton."

"The detective agency?"

Jo nodded. Her heart was still racing, the envelope trembling in her hands.

"Want me to read it?" Andy asked.

Jo handed it to her without a word, and Andy lifted the fold and pulled out what looked like three sheets of paper. She began reading the first sheet, her eyebrows rising higher and higher the longer she read.

Jo touched her hand. "Could you read it out loud?"

Andy smiled at her. "Sorry." She cleared her throat. "Dear Sir."

❖

June 1, 1891
Dear Sir,

I write to inform you of the successful conclusion of our investigation into the search for your wife, Mrs. Aurora Lemke, née Anderson, and her some-time companion, Miss Sarah Bell, both of Chicago, Illinois.

At your initial interview with the detectives at our San Francisco office last January, you suggested we start with the latter. That suggestion has led us to the former.

Miss Sarah Bell, alias S. Bell, alias Mr. S. Bell, was traced from Chicago to San Francisco soon after your own arrival in that city.

Upon arrival in San Francisco, Miss Bell as Mister Bell procured work at a tannery mere blocks from your home and place of employment. Further investigation and extensive questioning revealed a local apartment where "Mister" Bell was living, two streets away from your own. Interviews with and payments to Bell's coworkers and the general cleaning and board mistress of Bell's living establishment revealed the following:

1) That Miss Bell (known as Mister Bell) was actively pursuing and observing someone in the city. Further investigation and local interviews made it clear that Bell was watching someone at both your place of work and at your place of residence, suggesting that it was you Bell had pursued and watched. This last is a supposition, but we believe it a valid one, nonetheless. Insofar as you were searching for her, you can also understand that she was searching for you, found you, and observed you for some months.

2) Miss Bell, once summoned by your wife, Mrs. Aurora Lemke, thereafter left San Francisco and joined her in her new place of residence in Estes Park, Colorado.

Evidence for (2) is provided in this envelope in the form of a telegram provided (with payment) by the said cleaning mistress of "Mister" Bell's apartment, left behind in her hasty departure. The telegram will reveal that your wife, aka Rory, asked for Miss Bell to join her in Colorado in July of 1889. Subsequent inquiry along these lines provided definitive evidence that both women can still be found in that city, Estes Park, under their own names, as of the date of this document.

The following pages will give you a detailed description of our methods and the expenses occurred therein, as well as a detailed map regarding the establishments and the apartment mentioned in San Francisco in relationship to your home. You will also find the remainder of the retainer you provided here as a bank cheque, payable to you in full at any reputable banking establishment in all states and US territories.

It has been our pleasure to serve you. Should you have any questions regarding our methods or the costs incurred, please visit or write to your nearest Pinkerton office with your case number and this entire document.

Our sincerest pleasure,

The Pinkerton National Detective Agency

After a brief glance at it, Andy held the rest of the document out to Jo, and she flipped through it almost numbly. The methods detailed here suggested bribery, coercion, and occasional violence to achieve their means. While the Pinkertons had a much better reputation now, Jo remembered from some historical documentary that they had been something like a paramilitary force at times, employed as violent strikebreakers and semi-professional law enforcement in the later nineteenth century. It didn't surprise her to read that they had done whatever was necessary to track down their woman, in this case.

"Jesus Christ," she finally said, her voice almost a whisper.

"So Sarah led him right here," Andy said.

"Out of carelessness. If she hadn't left that telegram…" Then what? She scratched her cheek. Clearly the contents of this coffee can revealed that Henry had tracked his wife here, but what had happened after that?

"Is that all?" Andy asked, moving the papers aside. "Nothing else?"

Jo shook her head. "I've already looked. I'm surprised this stuff survived at all. Why would he bury it out there? In that spot, of all places?"

Andy seemed as lost as she was and didn't reply.

Jo shifted through the contents of the coffee can again, frustrated to the point of anger. They seemed to find nothing but more puzzles. Why couldn't anything be easy? Why hadn't Aurora or Sarah simply written everything down? The thought gave her pause, and her anger drained away almost at once, replaced with a cold dread as she sat there considering the implications of Henry's sudden arrival in Estes Park.

Someone wouldn't write something down for a lot of reasons. After all, it wasn't as if anyone would know Jo's day-to-day life in the future. The two women had been together by 1891. Why would they have to write letters to each other anymore? They hadn't found any diaries, so why *would* they have written about Henry's appearance, especially if something had happened? She stood up, suddenly breaking into a chilling sweat.

Andy jumped. "What? What is it? Did you think of something?"

Jo hesitated. The idea, which had been so clear, had slipped away before she could grasp it. She shook her head, almost groaning with frustration. "Damn it. Just for a minute, I thought I knew…I thought I had it, but now I'm afraid I'm leaping to conclusions." She sat back down and took Andy's hands. "Look—let's say we're Rory and Sally."

Andy grinned. "Okay, but I'm Sally."

Jo grinned back at her. "Sure—you're Sally, and I'm Rory. After months apart, we're finally reunited. Time passes, and we think we're in the clear—no cruel, abusive husband to beat me, you, or the kids."

"And our own place—somewhere that's ours, something we've earned."

"Exactly," Jo said, glad Andy was playing along without explanation. "More time passes—long enough to make our business a real success. Something we can live on, together, and support our two boys."

Andy squeezed her hands. "I like this story."

Jo nodded, and then that same cold dread swept over her.

Andy frowned. "What's the matter?"

Jo licked her lips. When she spoke, she was almost whispering, almost as if someone was listening to them. "Then let's say my husband shows up—all of a sudden—totally unexpected. He might have even walked up that same damn trail we use."

Andy's face fell. "That would be awful."

"And I'm sure he was really angry—furious, even. Here we are, happy as clams, and he's been hunting us for years. He probably charged right inside this cabin without bothering to knock. He might have even tried to hurt one of us again."

Andy was even paler now. She stood and walked over to the photograph hanging above the fireplace. "Maybe he hurt you. Maybe he gave you the scar there on your face." She pointed at the picture of Aurora and traced a line down the side of her cheek, matching the scar shown on the face in the photo.

Again, Jo's stomach knotted. She and Andy stared at each other for a long time, not speaking.

"What would you do?" Jo finally asked. "If he did that to me?"

Andy didn't hesitate. "I'd kill him."

CHAPTER TWENTY-SEVEN

Jo sat back on the couch, feeling as if someone had just knocked the wind out of her. "So would I."

Andy's face was still tense, and she plopped down again, taking Jo's hands.

"You think they killed him?"

Jo lifted her shoulders. "I mean, I don't know, but it would explain a lot of things."

"Like what?"

Jo gave her a weak smile. "It would explain why he's so angry— so upset."

"An avenging spirit," Andy said, smiling slightly.

"Exactly."

Andy's smile faded and she nodded. "It fits."

Jo sighed and stood up, her anxiety making her restless. She started pacing, hands behind her back. "It does fit, but so would a lot of other explanations."

"Such as?"

"Maybe he never made it here. Or maybe he did, and they managed to make him leave. Or maybe someone warned them he was in town, and he was driven away somehow, or arrested." Jo stopped pacing and met Andy's eyes. "How could we ever know, one way or the other?"

Andy patted the spot next to her on the couch, and after hesitating, Jo rejoined her.

"Look," Andy said, "you're right, of course. We can't know for sure. We can know only what we can see. The stuff in the can suggests that he was here. A photo two years later shows Aurora, Sarah, and the boys—no Henry. Sometime between 1891 and 1893, he disappeared. I can't think of any reason he would have left in peace after searching for his wife for so long, especially if she was living with someone else, and a woman, to boot. He must have known what that meant."

"Maybe they paid him off," Jo said. "From what Kevin said about their business, they were making a lot of money by then."

"How about bank records? Maybe we could see if they made a big withdrawal or something."

Jo sighed. "Sounds like another wild-goose chase." She frowned. "Anyway, I just can't imagine him taking a bribe, not after hunting all over the country for her. If anything, I'm surprised Aurora and Sarah survived."

"So we're back to the other idea: they killed him."

Jo rubbed her face. "Jesus. Can you even imagine?"

Andy nodded, going pale again. "I can. I absolutely can."

Jo's stomach fluttered, and she rubbed the back of Andy's hands with her thumbs. Andy's eyes were distant, unfocused. Then her eyes filled with tears, and she blinked quickly and shook her head as if to clear it.

"I'm sorry."

Jo shook her head. "Don't be. I'm the one who's sorry. I'm sorry this whole thing," she gestured around the room, "is bringing up so much for you. I wish I could go back in time and stop it."

Andy focused on her again, and Jo saw something dark in the beautiful blue depths of her eyes. Her troubled expression cleared and settled into a more obvious fury. Color rose to her cheeks and her lips tightened.

"At the end," she whispered, "after the last time she hit me…I had a gun. Left over from my days in the service. I got it out and put a bullet in it." She paused, her eyes filling with tears again. "I almost did it, Jo. I almost killed her. I stood outside our bedroom door all night, wanting to go in there and blow her brains out. I don't know how I stopped myself." She licked her lips, swallowing a few times as if to get her breath back. "In the end, I made myself leave. I didn't take anything. I didn't tell her. I just left. It was the worst day of my life."

Tears slipped out of Jo's eyes without warning. She pulled Andy into a rough embrace. Andy's shoulders were shaking with silent sobs, and Jo's sorrow felt fathomless. Finally, she drew back, gripping Andy's shoulders.

"You didn't deserve that, Andy. I hope you know that."

Andy nodded, wiping her face, her eyes rooted on her hands twisting in her lap. "I know. I know now, anyway. It took me a long time to get over her, Jo, over what she did to me. Sometimes I still wake up, wondering what mood she's in, how I can make her happy… happy enough to avoid…" She sighed. "I still can't believe it's over, not all the time, anyway." She looked up, that dark anger back, burning in her eyes. "But yes—I can understand wanting to kill someone. I can understand, and I can believe it, because I've been there. In some ways, that's the worst part—that she drove me to that. That's not me, Jo, not me at all. I was in the service, but I'm really a pacifist. She made me like that—angry, aggressive, broken."

A rage that swept through Jo in a wave of heat replaced her sorrow. The very idea that someone, some bitch, had done that to Andy, had made her feel like murder was the only option, was so horrifying she could hardly breathe.

"So they killed him," Jo said simply.

Andy nodded. "I think so, yes." Her brows lowered. "No—I know it."

Jo let herself absorb this idea, surprised that she could accept this possibility with few qualms now. She glanced over at Andy, whose eyes were distant again, unfocused, and the tender sympathy she felt suddenly overwhelmed her. She had to blink again, and the movement made Andy glance up. Her face fell even farther when she saw Jo's tears.

"Please don't cry, Jo," she said. "It's all in the past now. We're here. I'm safe. I'll never see her again. She can't hurt me anymore."

Jo managed a weak nod and wiped her eyes. "Okay, Andy. And my offer still stands—whenever you want to talk about her—"

"I know. And I will, Jo, just not right now. I-I feel like we're on the brink of something. I don't want to let her derail this. I almost feel like…" She knit her brows, frowning.

"What?"

Andy met her eyes, her jaw clenched. "I'm part of this now, whatever's happening here. I was destined to be here with you. My past brought me here." She glanced away, her cheeks pink. "I sound superstitious and hokey, but—"

"No. You're right. You're part of this as much as I am. I would never have gotten this far without you." She gestured at the room. "This place…seems to have planned for us to be here together right now."

They were quiet for a long time. Jo wanted to ask Andy about her past, about the woman who had hurt her, but she managed to keep her mouth shut. What she'd said several times needed to be true—she would be ready to hear the details whenever Andy was willing to tell her, but she wouldn't force her. It was Andy's story, not hers.

Andy examined the contents of the coffee can, sifting through them, rereading everything, her features calm. Jo decided to heat some water for something caffeinated and hot, hoping the urge to ask questions would fade.

The electric kettle was out of water, and when Jo checked the inside of the little bucket she'd filled this morning, she groaned. It too was empty.

"Goddamn it," she said. She got down on her knees in front of the sink, opened the cabinet, and saw that she'd left the wrench in there from earlier. At least that was something—she wouldn't have to go looking for it. She scooted forward, wrench in hand, and then hit her head on the edge of the cabinet so hard she saw stars.

"Fuck!" she yelled, leaning back and slapping a hand over the pain.

"What happened?" Andy called, clearly alarmed.

"I hit my head trying to—" She stopped speaking. An idea rose in her mind, so swiftly and with such assurance, she was certain she was right. She had to be.

"Holy shit," she whispered.

Andy appeared around the kitchen counter. "What is it? Are you okay?"

Jo almost leapt to her feet, racing over to Andy and drawing her into a quick embrace. She kissed her once, hard, and Andy laughed.

"What is it? You look, I don't know, like you won the lottery or something."

"I know where he is," Jo said. "I know where to find the body."

Why hadn't she thought of it before? Earlier, when they'd walked by the well toward the cemetery, she'd avoided it. Her evasion had even seemed reasonable—she was afraid of it. After all, she'd nearly died there. Her death would have seemed like a suicide, even, which would have been devastating for her friends and family. But now she knew better.

She started gathering her gear and gestured for Andy to do the same. Andy, however, stood there, unmoving.

Jo sighed. "It's the well. It was always the well."

Andy's face cleared, and she nodded. "Of course." She opened her pack to check her gear as Jo finished examining her rope, harness, and other climbing equipment. When they finished, Jo gestured at the door, and Andy followed her outside.

"The explanation was there all along," she told Andy, hurrying down the trail, Andy just behind her.

"What was?"

"The other part of all this—the water. The sink was turning on by itself—Daniela and I both saw that, and we knew it wasn't some mechanical malfunction. Something was turning it on."

"Or someone," Andy added.

"Exactly—someone. It was another clue. Aurora was telling us where to go."

From behind, Andy grabbed her shoulder, making her stop. Jo turned around to face her, her impatience making her almost angry. Andy, clearly seeing some of this emotion, held up her hands.

"Hold on, will you? Don't you think we're rushing into something? Shouldn't we talk about this first?"

Jo almost groaned. Why couldn't she see it? "What do you mean?"

Andy's eyes hardened into fierce shards of turquoise, and she touched Jo's arm. "Just listen for a sec, okay? Think about what we're doing."

Jo stared at her, her frustration mounting.

Andy sighed. "Jo, I get it, and I agree. Something's in the well. But what's the plan? You're just going to climb inside and find his body? Then what?"

Jo opened her mouth to protest and then snapped it shut. She had a point. "What do you suggest?"

Andy stared off into the woods, hands on her hips. Here, in the dim light of the cabin, the blue of her eyes was almost dark and frigid, like a crevice in a glacier. Finally, she looked at Jo, that hard azure focusing in on her like blue ice. "Okay. As I said, I agree with you. But consider the facts." She held up one hand and began counting off on her fingers. "The last time you went near the well, you lost control of yourself. You almost jumped in on your own. You felt that same cold, saw that same darkness Meg saw before she was pushed off the cliff, smelled that smell."

"Okay."

"But haven't things changed since then?"

Jo frowned. "How so?"

Andy met her gaze and held it. "Henry's stronger now, Jo. You can see him, for one thing, and he's not afraid. He can even come inside the cabin."

Jo mulled these points over and finally recognized Andy's words for what they were: the truth. Andy, as if sensing this change, took a step toward her, her eyes softening even further. She held her hands out, and after hesitating, Jo took them in hers. Something inside her relaxed, and the rest of her impatience faded away. Andy rewarded her with a broad, warm smile.

"Thanks," Jo finally said.

"For what?"

"For stopping me. I was ready to climb down there this second. But you're right. We need to be careful. We need some kind of plan."

Andy glanced at her watch. "We still have some daylight left, but not much—two hours, tops."

"I don't think I can wait until tomorrow. I won't sleep."

Andy hesitated. "I also don't think it's *safe* to wait. Not when just the two of us are up here."

"What should we do? Do you have an idea?"

Andy's eyes hardened into deep blue again. "You're not going to like it."

Jo waited, staring at her. Finally, Andy spoke again. "I'm the climbing expert, Jo. I'm the one who needs to go down in the well."

Jo let go of Andy's hands and took a step away from her. "No fucking way. I would never let you—"

"Why? Because it's too dangerous? How is it any different for you?"

"Because…" Jo shook her head again. "It just is."

Andy rolled her eyes. "It isn't different, Jo, and like I said, I'm the one who knows what she's doing."

"I can climb—I've done it lots of times."

"Yes, you have. But you don't have as much experience as I do. I teach people how to do it, for God's sake—how to avoid panic, what to do in an emergency. I've experienced just about everything that can happen to a climber."

Jo's eyes filled with tears. She couldn't allow this, *wouldn't* allow this to happen. The idea terrified her so much she wanted to wrap Andy in a blanket and hide her away somewhere.

She took a deep breath, trying to calm her fears. "Andy, I hear what you're saying, but I can't let you do it. The risk is too high, and it's my problem, not yours."

Andy looked like she wanted to stamp her foot. "Don't you remember? I'm part of this, too, Jo. Not as much as you, but I'm definitely in this somehow. I have been, almost since the beginning."

Jo was shaking her head, but Andy cut her off before she could say anything. "Jo, I'm not arguing with you. It has to be me. And you're not letting me—you're helping me." Those blue eyes were back on her, but her gaze was even, her face relaxed. She seemed confident now, sure of herself, no longer angry. She stood up straighter, squaring her shoulders. "We'll do it my way or not at all."

Jo's stomach clenched. "What do you mean?"

"Exactly what I said. Either I go down, or I'm not helping you. I won't let you kill yourself."

Jo went cold, so full of rage, every muscle grew rigid. She clenched her fists and started to shake.

"Fine," she managed to say, her voice almost a whisper. "Go."

Andy flinched. "What?"

"Leave. I can do it on my own."

Jo started walking away, hardly able to see for the blood pounding in her veins.

"Jo!" Andy called, already far behind. "Jo! Wait! Don't do this!"

Jo was vaguely aware of running steps catching up to her and two strong arms grabbing her from behind. Like the thing in the bedroom this morning, Andy pinned her, and Jo wrenched against her, thrashing around in her arms. Andy let go unexpectedly, and Jo stumbled forward, falling to her knees. Andy was next to her, kneeling, in seconds. Jo turned to her, ready to push her away, and then their eyes met, and she burst into tears. Andy drew her into her arms, kissed the side of her head, and Jo let herself relax into her, hugging her in return.

Andy pulled away first, her eyes teary and red. "Jesus Christ, you're stubborn."

Jo managed a weak laugh. "It's one of my character traits."

"More like a flaw. Damn. You were actually ready to leave me, weren't you? You would have done it on your own if I didn't help you."

Jo nodded, and Andy shook her head. "You're crazy. You know that, right?"

Jo sniffed and wiped her face. "You're the one who's crazy, Andy, if you think I'd let you go down there instead of me."

Andy threw her head back, sighing dramatically. "For God's sake, Jo. How is it any different if I let you do it? Don't you know how much I care for you? It would kill me if—"

Jo stopped her mouth with a kiss. Andy tensed against her and then relaxed into it, kissing her back. Jo put her desperation, her horror into that kiss. She had to convince her, once and for all, to listen to her.

After a long while, Andy pulled away and then rested her forehead against Jo's. "Okay, Jo. We'll do it your way. I know I'll regret it, but I'll do it. I'll help you."

Jo tried to hug her, but Andy pushed her away. "I have one condition."

"What? Anything."

Andy met her eyes, her expression hard and serious. "You have to listen to everything I say, Jo, and I mean everything. This is life and death here. You know that."

Jo nodded, her relief so great she would have agreed to anything. "I'll listen. I promise."

Andy continued to stare at her for a long beat before she finally nodded and sighed, getting to her feet. She held a hand out for Jo and helped her up.

"Our first fight, and we end up in a wrestling match."

Jo managed to laugh. "Too bad it's the wrong kind of wrestling."

Andy smiled in return, but her expression faded. "I'm scared, Jo."

"Me, too."

"You better not get hurt."

"I won't. I promise."

They continued toward the well, Jo's heart now racing. Andy was right. The stakes couldn't be higher. This could very well be the end of everything.

The well came into view, and they both stopped. Andy clenched her hand, squeezing it almost painfully, and Jo squeezed back. She started walking first, extending her arm backward until Andy finally joined her, and they walked side by side, closing in on the circle of stones.

It was late afternoon now, sliding into evening, but to Jo, it suddenly seemed much earlier, much brighter outside. Some of the tension she'd been holding in her body relaxed, and as they walked the last distance toward the well, she caught a whiff of something sweet, almost cloying, coming from the woods. She paused some ten feet from the well, turning her head toward the trees, inhaling deeply.

"What is that scent?" Andy asked, her voice strangely slurred.

For Jo, it seemed to take an eon to rotate her head in Andy's direction. She saw little trailers in her vision as the world caught up with her eyes, almost as if what she could see was stuck a few seconds behind. When her vision finally matched the direction of her eyes, she was amused to see Andy's sleepy, almost dopey grin. Andy blinked a few times, slowly, almost as if she were having a hard time staying awake.

"That scent...it reminds me of..." Andy said, then yawned, her mouth incredibly wide. She yodeled and slowly closed her mouth. Her lips were twisted in a crooked, drunken grin, and she shook her head as if to clear it, then staggered slightly. "Think I need to sit down."

Her words were slurring together, yet Jo eventually understood what she'd said. Jo laughed, so tickled by Andy's stupor she could hardly stay upright from her laughter. She watched as Andy sat down on the ground, quite heavily, then pitched over on her side in a heap. Jo laughed again, so hard she bent double, clutching her stomach and short of breath. She lost her balance and then was down on the ground.

The sun was almost too bright for her eyes, and her laughter finally dissolved into light chuckles as she closed them against the glare. The warmth felt nice on her face—neither hot nor cold, but comfortable. The perfect nap weather, in fact. She'd managed to tumble on top of a soft pile of fallen leaves, and she lay back, making herself comfortable by scooching her back and shoulders into the pile. She forced her eyes open again and stared up at the blindingly blue sky, smiling to herself. Her eyelids were growing heavy again, and she let them close. Sleep had never seemed more appealing.

CHAPTER TWENTY-EIGHT

This was Rory's favorite time of year. Snow still dotted the ground in small patches, and while they could probably expect one or two more snow showers, the winter—the real winter—was over. It would be a couple of weeks until they might consider digging up the ground for their vegetable garden, but the sun didn't seem to care about that today. It was bright and warm, nearly summery, and the fruit trees were in full blossom. Their scent was heavy, even here half a mile from the orchard. She had a list of tasks to accomplish, but that was for later. Today was for rest. She could very easily sit here reading on her porch forever—it was that pretty. She might take a little walk later with Sally, but for now this was exactly where she wanted to be.

She picked up her book and rocked back in her chair. Sally had built this rocker for her as a surprise. She'd been so secretive while she was working on it, so sly even, Rory had at first worried that she was hiding something significant from her. Then, when she'd finally presented the rocker their first day of spring celebration last month—bashful and proud—Rory hadn't been able to stop herself. She'd kissed her right in front of everyone at her party. But what of it? All of their friends knew what they were, as of course the boys did. And it had been all right—no one was upset. And Sally turned such a pretty shade of pink when she was embarrassed.

The door to the cabin opened, and Sally and the boys nearly tumbled outside together. They were laughing over some shared joke, little Robert almost squealing with joy. Rory took the moment she was unseen to observe the three of them—her boys and her lover. John was tall now, taller than his father had ever been. Almost a man now, he showed the first signs of a mustache on his upper lip. All three of them were dressed in their buckskin leathers, guns slung over their shoulders.

Sally spotted her first, and her grin transformed into a wide smile. Then, almost as if she'd remembered something, she put a hand over her mouth. She was still sensitive about her scars and missing teeth.

Rory pushed herself up and out of the chair. Her boys stopped giggling and stood straighter, awaiting inspection.

"And where are you off to this morning?" Rory asked. She directed the question at John.

"Sally's taking us hunting. She saw a big buck down by the river."

"I get to take the first shot at him!" Robert added. "John promised."

Rory ruffled Robert's hair and turned to Sally. "Hunting? Today? On a Sunday?"

Sally nodded, the ghost of humor still making her eyes dance. "Yes, ma'am."

"Did you get the breakfast I cooked for you?"

Sally patted the little bag tied at her side. "Corn cakes and ham."

"I'm carrying the beer," Robert added, clearly proud of himself.

John shoved his shoulder. "You ninny! You weren't supposed to tell her that."

"Oops," Robert said. The corners of his mouth drew down in a deep frown, and he looked up at his older brother, clearly terrified.

Rory raised her eyebrows at Sally. "Beer?"

Sally had gone that pretty shade of pink. "Yes, ma'am."

Rory shook her head, pretending to be upset. Truthfully, she didn't care what anyone did or drank on a Sunday, but all three of them enjoyed themselves more if they thought they were getting away with something naughty.

"You boys run on ahead," she told them. "I need to talk to Sally on our own."

John pushed his brother's shoulder again and stalked away in disgust. Robert's eyes sparkled with tears.

"I'm sorry, Sally," he said, then ran to catch up with his brother.

Rory waited until they'd cleared the first line of trees down the trail, then grabbed Sally and kissed her—deeply, tenderly—running her fingers through her short, blond hair. Sally had offered to grow it out again, but Rory asked her to keep it short. They both liked it better that way.

"I thought we were spending some time alone today," Rory whispered.

Sally's face became even rosier. "We are. I'm going to show them where to hunt, and then I'll come right back. They'll be gone all day. We'll have the place to ourselves until evening."

Rory took a step away and swatted her bottom. "Best not keep me waiting."

Sally shook her head. "I won't. I'll be back before you know it."

As if to prove this point, she took off running, and Rory laughed at her retreating form. Sally disappeared into the woods in almost the exact spot she'd appeared just shy of two years ago. At the time, Rory had convinced herself she'd never see her again, so that when she did arrive, she almost didn't believe her eyes. It didn't help that Sally had been hard to recognize. Cut up and scarred and so dreadfully thin, she'd been like one of the tramps they sometimes got around here asking for food or work. Then, something about the way Sally held her shoulders and the way she walked had made Rory recognize her. They'd run at each other with open arms. She'd never cried so hard before or since.

And now here they were—a little family made of love. A little family with friends and supporters. A little family with a steady income. They had their own place, their own money, their own life. Their past, that ugly eternity, was over and done with. They had the rest of their lives to be happy together. Nothing could be better.

She turned toward her rocker but stopped before sitting down again. She might have felt like wasting the beautiful morning before, but her family's energy seemed to have rubbed off on her. Maybe she'd take that walk now and settle herself to wait for Sally later. It would, after all, make the time go faster.

She went inside for her bonnet and shawl, knowing as she tied them on that she was being silly. Sally didn't care if she kept her skin pale, but the habit was ingrained. She'd only recently stopped wearing a corset—another forced habit, but one she was more than happy to leave behind once she got used to the lighter, more breathable chest stays.

She went outside, leaving the door open to air the cabin. Too early in the season for bugs, and with the smell of breakfast still lingered inside, it needed a good airing. She stepped off the porch and debated. She could climb up to the peak—it had the best views, after all. But after hesitating, she decided she'd rather go see her maple tree. She'd planted it last autumn, just beyond the well on a little flat area overlooking the eastern valley. Sally planned to put a small bench there once the tree grew a little. Rory had checked on her tree once after the last big snowfall, pleased to see it still there, still thriving despite the hard winter. Today seemed like a good day to reacquaint herself with it.

Robert now fetched the water and kept the path to the well clear, and she was pleased by how nicely he'd maintained it. The woods were deeper here than elsewhere on the top of the mountain, yet the trail was easy to follow. She passed the well and walked on, the trees suddenly breaking into the pretty little clearing on the side of the cliff. Her maple had shot up some six inches or more since she last saw it, and her heart warmed. Sally was in charge of all the other trees—the fruit trees that provided them a decent secondary income—but this maple was hers alone.

As she walked closer, she smiled at the leaves starting to bud. The maple was probably too young to flower much this year, but next, maybe, she could expect some pretty pink blossoms. Sally had thought the choice of a maple a strange one for this climate and elevation, but Rory knew now that she had been right to think it could thrive here.

She could still put her hands around the trunk fairly easily at her height, but it had already thickened dramatically nearer the ground. She patted the bark, as if touching a beloved pet, then rested her forehead against the trunk, closing her eyes. The sun beat down on her neck, and she pulled her shawl up farther to cover the skin there.

"Hello, Aurora," a voice said behind her.

The warmth of the day faded at once as a deep chill ran down her spine. She knew that voice. She opened her eyes and turned, slowly, still hoping she was wrong, but she wasn't.

It was Henry.

His skin was sallow and dirty, his clothes hung on him in tatters, and his beard was positively wild. Physically, he'd undergone a complete transformation. He was, in fact, almost unrecognizable. But that look in his eyes and that devil-like grin were the same she'd seen repeatedly in her darkest nightmares. She would have known that expression no matter how long it had been since she'd seen him or how much he'd changed.

"Henry," she said, making herself sound more confident than she felt.

He took a step toward her, and she flinched. Seeing her reaction, his grin broke into a smile, and he laughed. He held his hands up and stayed where he was.

"No need to be scared. I ain't here to hurt you."

"Then why are you here?"

His smile disappeared, and his face clouded over. "To take back what's mine, to get what was stolen from me."

Rory threw a quick glance over her shoulder, wondering if she could run, but she was too near the edge of the cliff to escape. He had likely approached her here knowing she would be trapped.

"And what's that? What was stolen?" she asked, still searching for somewhere to run.

"Stop that," he said, his voice dark with the familiar, angry firmness. "Stop looking around. You ain't gonna get out of this so easy. I came here for my property, and I mean to take it."

The air seemed to have been punched out of her. "What property? What are you talking about?"

"You. The boys. You're mine." He sneered. "Not that fucking *freak*'s. I saw you two, you know, out there on the porch. That kiss before she left." He spat. "To think you let her touch you with that filthy mouth. Makes me sick." He took another step toward her. "Going to have to wash you in bleach water to get her filth off you."

Rory ducked down and grabbed the first thing her fingers found before standing up and throwing the rock at him as hard as she could. It managed to connect with his forehead, and he recoiled, cursing. She started running too late, and he grabbed her arm, twisting it hard. She crumpled to the ground, screaming. He flung her arm away and kicked her once in the side.

"Fucking bitch!" he roared, and slammed into her again.

Rory rolled away from him, desperate to get up on her hands and knees, but his boot connected with her rear end, and she went flying, her face skidding into the dirt. She bit her tongue against the pain and then heard him walking closer. His shadow fell across her, and she rolled over on her back, peering up into his face. The rock had pierced the skin on his forehead. One side of his face was coated with blood.

"I ought to kill you for throwing that rock," he said, then spat on her face. "Seems you lost you some of those manners I taught you when we lived together. I'll have to take you in hand again. God knows what you're teaching our boys."

The thought of her children made Rory go wild. Sitting up as quickly as she could, she grabbed his leg and sank her teeth into his calf. She tasted dirty cloth first but soon felt his flesh. Henry uttered a howl and kicked her away from him. She rolled with his kick, bracing for what she knew would follow, and he kicked her again. She saw the edge of the cliff coming toward her, and then she was falling.

She had just enough time to let out one shriek before she was sliding along the rock face. She landed, hard, on a little jutting ledge a short distance from the top and only just managed to keep herself from rolling off it and into oblivion.

Cut and scraped and bleeding all over, she checked her body for signs of broken bones. Both her ankles hurt, and the ribs on her right side screamed with pain. She bit her tongue to keep from calling out, hoping to God he wouldn't hear her down here.

She saw a shadow above and almost screamed when she saw his face twenty feet above, poking over the side of the cliff. Even beneath the beard, and despite the distance, she knew that look on his face. She'd seen it before and knew things were only going to get worse.

"Goddamn bitch!" he screamed. "I'm going to climb down there and kick your teeth in! If you think you can get away with throwing something and biting me, you're wrong!" He paused, as if for breath. "And anyway, I don't need you. More women in the world than you— prettier and younger ones. I could just take the boys and leave you down there to rot. And kill that fucking freak on the way."

She tried to get enough air in her lungs to argue, but her voice, when it came, was almost breathless. "No."

Henry cupped a hand around his ear. "What was that?"

She took a deeper breath, her ribs protesting. "No!" she screamed.

He laughed, throwing his head back and disappearing before he leaned over again. "You ain't in any position to argue with me, missy. As I see it, you got two choices. You can stay down there and die, or I can help you up here and we can talk. Which will it be?"

Rory knew she wouldn't stay alive very long if he left her here. She'd likely punctured a lung, either on the drop down or from one of those kicks. A coppery, bloody flavor filled the back of her mouth.

"Hey! I'm talking to you. What will it be?"

Her eyes filled with tears. "Help me," she said.

Again, he cupped his ear. "What's that?"

"Help me!" she managed to scream.

"I will help you, my dear. But I got some conditions."

Whatever they were, he didn't get a chance to say them. She heard a loud, thunderous sound, and suddenly a fine mist of bloody, red gore rained down on her. Henry's head disappeared, but his body stayed upright for a second before dropping down at the top of the cliff. His headless shoulders hung over the edge, his body nearly slipping over.

Rory screamed, frantically wiping at the blood and tissue coating her face and body. She heard movement at the top of the cliff as someone dragged Henry's headless body back off the edge, and then Sally's face appeared above, eyes huge at the sight of her.

"Is that yours?" she called. "All that blood?"

Rory shook her head. "It's his."

"You okay?"

She shook her head again. "I think I broke something. Inside. Blood in my mouth—my blood, I mean."

Sally cursed. "Let me go get some rope. I'll be back."

"Don't leave me down here!"

Sally frowned down at her. "I'll be right back. I swear it." And then she was gone.

Rory never knew how Sally managed to get her to the top again. She was in too much pain to pay attention. She remembered passing out, then waking up when the excess rope slapped down on top of her. The journey up was a hazy trip through a pain-filled hell, and she lost consciousness for most of it. When she came to again, Sally crouched next to her on the ground, holding her hand, the maple tree framing the sky behind her.

Sally's hair was sticking out on the sides of her head in all directions, partially smeared with bloody gore. She must have run her hands through it while she waited for me to wake up, Rory thought. She did that when she was nervous. Despite Sally's appearance, Rory had never seen anything more beautiful.

"Here," Sally said, pulling out her handkerchief. "Let me clean your face a little."

Rory stopped her hand, squeezing it. "Lay off a minute, would you? I just want to see your face. I feared I'd never see you again."

Sally was pale, clearly terrified. "We have to get you to a doctor."

Rory shook her head. "Not possible. We'd have to explain…" She shook her head more firmly. Suddenly, she remembered, and she craned her neck around, spotting Henry's body some ten feet away, with nothing above his shoulders. She looked back at Sally quickly. "No one can know. They'd hang you without asking questions."

Sally opened her mouth, but Rory cut her off again. "No one, not even the boys, can know about this."

"We could say you had an accident," Sally said, almost blubbering. "You fell off the cliff and—"

"No one would believe us. The boys might, but no one else will."

Sally's eyes filled with tears, and she gripped Rory's hands with hard desperation. "I don't want you to die."

"I won't die. I know what to do. I've fixed enough ribs in my day."

Sally shook her head. "On animals. That isn't the same thing."

"It is. I'll talk you through it."

Rory was proud of how sure she sounded. She was actually fairly certain she would die, but it was a small price to pay to keep a rope from Sally's neck. She'd much rather be dead.

"What about…?" Sally lifted her chin at Henry's body. "I could push him over the edge."

Rory shook her head. "No, not certain enough. Someone might find him. We have to hide him."

Sally's eyes narrowed and she looked away, as if considering. Finally, she said, "I know a place."

"Where?"

"Never you mind. I'll hide him, and then only one of us will know. You aren't in any shape to help."

"When will the boys be back? Do you have enough time?"

Sally hesitated and then nodded. "If I start right away. But I don't want to leave you lying here. You should be inside."

"Lying here or lying in bed is the same thing. You commence on his body. That's the main thing. I don't want the boys to see him like that, or at all, if we can help it."

Sally opened her mouth as if to argue before her shoulders finally sank in defeat. "Okay, but I'll check on you. You just rest here." She pulled off her buckskin jacket and laid it over her. "I wish I had a pillow."

"I'm cozy enough. Get going."

Sally nodded and rose to her feet. The rest of her leathers were splattered with blood and chunky gore, and they'd be worse before this was all over. Still, it was a small price to pay for her safety.

"Hurry back. And make sure he didn't leave anything lying around. He might have a pack somewhere."

"Okay. I'll look for it."

Still Sally hesitated, clearly not willing to leave her, and Rory shooed her on. "Get going. The boys could be back any time."

Sally's face hardened, and, silent, she got to her feet. By twisting her neck at an incredibly awkward angle, Rory could just watch her as she worked. She spent a few minutes gathering her rope again, carefully looping it over her shoulder before tying it off. Next, she stooped and grabbed Henry's remains under the arms. She dragged him away, back toward the cabin, the rope still looped over her right shoulder. She winced against the pain, eyes squeezed shut, and when she opened them again, Sally and the body were gone.

She relaxed her neck and stared into the sky, suddenly certain she would die out here, all alone. Some cowardly tears trickled out of the corners of her eyes, and she brushed them away impatiently. After all, she didn't have anything to fear. Her only concern was Sally and the boys. But they would be okay in the end, regardless. Maybe Sally would find someone new—not soon, but someday. Some pretty little woman like herself to help her run this place and raise her boys.

She sobbed, then laughed. "Aurora Lemke, you fool," she said. She stared into the bright blue of the sky, letting its peaceful beauty wash over her, suddenly thinking that perhaps she would make it through this. She fought her eyelids and then passed out.

CHAPTER TWENTY-NINE

When Jo opened her eyes, the sky above her was the crystalline blue that shows itself only in the mountains. She blinked, confused, and then, as if remembering something, she put her hands on her side, feeling for broken bones. She let out a relieved gasp and sat up, head spinning.

Andy lay crumpled on the ground a few feet from her, her face peaceful, serene, with a slight, almost amused lift to the corners of her mouth. Jo crawled over to avoid standing up and touched Andy's hand. Andy's sleepy grin turned into a smile. She opened her eyes, blinked several times, and then sat up all at once. She put a hand to her head and closed her eyes.

"Jesus," she said.

"Dizzy?" Jo asked.

Andy nodded. "Like I just got off a merry-go-round." She frowned. "What happened? Why are we on the ground?"

"You don't remember passing out?"

Andy frowned, her brows lowered. "The last thing I remember was the smell of apple blossoms." She shook her head. "Nothing after that."

"Did you have any dreams? While you were out?"

Andy looked even more confused. "Dreams? Like what?"

Jo had a fleeting sense of disappointment. She'd hoped they'd shared the dream, or vision, or whatever it had been. To Jo, the experience was as clear as a recent memory—she'd lived it, in fact, inside Rory's body. She'd hoped Andy had been there, too.

"Let's try to get up," she said. She rose on wobbly legs, but her sense of equilibrium returned almost at once. Andy likewise stumbled, but she was steady once more after pacing around, shaking the sleep from her limbs. After a few seconds, the only evidence of what they'd just gone through was a few leaves on her jacket. Jo stepped toward her and brushed them off.

"What happened?" Andy asked again.

"I'll have to tell you later. If we don't go into the well now, we won't have time before dark."

Andy opened her mouth, and then, as if seeing something in Jo's eyes, her mouth snapped closed, and she started walking toward a large pine tree about fifteen feet from the well. Jo followed slowly, her legs still tingly and weak. She watched Andy circle the tree a couple of times before she gestured at it.

"We'll tie the line here."

Jo, suddenly terrified, barely managed to acknowledge what they planned to do. Standing this close to the well, her old terror reemerged. She could hardly look at it. How on earth could she go down there?

She spent the next few minutes setting up the ropes and putting her harness, helmet, and the rest of her gear on. Andy did most of the work with the ropes, while Jo just stood there as a secondary assistant, holding whatever was asked of her and getting out of the way when needed. Throughout this procedure, she kept her eyes off the well, hoping the sight of it wouldn't shock her as much as the next time she saw it.

But it did. In fact, focusing on the well, staring directly at it, terrified her even more than before.

"Jesus, Jo," Andy said, touching her hand. "You're as white as a bedsheet. What's the matter?"

Jo's teeth were clattering, and it took some time to respond. "Scared."

Andy grabbed her shoulders and somewhat roughly turned her away from the well. "Goddamn it, Jo, you can't climb in this condition. You'll get yourself killed. You're shaking all over."

Jo shook her head. "I-I'm okay. I'll b-be okay."

"No, you're not, and you won't be. Get that damn harness off and let me do this. You're in no shape for heroics." Then, not waiting for a reply, Andy unclipped the rope and wiggled the harness down off Jo's hips. Almost listlessly, Jo stepped out of it. She watched, completely detached, as Andy pulled the harness onto her own hips and clipped it into the rope.

She grabbed Jo's shoulders again. "You have an important job,

Jo. You need to watch the rope and make sure I have what I need. I'll call up with instructions, and you need to do whatever I tell you to do without arguing. Okay?"

Jo had no will to argue. Even now, with her back to it, the well filled her with dumb horror, a terror so wide and deep, it felt ready to crush her whole. She continued to watch Andy's preparations, feeling removed in her fear, not particularly concerned that this woman was risking her life for her. She watched, unmoving, as Andy put her own shoes and helmet on before removing the lid. It was still attached on one side by the second lock, but Andy managed to swing it off the hole so that it leaned on one side of the raised lip of rocks. She peered down inside the well, leaning at a dangerous angle, before she stepped away and back toward Jo. After rummaging around in her backpack, she pulled out what looked like a road flare. Jo's guess was confirmed when she took off the flare's plastic cap to strike at it and light it, a little like a match. She walked back over to the edge of the well and threw the flare inside. A few seconds passed before the splash. Andy continued to peer inside before pushing off the rocks and coming over to Jo again.

"Okay. I'm going in. It's bright enough inside now. Between the flare and my headlamp, I should be able to see just fine."

"Can you see his body?"

"Not from up here. If it's in the water, I'll find it. I spotted the bottom, so I hope the water is pretty shallow."

"How far down?"

"Hard to say, maybe forty or fifty feet."

Jo focused on the rope, that strange detachment keeping her distant, almost unconcerned. "Do you have enough rope?"

"Plenty." Andy kissed her. "Okay. I'm going in. Listen for instructions, okay? You don't have to stand right next to the well, but you need to be close enough to hear me. The echo should help, but you might want to stand over there a bit."

"All right."

Andy's face crinkled. "Are you okay? You seem…distant. Are you upset that I'm doing this?"

Jo shook her head. "No—not upset at all. You're right. It's safer this way."

If Andy found her complete turnaround on this topic strange, she didn't stop to argue. Instead, she walked back to the well and, without hesitation, threw her rope inside. Leaning on the rocky lip, she peered inside, ostensibly to check that the ropes weren't tangled, and then she pushed herself up onto the lip of rocks. Seconds later, she was walking backward into the hole, rappelling out of sight.

Once she disappeared, Jo's lethargy disappeared. She ran to the well, almost screaming, and stared inside. Andy was already a good distance down, walking slowly on the wall of the well. It was too late, but Jo couldn't help the little groan of terror that rose to her lips.

Andy looked up. "You okay? Everything all right up there?"

It was pointless to stop Andy now, but Jo sobbed, once. "I'm okay."

Andy had stopped moving. "You don't sound okay. Want me to come back up there?"

Jo shook her head and then, realizing she was probably backlit, managed to say, "No. Keep going."

She watched the descent as long as she was able. The farther Andy went, the smaller and more vulnerable she appeared. Jo fought a wild, almost desperate urge to call her back up, back to safety.

The idea of safety gave her pause, and she wrenched her eyes away from the hole, searching the woods in all directions. She wasn't, after all, any safer up here. Whatever power Henry had, he seemed strongest in the woods, here at the surface. He'd controlled her before from here.

Suddenly terrified they'd overlooked something, she raced back to the pine tree where Andy had tied her line. It was perfectly whole, the rope tense now but clearly sound. The tree didn't seem to mind the strain, as it wasn't even moving with Andy's weight beyond a little trembling in the needles. Still, Jo couldn't shake the feeling that they'd forgotten something crucial, something obvious, that would cause trouble.

She rushed back to the edge of the well and leaned over to peer inside again. Andy looked very small and far away now. Jo could just make out the movement of her head as she reacted to the changing light at the top.

"Everything okay?" Andy called. Her voice sounded weak, much farther away than the actual distance.

"I'm fine, but please hurry. Something isn't right."

"Something's bright?" Andy yelled back.

Jo sighed in exasperation. "Something's not right!" she said, much louder.

"What? What's not right?"

"I don't know. It's just a feeling."

"A what?"

"A feeling!"

"Okay. I'm almost to the water. Just a couple more feet."

Andy was too far down for Jo to make out much detail, but she saw the water ripple as Andy entered it. She heard some splashing, and then the rope relaxed slightly next to her.

"I can stand up!" Andy called from down below. "The water just hits my knees."

"Can you see his body?"

"No, but I do see something. Let me look."

Jo briefly recognized what was going to happen before it did. The circle of stones that lined the edge of the well had stood in this place for over a hundred years. It had been set there in place as the need arose to dig deeper and deeper for water. Eventually, the top of the well had needed shoring up, and these stones had been set up here, held in place by a version of homemade concrete. That concrete had safely held the mismatched stones in place for more than a century.

Until today.

Jo would wonder later if Andy's weight had set off the accident, or if something, or someone else had done it. But with the first crunching, grinding sound, she knew what was going to happen. Using her arms, she pushed backward as hard as she could, jumping and pinwheeling them to land upright. The stony lip of the well caved inward at the site of the rope, the rocks slipping down and dropping inside the hole in a cascade of dust, dirt, and stone. The stones pulled up a lot of the ground at the base of the mouth as they caved in, and the sound as they fell and tumbled inside the well was like a series of echoing bombs. Jo was certain she heard Andy's piercing shriek before the long, horrible silence that followed.

Throwing herself on her stomach, she inched toward the well, the ground now loose and sliding under her. She grabbed the rope, braiding her fingers around it, so that if she felt the ground give way completely, she might be able to hold on. The ground now sloped down here, toward the hole of the well, so when she reached the edge, she couldn't get her head over the hole. No matter how far she craned her neck, she could not see the bottom of the well.

"Andy?" she called. "Andy? Are you okay?"

No response.

Sobbing, Jo scooted backward, away from the gap in the edge of the well, and rushed around to the other side. About a third of the stone lip had collapsed, and the rocks on this far side still felt solid, but she was afraid to put her full weight on them. Steeling herself, she rested her forearms on the rocks and, by standing on her tiptoes, managed to look down inside.

The debris had apparently buried the flare, as she saw no light source below. Andy's headlamp was likewise obstructed. The sunshine, revealed only the area ten or fifteen feet down from the top.

"Andy!" she yelled, louder this time, but she heard no movement or sound.

They'd used Jo's gear for Andy's descent only because Jo was originally supposed to go down. Andy had even used her harness. But Andy had a full set of gear in her backpack, and Jo raced toward it, throwing herself onto her knees and tearing it open. After flinging aside several unnecessary supplies, she finally found the rope. She yanked it out of the bottom of the bag, sending the rest of Andy's supplies flying, then leapt to her feet and ran toward the pine tree.

Jo had tied this kind of knot hundreds of times. Long before she'd even climbed, she'd spent hours with Meghan, who'd quizzed her on knots. Still, she had to pause to remember every step, taking long, deep breaths to clear her mind. Her fingers were shaking when she began, but she kept her eyes rooted to the knot Andy had tied, using it as a mental guide. She had to start over once, recognizing a mistake, but she finally managed to tie the rope to the tree, just under the line Andy was attached to. With all these ropes, it would be very easy to get things tangled. It might be safer to anchor somewhere else, but she didn't have time to think about it. She found Andy's harness and tightened some of the straps to fit her smaller frame.

She started walking toward the well, holding the rest of the rope to keep from getting it jumbled with Andy's. Stopping a couple of feet from the spot where the ground had caved inward, she realized she wouldn't have yet another of Andy's advantages. Without a light at the bottom, she would be basically walking backward into the dark. She shuddered, the thought making her almost ill. She couldn't risk dropping another flare inside, but she might have a glowstick in her pack. It wouldn't be nearly as bright as a flare, but it would be something to aim for, anyway, and might provide some clue as to Andy's condition.

She dropped the rope onto the ground and sprinted to her pack, kneeling next to it almost reverentially. If she didn't find a glowstick inside, if she'd used it earlier for some silly reason, she'd be going down in the dark. Hands shaking, she uncinched the top of her backpack, digging around inside until she found the little orange stuff-sack she used for the extra odds and ends she needed when camping. She unrolled the top, and the first thing she pulled out was a thin, foil pack with a yellow glowstick.

"Thank Christ," she breathed.

She unwrapped it, then snapped and shook it to life before walking over to the well and throwing it in. Even if it hit Andy directly, it couldn't hurt her. The rocks here at this part of the lip still looked solid, so she gingerly leaned on them to peer inside.

The sickly, greenish-yellow light from the glowstick made the bottom of the well seem eerie, otherworldly. It was dim, but Jo could just make out Andy's crumpled form, or at least part of her—her helmet and one arm. She wasn't moving.

"Andy?" she called again. Nothing.

Panic and anxiety threatened to overwhelm her. Never had she wanted Carter and her clear, calm mind more. Carter would know what to do. Carter would know if it was better to go down there or get help. Carter would also be able to accomplish this rescue, if that's what she had to do, far better than she would be able to. But Carter wasn't here. This was up to her.

This simple truth made her heart rate slow, and she stood up straight and began checking her gear again. At the last moment, she remembered to grab a first-aid kit and a bottle of water, and then, without letting herself pause and think about it again, she clipped her harness onto the carabiner and starting walking backward toward the hole again.

The ground was eroding quickly, and she slipped a few times on the loose soil before her shoes finally found purchase on the stony surface a foot or two inside the well. She walked slowly, carefully downward until she felt stable, and then she rested, suspended over the hole.

CHAPTER THIRTY

From here, Jo could see the full extent of the damage. The cave-in had not only pulled in about three feet of stones and rocks from the lips of the well; it had also dragged about a foot of the stony surface inside the well with it. The tension on the rope could cause the damage to spread. Still, with the angle of her rope, if more of the rocks from inside fell, their impact would be minor. The rest of the stones that jutted above the surface seemed stable enough, but she wouldn't trust any weight on them.

She rappelled in steady silence for several feet, then paused again, listening for the sound of moving rocks. But only the slight rustling brush of her rope and the squeaking rubber of her shoes greeted her. She continued, throwing a glance downward every minute or so, relieved to see the circle of greenish light growing closer.

When she was nearly halfway, about twenty feet above Andy, a dark shadow passed over the sunlight at the top of the well. Knowing what she'd see, she snapped her eyes upward and her headlamp, after she'd positioned it correctly, finally revealed Henry's grinning face.

Seeing him seemed to produce the dank, putrid smell that suddenly filled her nose, and she flinched away from it. Worse than carrion, the odor was the essence of darkness, of fetid decay. It was the scent of death.

The cold spread through her next, chilling her almost immediately. Before, the well had held a damp coolness, but this was different, a cold so deep and painful, her limbs recoiled. This kind of cold could kill you if you stayed in it too long.

Gradually, the sunlight behind his head seemed to cloud over and almost disappear, the remains of the day slipping into twilight, almost as if he were controlling time itself. He was perhaps twenty feet from Jo, but she could make out the black, rotten edges of his teeth beneath his dirty, matted beard. He remained motionless, simply grinning.

"What do you want from us?" she yelled. "Leave us alone!"

His lips parted slightly in something like a smile, and then he jerked up and out of sight.

"Shit," she whispered, peering around. She knew exactly what would happen next.

Most of the climbing she'd done with Carter and Meghan had either been in the climbing gym or on low, natural rock faces. Descending the wall of a well was something else. The stones had been put in place to create a smooth inside surface. Jo didn't know how this was done, precisely, but whoever had created the inside of this well had done an impeccable job. There was very little space between the stones, the surface almost as smooth as if it had been sanded down. Still, after jerking herself forward, she managed to find a hold with her fingers and toes, and at almost the exact moment she managed to rest her weight on her hands and feet, the rope above her relaxed. A few seconds after that, it slid down into the well, and she braced herself as it fell behind her. The impact of the rope hitting her and then crashing below almost made her lose her grip, but she managed to hold on to the edge of the well. It yanked at her waist when it hit the bottom, and again, her fingers almost slipped, but she held on.

"Fuckety fuck," she breathed.

Her heart was hammering, but she wasn't afraid. Managing to hold on gave her a trill of confidence, made her more certain, in fact, than she'd been when she was safely on the rope.

The rest of the distance down to Andy took far longer than the same distance she'd rappelled. Still, while the surface of the inside of the well was remarkably smooth, it wasn't entirely so. This had been handmade, after all, and she eventually found purchase between the stones.

She managed to jump the last few feet, aiming away from Andy, but the rocks she landed on were piled unevenly, and she slipped, landing on one wrist and her tailbone with a jarring pain. She tried to get up but slid into the water. The stones had filled in the bottom of the well somewhat, but there was still plenty of liquid here.

Andy stirred to life at the movement of the rocks and water, raising her head and sending little stones and pebbles sliding off her helmet.

Her legs were buried under the rocks, and Jo stood up to remove them more quickly. Andy was soon able to help, moving the stones aside and freeing her legs.

"Are you hurt? Is anything broken?" Jo asked, helping her stand.

They hugged, briefly, before Andy drew away and, wincing, bent down, inspecting her legs with her hands. In the eerie light of the glowstick, she was ghostly, almost apparitional. Finally, she stood up, shaking her head. "I think I'm okay. A little bruised, maybe, but nothing worse. No cuts or breaks, as far as I can tell." She rubbed her shoulder. "This hurts the worst—a really big rock hit me here. I think that's why I passed out, though I do remember getting hit on my helmet, too. Might have been a shock concussion that did me in."

Jo had never been more relieved. The whole distance down here, and up at the top, she'd continued to tell herself that Andy was wearing a helmet, that Andy would be okay. But only part of her had believed that possibility. The darker part of her had imagined she would get down here and find a dead body.

She remembered the purpose of this whole misadventure and peered around on the ground. "Did you find him? Is he down here?"

"I don't know what I found, except a metal box. Here, under these stones. I was just about to figure out how to open it when the cave-in started."

They both began shifting the loose stones away to the other side of the well, their movements hampered and awkward because of the close quarters. They found the spent flare, and Jo could have kicked herself for not bringing a second as a backup. Finally, she shifted a sizable flat stone aside, revealing the top of what looked like a large box, about three feet on all sides.

"What on earth?" Jo asked.

Andy shrugged. "That's what I thought when I saw it. I can't budge it—it's too heavy. I felt seams, though, so maybe there's a lid or something."

Jo knelt down in the water, feeling around on all sides of the box. She located the seams Andy had mentioned, then finally found what felt like a metal handle on the side facing her. She inched her fingers along the face with the handle and detected a circular knob, then stood up, hands and sleeves dripping.

"It's a safe. No wonder you couldn't budge it. Must weigh hundreds of pounds."

Andy was frowning, staring behind Jo. She bent over and stood up, holding the rope. "Wait a minute, is this mine?"

Jo explained how she'd used Andy's rope to climb down and what had happened. "I guess he untied it."

Andy gave the rope she was hooked in a tug. "The one I used is still tied. Feels totally fine."

"That's what he wants us to think. He wants us to use it to climb back up, and then he'll untie it at the last second." She gestured helplessly. "We're going to have to get out of here without a rope."

"Carrying that thing?" Andy said, gesturing at the safe. "No way. I could get out of here—my harness has some metal anchors we can clip into from inside here—but I just can't imagine how we'll do it with that thing. I'm not even sure we'll be able to move it."

Jo knelt in the water again, feeling around at the base of the safe. After groping for a while, she found what she'd suspected. The safe was bolted in place.

"Motherfucker," she said, and stood up. "It's attached to the floor. No way we could get it out of here without tools."

"So someone put this safe down here?" Andy asked.

"Looks that way."

"But I thought this well was used until the twentieth century."

Jo realized where she was going and frowned. "You're right. She wouldn't have put it here if they were still drinking this water."

"Who? What do you mean by she?"

Jo shook her head. "It's too complicated to get into. Anyway— someone must have brought it down later, after the other well line was dug."

"When was that?"

Jo thought. "The 1920s, I think."

The two of them stared at the safe, both, Jo thought, realizing the same thing. Aurora and Sally were dead by the 1920s. That meant one of their kids, or maybe a family friend, had hidden this safe here after the two women died. Someone had known what Sarah had done and decided to hide the evidence.

Jo let out a long whistle. "Holy shit."

"No kidding—talk about a family secret."

"Maybe John, or whoever, found the body after Aurora passed away, already tucked away in this safe, and decided to hide it here. No one would use this well again, after the other, deeper one was drilled."

Jo paused, frowning, and then shrugged. "I don't know if we'll ever know all the details. For now, we just have to get it out of here. Henry seems to want to stop us, so that must mean we're on to something."

They were quiet, just staring at it.

"You could see if you could open it, I guess," Andy said. "Wouldn't hurt to try, anyway. Maybe the locking mechanism is broken."

Jo knelt in the water again, this time twisting her headlamp down so the light shone onto the box more directly. Her hands were greenish in the water, a result of the glowstick or the water itself, and the sight gave her a pinched, hollow feeling in the pit of her stomach. That's what your hands would look like if you were dead, she thought.

"Stop it," she whispered.

"What?" Andy asked, kneeling beside her.

"Nothing. I'm just creeping myself out."

She tried the handle, pushing down and pulling up on it, but nothing happened. The knob spun easily, however, suggesting that it hadn't, at least, rusted shut.

"It's locked. It's not rusted, at least, but it's definitely locked."

Andy stood up, her knees popping in protest, and Jo joined her. Andy drew her into her arms, kissing the top of her head. "I can't believe you came down here for me."

"What else was I going to do?"

Andy nodded on top of her head, her arms still tight around her. "Still—thanks."

"Although now we're both stuck down here," Jo said, trying to laugh.

Andy shook her head. "No—not stuck. I have some tricks up my sleeve. Like I said, I have some anchors here in my little fanny pack, and we have rope. It will be slow going, but we can get out."

Jo pointed at the safe. "But what about that? After all this, we're just going to leave it here?"

Andy raised her shoulders. "What else can we do? Unless you know the combination, whatever's inside will have to stay here for now. We can get someone else to pull it out and open it later."

Jo stared down at the safe, her frustration a living, breathing heat that twisted her insides. How on earth could she just leave it? They'd both almost died for it. It wasn't fair.

"How many numbers do you think are in the combination?"

Andy lifted an eyebrow. "No idea. My school lockers always had three, but I don't know if that's standard. There's no way to know."

Once again, Jo knelt down into the water. She couldn't tell if it was her imagination, but the water seemed colder than before. Perhaps the long-term exposure was chilling her from the knee down, but the temperature seemed to have, in fact, dipped. Henry was still here and getting closer. The smell wasn't here yet, but once it was, they wouldn't be able to do much to stop him.

She pushed the thought aside and closed her eyes, thinking back on her day in the museum with Kevin. She'd read Aurora's full birthday, she knew she had, but she couldn't quite remember the day of the month. Still, it was a place to start. She started with 6-1-55, moved on to 6-2-55, and continued. On 6-10-55, her nose caught the first hint of the rotten stink. She pulled her hands out of the water to warm them and rubbed them together to revive feeling in the tips. Andy put a hand on her shoulder.

"Do you smell that?"

"Yes. I'm hurrying."

Andy squeezed her shoulder. "Don't rush. It's okay. He can't do much more to us down here."

"Don't be so sure," Jo said, and plunged her hands back into the water. She tried 6-11-55, 6-12-55, and on and on until the end of the month.

"Damn it," she said, slapping the water. "I did all of June. I thought for sure it would be Aurora's birthday."

"We can't wait," Andy said, her voice a little pinched. "We need to get out of here."

Jo could feel it, too. The chill, which had been unpleasantly cold mere minutes ago, was now verging on frigid—that icy frost she'd felt while hanging above, and in the bedroom this morning, and out by the well days ago. The wretched, foul scent was now nearly overpowering, making her fight her gag reflex.

He's trying to drive you away, Jo thought. He's trying to scare you. Keep going.

She pinched her eyes shut, searching her mind for some clue, some idea about the combination. She couldn't accept that she could have been led here, gone through all this, only to fail. Some part of her insisted that she must know the combination.

She snapped her eyes open. She knew.

She put her hands back into the water, found the combination lock, and quickly put in 3-14-82, her birthday, and Carter's. She pushed down on the handle, which gave at once. She had to back away from the safe to open the door, and when she plunged her hands into the safe, she felt something inside.

She stood up, pulling the sack out with her. It had stayed remarkably dry inside the safe, so that it was only slightly damp from its quick plunge. The bag itself was made of a rough burlap, cinched at the top with what looked like a leather belt.

Andy flinched away, covering her nose and mouth. "Jesus Christ, does that stink! What's in it?"

"This is Henry—or what's left of him."

Andy's grimaced. "Yuck. Really?"

Jo nodded. "Sarah must have cut him into pieces and put him in the safe."

Andy grimaced. "Gross." She paused. "We're bringing it with us?"

Jo nodded again. "It has to come. We have to get rid of it, or him— get him away from this place, once and for all."

Andy didn't argue. Instead, she stared upward, straight up at the top of the well, before meeting Jo's eyes again. "Do you think you can do this?"

"Yes."

Andy smiled. "Good. I guess the other question is—do you think he'll let us?"

"What do you mean? What else could he do?"

Andy lifted a shoulder. "Lots of things. There's still plenty of rock up there at the top. If he made the rest of it cave in, we wouldn't have a chance."

"But we'll be tied in, right?"

"Once I get an anchor in the wall. But not before that. If he decided to throw something down here before I get one in, nothing would stop me from falling." She shook her head. "I don't know what I was thinking. I should have put in anchors on the way down."

Jo squeezed her arm with her free hand. "You can't think that way—we couldn't have known this would happen."

Andy nodded, still looking guilty and shamed. Finally, she shook herself. "Okay. I'm going first. I'll put in an anchor about twenty feet up, then the next another fifteen above that, and then I'll help you up." She turned as if to do just that, but Jo grabbed her shoulder, spinning her into an embrace.

"Be careful," she said, and kissed her.

CHAPTER THIRTY-ONE

Jo's neck hurt from watching. Andy was still climbing, her progress slow but steady, her movements reflecting that same, careful grace Jo had seen a hundred times before. She took long pauses between reaching upward for the next handhold, and when she did, it looked almost effortless. She had to be struggling by now, as she'd been holding herself on the wall with nothing but her fingertips and toes this entire time, but she seemed steady, certain. Jo was almost convinced this would work.

The cold and the awful smell were still here, but, like anything terrible, she was almost used to both now. She'd once spent nearly a month next to a high-capacity feedlot for a work assignment, and within a week she'd hardly noticed the smell of feces and decay. After all, no matter how awful, it was just a smell. It couldn't hurt them. The cold, on the other hand...

"How are you doing?" Jo called up.

"Okay," Andy said, her voice sounding clipped, almost short.

Jo shouldn't have said anything, but she couldn't stop herself. She was shivering harder, and her feet and lower legs, submerged in the icy water, were almost completely numb. Andy might be tired, but she was probably warmer.

"All right," Andy called down. "I'm about to hammer in the first anchor."

Jo's breath caught as she watched. Andy had been holding on with both hands, but now she released one and dug around in her little fanny pack. She pulled out a metal anchor, slipped it into the hand holding on to the wall, and then pulled her hammer from her belt. It was like watching a magician. Somehow, despite having a third of her weight resting on the one hand, she got the anchor in place and started hammering it into the rock with her free hand. The sound was harsh, almost deafening inside the closed space of the well, and a little drift of dirt and dust rained down from above. The whole process was terrifying, but Jo forced herself to keep watching. She needed to know what to expect.

"That's one," Andy finally said. She'd tied the second rope to her belt, and Jo watched as she clipped it onto the anchor. The next part was the scariest, as Andy grabbed the rope and leaned backward, her entire weight now on the anchor she'd hammered in.

"It's steady," she finally said.

Jo let out the breath she'd held and almost staggered with relief. "Is it safe?" She couldn't help but ask.

"As steady as it can be. I hammered it into the space between the rocks, into whatever is behind it. It must be stone as well, since it felt much harder than dirt. We'll just have to hope I'm right. I'll get the next one in, but really, I'm just putting them in for safety. If I fell, it should hold, or at least slow me down, but I don't trust it to hold either one of us entirely for very long—just give us long enough to grab the wall."

"What does that mean?"

Andy peered down at her, now holding on to the wall again. "It means I need to get to the top and pull you out."

"What?"

She frowned. "It's the only way, Jo. An anchor like this wouldn't hold you the entire way, so we can't take that risk."

"But I could climb up, too! Like you're doing."

Andy continued to stare down at her before finally shaking her head. "No, Jo. I don't doubt that you could try, but I do doubt that you'd make it the whole way. Not without a long rest some place. It's almost fifty feet." Then, as if to prove that the argument was over, she started climbing upward again with her slow, certain pace.

"Goddamn it, Andy! I can't let you do this! You can't keep taking all the risks for me!"

Andy didn't respond. She simply kept going.

"Stop it! Stop it right now, or I'm coming after you."

Andy paused, but Jo had a hard time seeing her expression. When she spoke, her voice was firm but still warm.

"Jo, listen to me. I know you want to help, but sometimes you have to accept your limitations. You can't do this. I can. Let me get to the top. Let me help you. The longer we argue, the harder it will be for me to make it. I'm really tired, and my shoulder hurts like hell."

Jo sobbed, putting her hands over her mouth to stifle another argument. Andy was right, but it didn't make her feel better. Andy had already almost died today, and now here she was, putting her life on the line again.

Almost as if she'd made it happen, the other rope, the one still tied to the tree, suddenly started to move on its own. Jo knew what to expect, and she called out a warning to Andy above. A moment later, the rope was falling into the well, slipping past Andy to land on top of Jo's head and shoulders. It didn't hurt much, but when the other end of the rope came, it slapped her face, which stung.

"You okay?" Andy called.

"Fine. Glad we didn't try using it."

"You were right. He's waiting for us up there."

Jo didn't respond. Already, despite the dim light and the distance, she could see that Andy was moving steadily upward again. Regardless of the danger, she was still set on making it to the top. Jo ground her teeth, frustrated and disgusted. If she'd only spent more time in the climbing gym, she could be the one risking her life. What would he do to Andy when she made it outside? Little panicky tears tickled at the corner of her eyes, and she stifled another protest. She couldn't do anything now but wait.

"Jo?" Andy finally called. Her voice sounded hollow—much farther away than the thirty or forty feet above.

"Yes?"

"I'm putting in the second anchor now. My arms are really tired now, honey, so I need you to promise me something."

Jo was nearly breathless with panic. "What?"

"If something happens—promise me you'll be safe. You can get out of here if you're careful. Just don't put your whole weight on the anchors, or only do it for a couple of seconds at a time. Stop if you hear or feel one slide. Can you promise me?"

Tears were slipping down her cheeks now, but she managed to choke out, "I promise."

The sound of the hammering started once more, and again, dust and debris fell down from above, making her close her eyes and look away.

It seemed like decades before she heard Andy say, a little

breathlessly, "Okay. It's solid, at least for now. I'm going to rest here for a sec, and then I'm going out. I can see the top now, and I haven't spotted him yet. He's either going to let me climb out or wait until the last second to try to stop me."

They were quiet for a long time. Jo kept her eyes shut tight, her body rigid with tension. She should watch the last of it, make sure Andy got out safely. It was difficult now, with the angle, distance, and dark to see anything, but she could see if she tried. She only had to open her eyes.

"Jo?" Andy called down. This time, despite the distance, her voice was crystal clear, almost as if she were standing next to her.

Jo's heart slowed down almost at once. "Yes?"

"I love you. I know we just met, but—"

Jo opened her eyes in an instant and peered upward, into the empty blackness above her. "I love you, too."

Andy didn't respond. Jo could vaguely see her, dangling off the anchor she'd put in, but the angle of her head suggested that she was staring down at her. Finally, she leaned forward, back onto the stony surface of the well. She started climbing again, and this time, Jo wasn't afraid any more. She was worried, but the fear no longer pressed her down, suffocated. It also didn't seem as cold as it had, and she smelled something fresh and sharp in the air.

"Apple blossoms," she murmured. A hot flash of hope washed through her. Henry might be up there at the top of the well, but he wasn't alone.

Rory and Sally had come to help.

❖

The trip to the top was a jerking, seemingly endless process. Andy had rigged up a kind of pulley using the tree as an anchor. She tied off every ten feet to rest. As she did, Jo had to simply dangle, helplessly, over the chasm. Jo had clipped in to each anchor as she passed it with the second rope, but that precaution hardly made her feel less helpless and useless. She was being hauled out of the well like dead weight—almost as lifeless as the remains inside the stinking burlap sack she'd tied to her belt.

Despite the endless time that passed, the light at the top of the well became brighter and brighter as it grew closer. It seemed like the middle of the afternoon out there, not early evening. The water from the bottom of the well had done something to her watch, so she wasn't sure what time it was, but it must be quite late by now.

Andy's face suddenly appeared at the top, about ten feet away, little spots of color in her cheeks from exertion.

"Oh, thank God. I wasn't sure I'd ever get you up."

"I could climb the rest of the way," Jo said.

Andy shook her head. "No. That last part was the hardest—I almost fell. The soil up here is too loose. Just let me get you out, honey." She didn't wait for a reply, simply disappeared. Soon, Jo was being jerked upward again, and her head snapped with each wrench.

The site of the cave-in finally appeared a foot or two above her, and Jo threw herself forward, snagging the exposed root of a tree. Andy appeared and grabbed her arm, and between the two of them, she managed to clamber out of the well, both collapsing onto the ground a few feet from the hole. Andy squeezed her hand painfully with her gloved fingers as they lay on their backs catching their breath.

"Jesus," Andy said, still gasping.

"No kidding. I'm never climbing inside a well again, I can tell you that. Don't even ask."

Andy managed a weak laugh and then propped herself onto an elbow, peering down at her face. "You goof."

Jo smiled up at her, but Andy's expression faded. She sat up and kissed her. "Why the long face, lady?"

Andy gestured around them. "Notice anything?"

"What? You mean the glaring sunshine and green, leafy trees? No, I hadn't."

Andy didn't even smile. "Jo—be serious. An hour ago, it was almost evening, and now it looks like late morning. It was autumn, and now it's like spring or early summer. What do you think it means?"

Jo sat up more fully, scooting her legs up and sitting on her bottom. She waited for Andy to do the same. They sat cross-legged on the ground, their knees touching, staring into each other's eyes.

She took Andy's hands in hers. "It means we're safe, Andy. That's what it means."

Andy frowned. "How do you know?"

Jo laughed and waved a hand vaguely around them. "Because of this. It's the opposite of Henry. It's them—Aurora and Sarah."

Andy was still frowning. "You mean like they're here somewhere?" She glanced around. "Helping us?"

Jo nodded.

"Can you see them?"

She shook her head. "No—but I know they're here. They're protecting us."

Andy still seemed skeptical, but Jo laughed and climbed to her feet. She held out a hand and helped Andy get to her feet, concerned to see her wince with pain.

"Is it your shoulder?"

Andy nodded, her face pinched. "It's really bad. It wasn't dislocated, but it almost was. It hurts something terrible."

"We need to get it checked in Estes. And we need to get this damn thing," she touched the burlap sack, "the hell off this mountain."

Andy's frown deepened. "And then what? Throw it in a river?"

Jo shook her head. "No—too many things could go wrong. We'll have to take it to the police. I'll say we fished it out of the well because we thought something fell in when the side collapsed."

Andy paused, then nodded. "Sounds like a solid plan. Do you think it'll be that easy?"

"You mean Henry?"

She nodded. "Don't you think he'll try to stop us?"

Jo shook her head. "He might try, but I think he's done here. As long as it's warm and clear out, we'll know we're safe."

Andy smiled slightly. "And as long as it smells like apple blossoms."

Jo nodded. "Exactly. Let's get going."

She turned to do just that, but Andy grabbed her hand. "So that's it? That's the end?"

Jo laughed. "You wanted something more dramatic?"

Andy chuckled. "I guess so. Not wanted, so much as expected."

Jo smiled. "Me, too. But let's count ourselves lucky and get the hell out of here before he comes back."

Andy made her wait until she repacked her backpack, worried that they might eventually walk into the dark somewhere. Soon, however, they were hiking down the trail toward Andy's truck. Despite the fact that it was almost October, anyone could have told by the warmth in the air and the scent of new growth that it was springtime in the Rockies. Jo had been up here many times and seen the trees and foliage exactly like this in late April or early May. As much as she loved autumn and winter up here, the world around them was gorgeously fresh. Jo was walking in front of Andy, the two of them occasionally stopping together to take in the beautiful flowers and trees. The warmth of the day was almost too much for the heavier clothes she wore. She rounded one of the last major corners of the trail, just before the last long descent, and froze. Andy almost ran into her from behind.

"What is it?" she asked. "Do you see something?"

Jo couldn't breathe. In a little clearing in the middle of the aspen grove, a group of people stood waiting. Jo could actually see the trees behind them through their translucent, glowing bodies. She counted at least twenty of them, all of them bathed in a warm, bright sunshine. She glanced back at Andy, who was peering ahead, clearly not aware of them.

Jo turned back to the group of people and took a couple of wary steps forward. They were all smiling, all seemingly happy. The crowd parted a little, and several young men stepped forward. They resembled each other very strongly—clearly brothers, if not twins. One of them moved a little bit farther ahead of the others, walking directly toward Jo and smiling quite broadly, and she suddenly recognized her grandfather as a young man. He had that same funny scar above his eyebrow he'd gotten as a kid, the one she'd run her fingers over many times while sitting on his lap as a child. She'd seen photos of him at this age in his army uniform, but even so, she would have known him immediately. She sobbed and ran toward him, but he jumped back and held his hands up in a warding gesture. She stopped about five feet from him, tears falling from her eyes.

"Grandpa? Is that you?" she asked.

He nodded and gestured around him. He'd had several brothers, and though Jo hadn't seen many of them since she was young, she knew these must be them.

"It's so great to see you," she said. "I'm glad to know you're… happy."

He beamed, his smile so wide she could see every tooth, and then he stepped to the side and gestured behind him at the crowd. A beautiful woman about his age came forward, and he put his arm around her shoulders. It was her grandmother, younger than Jo was now.

Jo sobbed louder and put her hands to her mouth, tears now falling freely. Her grandparents backed away a little and to the side, allowing one of Jo's uncles to step forward and nod at her. He'd died when she was very young, but he'd always been her favorite. He smiled before he too moved away and back into the crowd.

The crowd had parted entirely now, and Jo saw a group of four people she had seen many times now in the photograph over the fireplace and in her vision this afternoon. Aurora, Sarah, Robert, and John, all of them seemingly the same approximate age, stood in a group together holding hands. Like her grandparents and great-uncles, they seemed positively joyful at the sight of her. Again, Jo stepped toward them, but like her grandfather, Aurora held up a hand to stop her. She was shorter in person—much shorter than Jo had expected, perhaps five feet tall. She had beautiful, wavy black hair, and her dark-brown eyes were the exact shade and shape of her father's, brothers', and sisters'.

"Aurora?" she asked.

She smiled and nodded.

Jo couldn't help but stare at the butch, blue-eyed, blond woman next to her. Seeing her was like gazing into a crazy, funhouse mirror. She looked almost exactly like Carter, and, she knew by extension, almost exactly like herself. Only the thin, pencil-line scar that ran the length of her face differentiated her from any photo she'd ever seen of herself or Carter. To call the resemblance uncanny was a serious understatement.

"Sarah?" she managed to ask. Her voice sounded weak and uncertain.

Sarah grinned and dipped her head.

Jo gazed back and forth between the two of them, her heart welling with pride and dizzying elation. Tears were still falling, unheeded, from her eyes, but she suddenly remembered something and spun around, looking for Andy.

Andy stood where she'd left her, her eyes seeming dazed and unfocused. Jo waved a hand at her to no effect and realized that all of this, this entire gathering, was for her alone.

She turned back to Aurora and Sarah and smiled at the young men next to them—Robert and John.

"Is this right?" Jo asked, touching the bag of remains still tied to her belt. "Is this what I'm supposed to do? Get rid of him?"

All three of the original Lemkes and Sarah nodded vigorously.

"Okay," she said, her voice breaking.

She wanted to stand here with them forever. She wanted to know them, talk to them, become friends with them. These women felt like part of her now, as close as she was to Carter, even. She loved her family, got along with just about everyone incredibly well, but having women like this in her life to admire and to know and follow would make her life richer, deeper.

She had to swallow a couple of times before she managed to ask, "Will I see you again?"

All of them simply smiled before they began walking away. As the crowd approached the far side of the clearing, each person gradually faded into a more obvious translucence before, about ten feet beyond the aspen grove, they disappeared entirely.

Aurora and Sarah waited, just beyond the edge of the trees, for the rest of the family to disappear. They waved at her one last time before turning around and fading from view.

Once they'd disappeared, the sunlight gradually faded out of the sky, almost as if the sunset were on fast-forward, and she was plunged into the chilly, nighttime air.

"What? What happened?" Andy said.

Jo could just make her out in the dark, and she walked toward her, holding out her hands. Andy grabbed hers and drew her into a tight hug.

"It's complicated," Jo finally answered, then kissed her with a fierce, almost painful joy.

EPILOGUE

It was extremely cold, far too cold to sit outside in usual circumstances, but several gas heaters were set up around the fire pit, so that even Rachel, who had never been through a Colorado winter, claimed she was perfectly comfortable. The forecast called for snow later this evening, but everyone was staying for the remainder of the long holiday weekend, which meant the likelihood of getting snowed in was actually welcome. Already, the late-afternoon air had that sharp, wet smell that foretold a storm, and the darkening sky was a solid slate gray. Carter had recently splurged on a nice set of outdoor furniture for the cabin, and the new chairs meant that each of the four couples got to sit next to their partner on cushioned love seats with a cheery red, wool blanket over their knees.

"Thank God," Rachel said, settling back on her chair. "I thought I'd never make it up here."

"Was it that bad?" Meg asked.

Rachel nodded. "A whole week of my mother nagging me to move back to California, followed by the worst Korean Thanksgiving food I've ever eaten, courtesy of my sister, the world's worst cook." Everyone laughed, and Rachel managed, for the first time, to smile.

She squinted at Andy. "You stayed here in Colorado, right?"

She nodded. "Yep. My first Lemke Thanksgiving."

Rachel eagerly sat forward. "And? How was it?"

Everyone was staring at her now, and Andy colored. Her eyes shifted nervously to Jo, and Jo laughed. "It's okay, hon. You can be honest."

Andy lifted an eyebrow. "You say that now…" She winked. "I'm kidding. It was fine. I was grilled a bit, and I met about a thousand people, but everyone was really nice."

Jo sighed and squeezed her hand. "My parents and my siblings spent all morning asking her questions, and then the rest of the family showed up, and she had to answer them all over again."

Andy shook her head. "It wasn't a big deal. You prepared me for it."

"There were a thousand people there?" Rachel asked.

"No. I'm exaggerating."

"How many people were there?"

Carter and Jo shared a look, and Jo shrugged. "Sixty? Maybe seventy throughout the day? Everyone kind of comes and leaves when they feel like it. Usually at most like forty at a time."

Carter nodded. "That sounds about right."

Rachel's eyes opened even farther. "Wow. You're really brave, Andy." She shifted her gaze to the men. "How about you guys? What did you do?"

"We did the family thing, too," Drew said. "My parents have met Kevin before, but this was the first time I'd met his family."

"My parents are divorced," Kevin added.

"So that meant we had to go to three dinners." Drew grimaced. "I'll be happy if I never eat turkey again as long as I live."

Rachel turned to Meg and squeezed her knee. "We thought about doing that this year, having Meg fly with me, or me stay here with her, but it seemed—"

"Too soon," Meg said, frowning. "Not that we're not serious about each other, but my mom—"

"And my whole family—"

"Are kind of jerks," Meg said. She shrugged. "Maybe next year."

Everyone was quiet for a while, and Jo closed her eyes, enjoying the peaceful mountain air. The chill on her face felt wonderful in contrast to the warmth of the heat lamps and the crackling fire, and for the first time in days, she started to relax. She loved her family, and she loved being around them, but introducing them to Andy had been stressful, especially with the other news she had to share. She'd taken her parents aside after everyone left last night and told them privately. They'd been supportive, but she'd worried about it for days beforehand. Now she planned to tell everyone here.

She opened her eyes and found her gaze drawn to the cabin. She was facing it almost directly, and the sight of it gave her that warm wholeness again—that comfort she'd always felt when she was up here before the events of two months ago. After the police had finished their investigation at the well, she'd received a slap on the wrist for moving Henry's remains. She and Andy had finished the next two comfortable, serene days up here together before returning to work, as if the events of those two weeks had never happened. That feeling had returned on her first trip back to the cabin with Andy after her weeks on fire duty, and she had driven up here almost every night the cabin had been free since. Just last weekend, she and her friend Ronnie had come up for a night on their own. She couldn't get enough of it. She'd have driven up the canyon to Estes regardless, to see Andy, but the two of them spent almost all their time together here instead of at either of their apartments. It was, as much as a part-time place could be, their real home.

The others here tonight obviously could feel the cabin's draw again, too. Ever since that crazy afternoon at the well, she and some of the others, but more often all eight of them, had met here almost every other week. Often, all eight of them had stayed overnight together, crowding into the three rooms quite happily, content just to be together. She knew why she and Carter were drawn to it—the place was part of them, after all, but the others seemed to have begun to feel its almost magical draw. Even Meg, who had once sworn she would never return, had come back as often as anyone else. This was their place almost as much as it was her family's. Soon, Jo knew, she would be able to come up here even more often.

She opened her mouth to tell her friends what she'd told her parents last night, but Carter spoke up first. "Oh, so guess what, everyone? Daniela and Kevin found something in the archive in Longmont last week."

"In Longmont?" Meg asked, obviously confused.

Daniela nodded. As she signed, Carter interpreted. *Yes. Kevin and I had the idea to check there when we didn't find more photographs in the Estes archive.*

"I'd heard that some of the historical photos ended up there before Estes developed its own historical society," Kevin added.

It seemed like a long shot, but it was almost like we were meant to find them.

"They were in the first box we checked. An entire set of photographs of Aurora and Sarah, the kids, the cabin, and some photos of their business."

We could hardly believe it.

"Anyway, we've made copies, and I brought them with us."

Daniela had texted her pictures of a few of the photographs when she'd found them, but Jo was eager to see the professional, large-sized copies. She'd asked Kevin to make several books of photographs to give them to their family, so it meant that each couple here had a book to examine together.

"Talk me through what I'm looking at," Rachel said.

"Okay," Jo said, opening to the first page. It featured a family photograph very similar to the one that already hung inside the cabin, but it had been taken a bit later. "This one is from 1897. That's Aurora seated on the right and Sarah on the left, with Robert and John behind them."

Rachel was peering closely at the photo, her nose mere inches from the page. She sat back and shook her head. "It's really crazy. I mean, you can hardly believe it. She looks just like you and Carter."

Jo and Carter smiled at each other. The revelation that the two of them were basically doppelgangers for their great-great-grandmother's lover had shaken things up considerably at Thanksgiving yesterday. They'd both told their parents long before the reveal to the more distant family, but the resemblance still seemed to upset just about everyone. Truthfully, it still gave Jo a strange dropping sensation in the pit of her stomach when she dwelt on what it meant.

Almost everyone else in their entire immediate family on their father's side resembled either John, Robert, or Aurora. In many cases, the resemblance was almost creepy. Her father, for example, was basically a dead ringer for the older brother, John, in this photograph, and her brothers and several of her male cousins looked like one or the other as well. Most of her female cousins and both of her sisters, especially Annie, resembled Aurora. She and Carter had always been the outliers, the strange ones, or, as one of her grandmothers claimed, the changelings. With their fair hair and light eyes, no one outside the family ever suspected that she and Carter were related to anyone but each other. And now, to find this stunning connection to a woman they weren't literally related to was earthshattering. No one had a reasonable, practical explanation. In fact, when she'd told Carter what she'd learned during her visions, Carter hadn't believed her. She might never have believed her entirely except for these photographs.

The next photo was even more obvious. It was a portrait of Sarah "Sally" Bell at forty years of age. Jo saw the others visibly react to the photograph. Rachel and Meg actually flinched, and Drew's eyes seemed likely to bug out of his sockets.

"Holy shit!" Drew said, and let out a long, low whistle.

"It's crazy, right?" Andy asked.

In the photo, Sally was staring directly at the camera. The picture focused on her upper body, from the waist up. Her expression was wry, almost sarcastic, as if she'd just stopped laughing or was about to start. Jo had seen that expression on Carter's face a million times. Sally looked so much like her, it was difficult to distinguish between the woman in the picture and the woman sitting next to Daniela. Of course, Carter, Andy, and Daniela claimed that Jo looked just as much like Sally as Carter did, but it was harder to see a resemblance when it was you.

Meg shook her head and closed the photo album. "It's kind of creeping me out."

"Oh, no!" Drew said, shaking his head. "Don't think of it like that."

"Like what?"

"Like a bad thing." He peered around at each of them, frowning. "You guys are treating this like it's some kind of curse. It's not. It's the exact opposite."

"A blessing?" Meg asked.

He pointed at her. "Bingo—or something like that, anyway."

Everyone was still staring at him with either confusion or hesitance, and he sighed. "Guys, come on. Think about this: Aurora and Sarah went through hell together. I mean, Christ! All the shit they had to do just to live together, just to escape that crazy bastard. It boggles the mind. Yet they did it. They persisted. They survived and thrived. They had a family together, a family that gave us all these two women here, at the very least, not to mention all the other Lemkes that came before and since. Then, sixty years after they die, their relationship is recreated in these two women. Carter and Jo are the spiritual manifestation of that love made human."

Carter's eyes filled with tears, and she reached over to squeeze his hand. "That's beautiful, Drew. Thank you."

Drew grinned, clearly self-satisfied, and Kevin rolled his eyes. "It was a lovely thing to say, babe, even if it does sound a little bit like superstitious mumbo-jumbo."

Drew threw his hands in the air. "What other explanation is there? After all the crazy shit that went down up here, this is the thing you find hard to believe?"

Kevin lifted one eyebrow and then nodded. "I guess you have a point."

"You're damn right, I do."

Meg seemed to relax, and she opened the album again as either Carter, Jo, Daniela, or Kevin explained what they were seeing. They discussed several photographs of the family, some of Robert's many kids—including Carter and Jo's grandfather—as well as several of the cabin over the years. In the later photos, the two women were clearly older, but spry and healthy, wrangling horses and cattle and talking to customers at their horse-rental business. Every picture showed a happy, fulfilling life with smiles and barely suppressed laughter.

As the others around the fire joked, refilling their drinks and gathering the materials for the dinner they were cooking over the fire, Jo let herself reflect on what Drew had suggested. She didn't know if what he'd said was right, or if some other explanation for why she and Carter seemed to share some kind of genetic link with Sarah Bell existed, but she realized then, perhaps for the first time, that she could choose to do exactly what Drew suggested and be grateful for that link. She and Carter's eyes met, and without sharing a single word, she knew Carter had just realized the same thing. Carter gave her that identical, almost sarcastic grin she'd just seen Sally give the camera, and Jo winked back.

Drew was either right or he wasn't—it didn't matter. The only thing that mattered was that, regardless of the explanation, she and Carter would have a happy, loving life, just like their great-great-grandmother.

Andy put a glass of champagne in her hand and sat down next to her, taking her free hand. Daniela passed the others similar glasses, then rejoined Carter on their seat.

"Hey, swell, what's the occasion?" Rachel asked.

Jo has some news to share, Daniela explained.

Carter seemed surprised, and Jo warmed from within. She'd told Daniela her news yesterday. They'd taken a quick trip to the grocery store together for last-minute yams, and she'd asked her for advice on how to break the news to everyone. Daniela had kept her secret for the last twenty-four hours, which meant a lot. They were beginning to trust each other again.

Everyone was staring at her expectantly, and she had to look away from Daniela to stop from tearing up.

"What is it?" Rachel asked.

"It must be good if we're getting the good champagne," Meg said, grinning.

Jo cleared her throat and turned to Andy. She was telling everyone, but she was actually telling Andy.

"I put in my notice at work."

Andy's eyebrows shot up, and everyone around them started talking at once. Jo held up a hand and waited for them to stop, still staring into Andy's eyes.

"I asked for a transfer, and it was finally approved. Starting next week, I'm an employee of the town of Estes Park."

Andy's eyes filled with tears, and she pulled Jo into a rough hug, upsetting both of their glasses of champagne. Everyone around them clapped and whistled, and when they drew apart, Jo's eyes felt wet and hot.

"Does that mean…?" Andy asked.

"Yes. I want to move in with you. As soon as possible. Monday, if I can."

Amid more cheers and hollering from the others, Andy kissed her and nodded eagerly.

"Yes," she finally said. "A thousand times yes."

When they'd both calmed down and were wiping their faces, Drew suddenly seemed to realize something. "Hey—wait a minute! Does that mean I'm getting kicked out of *my* apartment? Where am I supposed to go?"

Andy's face fell, but Kevin elbowed him hard in the ribs. "Be quiet, you bastard. You know I've asked you to move in to my place like a million times."

Drew nodded, his lower lip puckered. "True. I keep meaning to do that."

Kevin kissed him. "I know you do. Now you have to. One day of getting up early and we'll have you installed at my place lickety-split."

Drew put a hand to his forehead, dramatically. "Not getting up early! Anything but that!"

Carter stood then, lifting her glass. "Okay, then, this is good news. Andy, I'm so happy we had those flat tires. And Jo—you're one lucky woman." Daniela swatted her leg, and everyone laughed. Carter grinned at her and then looked back at Jo and Andy. "But seriously, guys, congratulations. Here's to the first step in the rest of your lives together."

"Hear, hear!" the others said.

Jo listened as the others exclaimed and talked animatedly about the tabletop game Rachel had brought up with her for the weekend. She didn't feel the need to join in. Instead, she watched while everyone talked as if they'd all known each other their entire lives. She couldn't believe this was her life. Something, or someone, seemed to have made this day, this moment, just for her.

Her gaze drifted over to the cabin, and for a second, she thought she caught a glimpse of someone inside watching them. The firelight flickered, and from this angle she could see directly into the living room, right at the spot where the photograph of Aurora, Sarah, John, and Robert hung above the fireplace. They were part of this, too, and they were happy for her—just as happy as the people sitting here. Their happiness, more than anything else, was their legacy, and she was part of it.

About the Author

Charlotte was born in a tiny mountain town and spent most of her childhood and young adulthood in a small city in northern Colorado. While she is usually what one might generously call "indoorsy," early exposure to the Rocky Mountains led to a lifelong love of nature, hiking, and camping.

After a lengthy education in Denver, New Orleans, Washington, DC, and New York, she earned a doctorate in literature and women and gender studies.

An early career academic, Charlotte has moved several times since her latest graduation. She currently lives and teaches in a small Southern city with her wife and their cat.

Books Available From Bold Strokes Books

All She Wants by Larkin Rose. Marci Jones and Tessa Dalton get more than they bargained for when their plans for a one-night stand turn into an opportunity for love. (978-1-63555-476-2)

Beautiful Accidents by Erin Zak. Stevie Adams doesn't believe in fate, not after losing her parents in a car crash. But she's about to discover that sometimes the best things in life happen purely by accident. (978-1-63555-497-7)

Before Now by Joy Argento. The instant Delaney Peyton and Jade Taylor meet, they sense a connection neither can explain. Can they overcome a betrayal that spans the centuries to reignite a love that can't be broken? (978-1-63555-525-7)

Breathe by Cari Hunter. Paramedic Jemima Pardon's chronic bad luck seems to be improving when she meets police officer Rosie Jones. But they face a battle to survive before they can find love. (978-1-63555-523-3)

Double-Crossed by Ali Vali. Hired thief and killer Reed Gable finds something in her scope that will change her life forever when she gets a contract to end casino accountant Brinley Myers's life. (978-1-63555-302-4)

False Horizons by CJ Birch. Jordan and Ash struggle with different views on the alien agenda and must find their way back to each other before they're swallowed up by a centuries-old war. Third in the New Horizons series. (978-1-63555-519-6)

Legacy by Charlotte Greene. In this paranormal mystery, five women hike to a remote cabin deep inside a national park—and unsettling events suggest that they should have stayed home. (978-1-63555-490-8)

Somewhere Along the Way by Kathleen Knowles. When Maxine Cooper moves to San Francisco during the summer of 1981, she learns that wherever you run, you cannot escape yourself. (978-1-63555-383-3)

Blood of the Pack by Jenny Frame. When Alpha of the Scottish pack Kenrick Wulver visits the Wolfgangs, she falls for Zaria Lupa, a wolf on the run. (978-1-63555-431-1)

Cause of Death by Sheri Lewis Wohl. Medical student Vi Akiak and K9 Search and Rescue officer Kate Renard must work together to find a killer before they end up the next targets. In the race for survival, they discover that love may be the biggest risk of all. (978-1-63555-441-0)

Chasing Sunset by Missouri Vaun. Hijinks and mishaps ensue as Iris and Finn set off on a road trip adventure, chasing the sunset, and falling in love along the way. (978-1-63555-454-0)

Double Down by MB Austin. When an unlikely friendship with Spanish pop star Erlea turns deeper, Celeste, in-house physician for the hotel hosting Erlea's show, has a choice to make—run or double down on love. (978-1-63555-423-6)

Party of Three by Sandy Lowe. Three friends are in for a wild night at billionaire heiress Eleanor McGregor's twenty-fifth birthday party. Love, lust, and doing the right thing, even when it hurts, turn the evening into one that will change their lives forever. (978-1-63555-246-1)

Sit. Stay. Love. by Karis Walsh. City girl Alana Brendt and country vet Tegan Evans both know they don't belong together. Only problem is, they're falling in love. (978-1-63555-439-7)

Where the Lies Hide by Renee Roman. As P.I. Camdyn Stark gets closer to solving the case, will her dark secrets and the lies she's buried jeopardize her future with the quietly beautiful Sarah Peters? (978-1-63555-371-0)

Beautiful Dreamer by Melissa Brayden. With love on the line, can Devyn Winters find it in her heart to stay in the small town of Dreamer's Bay, the one place she swore she'd never remain? (978-1-63555-305-5)

Create a Life to Love by Erin Zak. When sixteen-year-old Beth shows up at her birth mother's door, three lives will change forever. (978-1-63555-425-0)

Deadeye by Meredith Doench. Stranded while hunting the serial predator Deadeye, Special Agent Luce Hansen fights for survival while her lover, forensic pathologist Harper Bennett, hunts for clues to Hansen's disappearance along the killer's trail. (978-1-63555-253-9)

Endangered by Michelle Larkin. Shapeshifters Officer Aspen Wolfe and Dr. Tora Madigan fight their growing attraction as they work together to destroy a secret government agency that exterminates their kind. (978-1-63555-377-2)

Incognito by VK Powell. The only thing Evan Spears is focused on is capturing a fleeing murder suspect until wild card Frankie Strong is added to her team and causes chaos on and off the job. (978-1-63555-389-5)

Insult to Injury by Gun Brooke. After losing everything, Gail Owen withdraws to her old farmhouse and finds a destitute young woman, Romi Shepherd, living in a secret room. (978-1-63555-323-9)

Just One Moment by Dena Blake. If you were given the chance to have the love of your life back, could you ignore everything that went wrong and start over again? (978-1-63555-387-1)

Scene of the Crime by MJ Williamz. Cullen Mathew finds herself caught between the woman she thinks she loves but can no longer trust and a beautiful detective she can't stop thinking about who will stop at nothing to find the truth. (978-1-63555-405-2)

Fear of Falling by Georgia Beers. Singer Sophie James is ready to shake up her career, but her new manager, the gorgeous Dana Landon, has other ideas. (978-1-63555-443-4)

Daughter of No One by Sam Ledel. When their worlds are threatened, a princess and a village outcast must overcome their differences and embrace a budding attraction if they want to survive. (978-1-63555-427-4)

Playing with Fire by Lesley Davis. When Takira Lathan and Dante Groves meet at Takira's restaurant, love may find its way onto the menu. (978-1-63555-433-5)

Practice Makes Perfect by Carsen Taite. Meet law school friends Campbell, Abby, and Grace, law partners at Austin's premier boutique legal firm for young, hip entrepreneurs. Legal Affairs: one law firm, three best friends, three chances to fall in love. (978-1-63555-357-4)

The Last Seduction by Ronica Black. When you allow true love to elude you once and you desperately regret it, are you brave enough to grab it when it comes around again? (978-1-63555-211-9)

Wavering Convictions by Erin Dutton. After a traumatic event, Maggie has vowed to regain her strength and independence. So how can Ally be both the woman who makes her feel safe and a constant reminder of the person who took her security away? (978-1-63555-403-8)

A Bird of Sorrow by Shea Godfrey. As Darrius and her lover, Princess Jessa, gather their strength for the coming war, a mysterious spell will reveal the truth of an ancient love. (978-1-63555-009-2)

All the Worlds Between Us by Morgan Lee Miller. High school senior Quinn Hughes discovers that a broken friendship is actually a door propped open for an unexpected romance. (978-1-63555-457-1)

Falling by Kris Bryant. Falling in love isn't part of the plan, but will Shaylie Beck put her heart first and stick around, or tell the damaging truth? (978-1-63555-373-4)

An Intimate Deception by CJ Birch. Flynn County Sheriff Elle Ashley has spent her adult life atoning for her wild youth, but when she finds her ex, Jessie, murdered two weeks before the small town's biggest social event, she comes face-to-face with her past and all her well-kept secrets. (978-1-63555-417-5)

Cash and the Sorority Girl by Ashley Bartlett. Cash Braddock doesn't want to deal with morality, drugs, or people. Unfortunately, she's going to have to. (978-1-63555-310-9)

Secrets in a Small Town by Nicole Stiling. Deputy Chief Mackenzie Blake has one mission: find the person harassing Savannah Castillo and her daughter before they cause real harm. (978-1-63555-436-6)

Stormy Seas by Ali Vali. The high-octane follow-up to the best-selling action-romance *Blue Skies*. (978-1-63555-299-7)

The Road to Madison by Elle Spencer. Can two women who fell in love as girls overcome the hurt caused by the father who tore them apart? (978-1-63555-421-2)

Dangerous Curves by Larkin Rose. When love waits at the finish line, dangerous curves are a risk worth taking. (978-1-63555-353-6)

Love to the Rescue by Radclyffe. Can two people who share a past really be strangers? (978-1-62639-973-0)

Love's Portrait by Anna Larner. When museum curator Molly Goode and benefactor Georgina Wright uncover a portrait's secret, public and private truths are exposed, and their deepening love hangs in the balance. (978-1-63555-057-3)

Model Behavior by MJ Williamz. Can one woman's instability shatter a new couple's dreams of happiness? (978-1-63555-379-6)

Pretending in Paradise by M. Ullrich. When travelwisdom.com assigns PR specialist Caroline Beckett and travel blogger Emma Morgan to cover a hot new couples retreat, they're forced to fake a relationship to secure a reservation. (978-1-63555-399-4)

Recipe for Love by Aurora Rey. Hannah Little doesn't have much use for fancy chefs or fancy restaurants, but when New York City chef Drew Davis comes to town, their attraction just might be a recipe for love. (978-1-63555-367-3)

The House by Eden Darry. After a vicious assault, Sadie, Fin, and their family retreat to a house they think is the perfect place to start over, until they realize not all is as it seems. (978-1-63555-395-6)

Uninvited by Jane C. Esther. When Aerin McLeary's body becomes host for an alien intent on invading Earth, she must work with researcher Olivia Ando to uncover the truth and save humankind. (978-1-63555-282-9)